AUTHOR'S NOTE.

Big Mama is my eighth book and it is a very different kettle of fish from my earlier works. The first books I wrote were a saga telling the story of Billy Hopkins' family over a period of more than a century (1886 – 2008) and, although there were seven books, they were really one story in seven episodes (a so-called *roman-fleuve*).

The present work, *Big Mama*, is a completely different genre. I am also using a new publisher on this occasion since Headline, my previous publisher, felt that the new genre might prove too much of a change for many of my regular readers who have come to expect homely family stories from me. I hope that those of you who have been hoping for more of the same won't be disappointed by this present effort. At least, you have been warned to expect something very different from the usual Hopkins family saga!

Big Mama is a political thriller which takes place around the present time in a fictitious African country, Zambelia. The country in which the story is set, is not be found on any map, and the characters, together with the members of the British government delegation described therein, are equally imaginary.

BACKGROUND TO THE STORY

The history of Africa in the second half of the nineteenth century was characterised by the so-called scramble for Africa as the big European powers squabbled with each other for bigger slices of the continent's cake.

The second half of the twentieth century witnessed a frenetic dismantling of Africa as the same powers vied with each other in their rush to hand back freedom to the indigenous peoples. The nineteenth-century colonial map-makers had drawn straight lines of demarcation which cut arbitrarily across natural features like mountains, lakes, forests, and social entities like extended families and tribes bequeathing a legacy of tribal tension and hatred. Given this situation, our present administrators have tried to graft a series of nation states on to territories whose borders relate to no social or historical boundaries. In addition, models of European-type democracy – evolved over centuries of struggle and compromise - have been forcibly introduced to the new states. The slogan 'One Man - One Vote - ONCE!' became the sick joke of Africa as country after country reverted to its traditional pyramidal social and political power structure. Dictatorships supported by large 'school-certificated' bureaucracies sprang up everywhere. The sole route to wealth and possessions (for oneself and therefore naturally for one's extended family, village, and tribe) was perceived to be through education and participation (especially of the corrupt kind) in the government machine rather than through the possession of entrepreneurial and commercial know-how. It is against this backdrop that the story of *Big Mama* takes place.

***

BIG MAMA

Also by Billy Hopkins

Tommy's World
Kate's Story
Our Kid
High Hopes
Going Places
Anything Goes
Whatever Next!

(The above list is probably the best order in which to read them though not strictly essential as each book should stand on its own merit.)

Big Mama

Billy Hopkins

LEOPARD PRESS

First published in 2011 by:
Leopard Press
№ 633, PR8 3NG
Web-site: http://www.billysbooks.info
E-mail: billy@billysbooks.info

ISBN: 978-1-85988-070-3

A catalogue of this book is available from the British Library.

Printed and bound in Times New Roman
by the Leopard Press

DEDICATION

I dedicate this book to all the friends and colleagues
I came to know so well in the three countries in
which I worked during the period 1958-1985:
Kenya, Rhodesia (Zimbabwe), Malaŵi.

Acknowledgements

To a large extent, the production of this book has been a family affair and I wish to thank all those members who have been involved: first, my children, as follows: Stephen, Catherine, Laurence, Joseph, for their patience in reading, editing and commenting on the book when it was in its earliest and roughest form; Paul for type-setting the book and preparing it for printing and production; Peter, proprietor of Urmston Bookshop, for helping to promote and distribute it; my son-in-law, Steve Lovering (Art Direction) and his colleague Trevor Smith (Design), for the magnificent cover. Above all, I thank my wife, Clare, for her forbearance in not just reading the entire book several times and making the most valuable suggestions, but also for encouraging me through all my hesitations and self-doubt. Without their contributions, this book would not have been possible.

*****

However long the night, the dawn will break

African proverb

Chapter One

Students on the road. The Motorcade.

There were four of them: students on their way back to
university for the start of the new term. It was a journey
they'd done a dozen times or more and they knew every step
of the way but to-day, they were getting nowhere fast.

'With all these bloody refugees on the road, it's hopeless,'
sighed one of them. 'It's like swimming up the Limpopo
against a strong current. If we don't pick up a lift soon, we'll
never make Hekima before nightfall.'

'Don't be such a miserable sod, Bernard,' Eliud said.
'Try looking on the bright side for a change. Something's
bound to turn up, you'll see.'

'Yeah, sure. But four hitch-hikers with big suitcases and
haversacks! I mean, that's asking a lot of any driver who's
daft enough to stop,' Bernard retorted.

Daniel, the tall one of the group, joined in the argument. 'I
think Bernard's right, Eliud. You know, we'd stand a much
better chance if we split up. Suppose you and I speed up and
go on ahead and the two brothers can follow on behind.'

'That's the best idea I've heard all day,' replied Andy,
Bernard's brother. He grinned mischievously. 'Though I
think you got the order wrong. I mean, whoever heard of
English Lit. students like you two boneheads being ahead of
brainy Medics like us?'

'Andy, did anyone ever tell you that you were corny?'
Daniel laughed.

1

'Not till now,' Andy said. 'But OK, let's try your brilliant plan. And though we may be *behind* you, anything going in the direction of Hekima is bound to see us first.'

'That's obvious even to boneheads like us,' said Eliud, lengthening his stride. 'So if you're picked up by a big truck or van, don't forget to tell the driver to keep an eye out for us so we too can hop on board and cadge a lift.'

'OK, will do,' Andy said. 'Right, Bernard, you and I'll slow down so they can get ahead.'

Daniel and Eliud quickened pace and soon put a good distance between themselves and the two brothers.

On the main road and over the horizon as far as the eye could see, a stream of refugees stretched far off into the distance like an endless column of safari ants. A silent mass of people stumbling along and away from the civil war in Umbali. Their limbs were like sticks, their bodies skeletal and so shrivelled by famine that they looked like ghosts from another world. As they tottered forward in this grotesque game of 'Follow-my-Leader', there was in their withered faces an expression of apathy and resignation. Though their eyes looked out, they saw nothing; the eyes of a people without hope.

The gruesome silence was suddenly broken by the distant wail of police sirens. Far off on the brow of the hill could be seen the flashing blue lights of several big cars, their headlights on full beam, cutting a path through the mass of peasants stumbling along the road. As the cars got nearer, the wailing of the sirens and the hooting of the motor horns became louder and more strident. The motorcade was led by four military motor cycles whose outriders struck out wildly with their *sjamboks* at any wretches too slow to dodge out of the way.

'Clear the road, you idiots! Clear the road!' the soldiers yelled, driving young and old alike into the ditches.

The mechanized procession came to a bend in the road and, as it turned the corner, it almost ran into a small knot of

2

people gathered round a ragged old man who had collapsed exhausted in the middle of the road. The two leading soldiers dismounted and strode over to the group, pushing their way into their midst with their whips.

'What the hell's going on here? Come on, clear the way, you stupid bastards. Can't you hear the sirens? The President of Zambelia is coming through,' bawled the senior of the two.

'It's the old man,' muttered a dishevelled, bearded man speaking in a Chuzuni dialect. 'Looks as if he's dying.'

'Nothing to do with us,' snapped the soldier. 'Get him to the side. We must have a clear road through.'

By this time, the rest of the motorcade had caught up and come to a halt.

'Oh, God! Now, we're for it,' hissed the second soldier. 'Look out! Here comes the bloody "Hippo" himself!'

From the leading car, a Silver Cloud Rolls-Royce, there emerged a huge man, in the full military uniform and regalia of a colonel in the Zambelian Public Safety Police. He was young to hold such high rank, certainly no more than twenty-five. He was built like a mountain and he towered above his subordinates. His pock-marked face was screwed up in a scowl, partly in anger and partly in a vain effort to hold the gold-rimmed monocle in his right eye. He swaggered over, striking his thigh impatiently with his stick.

'What the bloody hell's going on here? Why have we stopped?' he bellowed. 'Against my express orders. I told you to keep the road clear and keep moving. If you can't do the job, I'll soon find others who can.'

Terrified, the soldiers sprang to attention and saluted smartly.

'Sorry, Colonel Kiboko. There's an old man lying in the road. They say he's dying.'

'Let's speed up the process and put the old bugger out of his misery,' the Colonel barked.

3

He pushed his way through the people, picked up the dying man as if he were a piece of old sacking and threw him roughly into the roadside ditch.

'If he's going to die, let him get on with it. He's holding up the motorcade. Right, now the wretch is off the road, perhaps we can be on our way again.'

He turned on his heel and strode back to the Rolls. The smoked window of the passenger door was wound down and an old man peered out.

'Why have we stopped?' he asked nervously. 'What's happened?'

'Nothing for you to worry about. A little difficulty up ahead but I've attended to it.'

'I have cramp in my leg. I'd like to take the opportunity to get out and stretch my limbs, Colonel.'

'Not advisable, sir. We have a tight schedule and we must be in Hekima by noon if we're to be on time for the opening of the Chamber this afternoon.'

'Not only do I have cramp, I need to pay a call. A call of nature, you understand.'

'Oh, very well. Best if you make it quick.'

The colonel looked around the road to make sure there were no refugees nearby, and then opened the saloon door. The president of Zambelia got out. He was an old man in his early eighties, dressed in a tailor-made blue safari suit, a silk cravat at his throat over which was draped a cheetah-skin cloak with matching fez. In his hand, he carried an ornately-decorated fly whisk which he now handed over to Kiboko.

'Hold on to that for a moment, Colonel. Sorry to hold things up like this but that's one of the afflictions of old age, you know. Weak bladder. You'll see one day. If you ever *reach* old age, that is.'

The president pushed back the velvet cloak, opened the fly-buttons of his tunic, and turned his back to urinate. At that precise moment, an assegai struck him full in the chest

4

entering his heart. He staggered back under the impact, clutching at the spear, fell to his knees, and keeled over dead, blood bubbling from his lips.

It happened so quickly that no-one had time to react. It was Kiboko who moved first.

'Oh, shit! Blast and damn!' he cursed. 'Stop that man!' he yelled frantically, pointing to the bearded man who was now fleeing and trying to lose himself in the crowd.

The two soldiers chased into the throng of refugees and soon emerged dragging the man along the ground by his matted hair. They threw him at the feet of the colonel who prodded him with his stick.

'Get up on to your two hind legs, you mad bastard! Up, I say!'

'Death to the tyrant!' the assassin shouted defiantly, now propped up between the two soldiers. 'Power to the People's Democratic Party! Today, I rid the world of a rat!'

Enraged, Kiboko replaced his monocle and glared down at the wretch.

'And, now, I rid the world of another,' he snarled.

He withdrew his revolver from its holster and shot the killer twice in the stomach.

'Throw his body into the bush and let him make the acquaintance of his friends flying above,' he said, gesturing towards the vultures which, attracted by the promise of a double or possibly a treble feast, were already gliding down from the sky to perch in a semi-circle not far from the scene.

From the Range Rover at the rear of the motorcade, a fair-haired man appeared. He was around fifty years of age, tall and thin, with a long forehead and a scar on his left cheek; his blond hair was cropped and his tight lips were adorned with a narrow moustache. His steely blue eyes were set in what would have been an expressionless face had it not been for the slight nervous tic.

5

'What on earth is going on, Kiboko?' he asked impatiently. 'We must get a move on if we're to make the twelve o' clock deadline.'

'Some lunatic bastard from the PDP has put a spear through the President.' Kiboko said impassively.

'Gott im Himmel! Not another one!' exclaimed the fair-haired man. 'That's the second this month! You were supposed to be guarding him. What a mess! Big Mama's not going to like it. She gave strict orders that we were not to stop under any circumstances. She'll play merry hell when she hears about this.'

'Look, Schneider, how was I supposed to stop him taking a leak? How was I supposed to know that there would be some crazy dissident waiting with a spear?'

'It's your job to know, Kiboko. You tell that story to Big Mama, your dear old Aunty Marianne, when you report to her and see how she likes it. Anyway, let's tidy things up before we move on. First, I suggest we remove the mantle from our dead president. No sense in wasting such a beautiful and expensive garment. Thank God, it's not been damaged but that assegai has made a mess of the tunic, I'm afraid. Pity about that.'

'We'll avoid identification by removing all clothing,' said Kiboko 'Then we'll throw both bodies to the scavengers.'

He snapped his fingers and his men obeyed his orders, carrying the two corpses away from the road and into the bush.

'We shall shortly be passing through another little town,' said Schneider. 'So, I suggest we bring up our reserve president right-away because the people will be expecting to see their leader waving his fly whisk as we go through.'

The colonel blew loudly on the whistle he carried on his lanyard. From the window of the Range Rover, a police lieutenant popped his head out.

'Yes, Colonel?'

'Send Sergeant Kanyuka,' Kiboko called. 'His presence is required.'

From the Range Rover, there emerged a replica of the late president - same age, same build, same features. He came trotting up to Kiboko and saluted.

'Yes, yes. Come along, you old buzzard,' the Colonel said, draping the mantle around his shoulders and tapping the mottled fez on to his head with his stick. 'From now on, you are President Matata, head of the country. Now, get into the Rolls. And here, don't forget this,' he added, handing him the fly whisk.

He turned to Doctor Schneider.

'Maybe now we can be on our way.'

'Not so fast,' answered Schneider. 'What about witnesses? Have you checked to see if anyone saw that little episode?'

'You don't mean these bloody refugees? They've nothing on their minds but getting their snouts into the troughs at the next food camp. No need to worry about them. They're like the three wise monkeys – speak no evil, hear no evil, and most important, see no evil.'

'All the same, it might be as well to make sure. If this gets out, Big Mama will have your guts for garters.'

'Oh, very well,' said Kiboko. 'We'll check.'

In a loud voice, he called out to the hordes limping along the ditches.

'Did anyone witness the incident? Please come forward if you did. You will be well looked after. We need witnesses.'

The refugees continued to hobble along the roadside, deaf to his appeal. But two young men carrying battered suitcases stopped and one of them waved.

'Yes, we saw the whole thing,' he called. 'If needed, we can give evidence that the President was murdered by the PDP. We saw that bearded man throw the spear.'

7

'Excellent,' said the Colonel. 'Your name, please?'

'I'm Andrew Zulu, and this is my brother, Bernard. We're medical students at the university - on our way back to college. We were hoping to thumb a lift when it happened.'

His brother Bernard tugged urgently at Andy's sleeve and whispered from the side of his mouth, 'Best not to get involved, Andy. Stay out of it. Could be dodgy.'

To the Colonel he called, 'No, no, we didn't see anything. It happened much too fast.'

'Don't be stupid, Bernard,' Andy rasped. 'You worry too much. Here's our chance to get to Hekima in double quick time – and in style.'

'That's good, Andrew Zulu,' Kiboko now called over. 'We shall be pleased to take you and your brother the rest of the way and we'll take down your evidence when we reach Hekima. There's room with Doctor Schneider in the Range Rover.'

'Come on, Bernard,' Andy said. 'It's our lucky day. Back to college in 4 by 4 luxury.'

Still reluctant, Bernard joined Andy in throwing their luggage on to the roof rack where a soldier strapped it down and they boarded. The motorcade continued on its way - lights flashing, horns blaring, sirens wailing, leaving behind a hundred vultures hopping and fighting over the carcasses left in the road.

It was a peculiar thing about vultures, Andy thought, as he looked back on the grisly scene they'd left behind. Nobody understood what it was they responded to when they detected that something had expired. It couldn't be simply a matter of their acute sense of smell or sharp vision because when there was nothing dead about the place, you could scan the sky with the most powerful binoculars and not a single bird would be visible. But let there be carrion or even a hint of it and within minutes, the air would be full of them. It was out of the question that they could scent it from so high up there in the stratosphere, or that they could see the dead remains. So if they couldn't see it or smell it, how in heaven's name did they sense it? That's one of life's mysteries, he reflected.

An hour later, the motorcade turned off the tarmac road through massive iron gates and into a gravelled driveway which wound through the neatly clipped lawns and under the tall trees of jacaranda and kaffirboom that were part of the extensive grounds of State House, Hekima. The line of vehicles stopped outside the solid oak entrance and the entourage began to dismount.

'Come along, you old codger,' said the Colonel opening the saloon door of the limousine. 'Your moment of glory is over. You return to the rank of sergeant until we need you again. Now, I'll take that presidential outfit, if you don't mind.'

He collected the garments and addressed the students.

'I suppose you two young men are hungry after your journey,' he said. 'If you'll come into the main drawing room, I'm sure, being medical students, you'll have a lot in common to talk about with our Doctor Schneider. My soldiers will unload your luggage and keep it safe for you. Meanwhile, I'll see if I can't organize some food for you in the dining room.'

'You're being really kind,' Andy said. 'I hope we can return your hospitality one day.'

'I'm sure you'll be able to repay us and serve your country somehow, one way or another.'

The youths followed the police chief into the palatial drawing room and settled down on the luxurious divan to wait for Doctor Schneider.

'I can't believe our luck!' Andy exclaimed. 'We really have fallen on to our feet and no mistake.'

'Hope you're right,' said Bernard. 'I'm not too sure I like the way things have panned out.'

After ten minutes or so, they were joined by the Doctor.

9

'Well now, young men, what are your names and how do you like State House?'

'I'm called Andrew and this is my brother Bernard. We've never managed to visit State House before and we are most impressed,' Andy gushed. 'I'm sure it's as good as anything Buckingham Palace can offer. I have never seen such luxurious furniture and the paintings on the walls must be worth a fortune.'

'So glad you like it,' replied Schneider, 'but it's not a patch on the palace the President has in the capital at Lundazi and the one he's having built at Lake Zambelia. Now *that* is something and it'll be the equal of any palace anywhere in the world. Our presidential hostess, Marie Antoinette, Marianne to her family and close friends, sees to it that its furnishings and its décor are the best. Why, the paintings she plans for the walls must be as valuable as those to be found in any major art gallery in the world.'

'I agree with Andy about the magnificence of this drawing room,' Bernard said. 'It will be hard for us to settle back in our little study bedrooms after sitting in a place like this. As for the other palaces, maybe one day we'll get to see them on an official tour.'

'We must see what we can do for you,' the Doctor smiled. 'I see no reason why such a tour cannot be arranged,' he said. 'It'll be small recompense for the vital testimony you can give to help bring this vicious P.D.P. organization to justice for the cruel assassination that you witnessed today. Now, I know it's stating the obvious and I do apologize for it but everyone can see that you are identical twins, which is a most unusual thing here in Zambelia. What's the story?'

'Ah, I think I know what you have in mind,' said Andy grimacing. 'In the old traditional Zambelian family, which ours is not I'm happy to say, it was the habit to kill first-born twins at birth.'

'Also babies born feet first or upside-down as they used to put it.' Bernard added, 'but such superstitions are no longer

10

practised, thank the Lord. In fact, anyone caught doing it today would be arrested for murder.'

'What was the reasoning behind such vile primitive thinking, I wonder?' Schneider asked. 'I mean, murdering babies at birth! I ask you!'

'Put it down to superstition,' Andy explained. 'Such babies were not considered human, and it was believed that they brought curses down on the extended family for generations to come.'

'I suppose too' Bernard said, 'there is in their twisted way of thinking, a sort of logic. First-born twins meant too much strain on the mother. A woman could not work so hard in the field while she was feeding one baby at the breast, carrying one on her back and maybe another in her belly.'

Andy said: 'Anyway, we're not first-born as we have an older brother, Jack, who, by the way, is following in the family footsteps like us, as he's a medical student at the university but he's way ahead of us as he's in his fifth year.'

'So you're both medical students! I was going to ask you what you were studying,' Schneider said.

'Yes, that's right,' Andy said enthusiastically and leaning forward. 'As I said, medicine seems to run in our family in a way for not only is our older brother, Jack, studying the subject but our late father was a doctor at Lundazi General Hospital for many years. It's through the money that he left us that we've been able to undertake the long medical course at the Uni. We shall be entering our second year this term.'

'Most interesting,' Schneider said. 'So that's all there is left of your immediate family, your brother and yourselves. What about your mother? Is she still alive?'

'Afraid not,' Andy answered. 'She died over twenty years ago, giving birth to Bernard and myself.'

'I'm sorry to hear that,' said Schneider gently. 'So what are you two hoping to specialize in?'

'I'm hoping to do Infectious Tropical Diseases,' Andy answered promptly. 'When I see the number of Zambelians, young and old alike, suffering and dying from things like malaria, sleeping sickness, river blindness, and so on, I feel a great desire to offer my life in giving what help I can.'

'Very worthy and commendable of you to think like that,' said Schneider. 'And don't forget HIV/AIDS which is prevalent in our part of the world though not specific to the Tropics of course. And what about you, Bernard? What do you hope to do?'

'My interest is in paediatrics, in children's diseases -. I see so many young infants here dying of diseases which are eminently curable in advanced societies that I want urgently to give help. I have in mind killer diseases like: diarrhoea, scarlet fever, measles, diphtheria, and the biggest of them all, malnutrition. I want to devote my life helping to eradicate such diseases.'

'Most interesting, most interesting,' Schneider purred. 'Medicine also runs in my family. Both my father and grandfather were in the trade. My own specialty was gynaecology or the study of womankind and also obstetrics and bringing babies into the world. I suppose this stemmed from my interest in the opposite sex,' he leered. 'My first studies were at Berkeley in California and later at two European universities - Munich and London. I was particularly attracted to the field of...

The discussion was interrupted by one of Kiboko's soldiers.

'Sorry to intrude, Doctor Schneider, but the Colonel wishes to announce that the students' dinner is now ready and I have come to escort them to the State dining room.'

'I think that's the end of our most interesting discussion,' Schneider said, 'but rest assured we shall be meeting again and soon, you can rely on that.'

'Hope so,' said Andy.

Bernard was still a little apprehensive and overwhelmed by the situation they had found themselves in so fortuitously. Not so Andy.

'Let me get to the grub,' he said, rubbing his hands together. 'I could smell it even from the drawing room.' Addressing the soldier, he added, 'Lead on, Macduff.'

The soldier led them to the large dining hall where Colonel Kiboko was waiting for them.

'I'm sure both of you must be ravenous,' he chuckled. 'We'll soon put an end to your hunger. So I shan't hold you back a moment longer.'

He left them sitting at the monk's bench before a polished oak dining table. Five minutes later, two big military chefs marched in with large plates of steaming-hot porridge, meat, and beans - the most appetizing meal the students had seen in months. They tucked in with relish, cleaning their plates with thick slices of bread.

When they had finished, Colonel Kiboko, smoking a cheroot, came into the room to join them while the soldiers-cum-waiters stood back respectfully against the wood-panelled walls.

'I trust you enjoyed your meal,' the Colonel said warmly. 'Richly deserved for your willingness to come forward and act as witnesses. But, tell me, apart from the actual assassination, did you observe the way we switched presidents?'

'Not really,' Bernard said quickly. 'We didn't look too closely.'

'Don't be silly, Bernard,' said Andy, digging his brother playfully in the ribs. 'Yes, of course we did, Colonel. We thought that was quick-thinking on your part.'

'Thank you. You are aware, of course, that you are now privy to a state secret. No-one outside the presidential guard knows that we use stand-ins when we think our leader might be exposed to a dangerous public appearance. I must, of course, insist that you swear an oath of secrecy on the matter. It is imperative that our enemies outside are not aware of our use of presidential doubles.'

'You can trust us,' said Andy earnestly.

'Good. Then there's no harm in your knowing that neither of the presidents you saw this morning was the real thing. No, the true one will arrive for the opening of the Chamber of Deputies later this afternoon - he will come by helicopter.'

'But surely, he too will be exposed to danger when he appears in public,' Bernard protested.

'Good point. But we surround him the whole of the time with dozens of Ngoma dancing women led by our official hostess and presidential consort, Marie Antoinette, whom we respectfully call Big Mama. No-one can get near him that way.'

'I've never realized that before,' said Andy admiringly. 'That's clever.'

'We think so,' said the colonel, smiling broadly. 'Now what about a dessert, boys?'

'Thank you so much,' the twins chorused.

'We have prepared a special surprise for you as a reward for your help.'

'You've already been too kind,' Andy said.

'Think nothing of it,' smiled the Colonel.

He gave a signal to the soldiers standing behind the students. The men stepped forward quickly and, with professional expertise, strangled the brothers where they sat, snapping their necks like twigs.

'Neatly done, men,' said the Colonel, puffing on his cheroot. 'Couldn't have done it better myself. It says much for your commando training. The element of surprise is crucial in situations like this. As you know, there was no choice in the matter and it had to be done for the good of the country. We couldn't take the risk of letting them out. Now gather their things together. There must be absolutely no

14

trace that they were ever here in State House. Meanwhile, I'll go and tell Schneider there are two healthy corpses for his Medical Research Bureau. At least, that should make Big Mama happy.'

****

Chapter Two

Aboard the 747. Sue meets Mike.

The 747 flew across the night sky, high above the Great Rift Valley.

The mixed scent of lemon cologne and fresh coffee pervaded the cabin as the stewardess took round hot towels to waken sleepy passengers in readiness for their next meal and to make them comfortable for the rest of the flight to Zambelia.

Sue, wide-awake after a sleepless night spent in a vain attempt to get comfortable, read the Halliday's letters for the umpteenth time.

'As you know, we work in the presidential palace in the state capital, Lundazi, and we're about a hundred miles from the university town of Hekima, which is nothing in African terms. We'll visit whenever we're free and whenever President Matata has duty at State House there. Hekima itself is one of the most picturesque little towns in Africa. You're going to love it. No city lights of course. The town has two banks, two superettes, one newsagent, one chemist, one baker, masses of Indian shops - sewing machine operators, cobblers, watch-repairers on shop verandahs (on our last visit, the repairer fixed the winder of my watch for ten centinos - about 5 pence - and made a damn sight better job than the 'several quid' effort of the jeweller I took it to in England!).

Lundazi, of course, is the shopping centre but even though it's the capital, it's no bigger than a small English market town. Lovely country of course, Sue. For most people it's

The Lake with its shore line as long as from Dover to Land's End and its clear, blue water and sandy beaches offering swimming, fishing, and bathing. For Helen and me, however, it's the Hekima Plateau - dense forests, rushing mountain streams (flanked by tree ferns and thick belts of indigenous woodlands). For me, also, it's a number of beautifully-sited, well-kept nine-hole golf courses. But for others, it's the tennis or the squash or the music or the drama or the bar at the local country club. Our Life President Matata runs the country very firmly and what he says, goes. For example he has banned television, I'm happy to say. You make your own entertainment. Or else......

Look forward to seeing you. Lotsa love, Peter. Now over to Helen.'

'Hello, Sue. Helen here. The above letter is Peter's angle on things. He forgot to mention Hekima market with its never-ending supply of fish, fruit, vegetables, and new potatoes all the year round. Strawberries too. Blackberries and 'golden berries' in season and you can pick them yourself if you want to in the wilder parts of the forested plateau behind the university. At present, peaches, mangos, bananas (we grow our own), paw-paws, granadillas, and the avocados are so plentiful they fall right off the trees...the list is endless.'

'Your salary of 20,000 matunda (about £10,000) is ample to lead the good life out here and Peter tells me you'll be receiving a special BED Gratuity as well for extra services rendered. That's the icing on the cake. We think you'll love it out here. Peter has mentioned that President Matata here is a very strict and eccentric leader and there are one or two whimsical rules to abide by but apart from those, life here is blissful. Can't wait to see you. We count the days. All my love, Helen.'

Sue tilted her seat back, closed her eyes and smiled to herself. BED Gratuity! That had caused a good deal of consternation and amusement at the Post Office when the clerk had read the telegram over the phone to her. As long as the job included the extra BED gratuity, she'd said to the bewildered clerk, that's OK. The British Expatriate Deferred Gratuity - 100% of her salary to be paid tax free into her British bank account at the end of the contract. On top of that an old-Colonial style house at a nominal rent. How had she managed to be so lucky! It sounded too good to be true. She was single, well-off, had no-one to answer to, and no longer had any ties to speak of.

Oh, it would be good to be back in Africa! It was four years since she'd lived and worked teaching English in Kenya. Livingstone had said that once you were bitten by the African bug, there was no getting it out of your system? Well, she'd been bitten by the African bug all right – no doubt about it and she'd found it difficult to settle down to life back in England.

She was going to miss her brothers, her friends and old familiar places of course but nevertheless, what a relief it had been to pack her bags and board that plane! What joy to get away from the industrialised North with its mean streets, its endless drizzle and the care-worn, grey faces. It had been so depressing. Then there was the traffic, the burglaries, the muggings, the breakdown in law and order. The crazy justice system that seemed to care more for the criminal than the victim. The selfish greed and the "what's in it for me" attitude. She was leaving it behind, at least for a few years. Off to a simpler, saner, society. People who thought Africa was primitive didn't know a thing. It was infinitely more civilised than lawless Britain!

As for the Polytechnic job she'd had there! What a job and a half that had been! Lecturer in Staff Development! Four hundred plus staff and not one had wanted to be developed! That last training course she'd organised had been the last straw. She'd persuaded some of the foremost experts in Britain to come and teach on it - no expense spared – and she'd put heart and soul into setting it up. At the last moment, the Principal had suddenly cancelled the whole thing. No reason given. That was it! Enough to bring out the stubborn Taurus and her Irish temper! Storming into his office, she'd blown her top, and given him a piece of her mind. She'd gone home and wept with anger and frustration. She loved teaching but what was the point of it all? It was 1998, she was thirty-nine years old, and her future had risen up in front of her like a brick wall. She could see herself destined to remain a spinster the rest of her life, teaching stuff that nobody particularly wanted to learn.

Her two older brothers had been forever at her to get married. 'When are you going to get hitched, Sue?' or 'Why don't you find yourself a nice rich bloke, Sue?' As if you simply went up to the meat counter in TESCO's and put one on your shopping trolley. None of them had ever seemed to realise that there was no way she was going to get a man whilst she was teaching all day, looking after an invalid mother at night, and at the same time completing her PhD thesis on the theme of political tyranny in Shakespearean drama. There had been one or two men in her life but it had never amounted to much. Odd encounters on Education courses she'd attended during the long, summer vacations. But all one-night stands and nothing permanent. She'd no qualms about permitting the occasional handsome man into her bed if he was attractive enough, which to her meant a good sense of humour and enough intelligence to conduct a half-decent conversation. In the end though, she'd come to the conclusion that maybe she'd set her sights too high and was suffering now because she wasn't prepared to compromise.

When this chance of a two-year appointment at the University of Zambelia had come up, it'd been the answer to her prayers and she'd taken about ten seconds to decide. Knew she had to go for it. Livingstone's so-called *mal d'afrique* was like those *'Wait-a-minute'* jungle vines, she'd read about somewhere. You couldn't see them but they grabbed you all the same, wrapped themselves around you and pulled you back. And she'd been grabbed by the African vine all right and no mistake.

It hadn't been easy to get away. There'd been the selling of her apartment and the storage of the furniture, the packing, the travel arrangements, and endless round of goodbyes and farewell parties. But now, it was behind her and she was free at last!

Her thoughts were interrupted by the stewardess offering coffee. She lowered her tray and took the cup, being ever so careful not to disturb the man sleeping contentedly next to her. He seemed not to notice her when he'd boarded at Rome some time back and he'd closed his eyes more or less immediately, opening them briefly only for refreshments. He was a slim, long-legged fellow, about forty years of age she guessed, though perhaps a little older since his dark hair was flecked with strands of silver which added a scholarly dimension to his presence. A sun-tanned face with gentle features. Sue didn't mind his snoozing and his apparent indifference towards her as she'd had her fill of talkative bores on past journeys. But she envied him this ability to nap so easily for she'd tossed and turned and found herself in all sorts of odd positions in her own futile efforts to get some shut-eye.

She managed to nod off at some point after Khartoum but she awoke with a start from a restless slumber and wondered how far they'd got on this long flight. She leaned forward, pulled back the shutter on the cabin window and stared out. There was no moon that night and from the cloudless sky, the cold, frosty stars looked down with their thousand million eyes on the dark earth, pinpricked with the tiny lights of countless village fires glowing in the black landscape. Far off on the distant horizon, she could detect the merest hint of light. As she watched, the pale light gradually became tinted, first with pink, then violet, yellow and red - faint at first but suddenly and breathtakingly radiant and resplendent, filling the whole sky with a glorious spectrum of colours. Darkness turned to brilliant gold. An African dawn!

She could imagine the scene thirty thousand feet below. The cocks crowing and the birds breaking into song. The blue smoke rising through the grass thatch of a million beehive mud-and-wattle huts to join the morning mist. A woman, baby on her back, pounding the corn with a steady rhythm whilst the porridge in the blackened pot cooked on the glowing logs. The man harnessing his oxen and cracking his whip. The young lad whistling and prodding the herd of hump-backed, hardy cattle from the kraal, raising the dust as they lumbered out to snatch at the close-cropped tufts of grass. The women walking with perfect, graceful poise, tin container on head, to the local well to gossip and fetch water for the day. The children hurrying barefoot along the miles of dusty, murram track to the ramshackle mission school, there to squat with their slates on the earthen floor and attend to their lessons reverently as if listening to the Messiah himself. The old men assembling under the big tree with their blankets and their *pombe* beer to talk away the hours. The sun was up. Africa!

'Beautiful, isn't it?'

Sue turned, startled for a moment as the man next to her continued.

'It breaks so suddenly. Is there anything on this planet more beautiful than an African dawn? Like watching a great artist paint a series of quick masterpieces using the whole sky as his canvas.'

'Yes' Sue agreed, 'and a different masterpiece each morning.'

'First time in Africa?'

'No. I've worked here before in Kenya. This time, I'm heading for the University of Zambelia at Hekima.'

'Really!' he exclaimed. 'Then we're going to be colleagues. I'm Mike Goodman. I lecture in the Faculty of Medicine.'

He offered his hand.

'Pleased to meet you. I'm Sue Delamere,' she said, taking his hand.

'Good to meet you, Sue.' He stole a quick glance at her. She was strikingly beautiful with auburn hair, lovely blue eyes in an oval face. Under the shapeless utility travel clothes she was wearing, he noted the suggestion of a fine shapely figure. With the right hair style and an up-to-date outfit from a fashion guru, she'd be very glamorous.

'And before you ask,' she said, laughing. 'I *am* related to the great Lord Delamere but only through long-dead, remote ancestors. I believe my great, great, great grandmother was the daughter of the Fourth Earl of Enniskillen and married Baron Delamere in 1899.

'In that case I shan't ask you too many questions about your royal connections,' he said enjoying the joke.

'You say you work in medicine? So, you're a medical doctor?'

'Yes. My colleagues and I help train doctors, nurses and medical orderlies. What about you? What's your field?'

'My contract is with the English Department and I teach Literature with special reference to Elizabethan England.'

'Fascinating! The students will love your subject. I'm sure they'll find much of it relevant to their own lives.' He said this without the slightest hint of irony. 'You say you've worked on the continent before. How did you find it working in Kenya?'

'An absolute joy - which is why I'm looking forward so much to going back. I found that African students were so grateful for all that you did for them - so unlike some of our British students.'

'Yes. I've read about how rough it can be teaching in certain British schools and colleges where students are unmotivated and apathetic. I often think they get things too easily whereas our African students have to work so hard to get any schooling at all, yet alone higher education. It's good you've worked on this continent before, so you won't have any pre-conceived notions that newcomers sometimes have of Africa.'

'What sort of notions?'

'Oh, you know. The usual popular Hollywood ideas of Africa: that the natives are primitive and run around with bones through their noses; or that you're likely to meet Clark Gable and Ava Gardner dressed in their safari gear on the streets of Lundazi recently back from hunting lion and elephants in the jungle. That kind of thing.'

Sue laughed. 'I'm hardly in that naïve category having spent so much of my childhood and early teaching career out there.'

'And thank the Lord for it. You'll probably fit right in from the start. But what do you know about Zambelia?'

'Not a great deal. Obviously, I've read the various travel brochures and official guides issued by the government and it all sounds exciting, I must say.'

'What about the political situation in Zambelia? What impression did you get from these official pamphlets?'

'Not very much. I know that there are two main tribes: the dominant Massuyu and the minority Chuzuni; that Zambelia is run by President Samson Matata who goes around in a cheetah-skin cloak and hat and I gather that he is something of a dictator which, in many ways, I welcome because I believe that without firm rule, a country can descend into chaos.'

'You seem to be pretty well clued up on President Matata. He likes to wear a cheetah hat and cloak because he reckons the cheetah is a cunning animal that never attacks head on but lurks in the grass and relies on a great turn of speed to dispatch its prey. He *is* something of a wild animal, a sort of cat that will enable him to remain in power for a long time. He likes to be called King Cheetah.'

Sue laughed. 'King Cheetah! That's a title that could have a double meaning.'

Mike joined in the laughter and said, 'True, but he prefers to be called cheetah in Swahili, that is *Duma*. But I agree with you about law and order to a certain extent as long as it's not overdone. Matata is an African leader of the old school who won, much to the surprise and against the wishes of the British government, the first and the only democratic election ever held so far; that was before independence about thirty years ago. He has dispensed with democratic elections ever since and now rules with an iron fist having got himself appointed as Life President by methods it's best not to ask too much about. He also has an official hostess or consort and no-one is absolutely sure whether she's his mistress or simply a companion. Behind her back she's been dubbed "The Regent of Zambelia" for her supposed power behind the throne and people accuse her of using her position to turn her family into the nation's richest and most powerful clique. But once again, it's probably hearsay. Interestingly she's named like the famous "let them eat cake" Marie Antoinette though I think those closest to her call her Marianne.'

'I'm intrigued,' Sue said. 'but I don't think Marie Antoinette ever uttered those immortal words "let them eat cake" when they reportedly told her that the peasants had no bread. I'm pretty sure the quotation is from an essay by Jean Jacque Rousseau. As for that name 'Marianne', didn't there used to be a popular song entitled 'Marianne' sung by Donny Osmond? Sorry, Mike, I've interrupted you.'

'I can see I'll have to watch my Ps and Qs with you. As for a song entitled 'Marianne', it might be best if you're not heard singing it in public as our rulers are mighty touchy on the subject.'

24

'What, touchy about a popular song? Surely not?' Sue laughed.

'Afraid so,' Mike said looking serious for the first time. 'Anyway, to get back to the subject of Matata. A dissident faction in the country claims he won the election by corruption, ju-ju methods and the use of terrorism but there's no proof. Another disgruntled group in the country reckon he's built up an adulatory cult of toadies and strong-arm men who prop him up and keep him in power. They are loyal to him because they have the most to lose if he goes. State radio and the press declare he is a "god" who can work miracles with his almighty powers.'

Sue nodded. 'In the two African societies I know about, there were always malcontents ready to plot against the boss. There's bound to be feelings of jealousy and envy amongst the losers who feel their noses have been put out of joint. Don't you think so?'

'Maybe you're right,' he said, none too enthusiastically. 'Tell me, have you any family or friends out here in Zambelia?'

'No. I have two older brothers back in England but both my parents have sadly passed on. But I do have some good friends there. Old family friends, the Hallidays, who work in the State House in Lundazi. What about you? Do you have family in Zambelia? I notice you're wearing a wedding ring.'

Sue indicated the ring on his left hand.

'No. Not now,' he shrugged. 'Divorced. My wife - ex-wife - works in Durban now - a dentist.'

'So sorry to hear about your divorce. I'm told it can be a bitter and painful experience.'

'No problem now. We split up about three years ago and though it *was* painful at the time, I'm over it now. As far as I'm concerned, it's in the past - ancient history.'

'Good to hear you're recovered. I know from friends of mine back home who went through divorce how rough it can be. Anyway, these old friends of mine in Lundazi paint a glowing picture of life out there; they're the ones who persuaded me to take up the post in Hekima. I can't tell you how glad I am to be back in Africa. From what the Hallidays tell me, it sounds like roses all the way.'

Mike looked concerned for a moment. 'Not forgetting that roses sometimes have thorns,' he said.

'How do you mean?'

'Well, snags, drawbacks, if you like.'

'What sort of drawbacks?'

'Well, for a start, it's a poor agricultural country producing tobacco, tea, sugar and maize. There are a few raw materials, like gold and diamond deposits but these don't amount to much. What little has been developed is held firmly in a government monopoly. How much of this wealth is used for the good of the people is anybody's guess. Precious little I'd say. In many ways though, being a poor country with few natural resources can be a blessing in disguise.'

'Sorry, but you've lost me there. How can being poor be a blessing in disguise?'

'Well, look at it like this. The more natural resources a country possesses, the more they seem to cause strife. You've only to look at Nigeria with its oil; Zaire with its vast mineral wealth; Zambia with its copper. They attract nothing but trouble. Sorry, if I appear to be riding my hobby horse.'

'Not at all. I've always found people on hobby horses to be the most interesting and the most passionate about things. But you were talking about roses and thorns, snags and drawbacks.'

'Oh, yes. I remember now. Take Zambelia's climate for example. On the whole, it's beautiful but sometimes capricious, producing floods and droughts. But you'll be used to that kind of thing. No, there are more serious problems. Look, I don't want to disenchant you before you've even set foot in the place.'

26

'Don't worry. You won't,' Sue laughed. 'Believe me, nothing could be as bad as the place I've come from.'

Mike smiled at her quizzically. He wasn't convinced but he was already regretting his thoughtless comments. She looked like a nice person and he didn't want to dampen her enthusiasm and spoil her return to Africa so early in the game. She'd find out for herself soon enough.

The sound of the tannoy interrupted them.

'This is Captain Evans speaking. We shall soon be commencing our descent into Lundazi International Airport and we expect to land there in about fifteen minutes. Local time is nine am. The weather there is fine and temperature is twenty degrees Celsius. Please, return your seats to the upright position and fasten your seat belts. We trust that you've enjoyed your flight with British Airways and we hope to welcome you aboard once again in the near future. Thank you.'

Then something unusual happened. A number of African men and women began altering their attire: the men took off jackets and ties and substituted safari tunics and cravats whilst the women removed their European-type wigs and hair extensions.

'What's all that about?' a puzzled Sue asked, observing this odd behaviour.

'They're returning Zambelians,' Mike grinned, 'and they're anxious to conform to the official dress code; it's referred to as authenticity. No European dress allowed for indigenous people as part of the Africanization programme that's attempting to reject all vestiges of colonialism. There are quite a few dress regulations. I'll explain further when we go through immigration. Now, I think it's time to adjust our seats into the upright position.'

'Well, here we go,' Sue said, relaxing with eyes closed giving Mike a chance to look at her more closely.

His first opinion of her beauty was confirmed. If anything, she was even more attractive now her features were so relaxed.

The rhythm of the great Pratt and Whitney engines changed abruptly and the plane began to descend steeply. Soon, the world turned topsy-turvy as they rushed at a crazy angle over daub-and-wattle villages, roads, railways, rivers, and bridges.

'What's that strange black river we just passed over?' she asked suddenly opening her eyes and peering through the cabin window. 'It looks like treacle flowing along a road.'

'That's not a river,' Mike chuckled. 'It's Zambelia's so-called M.1 motorway. And as for the treacle, that's the refugees fleeing from the senseless civil war in Umbali; they're on their way to the big refugee camp outside Lundazi. Zambelia, which has great problems feeding itself, is now forced to play host to a million refugees.'

He decided to stop there. He knew the camps only too well, spending much of his spare time administering to the needs of the sick and the dying there.

'How do they get across the border? Don't the Zambelian authorities stop them?'

'Impossible to do so. Some refugees have walked hundreds of miles. Many have simply crossed the road. You see, the road is the border between the two countries. One side is Umbali - the other Zambelia. Sometimes it runs through a tribe, a village, - even a family - thanks to our nineteenth century colonial mapmakers. Ah, here we go.'

A gentle thud and the deafening screech of brakes announced their landing.

The 747 eased down on the tarmac, bumped slightly, braked, turned, and taxied in towards the airport terminal. Uniformed airport staff wheeled out the disembarking steps, and an eager caravan of porters, baggage trucks, officials and *askaris* swarmed out towards the plane like a line of safari ants. The doors swung open, the officials marched on board, there was the usual bureaucratic delay, and then the passengers began to emerge, staggering down the steps, carrying their hand luggage and top coats, blinking and screwing up their eyes against the sudden glare of the tropical sun.

'Welcome to Zambelia, Sue,' Mike said. 'I hope you'll be happy here. I'm sure you'll find the life here more exciting and challenging than the one you've left behind.'

****

Chapter Three

Arrival Lundazi Airport. Meet The Hallidays.

In the arrival lounge of the airport, there were long queues.

'To get into this country, Sue,' Mike explained, 'we have to surmount three bureaucratic hurdles. First, immigration. Second, customs. Third, internal security.'

'What on earth's that last one - internal security?'

'Sorry. No words of mine could do it justice. You have to experience it to believe it.'

He recognized someone ahead of them in the line. 'Oh, there's a colleague of ours with his wife. I must introduce them to you as soon as I get the chance. They're from Arkansas and his full handle is Doctor Elmer Moroney but at the university, everyone calls him Bugsy Moroney.'

When she heard this, Sue could not suppress a fit of giggles. 'But isn't that the title of a gangster movie where the gangsters are kids? I loved that film and the battles between '"Fat Sam" and "Dandy Dan" with their splurge guns covering the victims in cream.'

Mike joined in Sue's laughter. 'That movie was entitled "Bugsy *Malone*" whereas our man is Bugsy *Moroney*. It's pretty close, I have to admit.'

'But why Bugsy?' Sue asked, still chuckling.

'Doctor Moroney is an entomologist and a good one at that. And since bugs are his business...'

'Naturally, he gets the pet-name, Bugsy,' Sue said, completing his sentence. 'But didn't his wife object?'

'She did at first but when she heard everyone calling him "Bugsy", she caved in and now she too adopts the nickname and thinks it's "kinda cute". He's a great bloke is our Bugsy but a bit of a dreamboat; most of the time he has his head in the clouds.'

'Judging from his lean and lanky appearance,' Sue grinned, 'that could mean both figuratively and literally. He looks as if he belongs in a circus.'

Bugsy was five or six places ahead of them in the queue. Hunched under the weight of the two heavy cases of hand-luggage, he was the strangest-looking creature Sue had ever clapped eyes on. He was around fifty years old, about six feet six inches tall though it could have been more, with a beanpole-thin figure which looked too long to be balanced on two normally-sized feet; a square head with a crew hair-cut, and a pale, flat face with rimless glasses through which he squinted giving him a bewildered and startled expression. To Sue, he looked for all the world like the ideal absent-minded professor straight out of a boy's science-fiction comic. Next to him with both hands free - stood his diminutive wife, wearing a dazzlingly bright green trouser suit, a matching shoulder-bag, jumbo-lensed, heart-shaped sun-glasses, and extremely long ear-rings.

Mike now tapped the tall man lightly on the shoulder. Despite the heavy luggage, he seemed to jump several feet into the air.

'What's that? What's that? Who's that?' he exclaimed, peeping nervously over his shoulder. 'Oh, yeah! Oh, yeah! It's you Mike!'

'Let me introduce a new colleague, Bugsy. Sue, meet Bugsy Moroney and his wife Betty Jo. Sue is with the English Department. Bugsy teaches biotechnology - he's a genetic engineer.'

31

'Sounds mysterious,' said Sue. 'Gene manipulation, and all that. But happy to know you both.'

'Oh, yeah! Oh, yeah!' said Bugsy. 'Hi. Great to meetcha. We'll talk some more when we get to Hekima. Say Mike, I went to a few conferences on avian mating patterns back in the States; learned a lot. Got myself a swell cam corder and a coupla CD players. Picked 'em up in Nairobi for a song; they'll be great for recording African songbirds. But right now, the problem is we gotta get past these goddam official guys.'

'Hi. Glad to meetcha, Sue, and welcome to Zambelia,' said Betty Jo, enthusiastically and ignoring her husband's concern about getting past the customs. 'We must have you over for dinner some time when we get back to Hekima. *If we ever get back to Hekima, I should say.*

Sue thought to herself: When someone in England says "we must have you over some time," it usually meant: "no way shall we ever have you over."

But Betty-Jo continued: 'Bugsy can show you his slides on African songbirds. See you soon. Now Bugsy, do you have the Employment Permits?'

'I had 'em somewhere here, honey, when we were aboard the plane. But I can't seem to locate 'em right now.'

'Oh, God! Not again!' sighed Betty Jo. 'This happens every time we go a-travelling. You guys had better go on ahead. Now come on, Bugsy, take everything out of your pockets. Because if we don't find that damn permit we're right up that famous creek again. If I weren't with you, you'd forget your head.'

Sue and Mike reached the Immigration desk. Mike handed over his passport and this was promptly stamped and initialled by a sullen-looking official. Sue presented her Temporary Employment Permit.

The morose Immigration Officer scrutinized the permit for an unconscionably long time - it might as well have been written in ancient Sanskrit. He looked up with a surly expression: 'This permit is for two years only. If you stay even one day over the due date, you will be arrested. Welcome to Zambelia.'

He stamped the permit making every object on his desk rattle. Sue collected the document.

'And thank *you*, kind sir' she said, emphasizing her words, 'for that warm welcome.'

A Senior Immigration Officer standing nearby had been watching the proceedings closely.

'Wait,' he bellowed. 'Come back. Come back. That stamp won't do. What sort of stamp is that for a newcomer?' Glowering at the junior officer, he spat noisily on the ink pad and stamped the permit again. This time several things *did* jump off the desk and he signalled imperiously to his now sheepish underling to pick them up.

'There,' the senior man said. 'That's much better. Welcome again to Zambelia.'

Behind them the Moroneys were still searching for their precious work pass.

'Are you sure you didn't leave it behind in Kennedy when you were looking for your passport?' Betty Jo sighed.

A happy, smiling porter approached Mike with a trolley.

'Jambo, Daktari. You want a porter for the *memsahib* and yourself.'

'*Asante sana*,' said Mike. 'Please take our luggage.'

'*Mzuri, Daktari.*'

The porter collected their baggage from the carousel and the trio made their way into the Customs Hall.

'Isn't there a green and a red channel to go through?' asked Sue

Mike laughed. 'You must be joking. In this country, Customs want to see everything. And I mean everything.'

Ahead of them a customs official was giving an Asian family a hard time.

'If you don't have the receipts for this camera and audio equipment, you must pay the full duty,' he was yelling at the unfortunate travellers. 'I could have you arrested for attempted smuggling.'

'Over here, please!' an officer called to Sue and Mike. 'Are you two together?'

'You may as well check us out together,' Mike suggested, 'for the sake of speed and efficiency.'

'Do *not* try to tell me my job,' the official barked. 'Now, Madam. Please open your suitcases and your hand luggage for inspection.'

'You mean *all* of it?' asked Sue incredulously.

'All of it!' he growled.

Reluctantly, Sue flicked open the catches on her cases. The officer rummaged through her belongings.

'Do you have anything which you have bought in the last six months?' he asked. 'Watches, jewellery, electronic equipment? That sort of thing? Presents for friends in Zambelia?'

'Nothing,' she replied.

'What about this silk underwear?' he enquired loudly holding up a black transparent negligee and a pair of lace panties. The lascivious eyes of the males in the customs shed - including Mike's – swivelled to the garments in question.

'Nothing, I said,' she snapped, flushing with anger and embarrassment.

'Very well,' he said, chalking her cases.

Mike passed through without any trouble. He'd learned his lesson the hard way in past encounters.

The Moroneys had now managed to survive the Immigration inquisition and were immediately behind them undergoing the Customs ordeal.

'Do you have anything new in your luggage?' they were asked.

'No. I guess not,' said Bugsy.

'But, honey, what about the two CD players we bought in Nairobi? Did you forget about them?'

Bugsy looked daggers at his wife.

'Oh, yeah. Oh, yeah. I clean forgot about them. I guess I'd better declare them though they're essential for my work at the University.'

'I cannot see why you need two players,' the official said.

'I guess you're right,' said Bugsy. 'Look, the Sony is for me and the Sanyo is for you. How about that?'

'That will be satisfactory,' the customs man replied with an oily grin.

Sue and Mike moved on leaving the Moroneys in the throes of a heated argument over the exact amount of the charges due on the rest of their electronic equipment.

'This is beginning to get me down,' said Sue. 'What a welcome after a long and tiring flight!'

'Sue,' said Mike. 'In the immortal words of Al Jolson, "You ain't seen nothin' yet". The next one - Internal Security - is the most entertaining one of all. Hold on to your hat.'

'You seem to be running the gauntlet successfully.'

'That's because *I* know the ropes and the things to avoid. I know the way these officials think.'

They entered a room marked "Zambelia State Security". Over in the corner, a European youth was having his hair cut by an African barber.

'What's that about, for heaven's sake?' asked Sue. 'Why a barber's shop in the so-called State Security Department?'

'Nothing to worry about,' said Mike. 'His hair exceeded the length permitted for males in this country. So they're correcting his coiffure so's he can be allowed in.'

'What strange laws!' she said. 'I thought I'd seen it all.'

'You wait. There's more to come.'

A smartly-dressed officer with the ZSS flashes on his shoulders beckoned them over to one of the long desks. High on the wall behind him was a massive beaming portrait of the Zambelian President emerging from the clouds dressed in his Savile Row safari suit and his mottled fez, and carrying the obligatory fly whisk; the poster of the benign, smiling Leader bore the legend: 'President Matata Loves You.'

'Shades of 'Big Brother' and '1984',' Sue whispered.

'Not really,' replied Mike. 'I doubt that anyone in this country has ever read that work since it's been banned ever since the President came to power. Notice too that the picture occupies the highest place on the wall; it's illegal for anyone to place anything in a higher position.'

Next to the portrait hung the Zambelian flag below which was a banner displaying the four 'foundations' of the country's one-and-only permissible political party, the Massuyu Conference Party: INTEGRITY, ALLEGIANCE, DUTY, ORDER.

The official came forward to greet them.

'Good morning, Doctor Goodman,' he said. 'I hope you enjoyed your holiday in Britain. It's about a month since we last saw you here, isn't it? Glad to be back?'

'Why, yes. And thank you. It *is* good to be back.'

'I trust you purchased nothing seditious or pornographic whilst you were abroad. Books, films, videotapes?'

'Not me. Not a chance.'

'Good. If you don't mind, I'll go through your things. A mere formality in your case.'

'But, of course.'

The officer examined Mike's belongings with a skilled hand.

'What's this book, Doctor Goodman?'

36

'Oh, that. *'Myles' Textbook for Midwives'*. It's a book on gynaecology - a medical textbook I'm reviewing for our student nurses.'

The officer flicked idly through the book and his eye alighted on one of the diagrams.

'But this is a picture of the female sex organ.'

'The vagina. Yes, of course, it is. Student nurses have to know about these things.'

'I am sorry, Doctor Goodman but I cannot allow the importation of this book. It is lewd and pornographic and likely to corrupt the morals of our young and impressionable nurses. I must confiscate it and report it to the Censorship Board of Zambelia.'

Mike was about to protest but thought better of it.

'I hope the Censorship Board will report back soon. Let's hope they find in my favour as I have need of the book for a medical course.'

The officer turned away and took Mike's heavy book over to a shelf which held the works that had already been confiscated earlier that morning. They made a bizarre juxtaposition of titles with Arnold Toynbee's *The Russian Revolution* next to *Kiss Me Deadly* by Mickey Spillane; and *The Complete Works of Oscar Wilde* beside *The Lady Couldn't Say No* by Tony Spoletti and George Orwell's *Animal Farm*.

Sue couldn't resist taking the mickey. She said sarcastically: ' "I know the ropes" he says. "I know the way these officials think" he says. I'm surprised you took the confiscation of your book so submissively. Why didn't you protest?'

'Last year, one of our staff - a Professor of English had an eyeball-to-eyeball confrontation with the chairman of the Censorship Board on the subject of proscribed literature. Next day, he was made a P.I. – a Prohibited Immigrant – and given twenty-four hours to leave the country.'

37

'You mean actually deported?'

'That's exactly what I mean.'

The officer now turned his attention to Sue.

'Good morning, Madame. Welcome to our country. I have a number of formalities to go through. First, are you or have you ever been a member of a subversive organization, like the Communist Party or Amnesty International?'

'Never.'

'Good. Now, if you'll excuse me, I must examine your things.'

He rifled through Sue's suitcases and her hand luggage. He took out her Pentax camera and held it up.

'This is a good camera, Madame. I trust you are acquainted with our regulations on photography. There are many things and places you are forbidden to photograph on penalty of deportation. Things like road and rail bridges, police and fire stations, radio masts, and so on. You will find a full list of tabooed activities in the enclosed paper. Now, I notice, you have a copy of *Cosmopolitan* in your hand luggage. This is forbidden and I must confiscate it - it could corrupt our youth if it fell into the wrong hands. And your copy of *Woman's Own* is allowed but only after the censorship officer at the desk opposite has checked it out.'

'*Cosmopolitan* I can understand - it is perhaps a little risqué. But *Woman's Own*! Surely not! Could anything be more innocent? It's meant for housewives and mothers.'

'I'm sorry, Madame. I don't make the rules.'

'I did warn you,' said Mike, grinning from ear to ear as they walked towards the censorship desk.

'Wait a moment,' called the Security Officer. 'Could you return here for a moment? I've noticed, Madame, that the length of your dress infringes regulations.'

'My dress!' Sue said angrily, her Irish temper flaring up. 'What on earth do you mean? The length of my dress is my own damn business.'

38

'Not in Zambelia, Madame. We are strict about our standard of dress and are careful not to give scandal.'

He snapped his fingers and a junior security officer came forward with a tape measure. He measured the length of the dress above her knee.

'Four inches,' he reported.

'This is ridiculous,' exclaimed an irritated Sue. 'The whole thing's just a farce. Where's Barbara Windsor and the rest of the Carry-On" team?'

'We take short skirts as a serious offence, Madame. Since you have just arrived, you will be permitted to proceed to Hekima. But I must warn you, if you do not lengthen your dress to cover your knees, you will be arrested.'

Sue turned abruptly on her heel giving the officer a quick flash of thigh which he wasn't slow to notice. Mike was grinning now like a jackass.

'At least, it's more entertaining than Heathrow,' he said. 'Come on. Now for the censorship man.'

Sue slapped her copy of *Woman's Own* on his desk.

'It's all yours,' she rapped. 'Now, let's see you find something wrong with that!'

The young censor turned the pages of the magazine. He stopped at an advertisement featuring a young lady in a swimsuit.

'Not allowed,' he announced, obliterating the legs with a thick felt-tip pen. He flipped through the pages and stopped at an ad displaying underwear. 'Not allowed,' he repeated, painting out the lower limbs. He handed the magazine back to Sue. 'Now, it's all right and conforms to regulations.'

By now, even Sue was beginning to see the funny side of it.

'I feel like Alice in Wonderland,' she said. 'We only need The White Rabbit and the Queen of Hearts. They should be going through here any time now.'

Then the Moroneys appeared.

'Boy, are we having a rough time but we're coming to the last hurdle,' Bugsy called over to them as he deposited his suitcases on the security desk. 'Don't think anything can go wrong here.'

The Officer looked over in Betty Jo's direction.

'You should know by now that women are not allowed to wear trousers in our country. Men must dress as men and women as women. You must change into a dress of regulation length as soon as you reach home or you will be put in gaol.'

'Yeah, yeah, I know all that. I'll change as soon as I get home,' Betty Jo sighed.

Meanwhile, the officer pulled a book out of Bugsy's hand luggage.

'What's this book, Doctor Moroney? *The Green Revolution*? It must be subversive with a title like that.'

'Yeah, Yeah, Yeah. I mean No, No, No. It's a book about the hybridization of maize and wheat.'

'We can take no chances in this field, Doctor Moroney. We cannot jeopardize the security of our country. I must confiscate the book and report it to the Censorship Bureau.'

'Oh, very well,' sighed Bugsy. 'Just let me outa here so I can get home. We've had a long journey from New York and I'm just about all in.'

The officer leaned forward and peered closely at Bugsy's tie.

'That tie, Doctor Moroney. May I see it, please.'

'Oh yeah. Oh, yeah. You like the tie, huh?'

'I gave him that for his birthday,' said Betty Jo proudly. 'You see the picture of the pig and the letters MCP. Male Chauvinist Pig. You like it, eh?'

The officer turned purple with rage.

'That tie is a great insult to our country, Doctor Moroney. The letters MCP stand for Massuyu Conference Party and you are implying with your tie that party members are pigs. It is offensive to our country and to our illustrious leader - our great Lord and Master, the noble Life President Samson Matata.'

'No, no,' protested Bugsy. 'I've always had the greatest respect for your country and the Life President.'

'You will please wait here whilst I fetch my superior.'

'What seems to be the trouble here, Kilele?' demanded the high-ranking officer.

'This man, Doctor Moroney, has subversive intentions. First he tried to import a book which preaches revolution, then he wore a tie insulting our glorious party implying we are pigs.'

'No, no, ' wailed Bugsy. 'You got it all wrong. The tie means....'

'Please accompany me to the interrogation room,' said the officer. 'We shall get to the bottom of this. And, if these accusations are true, you will be out on the next plane, I can assure you.'

'Please, please,' protested Bugsy as they led him away. 'I'm innocent, I tell ya.'

'There you are,' Betty Jo called over. 'What did I tellya? Every time we go a-travelling, we end up the creek without a paddle. Now, let's see him get outa this one.'

'Will he be OK?' asked Sue anxiously.

'Oh, sure,' said Betty Jo. 'Bugsy's the kinda guy who always falls on his feet. You'll see.'

Sue and Mike began to walk down a long passage towards the exit.

'That's the most bizarre experience I've ever undergone,' said Sue. 'What stupid censorship laws!'

They passed two uniformed policemen strolling along the passage hand in hand.

'Look at those two. Why aren't they arrested for public scandal?'

'You've got it wrong, Sue. According to official sources, homosexuality is not merely strictly taboo in Zambelia, it does not exist and for a good reason. The government imposes severe punishment on gay people: for a first offence – five years in prison; for persistent serial homosexual behaviour – execution. As for those two officers, they are probably circumcision brothers and related by a strong ritual bond of friendship. I doubt there's any homosexuality involved but of course I can't be sure.'

At that moment, the Moroneys appeared with three porters pushing their mountain of luggage ahead of them.

'We made it! We made it!' Bugsy yelled.

'But, how did you get them to drop the threat of immediate deportation?' asked Sue.

'Easy,' said Bugsy, stroking the open palm of his hand and touching his nose with his forefinger. 'Cost me two hundred matunda and I told 'em to keep the goddam tie and the goddam book for that matter. And now, it's Hekima, bath-tub, and bed - here we come! Whadda ya say honey?' They hurried on towards the exit.

'The way things are run in this country!' said Sue. 'It sounds like a madhouse. It's crazy.'

'Wait until you visit the cinema in Lundazi. Then you'll see how crazy these censorship laws are. For example, Zambelians find kissing offensive - that means any kind of kissing even between close relatives. Kissing in public is illegal and punishable by imprisonment. You'll find the censorship of films is truly extraordinary. Violence and foul language go uncensored but kissing scenes, even between brothers and sisters, are always cut. When the cut and the spliced film are shown on the screen the couple about to

42

embrace suddenly spring apart as though repelled by a particularly foul form of halitosis. It's so hilarious that it always results in howls of laughter and has the audience rolling in the aisles.'

'I suppose these things are the snags you were talking about earlier?'

'Afraid not. These are not snags; they're merely pinpricks. Snags come later on the menu. The security situation in this country,' he laughed, 'can be summed up in the story of a little dog story.'

'You mean a shaggy dog story?'

'Not quite. There was this little dog who applied to the Zambelia Immigration for permission to emigrate. "But why do you want to emigrate?" the officer asked. "You've got everything here. Good home. Good food. You're well looked after." "I simply want to bark". the dog replied.'

'Very droll,' Sue said, unable to suppress a giggle. 'One thing is obvious though. 'If I'm to survive and keep my sanity, I'm going to need every bit of my Northern sense of humour.'

****

Chapter Four

Drive to Sue's Hekima home

At the arrival gate, Peter and Helen Halliday waited for Sue. They had known her since she was a toddler when they had been the family's next-door neighbour in the small town of Machakos in the Ukambani District of Kenya. Sue's parents had worked at the Boys' High School where they had taught English and History. Peter, then a slim twelve stone, had been an officer in the Special Branch of the Kenya Police while Helen had taught Domestic Science at the Women's Teacher Training College. Over the years, the families became close friends even though they couldn't have been more different. The Hallidays had no children whereas the Delameres had three - two sons and a baby daughter. The Hallidays were highly extrovert, loving nothing better than a round of dinner parties and social engagements whilst the Delameres were a quiet couple and, on the whole, preferred a less exuberant life style. The two families complemented each other as they saw in the other those qualities they found lacking in themselves. Every year, they spent their holidays together in a hired cottage at Shanzu in Mombasa and there, the Hallidays became second parents to the Delamere children, especially the young Sue who believed for many years that she had been lucky enough to have two mothers and two fathers. The memory of those wonderful seaside holidays would remain with her forever - the swimming, the leaping through the waves, the boating, the beach games in the tropical sunshine.

Helen's dinner parties in the Machakos township were celebrated for their extravagance. Their neighbours Jim and Kate Delamere were always the first names on the guest list though Jim had privately described their dinners as "gargantuan". Helen was highly qualified in the culinary arts having completed not only a degree in Domestic Science but an Advanced Diploma in Cordon Bleu Cuisine at the Prue Leith Cookery School. Her favourite way of spending her time was dreaming up new recipes for the delight of her guests and her husband, whose expanding waistline had begun to bear witness to her culinary skills. On the Country Club calendar of events - the dances, the bridge parties, the beetle drives, the quiz evenings - the Hallidays were the leading lights and the organisers of many delightful functions. And when it came to raising funds for the Club swimming pool or the new Squash Court, it was always the Hallidays to the fore. Garden parties, fêtes, barbecues, no matter what. Helen had taken on the role of House representative on the Club Committee - Peter was the Golf Secretary.

When Kenya won its independence in 1963, the Delameres became worried about their children's future education and decided to return to Britain. The Hallidays had opted to take their chances under Kenyatta's government and stay on for further contract appointments. Things had turned out well for them in the new Kenya and they remained at their posts continuing to enjoy the social whirl of the expatriate community. They finally returned to England on reaching the age of fifty-five - the accepted age of retirement for colonial civil servants - to start a new life in Bournemouth. They did the usual things that retired couples do in Bournemouth: swimming in the mornings with the other old folk in the warm indoor baths of the large hotels, taking advantage of the cheap lunches at their local church, attending afternoon tea-dances and bridge parties, joining the other promenading pensioners as they processed in the evenings along the seaside front. Their one challenging, intellectual pursuit had been the study of Esperanto, the so-called international language, at the local technical college. After a year in Bournemouth spent in the company of these silver-haired citizens, Helen Halliday decided she'd had enough.

'Is this all there is?' she asked of no-one in particular. 'Are we to live out the rest of our days in an elephants' graveyard?'

She began scrutinising the Overseas Appointments Sections of the national newspapers until one day she spotted an advertisement inviting applications for a Supervisory Housekeeper and Social Secretary at the State House of Zambelia, in Lundazi. She applied and, to her astonishment, got the post. Peter, her husband, who wasn't too sure about the move, secured the job of Security Adviser - a post, he was sure they had invented in order to keep him happy and give him something to do. After much heart-searching and many sleepless nights, they came to the conclusion that life in Zambelia would be better than waiting to be allotted their bath-chair on the promenade. They took in a deep breath and decided to go. They found that Zambelia had not only the friendliest of people but the most spectacular scenery they had ever seen in their globetrotting careers. As for the job! It was right up Helen's street since it involved organising ambassadorial banquets and big social events connected with the palace and acting as general factotum of the palace staff. So happy were they with the country and their situation, they wrote glowing accounts to Sue Delamere, now an experienced lecturer. When Sue's mother died leaving Sue free of commitments and responsibility, it seemed the ideal time for her to break loose from the post she held in the UK and return to the Africa she loved.

Now as they waited for the BA passengers to disembark, Helen looked around the waiting crowd and noticed a handsome, well-dressed African youth holding a small

46

blackboard with the name 'DR SUSAN DELAMERE' chalked on it.

'Good morning,' she called out to him.

The young man turned and gave her a dazzling smile - gleaming white teeth, and eyes that sparkled and danced.

'Good morning, Madam,' he replied bowing politely.

'I notice that you and I are waiting for the same person on the BA flight from London - Doctor Susan Delamere.'

'Why, yes. I've been asked to meet Doctor Delamere, a new member of staff, along with a number of other lecturers returning from leave. I've come with the mini-bus to take them back to Hekima.'

'I see. You're a driver on the university staff, are you?'

'No, not exactly. The driver is outside looking after the bus. I'm a medical student at the university. My name is Jack Zulu.'

'Nice to meet you, Jack. I'm Helen Halliday and this is my husband, Peter. We work at the palace.'

They shook hands.

'How do you like being at the university, Jack?' asked Peter.

'I love every minute of it' Jack answered, flashing that smile again. 'We have a fine tutor in Dr Goodman and the work can be challenging, especially that in the refugee camps and in the leproserie on Mombo Island. I have two younger twin brothers, Andrew and Bernard, also in the same line of work. I'm in my final year and they're about to join their second.'

'You're all training to be doctors?' Helen asked.

'That's right. At the end of the course we shall be qualified general practitioners but we hope to become specialists one day. Who knows? Perhaps one day we'll get our chance...Ah, here come the passengers now,' he said holding up his board.

Peter and Helen stood on tip-toe and craned their necks over the crowd to get a better view. The passengers ambled through the gate in a dream-like state looking bewildered like humans returning from a distant planet and surprised to find themselves back on earth. It was Helen who spotted her trim, neat figure first as she came through with the porter by her side pushing the luggage trolley.

'There she is, Peter,' Helen called excitedly.

She pushed her way through the crowd impatiently and rushed to meet her.

'Welcome back to Africa, Sue,' she cried embracing her.

'Sue, you look as beautiful as ever,' said Peter affectionately as he kissed her on the cheek.

'Am I glad to see you two again?' said Sue. 'I never thought I'd survive that crazy obstacle race back there.'

'Look upon it as an initiation ceremony,' Helen laughed 'Anyway you're here now and we know you're going to love it.'

Mike Goodman cleared his throat to make his presence felt.

'Oh, sorry, Mike,' said Sue 'Let me introduce a colleague. Mike Goodman - my good friends, the Hallidays, Peter and Helen.'

There was handshaking all round.

'There's a young man here who's come out to meet you, Sue,' Helen said.

'Ah, I see you've already made the acquaintance of one of my students,' said Mike to the Hallidays. 'Sue, meet Jack Zulu.'

'Honoured to know you, Doctor Delamere,' said Jack. 'I've come to escort you to Hekima. I have the minibus at the main gate.'

Sue shook his hand warmly.

'If you'll excuse me for a moment or two,' Jack said 'I'd better go on outside and help Doctor Moroney and his wife with all that luggage; from the look of things, they're going to need an extra couple of trolleys, I think. Nice to have met you, Mr and Mrs Halliday. Hope we meet again soon.'

'Likewise,' chorused the Hallidays.

'That young man is talented,' said Mike when Jack had departed. 'He'll make a fine doctor one day - as will his two younger brothers. Sue tells me you work at State House. How do you find that?'

'Hard work,' replied Helen, 'But satisfying. I do the social organising and Peter is in charge of security arrangements. So, we're kept pretty busy - which is how we like it. Big Mama insists on the highest standards of efficiency for the palace staff.'

Mike raised an eyebrow, 'Big Mama? And not the President?'

'It's an open palace secret,' said Peter. 'The President's getting on and he's not been too well for some time. Big Mama has been running the show as regent.'

'Who is this mysterious Big Mama?' Sue asked. 'And whose mother is she?'

Helen laughed. 'No, certainly not a mother. She is the eldest of five daughters of the late Karanja, a respected tribal chief, but she is the Official Hostess or Consort to the President - has been for many years.'

'Ah, yes, now I know who you mean,' Sue exclaimed. 'Mike has been telling me about your Marie Antoinette and I take it she's the Mama you're referring to.'

'That's right, Sue,' Helen nodded. 'the very same. Marie Antoinette but Marianne to family and close friends. And to people in the country as a whole she is known as Mama which is a term of great respect. Folk call her *Big* Mama, not because she has a big body, but because she's highly

49

respected and, in some respects, considered to be a sort of Big Mother and protector for everybody in the land.'

'I hope that's not like a female version of George Orwell's Big Brother in *Nineteen Eighty Four*.'

'Hardly,' Helen said, looking serious for the first time.

'I'm sorry to break up our little party,' said Mike, 'but I think I can see them waiting for us in the college Land Rover. We'd better be making tracks, Sue.'

'Perhaps we'll all meet again.' said Helen, hugging Sue once more, 'when we come down to Hekima. I can't tell you how happy we are to have you here in Zambelia with us. I know we can look forward to some good times together.'

'And thank you both for telling me about this lovely place,' Sue replied. 'I know I'm in for a great time.'

Jack Zulu was back. 'Sorry to break up the welcoming party,' he said, 'but it's a two hour drive to Hekima, so we'd better be on our way.

***

'I shall be taking the scenic route,' the driver announced, 'along minor roads to avoid the refugees. It's longer but the scenery's more interesting.'

The mini-bus sped through Lundazi - the streamlined city. The austere lines of the contemporary glass-and-concrete structures were softened by the blur of colour from flowering trees along the wide city streets - from the brilliant red flamboyants to the lilac jacarandas. Soon they were out in the country and the air was rich with the smells of earth and grass.

From her window, Sue watched an ever-changing kaleidoscope of African scenes. Rolling grasslands, hump-backed Zebu cattle grazing at a water meadow, women energetically turning a huge wheel to draw water from the well, a dilapidated mud hut with the pretentious title of '*The Las Vegas Bar*', the ragged boy pushing his home-made wire-model toy merrily along the street, the men playing at the Bawo board outside the barber's shop.

'I see that Mona Lisa smile again,' Mike said, sitting by her side 'More secret thoughts?'

'Just enjoying the passing scenes. Mike, such as that grotesque, upside-down tree I saw a moment ago. Straight from a horror film. Why, each of its arms would form the trunk of a large tree.'

'The baobab? That's right and it's amazing to think that that particular tree was probably a young sapling about the time Christ was born.'

The bus climbed a steep hill and, as it negotiated a bend in the road, they beheld verdant valleys dappled with the shadows of drifting white clouds, and the distant purple hills on the horizon.

Mike guessed that Sue wanted to be quiet and simply drink in the beauty of the landscape so he made no further attempt at conversation. He was right. Sue was only too happy not to talk, and not to have to yell to make herself heard over the sound of the engine. Despite the red dust thrown up by the Land Rover as it bounced its way along the corrugated murram road, she was content simply to be left to take in the sights: the twisting streams and little rivers, the tall, majestic cedars and the simple thatched huts of the native *shambas* with their banana trees and fields of ripening maize, the herds of braying goats and bleating sheep; the inevitable ubiquitous Indian *dukas* selling everything including the kitchen sink.

Two and a half hours later, she caught her first glimpse of the Hekima Plateau dominating the region and towering above the picturesque little town from which the mountain derived its name. In the distance could be seen Mount Chimungu devoid of mist cloud and standing proud and clear against the clear blue sky.

'Is it any wonder,' said Mike, 'that the Zambelian people believe that Chimungu is the home of God? If I were God, I think that's where I'd choose to live.'

'Mike,' Sue sighed. 'It's good to be back.'

'Let's hope it stays that way, Sue,' he said softly. 'So now. This is it. Hekima! Where you are to spend the next two years - happy years - I trust.'

'I'm sure they will be, Mike. I cannot imagine anything that could spoil them.'

'When you're settled in, I hope you'll allow me to drive you up to the Hekima Plateau. There's a superb hotel perched on the top and the view from up there is, well, in that clichéd phrase, out of this world. And, come to think of it, the lunch isn't bad either.'

'I'd love that, Mike.'

The bus climbed a steep, narrow path and stopped outside an old colonial-style house with a red-tiled roof, gleaming white walls, and a long, wide veranda that looked out on a terraced garden clothed in pink and purple splendour: cinerarias, azaleas, fuchsias, anemones, stocks, aloes, and proteas all competing for attention. The bus continued round to the back of the house where it came to a stop. A small African man dressed in a white apron stood at the kitchen door smiling in welcome.

'Why have we stopped?' asked Sue. 'What is this place?'

'This,' said Jack Zulu, smiling broadly and walking down the aisle towards her, 'is your new home, Doctor Delamere. And the man at the kitchen door goes with the house; he's your manservant, Sikio.'

Sue looked perplexed.

'Sorry, I don't understand. My house...my servant..? No-one said anything to me about house servant...'

'Yes,' said Jack. 'I was told to bring you to this house; it has been allotted to you. And Sikio belongs to the house and its occupant. I must apologise, if you don't approve, Doctor.'

'Approve? Of course I approve. I'm overwhelmed by it all. I was told I would be allotted a government house but never in my wildest dreams did I expect one anything like this. It's like something out of the musical *'South Pacific'*.'

'Great,' said Mike, 'as long as you don't expect me to break out with "*Some Enchanted Evening.*" Now let's get your luggage off the Land Rover and we'll leave you to rest and recover from your shock as well as your jet lag.'

'Welcome to Hekima, *memsahib*,' said Sikio bowing politely and taking the luggage from Mike and Jack. 'I have the honour to be your house servant and it will be my job to look after you.'

'Thank you so much, Sikio,' said a delighted Sue.

'I'm sure you'd welcome a good night's sleep after the excitement and the long journey, Sue,' Mike said. 'You should find that the University office has left you basic foodstuff in your fridge but I'll come back at week-end after you've had time to settle in and help you shop for provisions. It'll give me a chance to show you around Hekima market. I think you'll enjoy the experience.'

'Thanks for everything, Mike. I don't know what I'd have done without you. What I long for now is a nice hot bath and a good night's sleep.'

'I know you're an experienced traveller,' he said, 'but don't forget to tuck your net securely round your bed when you finally turn in. There's lots of mosquitoes about at the present time and you don't want to start off the new term by going down with malaria.'

'Thanks for that, Mike. Must admit the matter had slipped my mind but I think Sikio has already done it. Goodnight, Mike. I'm bushed.'

'See you at week-end, Sue Pleasant dreams on your first night back.'

The bus drove off leaving Sue in her new home.

She began by examining every corner of the house: the high-ceilinged living-room and bedrooms; the large, tiled bathroom; the spacious and fully equipped kitchen with its wood-burning stove; and the sturdy, sensible, hardwood furniture.

She stepped on to the veranda. She could not believe her eyes. The garden was a potpourri of exotica - brilliant aloes, bright red poinsettias, bougainvillea, and frangipani that would later fill the evening air with its heady scent. Beyond the velvet lawn, she beheld a vista of lush valleys and a panoramic view of majestic Mount Chimungu now shrouded in cloud and mist.

A flamboyant, red-and-green long-tailed lori glided across the garden and perched on a nearby tree where it cawed and croaked a raucous song of welcome.

'What was it Churchill wrote about Africa?' Sue asked herself. 'Something about 'Birds as bright as butterflies; butterflies as big as birds.'

'I have heated up the water for you, memsahib, and I have run your bath,' Sikio said softly, awakening her from her reverie.

'I think I must have died and I'm now in paradise,' she said to him, as she went into the bathroom.

'Yes, *memsahib*,' replied Sikio impassively.

***

As promised, Mike called to pick up Sue at the week-end. Saturday was market-day in Hekima and the town became a buzzing, bustling bazaar teeming with Zambelians of every age and from every part of the region. Early in the morning, streams of men and women poured in from the surrounding villages converging on the reserved central ground, the women loaded with heavy sacks of maize, bananas, potatoes and yams. They came in their hundreds: a laughing, joking crowd jostling and elbowing their neighbours in their desire

54

to spend their few centinos on the merchandise on display. And what a display was set before them! This market sold everything. Bicycles, buckets, and baskets. Milk, mats and mangos. Clocks, clothes and cockerels. Anything for which there was demand. And such a largesse of fruit and vegetables at the "knock-down" prices called out by eager traders who thrust their produce into the hands of vacillating customers. The women sat in groups with legs straight out on the ground, their produce spread out beside them while the men sat relaxed in the shade behind their stalls. Ragged urchins tailed visitors everywhere offering their services as carriers and hoping to snatch up any stray items that fell from overloaded baskets.

'I've never seen such a variety of goods!' Sue exclaimed, as they strolled through the stalls and around the kneeling peasant women. 'Why, I don't even recognise many of them! It feels weird to wander through a market like this and not have a clue as to what the things on display are. What in heaven's name are fermented locust beans? Why, they look like meatballs.'

Mike laughed. 'Simply add a spot of spaghetti and sauce and hey presto! You have an appetising meal.'

Sue revelled in the experience of wandering round this local bazaar. 'This place brings back so many happy memories,' she exclaimed.

They passed a home-brew stall.

'Try a taste of *pombe*, Madame?' a local brewer urged. 'Only one matunda a calabash.'

Mike chuckled. 'Go on! Live dangerously.'

'If that *pombe* tastes anything like it looks,' Sue giggled, 'it probably is "living dangerously". But OK, I'll give it a go.'

Mike handed over a *matunda* to the vendor and Sue took a sip. Her reaction was swift. 'Ugh! It tastes like sour porridge. I don't think I'd fancy getting squiffy on that.'

'It's an acquired taste, I think,' Mike said, downing the remainder of the calabash. 'I like it but in small quantities. Nothing to worry about drinking the stuff because after all, it's nothing but fermented maize.'

They moved on to the recycling section of the market. This was a waste-not society. Nothing was thrown away. If a thing had the remotest use, somebody picked it up and re-cycled it. Here was a man selling bottles of every shape and size; over there, another making rubber sandals from discarded car tyres; one offering old tin containers; yet another, rusty nails and screws which he had patiently collected, straightened out and, in an effort to promote them, exhibited his wares on little fancy white lace-doilies . It was a colourful, fascinating spectacle and over the scene there hung the rancid smell of cassava, and dried fish. Plus a billion swollen-bellied bluebottles.

'This beats Sainsbury's and TESCO's any day,' Sue said as she walked through the market with Mike and Sikio. 'I think I've got enough fruit, vegetables and fish to last a month. I even managed to buy a new mosquito net.'

'Only one?' Mike teased. 'What if you have guests?'

She laughed. 'They can damn well bring their own,' .

'I'll file that away in my mind for future reference,' he grinned.

As they came through the gate of the market, they met a blind, leper woman sitting on the stone step, her right breast exposed as she fed her baby. She held up a claw-like left hand begging for alms. Mike thrust a five matunda note into her palsied fingers.

'There you are, Liza,' he said. 'How's your husband?'

'*Asante Daktari* Goodman,'   she croaked. 'Jonathan is fine, daktari. He's sitting over there on the opposite step.'

'Right, Liza. I'll say hello to him on the way out.'

'How come they know you?' Sue asked.

'They used to be patients of mine at the College. They are both burnt-out cases now but their fellow-Africans are still terrified to go too near them even though they're aware the disease has passed. As for any new cases we carry in our ambulance, the populace runs a mile when they see us coming. The dread of leprosy stretches back into antiquity. Today, drugs such as the sulfones and rifampin not only arrest the disease but make the patient non-contagious. Nevertheless, the ordinary man won't accept that the disease is under control and no longer dangerous. Old habits die hard and the average Zambelian is filled with dread if he thinks there's even the remotest chance he'll contract it.'

On the way out, they made a point of seeking out Liza's husband who was sitting a couple of yards outside the market.

He was a much worse case than his wife. His nose had been completely eaten away by the disease and was no more than a red-crusted, angry aperture whilst his mouth was twisted into what looked like a permanent scowl. He earned his living by peddling crudely-carved figurines at the same time holding out a tin begging-cup for those who preferred to forgo the statues and simply give as charity.

''How's it going, Jonathan?' Mike said cheerfully, dropping a five matunda note into his hat. 'Are you making a fortune here on the edge of the market?'

'Soon be buying a Rolls Royce,' Jonathan managed to utter though the words sounded more like a snarl than a friendly reply.

'Good for you, Jonathan. Be seeing you soon,' Mike said as they exited through the market gateway.

***

On Sunday morning, Mike took her to hear the choir at the Hekima Cathedral. She was profoundly moved by the experience. The deep resonant tones of the African basses that blended with the soaring, impossibly-high notes of the coloratura sopranos reached into the depths of her soul

57

bringing tears to her eyes. They arranged to return a fortnight later when an even bigger choir would be performing to celebrate the visit of Lundazi's Archbishop Pius Kazembe.

'If this first week-end is any indication of what is to follow,' Sue said as they parted at her doorstep, 'then I know I made the right decision coming here. I feel as if I've been re-born and my life has begun again.'

'You know what they say,' he murmured. 'Tomorrow is the first day of the rest of your life. Soon, if you'd like it, we could let you see something of the other side of the coin by visiting the refugee camps and the leproserie on Mombo Island. I think you'd find such a visit an eye-opener. Jack Zulu and I could pick you up on Friday afternoon and take it from there. What do you think?'

'That sounds fascinating, Mike, and I'd love to come and see what you do. It's a date. Now, I must get an early night as it's been a pretty hectic week-end. I start work in the English Department in three weeks' time and I've got an awful lot of preparation to do. Must admit I'm a little nervous about what to expect.'

'You'll cope, Sue, I'm sure. Never fear. Now goodnight,' he said, hesitating and then kissing her gently on the cheek. 'See you next week-end.'

'I hope no-one saw you do that, Mike, or we might both be arrested,' she laughed. 'I'll see you soon. Now, goodnight, Mike, and thanks for a truly wonderful introduction to Zambelia.'

****

58

Chapter Five

Braaivleis at the Moroneys

Sue's first three weeks in Zambelia were free as teaching at the university was not due to begin until the beginning of the following month and so she seized the opportunity to make the most of the facilities Hekima had to offer. After the visit to the Cathedral, she and Mike enjoyed the sports at the Country Club: tennis, squash, and attempting to play a decent round of golf on the nine-hole golf course. Sue relished every moment.

'Mike,' she said one day after she'd putted the ball on the fourth green. 'I'm really enjoying this three week interlude before classes begin. Hekima is a great little town and so is its Country Club with all these amenities. Why, I haven't played golf for about six or seven years.'

'Yes, I can believe that,' Mike grinned. 'It shows.'

'I'll ignore that snide comment,' she laughed. 'Anyway, as I was saying. Things have been going great. I'm waiting for my advance baggage to arrive from England so I can finish making my home comfy, and then my life here will be complete. I hope I don't have problems with customs and censorship and all that stuff. The experiences at the airport were enough for me.'

'With luck, Sue, there shouldn't be any problem there. The Zambelian authorities are illogical in this respect. Personal effects coming in as cargo by sea and rail tend to attract minimal screening and avoid the stringent going-over that air freight does. Doesn't make sense, I know, but that's this country all over.'

Each day they rounded off their sporting activity with a swim in the club's superb, open-aired, Olympic-sized pool where Mike introduced her to the social set. Doctor Bugsy Moroney and his wife Betty Jo were there one afternoon and invited them to a Sunday braaivleis.

'Oh, yeah. Oh, yeah,' Bugsy rambled. 'Pleased to meetcha again. Sorry I couldn't socialise at the airport but the army of officials there kinda kept me busy and I had a lotta things on my mind.'

Betty Jo laughed. 'If you ever find out what's on Bugsy's mind, you let me know, d'you hear? Anyways, we're having a few colleagues and a few buddies over on Sunday afternoon and we'd love it if you and Mike would join us, say around three o'clock'

'I'd love to come,' Sue said.

'Same goes for me,' said Mike.

'Look forward to seeing you both,' Betty Jo gushed, 'provided Bugsy remembers to get the charcoal and stuff in and doesn't set himself and the guests on fire during the afternoon.'

As they drove away, Sue said, 'I don't like saying this, Mike, but I hate barbecues and its South African version, the braaivleis, which literally means burnt flesh.'

'I'm inclined to agree with you,' Mike laughed, 'but I suppose we'll have to show willing and go.'

'I can remember these braaivleis in Kenya. They always seemed to cook everything together: boerevors sausage, kebabs, and marinated chicken, and pork and lamb chops – you name it - and burnt to a cinder on the surface and underdone on the inside.'

'You sound as if you feel strongly about them, Sue. Why's that?'

'I suppose it's because I often ended up with a gyppy tummy. I could never see the point of standing around twelve feet from the grid and subjecting the entire neighbourhood to the smell and the smoke. I always found that no matter which way the wind was blowing or where I was standing, the smoke invariably followed me and got into my eyes. Now, I don't mind taking my food and *eating* it outside but why we insist on *cooking* it out-of-doors, I'll never know.'

'Beats me, Sue. Perhaps it's a throw-back to our hunter-gatherer Neanderthal roots. There shouldn't be a problem with food poisoning as long as the meat's cooked correctly but that depends on the skill of the one doing the cooking.'

'If I remember rightly, Mike, it was always the men who took over the outdoor kitchen by making the charcoal fire and cooking the meat while the women ferried the Tusker and Castle beers to the men, and looked after the kids.'

'Your best bet, Sue, is to eat a little sausage or two so as to keep the Moroneys happy. A couple of glasses of wine should wash away the foul taste.'

Mike thought that she seemed so worked up in her antipathy towards braais, it might be best to keep *shtum* though secretly he enjoyed the occasional cook-out if the meat had been thoroughly done.

***

The Moroneys' house was similar to Sue's. Inside it was spacious, cool and contained the usual basic university furniture: tiled wood floor, large stone fireplace, dining room suite, and three or four wooden easy chairs with washable cushions. There was a huge garden and it was there that the Moroneys had set up their braai equipment of brick-built canopy, extractor and several rotisseries. In the middle of the lawn, there was a long table with seating for a dozen people or more, and a number of university colleagues had already arrived. Sue welcomed the opportunity to meet them before the term began. Maybe she could pick up one or two tips.

Wearing a plastic apron with the legend: FOOD EATEN HERE AT YOUR OWN RISK. Betty-Jo welcomed everybody. 'As is traditional,' she bubbled, 'some of the men have volunteered to do the cooking with Bugsy but he insists on playing the head chef role, God help us, and so I hope you've all brought your Alka Seltzer. Only joking of course – or am I?'

Sue arched both eyebrows throwing Mike a knowing look.

'Hi everybody,' Bugsy cried, large metal fork in hand and now attired in full hotel kitchen regalia complete with hound's tooth chequered pants, black waist wrap, and an apron similar to Betty Jo's except his said BURNT TO PERFECTION. A finishing touch was added to the uniform with a tall chef's white hat that added another twelve inches to his not inconsiderable height.

'I like your hat,' Sue said. 'It gives that professional touch.'

'Oh yeah. Oh yeah. Ya think so? It's called a toque. In olden days, it was useful for protection from fat dripping from the ceiling, not that we have a ceiling here today. Anyway, food'll be coming right up. Hope y'all have good appetites.'

Sue took a quick look at the food sizzling on the braai and wondered how she could get out of eating that meat since it looked charred to a cinder.

Mike pursed his lips and gave her an understanding wink.

'I don't have much of an appetite, Bugsy,' she said. 'Besides, I'm on a diet at the moment.'

''You gals,' Bugsy replied, 'always on a diet. How does that saying go? "Eat, drink and be merry for tomorrow we diet".'

'OK, Bugsy. Maybe I'll try a couple of those little sausages with a buttered roll and salad. And the apple pie looks good.'

'Coming right up!' Bugsy said.

Sue and Mike joined a few of their colleagues at the table. The man opposite had a long, saturnine face and gave the appearance of enjoying this braai about as much as Sue.

'Hello there. My name is Malachi Marimba. Nice to see you again, Mike.' He turned to Sue, 'And you must be our new member of staff. We've heard a lot about you - all to the good, I hasten to say - and how you'll be taking over the English Lit. classes.'

'Malachi's full title, I should add,' Mike added, 'is Professor Malachi Marimba, Head of the History Department. And whilst we're introducing people,' he continued indicating the bearded bespectacled man sitting next to him, 'the academic-looking bloke opposite is Professor Joel Mbithi, Head of the School of P.P.E.'

'Academic-looking, eh?' Joel Mbithi smiled. 'That's a new one. Not sure exactly what that means, Mike, but I'll take it as a compliment.

'Glad to meet both of you,' Sue rejoined, exchanging hand-shakes. 'Please call me Sue. What's that P.P.E. stand for? Sounds like something mysterious out of M.I.5'

'Nothing as exciting as that, I'm sorry to say,' Joel Mbithi laughed. 'P.P.E. stands for Philosophy, Politics and Economics. So, how're you settling in, Sue? Do you like our little town, Hekima?'

'Haven't been here long but love it so far.'

'You'll be looking forward to meeting your students, I'll bet,' Professor Marimba said. 'I'm sure you can't wait for term to begin.'

'I think Sue believes Hekima is a holiday resort,' Mike laughed. 'Up to now, it's been all play and no work.'

'I don't think any such thing,' Sue protested amiably. 'I'm looking forward immensely to taking my first class next week though I've got to admit, I'm feeling a little apprehensive about my first session.'

'I'm sure the students are going to love you!' Joel Mbithi said warmly. 'And lecturing in a subject like English Literature, you can't go wrong.'

'Sorry, I'm not with you,' Sue asked with a nervous smile. 'How do you mean "can't go wrong"?'

'When I say "can't go wrong,' Joel explained, 'I was thinking of the nature of your subject, English Literature, involving poetry, Shakespeare and all that Hey Nonny Nonny stuff. *Prima facie* not a politically sensitive subject. Pretty harmless subject-matter, I'd say, that is hard to go wrong with.'

'Her predecessor, Dr Frank Johnson did,' Malachy Marimba said with a frown.

Sue was a little worried when she heard this.

'In some ways, Sue, Frank Johnson was asking for it,' Mike said to reassure her. 'He set out to stir up the students and, at the same time, was writing provocative articles criticising President Matata in the British press. You can't get away with doing that sort of thing here in Zambelia or for that matter any third world country where presidents tend to be hyper-sensitive.'

Malachy continued, 'Now it's much more difficult to teach my subject, History, without getting our government hot under the collar. As you can imagine, I have to tread carefully when dealing with nineteenth century colonial history and the so-called scramble for Africa.'

'Same goes for me, Joel said. 'It's harder still to lecture in social studies neutrally when dealing with studies in Philosophy and Politics. We have to watch our step all the time or they'll soon have us in Tagooma Prison. That's what we mean when we say that English Literature is relatively harmless.'

'Now, in my subject,' Bugsy said, joining them at the table with a full plate of boerewors sausage and a macerated mess of various unidentifiable foods. 'we don't have this problem.

64

My field of study, entomology, is completely free of dodgy political issues.'

'Entomology must be a fascinating field here in Africa, Bugsy,' Sue said. 'Why, your subject matter is all round you.'

'That's true. For an entomologist, Africa is the nearest thing to paradise. Like working in a vast natural history museum with my material right outside my front door and always ready to hand.'

'I know it's a daft question, Bugsy, but out of the vast numbers of insects available to you, do you have a particular favourite that absorbs your interest more than any others?'

'That's one helluva question, Sue. There must be a trillion insects I could choose. From the Anopheles mosquito to the Zabalius bush-cricket. But if shove came to push, I'd have to say the siafu ant. Not the most popular insect, I suspect, but for me certainly the most fascinating.'

Bugsy's little speech attracted the attention of a number of guests round the table. He was a lousy cook but a great raconteur – an American version of David Attenborough.

'Why so?' asked a bespectacled lady who had sidled up to join the band of listeners.

'Hard to say,' replied Bugsy. 'I suppose it's because they give the impression of being purposeful and intelligent, like a well-organised army. When rain is imminent or food is in short supply, they leave their mound and form marching columns of up to fifty million ants which can travel around twenty metres an hour.'

'I've heard they can sometimes kill people and devour them,' the lady commented. 'Is it true?'

'There have been many cases of this, usually creatures that can't defend themselves, like newly-born chicks, or wounded animals. I've even heard of a case of a drunken man falling asleep in a chicken coop and being eaten alive by a swarm of them. What impresses me about them is their almost human organisation into colonies made up of smaller worker ants being flanked by the large soldier variety. They display all the characteristics of a highly disciplined community working together with one end in view, namely to protect and nourish their queen.'

'It sounds like a human society,' Mike chuckled, 'with us workers paying our taxes, being supervised by the various authorities in order to provide sustenance and upkeep for our superiors.'

'Oh yeah! Oh yeah!' Bugsy enthused. 'You could be right, Mike but as you already know, while *siafu* may be my chief professional interest, my greatest passion in life, apart from Betty Jo of course, is ornithology.'

'Any particular aspect,' asked Henry Muli's wife, Abigail, who had now joined the party.

'Oh yah. Song birds especially.'

'Is that because birds sing when they're happy, Bugsy?' Sue asked.

'That's not the reason birds sing, Sue. Like all other forms of life on this planet, birds are interested in two things: survival and reproduction, though they really amount to the same thing. When a male bird sings, what he's really asking of the avian dames in the district: "Would any of you gals out there like to have sex with me? Would any of you like to have my babies?" And if his song is attractive enough, one of them will respond with "Over here, big boy!".'

'If only it were that simple for us humans!' sighed Mike.

'And of all the songs that a bird can sing, without doubt, the most fascinating is that of the Australian lyre bird which can mimic the sound of its rivals - in fact any sound it happens to hear, including a motor car engine, a camera shutter, and even a chain saw. I have some pictures and recordings which I can show you later.'

'How did you come to be so interested in ornithology?' Malachy Marimba asked. 'After all, it's a far cry from entomology.'

'I came to birds through insects and the subject of symbiosis in nature. As you know, ecto-parasites, particularly ticks and other insects, feed on the backs of many African mammals. Birds such as the yellow-billed oxpeckers and mammals such as the wildebeest do each other mutual favours and we call this co-operation "symbiosis" and there are lotsa examples in nature. It's an arrangement that suits both parties: the birds provide a cleaning service and the mammal provides a sort of restaurant for the birds. Recently though there's been a certain amount of doubt cast on this mutualism and a little later this year, I expect to be attending a conference at the University of London on the subject.'

'And who will be footing the bill for that?' Joel Mbithi inquired with a wry smile.

'Why, the University of course, as I shall be studying the ticks and the parasites and so it comes under the heading of entomology,' Bugsy said with a mischievous grin.

'You cunning devil,' Mike said admiringly. 'Some people have all the luck.'

'Or know how to play the system,' Joel added ruefully.

****

Chapter Six

Four Cases for Big Mama's Court

Philip Thomas Gichuru, Head Gardener at the Lundazi presidential palace, sat in the public gallery of Hekima Traditional Court and watched his daughter, Charity, giving evidence. The tribal chief, dressed in black robes and tricorn hat, looked at her sternly over his half-moon glasses.

'You say that you wish to take the solemn Githathi oath, young lady. Before you do, let me remind you of what it means. It is the most powerful oath of our tribe and, if you commit perjury, if you tell us lies, it will not be you that will suffer. Mungu who lives in the great Mount Chimungu will curse your relatives and your descendants forever. It could mean death, not only for you, but for your father, your mother, or your brother. Do you still wish to take the oath?'

'Yes, sir, I do.'

'Very well. Clerk of the Court, bring the Githathi Stone.'

The clerk carried in a large polished oathing stone with seven holes in it and placed it on the table in front of the young girl.

'Now,' said the Chief gravely, 'put your hand in each of the seven holes and say each time, "If what I say is not the truth, may this oath kill me and my family".'

Seven times, the young girl repeated the oath exactly as she had been told. Only then did the Chief begin his cross-examination.

'Do you, Charity Gichuru binti ya Philip Thomas Gichuru, swear on this solemn oath that the plaintiff, Daniel Chitanda, is the father of the child you now carry in your womb?'

''I do, sir,' she said in a whisper.

'You must speak up, Charity, so that the court can hear your words.'

'Yes, sir. I'll try.'

'Good girl. How old are you, Charity?'

'I'm not sure, sir, but I think I'm seventeen. My father tells me I was born in the year of the great locust plague.'

'And when is your baby due?'

'In about six months, sir. According to the campus nurse.'

'You are a student at the University in Hekima, are you not?'

'I am, sir.'

'Tell us what happened, Charity.'

'It was on a Friday night, sir, about three months ago. The first-year boys had been drinking strong *pombe* in the village beer hall. When they came back to the campus, about six or seven of them knocked on the door of our dormitory and we let them in. They brought much beer with them and they said we would have a party. They asked us to drink and we did so. They kept persuading us and asking us until we agreed to do it.'

'Do what, Charity? You must tell the court.'

'Let them enter our bodies, sir.'

'By "let them enter", you mean you permitted them to have sexual intercourse?'

'Yes, sir.'

'And how do you know that it was the plaintiff, Chitanda, who, as you put it, entered your body?'

'He lay on top of me, sir, and I know him and his voice from the classroom. And his friends called over to him many times by name while he was doing it to me.'

'And what did they say?'

'They said things like: "How are you liking it Daniel?" and "Is she good, Daniel?" '

'So the boy Daniel did not force you to do it? You gave yourself to him willingly?'

'Yes, sir. It was because of the strong beer that I drank. I could not think properly and I let him do it.'

'Apart from that night,' the solemn-faced Chief continued, 'have you ever had sexual relations with any other boy? Remember your solemn oath on the Githathi Stone before you answer.'

'No, sir. I was a virgin before that night and I have been with no other man.'

'Very well,' said the Chief. 'You may step down, Charity. Bring Daniel Chitanda to the witness stand.'

A clean-cut young man, smartly dressed in grey flannels, white shirt with university tie and royal blue blazer, stepped forward. He was about eighteen years of age.

'I am Daniel Chitanda, sir,' he said, head bowed in humility.

'Well, Chitanda. What is your side of the story?'

'I admit that I was there on that night, sir. But I am not absolutely sure that I am the father of her child since it was dark and there were many girls and many boys. Any one of us could be the father since we lay with many different girls.'

'Are you willing to take the Githathi Oath as Charity has done?'

'I am of the Chuzuni tribe, sir, and we do not have oaths like those of the Massuyu. I am also a Catholic and taking such oaths would be against the First Commandment. So it would be of no use. I can only say that I may be the father of the child but no-one can be sure. Perhaps other boys lay with Charity Gichuru that night.'

Philip Thomas Gichuru leapt to his feet and shook his fist.

'That's a filthy lie and you know it, Chitanda,' he shouted furiously. 'You were the only one to violate my daughter. Admit it like a man!'

'If there is another disturbance like that in my court, Gichuru,' the chief said angrily, 'I shall have you removed by force. Now sit down and be quiet.'

For the next twenty minutes, the Chief conferred with his fellow Headmen on the bench while the families in the court awaited their decision.

'Very well,' he said at last. 'We have listened to both sides of the case. We think that there is strong evidence that Daniel Chitanda is the father of the child now living in Charity Gichuru's womb but we cannot be one hundred per cent sure since there is no conclusive proof. Many boys and girls were involved in this disgusting orgy. We leave it to the university authorities to take disciplinary action against the culprits but we cannot see anything that can be done by law to prove paternity. The case is dismissed.'

Philip Thomas Gichuru was dumbstruck. He could feel the bile rising in his throat and he began to tremble with impotent rage as the full implication of the Chief's ruling sank in. What sort of justice was this? He knew beyond any doubt that Daniel Chitanda had wombed his eldest daughter. She would never have sworn on the Githathi Stone unless she had been absolutely certain of her facts. He'd had such high hopes for her. She had talked of being a clerk in a big office in Lundazi one day - perhaps even becoming a primary school teacher if she could pass the diploma. But now all that was finished. Now she was ruined. Not only would she have to leave university, but there was the shame of it in the village. People would say she was a slattern who would lie with any man and who knew not the name of the father of the brat that bulged her belly. The disgrace would be intolerable.

71

And who was to support the offspring? He could not afford to do so, since he already had many mouths to feed, and had many other children still at school. She would never find a husband now. No man would touch her since she was tainted and soiled. There would be no bride price - no goats - no beer-drink and no marriage bargain settlement struck with the bridegroom's family. Philip Thomas felt sick to his stomach.

As he left the court dejected with his daughter, he met Daniel Chitanda with his father. There was no triumph in their eyes. Both of them looked unhappy and ashamed, their heads bowed in contrition.

'I am sorry, Charity,' Daniel said to the young girl. 'I am fond of you and, if it were up to me, I'd marry you. But my father will not accept that your child is mine and he refuses to agree to the traditional marriage ceremony.'

Whilst the young people were talking, the two parents were involved in an altercation.

'This is a sad day and a sad ruling for you, Gichuru,' said Daniel's father. 'but you must understand our position - my son is much too young to marry and take on responsibility. He must finish his university course and get his diplomas and certificates before he can support a family. If he'd been older, things might have been different.'

'Your son must learn to face up to life and to the consequences of his actions,' Philip Thomas said bitterly. 'The womb is his; *you* know it and *we* know it. We would have accepted him into our family if he had acted like a man. What about my daughter, Charity? What is she to do now? Today, an injustice has been done. Only you and your son can put matters right between us.'

'Maybe in a few years' time - when my son has qualified as a teacher or a clerk, perhaps we can do something to put matters right,' the older Chitanda murmured.

'A few years' time! That is an outrage!' shouted Charity's father. 'That is not good enough. What do we do in the meanwhile? No, I want justice now. Today! The Chief's

Court has failed to give it to me - but I know where I can get it.'

He would make an appointment to see his boss at the palace, Big Mama.   She would have the answer to his problem.

***

Washington Fundi looked sadly at his two adolescent sons, Franklin and Dwight, as they sat at the rickety table studying their schoolbooks by the feeble, flickering light of the paraffin lamp. He was a worried man and he had run out of ideas as well as money. He'd tried everything and he didn't know what to do or where to turn to next. He had no wife he could talk it over with - she had died of malaria eight years ago.

Everything had been going well up to a year ago - until the American professor had gone back to his home in Pittsburgh. Washington had worked as cook and general house servant for him for over fifteen years and he had prospered on the regular monthly salary, putting both his sons through primary and intermediate schools. His job had even included a small house with lavatory and washing facilities. He had also eaten well. Whatever food the professor and his wife had on the table, he'd had his share too - sometimes with their permission, sometimes not. And, if the *memsahib* threw a dinner party, which she was fond of doing, there was always enough food over to feed any African family in his village for a month.   Suddenly, the professor's contract had finished. One of his relatives - his Uncle Sam, he'd said - had run out of money. Washington knew the feeling; it was something he could understand.   He'd had a similar experience with his father's brother. The professor had gone back to the States, no doubt to a beautiful house and a well-paid job whilst he, Washington Fundi, had been left high and dry.

He would never understand these white men. When they entered manhood, they turned a deaf ear to the advice of their elders and entirely neglected their parents. They seemed to

73

think only of wives, and children, and their daily bread. Not like the Africans who loved their parents because they knew they had brought them into the world. And again, the *Wazungu* never let their wives carry any heavy burden – the men themselves carried the provisions for them when they went out shopping. If they went to visit a place like a restaurant, they offered the chair to their womenfolk first and allowed them to sit down before they themselves took their seats. Furthermore, white men were lazy and could not make a farm unless they had much machinery; they did hardly any work and expected the African servants to do it all.

He had heard many strange stories of their behaviour in their own land. Sometimes, occupants of the same apartment building did not talk to one another and would continue for a long time without speaking or accosting their neighbours. But the strangest thing he had been told was that, in America and in England too, people were paid large sums of money when they could no longer find work. A West African visitor had said that it was even possible to have many names and make many claims for the money that the government gave to the poor. You simply had to sign your name in a book and the post office in England handed over a fortune in pound notes. Washington did not know whether to believe the man or not. But when this Nigerian stranger went on to say that the government even paid large sums for each child, he knew the man was lying and trying to make a fool of him. Why, if a man was paid for having children, what was to stop him from siring a great number and sitting at home drinking *pombe* and smoking *murangi*. No government was that foolish!

The American professor had been generous when he'd left. He'd given Washington three months' wages amounting to over one hundred matunda, and in addition, an old suit of clothes and a few of his old shirts and socks plus sundry bits of furniture. The professor had written a reference on his *kipande,* or work permit, to say that he was a good, honest, and hard-working servant. At Washington's request, the

74

professor had also written him a chit certifying that the clothes and the furniture were genuine gifts, in case the local *askari* picked him up and accused him of stealing them. Washington had sold all the things, and the proceeds had kept him and his sons afloat for six months. He had even sold his most precious possession, his watch, to pay the balance of their school fees. Then things had started to get serious as the funds ran dry.

He had returned to his native village and asked his two brothers for help. They had been kind and given him what precious little money they could afford but they too had sons and daughters to think about. He'd come away more or less empty-handed.

Every day, Washington searched for a job but there was nothing to be had. One morning, he had resorted to stealing a lady's washing from the line to buy food. He had only escaped her wrath by leaping over hedges and running for all he was worth across the Country Club golf course. He had thanked God that his sons had been at boarding school where they were fed.

But that had been last year. Now his sons had been sent home for non-payment of fees. For Washington, this spelt disaster. Up to that time, he'd managed to get by himself with little food but now his two sons were home, he was at the end of his tether. Everyone in Zambelia knew how important education was. It was the white man's secret weapon to a better life, to a good job, and to security, not only for the student but for his parents when they became old and infirm, and too weak to work. Now his sons were going to lose their schooling. They were trying to keep up their studies themselves at home reading their books by oil lamps but it was not the same. What else could they do? Where was he going to find the two hundred matunda needed for fees?

The next day, he tramped the streets of Lundazi looking for work - any kind of work; he couldn't afford to be choosey. In the morning, he heard on the grapevine that there was a vacancy for a general handyman at the Lundazi Inn. He ran all the way, as fast as his legs would carry him, but by the time he reached the tradesmen's entrance, there were already fifty handymen ahead of him in the queue.

Next, he'd tried his luck by knocking on doors at random, what his friend, the wood-carver termed 'cold-calling', asking if there were any odd jobs he could do.

The first house he selected was on top of a hill and involved a long climb up a winding path. He had reached the kitchen door when he was attacked by a pair of vicious German Rottweilers. He dashed for all he was worth and succeeded in climbing to safety in the fork of a large tree where the hounds, foaming at the mouth, continued to leap and snarl in a frenzied effort to reach him.

Eventually, a bearded European dressed in khaki shorts and hunting jacket appeared and restrained both beasts by the collar.

'Who are you and what do you want?' he demanded.

'I'm looking for work, Bwana, and I wondered if you had need of a cook or a general handyman.'

'I don't need anyone,' the man rasped. 'What's more you are trespassing. If ever I see your face round here again, I shall set the dogs on you and this time I shan't hold 'em back. Now, get off my land! *Voetsak*!'

'Yes, master. Sorry, master,' said Washington, only too glad to make his escape.

At the second house, it was the house servant who came to the kitchen door. He was distinctly hostile.

'There is no work here for you,' he growled. 'The Madam would not employ a casual beggar like you. Besides, *I* am the cook here. Do you think she's going to dismiss me to make room for a ragamuffin like you? Be off with you and try somewhere else.'

The situation looked hopeless and Washington was beginning to look around for washing lines. What alternative was there? It was either washing lines or the lines of Lugandan refugees tramping to the feeding centre.

He thought he would try one more house and call it a day. He climbed up the steep, terraced garden to the kitchen door. The servant there was about to turn him away when the lady of the house happened to pass by the open door. She recognised him.

'Aren't you Washington Fundi who used to work for Professor Oppenheim at the University in Hekima?'

'*Ndiyo, memsahib*. That's me. I was his cook and house servant for over fifteen years.'

'But what happened to you, Washington? You were once so healthy and well-built. Now you look so thin and gaunt.'

'Professor Oppenheim went back to Pittsburgh last year. Since then, *memsahib*, I've been picking up odd jobs wherever I could find them.'

'I'm so sorry to hear about that, Washington. I can't offer you a permanent job, I'm afraid, as I already have somebody but I can give you a day's work chopping firewood and clearing the *shamba* of leaves and brushwood. Say for ten matunda.'

'Thank you, *memsahib*. That's kind of you. I'll take it.'

All that day, he worked at the back-breaking work of splitting the big logs to be used in the hot-water boiler. Ten matunda wouldn't begin to solve his money problems but it was better than nothing and at least it was a start and would allow him to get some *posho* and beans from the local *duka*. As he attacked the wood with his big axe, he thought how strange life was. Last year, he'd been in full employment and had enough money to meet his bills. Today, he couldn't even afford to keep his sons at school. He wondered how much the fare to England was. He would like to have a post office book that would give him money simply for signing his name. He knew how to write. And his sons could go to secondary school for nothing while he sat with a blanket wrapped around him watching the coffee grow in his English *shamba*. But what was the use of dreaming? He would never find the fare to England.

His day's work over, he went to the rear door of the house to collect his day's pay.

The *memsahib* came to the door with a few left-overs from her dinner table and she counted out the agreed ten matunda into Washington's big, knotted hands and added an extra three for he looked such a sorrowful sight.

'I've been talking to my husband about your situation, Washington, and there may be some hope for you. Have you thought about becoming a blood donor at the president's Medical Centre? We've heard that they pay generously, especially if you're a rare blood group. I used to be a nurse at Lundazi General and I know that the going rate for normal blood used to be six matunda though it's probably gone up by now – maybe to seven or eight.'

'I don't understand this about blood, *memsahib*. What is normal blood?'

'If I remember rightly from my hospital days, there are four main blood types.: O, A, B and AB. The first two O and A are fairly common; B is less so but AB is rare. You might get more money if you are a B type and even more if you are AB.'

'How do they know which type you are, *memsahib*?'

'They will test you at the Centre. You never know your luck. If your two sons are over fourteen, they could also give blood. It's worth thinking about. You make an appointment and report to Big Mama's office, we're told.'

'But, that is a wonderful idea, *memsahib*. I cannot thank you enough. It could be the answer to my prayers. As a matter of fact, I am of the same tribe and the same village as Big Mama. My father worked for many years on her father's *shamba*. I'll make an appointment to see her the first chance I get.'

For the first time in many long months, Washington went home with a smile on his lips and hope in his heart. But, of course. Why hadn't he thought of it before? Big Mama would help him.

**

It had just turned dusk and a little before seven-thirty on Wednesday evening, the police Land Rover dropped Colonel Kiboko off at a large detached house on the outskirts of Lundazi.

'Wait here,' he said to the driver. 'I shall be no more than ten minutes.'

The colonel rang the bell at the imposing iron gates. A smartly-dressed security guard appeared flashing a large Hunter torch.

'Yes. Who is it and what do you want at this time in the evening?' he asked suspiciously.

'This is Colonel Kiboko - state security police. Open up at once! I have an important letter for Mr Tulshidas from the Presidential Bureau.'

'But my master has gone into dinner with his wife, Colonel.'

'I don't care if he's dining with the Aga Khan. Open up immediately or it'll be the worse for you.'

'Right away, Colonel, sir.'

Tarak Tulshidas was a small man in his early fifties. He had short, dark hair, and a smooth face with olive skin. He wore the finest silk shirt, a designer-tailored tuxedo, and the slight bulge of his stomach under his cummerbund was witness to his easy, comfortable, life style. There was about him an air of calmness and quiet confidence.

He had lived in Lundazi all his life and was fourth-generation Zambelian. His great grandfather had been forcibly brought over from India at the turn of the century to work as a coolie on the Great East African Railway but had stayed on when the work had been completed. The small general store which he had opened at the railway terminus, and which sold everything from calico to coffee, bacon to blankets, had soon prospered. The store had been extended by his grandfather and expanded yet more by his own father. When the business eventually had come into Tarak's hands, he had enlarged the enterprise even more by shrewdly diversifying into hardware and building materials at the time when there was insatiable demand from the newly-independent government for its ambitious building programme. He had further advanced his wealth by acting on one or two pieces of insider information and investing in the London stock-market. He had determined, however, never to use this overseas capital for ordinary business transactions. Secretly, he had placed it in a large reputable Swiss bank as an insurance against things going wrong in Zambelia.

The President of the country had recognised that his nation's economic strength and employment prospects depended to a large extent on the capital and business acumen of people like Tarak Tulshidas. He had therefore encouraged the Asian community to settle and trade in the five main Zambelian towns. Tarak had not been slow to see the possibilities, and had used his matunda fortune to create a small chain of electrical goods shops supplying wind-up radios and tape-recorders to the newly prosperous African and Asian citizens. Tarak had the Midas touch and whatever he touched turned to gold. Today, it was all mobile phones, computers, DVD players, camcorders, and television sets. Envious compatriots put his success down to luck but Tarak knew that it was not so much luck as the ability to spot an opportunity and exploit it.

His major problem and the biggest obstacle to growth was the severe shortage of foreign currency. Several times, he had applied to the government's Ministry of Finance and Trade for an extra allocation - so far without success. In order to keep his shops supplied with goods, he had reluctantly done the occasional risky currency transaction, like cashing foreign cheques for expatriates at a ruinously high exchange rate and, from time to time, buying up electrical goods imported by newcomers with customs exemption. The recent underhand deal with the palace foreman, Paddy Reilly, had been an example of a regrettable but necessary act to keep his stores afloat. But puzzlingly, the Reilly chap appeared to have won the tacit approval of the palace authorities for his large importations of electronic equipment. Tarak was at a loss to understand it. The Irishman must have special pull at the palace, he thought.

As he settled down to dinner with his wife that night, he had pushed these business concerns to the back of his mind. They were about to begin the first course when they were interrupted by the front-gate security guard.

'What is it?' Tarak demanded irritably. 'You know I don't like to be disturbed during dinner.'

'Sorry, Master. But Colonel Kiboko wishes to speak with you. He says he has an urgent message for you from the Palace.'

Tarak's heart skipped a beat. 'Oh, very well,' he said, abandoning his fish entrée. 'Better see what he wants.'

He met the colonel in the spacious vestibule.

'Good evening, Colonel,' he said. 'Welcome to my home. May I offer you a drink of something?'

'No drink, Tulshidas. This is not a social call.'

'Well, Colonel. You have a communication from the palace, I'm told. I hope it's not *bad* news you've brought. Perhaps we should go into the study.'

He led Kiboko through a thickly-carpeted hallway and into a softly-lit office, decorated and furnished in tasteful oriental style. The beautiful tapestries hung on the walls seemed to combine and harmonize with the unspoken wealth of the surroundings.

81

'I shan't keep you long, Tulshidas,' said the Colonel curtly. 'Big Mama would like to see you in her office tomorrow at ten o'clock sharp.'

He handed Tulshidas the official summons.

'I have one or two important business appointments tomorrow morning.'

'Then you'd be well advised to cancel them, wouldn't you,' Kiboko snapped.

'Very well, if it's that important,' replied Tulshidas gently. 'Perhaps it concerns my application for an extra foreign currency allowance.'

'I have no idea,' the Colonel lied. 'I'm simply the humble messenger. Now, if you'll excuse me, I must be on my way. I have another communication to deliver.'

'I'll show you out,' said Tarak Tulshidas politely.

Tarak returned to the dining table.

'You look worried, my dear,' his wife said.

'It's nothing,' he said. 'Nothing to worry about. Big Mama wants to see me tomorrow, that's all.'

Somehow, he'd lost his appetite.

***

The wall clock in the bar of the Lundazi Inn chimed eight. Big Paddy Reilly, seated on his favourite stool, was already on his fifth Pilsner and a feeling of *bonhomie* had begun to creep over him. The thick tobacco smoke and the excited babble of twenty male voices talking at once combined to produce in him a deep sense of contentment and comradeship. He took a long pull at his pint, wiped his mouth with the back of his hand, and addressed his younger companion.

'You're going to like it here, Jamesy. You can be sure about that. Coming to this country was the best day's work you ever did.'

'Do you think so, Paddy?'

'Indeed I know so, Jamesy. I've been here for two years and I love the bloody place and everything about it.'

'What makes you say that, Paddy?'

'Well, I tell you Jamesy. For me, it's been the good life all the way. I'm on the pig's back working for President Matata. He's such a generous man, I'd lay down my life for him.'

'It's to be hoped that that's not part of the job specification,' Jamesy chuckled.

'Ah, you may laugh Jamesy lad but you've got to appreciate that we've both landed on our feet here in Zambelia. Take me, for example. Here I am sixty-two years of age and I ask myself what I'd be doing if I'd stayed in Northern Ireland.'

'And what answer would you be giving yourself, Paddy?'

'By this time, Jamesy, they'd have thrown me on the retirement scrap heap. I'd probably be sitting in Kelly's Cellar Bar in Belfast's Union Street getting pissed with a lot of other 'has-beens' and wondering if we're going to be blown to kingdom-come by some crazy terrorist's bomb.'

'B'gorrah, Paddy, you're right there!'

'Instead,' the older man continued. 'I'm District Foreman with the Zambelia Ministry of Works and attached to the presidential palaces. Look at what I've got. A lovely house with swimming pool in two acres of garden - built with my own two hands and I won't say whose materials. Three servants and an eighteen-year old Massuyu maiden at home and ready to cater for all my needs.'

'*All* your needs?' Jamesy asked with a sly grin.

'When I say *all* my needs,' Paddy leered, 'I *mean all* my needs. Life is great here. Just great. Name me one thing that I lack.'

'Well, there's Guinness for a start.'

'Ah, Jamesy lad, you've put your finger on the one thing we don't have here - draught Guinness,' he said, draining his glass. 'Which reminds me. Time for another round. What'll it be? Same again?'

'That would suit me fine, Paddy.'

Paddy signalled to the barman who had been listening intently to their conversation.

'Fisi, you big-eared old bastard, bring us two more Pilsners. *Upesi sana.*'

'*Ndiyo, bwana.* Right away.'

'As we were saying, Jamesy. Draught Guinness - that's the one thing I miss over here.'

'But you can't have everything, Paddy. And judging from what you've told me about the job I've signed up for, that more than makes up for the lack of Guinness.'

'Make no mistake about that, my boy. It's the cushiest job *you've* ever had. We're responsible for the building work in the palaces - repairs, extensions, and all that stuff. We oversee a huge gang of labourers and we're paid top whack. And that's apart from the bit of Nero-in-Rome stuff, you know - the odd fiddle or two,' he added, tapping his nose with his finger.

'Fiddle or two, Paddy?'

'Now, don't come the old innocent with me, Jamesy. You know well the fiddles we can get up to in the building trade - with supplies and invoices and all that. Building materials landing up in the wrong place. I'll say here, on the QT mind, that I've never yet paid for petrol or servicing for my Volvo. And I've got nice little numbers going with Tarak Tulshidas and Ibrahim Suleman, the biggest Asian traders in Zambelia.'

'What about the state police, Paddy? Don't they worry you?'

'Not at all. Not at all. A little baksheesh here and there, and they turn a blind eye.'

'Like Lord Nelson at Trafalgar, eh, Paddy!'

'Dead right, Jamesy. As long as you play your cards right and make sure Big Mama doesn't get to hear about it.'

'Why do they call her Big Mama, Paddy?'

'I suppose it's because she's over six feet tall like those Bluebell Girl Dancers who used to perform in Paris. She's also "big" meaning important and powerful. But I don't really know, Jamesy. The most important thing is to be on your guard and trust no-one. Her spies are everywhere. There's something else, I must bring to your attention, Jamesy,' he said, pointing to the massive portrait of President Matata beaming down on them from above the bar. 'Never, never insult that man. Always pay your respects and you'll have no trouble. Never forget, Jamesy, that, in this country, he's the top man, the boss - the bloody gaffer. I drink to his health.'

He raised his pot and, as he tilted his head back to drink, he saw through the bottom of the glass a hated figure threading his way through the crowd and heading towards them.

'Don't look round, now, Jamesy,' he said. 'But do you know this man coming towards us?'

'No, Paddy, I do not.'

The figure reached the bar.

'Good evening, Reilly,' the intruder said

'Good Evening, Colonel Kiboko,' said Paddy. 'Can we offer you a little liquid refreshment?'

'No, thank you,' the Colonel answered coldly. 'I've come simply to pass on a demand from Big Mama. She wants to see you in her office tomorrow morning at ten-thirty sharp.'

'By all means, Colonel. Any idea of what it's about?'

'No use asking me, Reilly. If Big Mama says she wants to see you, you don't ask questions. Just be there! She has a busy programme and so you'd better not be late. You know what she's like.'

'Have no fear,' said Paddy. 'I'll be there. And I won't be late. You can be sure about that.'

He knew what Big Mama was like all right.

****

Chapter Seven

Sue gives lecture on Macbeth

After three weeks, a high degree of understanding developed between Sue and her house-servant, Sikio. He anticipated her every need - had her meals ready on time, ran her bath, made her bed, let down her mosquito net at night, and brought her tea in the morning. She'd spent her first few days in Hekima settling in, putting up her photographs and hanging her pictures and various knick-knacks to give the place a more homely, familiar look. With the help and advice of Sikio, she strengthened locks and fitted security alarms to doors, and attached plugs to the various pieces of electrical equipment, like radio/CD player and hair drier that had recently arrived in her sea freight from England. She'd walked into the little town several times acquainting herself with its geography - the location of the 'superettes', the Indian shops, the bank, the baker's. In the evenings, she prepared her lectures.

On the first morning of the new term, she was up with the lark. She swallowed her daily anti-malarial paludrin and ate the fruit breakfast of avocado and paw-paw Sikio had prepared. When the Peugeot station wagon came to collect her, she was ready and waiting, wearing her smartest outfit, brief case already in hand. She was feeling apprehensive about her first day in the Department even though she knew that she couldn't have worked for a better boss. Professor Henry Muli was not only a distinguished African academic but was known to be a warm, kind-hearted man into the bargain. He greeted her in his office as if she were a long-lost friend and then took her into the small staff-room to meet the rest of the staff of five lecturers - two women, three men.

'Ladies and gentlemen. It gives me great pleasure to introduce you to Doctor Sue Delamere, the new member of staff we've been waiting for. As you know, she'll be replacing Frank Johnson. As was explained to you last term, she has wide experience in the teaching of English both in the UK and on the African continent - Kenya in particular. Her specialist field is Elizabethan drama in which she holds the PhD of the University of Manchester.'

The colleagues smiled, nodding in friendly welcome which she acknowledged by returning their nods.

'She'll be teaching English Literature to the Honours students at all levels. We think we've been most fortunate in securing her services and we hope she'll be happy during her time with us.'

They clapped politely and there were murmurs of 'Hear, hear.'

The professor continued with the business of the meeting in much the same way as every other departmental conference that Sue had ever attended. He allocated lecture and tutorial duties while colleagues raised the usual questions: the shortage of library books; students coming late or cutting lectures; essays not being handed in on time. All meat and drink to her. She felt at home and knew she was going to like it in her new job.

At the end of the conference, Professor Muli thanked everyone for attending and wished them a successful term. When the staff had dispersed, he turned to Sue.

'You give your first lecture this morning, Doctor, and so I shall walk across with you and show you where the lecture theatre is.'

'That's kind of you, Professor; that'll be most helpful.'

As they made their way along the corridor, they met Bugsy Moroney walking the other way. He was looking dazed, turning his head from side to side as if trying to locate his whereabouts.

'Good morning, Doctor Moroney,' Henry Muli called. 'You appear to be lost. Can I be of assistance?'

'Oh, yeah! Oh, yeah! Good morning, Professor Muli. Lost? Oh, no! Oh yeah! I know which room I'm going to but don't know where it is. I'm looking for Room 32A.'

'But that's in the Annexe, Doctor, in the other building and you're going the wrong way.'

'Right! Right! In the Annexe! They must've changed the theatre. Why doesn't someone tell me about these things?'

'But you were informed at the last faculty meeting.'

'I was? Oh, yeah! Oh yeah! Which faculty meeting was that? Oh yah! Now I remember.'

'Good morning, Doctor Moroney,' Sue called to him. 'I met you on the plane out here. Remember?'

'Oh yeah! Oh yeah! You were with Mike Goodman, right? Must get going. My class'll be waiting for me.'

Bugsy ambled off down the corridor, head in the air and looking as distracted as ever.

'That man,' said Professor Muli, 'is one of the foremost authorities in his field, a brilliant academic and teacher but I don't think he knows what day it is, nor even which year.'

They reached the theatre where Sue's class of a hundred-plus students was waiting.

'I shall leave you here,' Henry Muli said. 'May I wish you the best of luck. I'm sure you'll find your students a most receptive audience.'

***

The English Lit. class had been waiting for the replacement to Frank Johnson for several months since he had been driven off by plain-clothes policemen from the

Public Safety Unit. What would this new lady lecturer be like? they wondered. Probably an elderly blue-stocking type with about as much sex appeal as one of Shakespeare's toothless old witches. The door of the theatre opened and in walked Sue Delamere. There was an audible gasp when they saw her and one of the students expressed his appreciation by giving a loud wolf whistle. Dressed in an exquisitely tailored two-piece suit in green, she strode to the front of the room. The students stopped talking among themselves and all eyes turned to her. There was a hush of expectancy as she stepped on to the raised platform and placed her notes on the lectern. She gazed around the room at the eager black faces before her and the young students grinned back in welcome, their pens hovering over their note-pads.

'Good morning, students. My name is Sue Delamere and I've come from England, and in particular from Manchester.'

A male voice at the back called out: 'Manchester United! Bobby Charlton!'

There was a ripple of laughter which Sue joined in.

'So glad you recognise my home town. We actually have two teams in Greater Manchester. Don't forget the other one – the Blues – Manchester City. But there's more to Manchester than its football teams,' she chuckled. 'Don't forget the City of Salford next door to it, famous for its inland docks and one or two writers like Walter Greenwood and Shelagh Delaney. And remember our distinguished Salford artist, L.S. Lowry, of "matchstick men" fame. But to business, students. I am here to teach your course on Shakespearian tragedy. Now, it has been said by some wit or other, probably Oscar Wilde, that the lecture is the means by which the notes of the lecturer are transferred from *her* notebook to *those* of the students without the subject matter passing through the minds of either party.'

Most of the audience laughed heartily but two mature-looking students sitting on the back row frowned at this levity. One or two others didn't get it and wrote it down as part of their studies.

'But I don't want you simply to write down everything,' Sue continued, 'without thinking about it. That's a waste of time. Better if you listened and tried to understand what's being said. Let's now turn to the subject of the lecture - Macbeth. I have been told that you have already made a preliminary study of the play with my predecessor, Doctor Frank Johnson. I shall take it then that you are reasonably familiar with the text. Before I begin, could I please ask you to switch off your mobiles? I find it distracting if they should start ringing during my lecture.'

Many students grinned as they took out their mobiles to check they were switched off.

'Thank you so much,' Sue said. 'Now to the subject of our studies. Each society has its own notion of law and order and those societies who consider themselves to be under threat are often terrified of anyone or anything that challenges that view. That goes for new ideas as well as potentially rebellious forces. After the violent murderous reign of the Catholic queen, known as Bloody Mary, her half-sister Elizabeth, daughter of Henry the Eighth and Anne Boleyn, became queen as Elizabeth the First and ruled England with an iron hand and firm central control - a position that could only be maintained at the expense of the liberty of her subjects. Throughout her reign, there was the constant fear of rebellion and intrigue to re-install the "Papist" Mary on the throne and a never-ending procession of citizens were arrested and burned at the stake for suspected conspiracy against the official religion, this being the Protestant faith established by her father, Henry. It mattered not if the accused were innocent or guilty, for rivals were easily dispatched with false, trumped-up charges. The most effective strategy employed by Elizabeth's government was to link or frame the rival or enemy with a proscribed religious or political group such as The Roman Catholic Church or a Republican Movement.'

A few students began to wink and exchange knowing glances with each other.

'You can see how in this atmosphere, the play *Macbeth* had such instant appeal since it's a play about political intrigue and ambition. For the audiences watching early performances of the play at The Globe Theatre in London, it was meat and drink. Here was a work that was all about their own political situation in Elizabethan England. So, what is *Macbeth* about? It can be summed up neatly, I think, in a single quotation, namely:

> *"Vaulting ambition, which o'er leaps itself*
> *And falls on the other"* '

Sue was now in her element and getting into her stride. She walked away from the lectern and began pacing up and down the dais.

'With every murder,' she continued, looking straight at her spellbound students, 'Macbeth thinks he has attained his goal and it will be his last murder. But he suffers from self-delusion, and, urged on by his sneering wife, Lady Macbeth, he is not satisfied. His ambition is insatiable. Having attained the throne, he must go on and on. He has little aim in office other than to hang on to it and make it a family possession. He has murdered for the power and he must keep it in the closed circle of his own kin, in his own dynasty. One more murder should do the trick, he tells himself. But there is no end to it. Evil feeds on itself.'

There was now vigorous nodding from her audience and one or two shouts of 'Exactly what's happening here in Zambelia!' The two students frowning at the back of the class were writing furiously.

'The play is also about the theme of power behind the throne. At the beginning of the story, Macbeth is strong, intensely patriotic, and thinks only of the good of his country, but as the play goes on, he becomes less and less concerned with his country and more and more with his own selfish ends. He becomes weaker as a character, almost senile, whilst Lady Macbeth becomes stronger. She has no regard for consequences but pushes her husband deeper and deeper into evil and wickedness. Perhaps you say, "But this is merely a play about Elizabethan England. It has no relevance for us today." That's not true for there have been many parallels in the past, such as the Borgia family who were accused of corruption during the Renaissance and of many other different crimes, such as <u>theft</u>, <u>rape</u>, <u>bribery</u>, and <u>murder</u> (especially murder by <u>arsenic poisoning</u>). But we don't have to go so far back in history for corruption like this. In the present we have had examples like Ferdinand and Imelda Marcos in the Phillipines, Nicolae and Elena Ceaucescu in Rumania, and Juan and Eva Peron in Argentina.'

'And Samson Matata and Big Mama in Zambelia!' a voice bawled. Sue was taken aback by this bizarre behaviour on the part of her students. Her lectures had never been received like this before.

A little disconcerted by this unusual response, she ploughed on. 'The play is a fine example of tragedy which goes to the root of things. The struggle in *Macbeth* is symbolic of the struggle between good and evil in man. It is a play about the fall of man and his recovery. Good is personified in Malcolm who is needed to supplant evil. Macbeth's tyranny is the practice of devilish wickedness, his advisers are the "instruments of darkness" and his unnatural rule can be opposed only with the help of God. The play shows how even a good man like Macbeth with fine qualities is pathetically vulnerable to the seductive and destructive possibilities of power. "Power tends to corrupt and absolute power corrupts absolutely".'

93

Several students were on their feet crying out, 'Hear, hear!' 'Absolutely right!'

Response to the rest of her lecture continued along the same lines.

'As we know,' Sue said forty-five minutes later, winding down her talk, 'good triumphs over evil in the end when Macduff brings Macbeth's head in front of the army and Malcolm, the new king, pledges that he will bring peace and order back to Scotland.'

She had come to the end of her first lecture and she collected her papers together and closed her folder. As she stepped off the platform, the students, with the exception of the two frowners at the back, were on their feet cheering and clapping for all they were worth. She had never before received a standing ovation for a lecture. She left the lecture hall gratified but at the same time mystified by the sustained applause. After all, it was a lecture in literature, not a political speech.

An hour after the lecture as she sat in her office reading, looking over her notes and preparing her work, there was a knock at the door. It was Professor Muli.

'I wondered if you'd like me to give you a tour of the department and show you where everything is. It'll give us a chance to have a chat. I suggest we begin with a short walk in the grounds around our faculty.'

Outside, they strolled around the perimeter of the lawn for a while.

'It's good of you to spare me the time like this, Professor Muli,' she said.

'I asked to see you,' he said gravely, 'not to show you round - but to warn you.'

'Warn me?' Sue said with a puzzled frown. 'Sorry, professor, I don't understand.'

'To warn you,' he continued, 'to be on your guard. You must be careful. Frank Johnson, the lecturer you are replacing, is at present in Tagooma prison and God knows when they'll let him out, if ever. They put him behind bars for collaborating with one of his students in the writing of so-called seditious poetry which is supposed to have challenged and undermined Matata's authority. When it was published in a British literary magazine, he was accused of promoting subversive ideas in his writings and in his lectures – in short, of inciting the students to revolt. Both he and the student have since been arrested and are now in prison.'

'My God!' exclaimed Sue. 'I didn't know any of this. Were any of the accusations true?'

'True? Of course they weren't true. But if The Public Safety officers say they are, there's no appeal. Your office here in the department is bugged. Your phone, including your mobile, is probably tapped. That's why we are talking in the open and not inside. Your home also is most probably wired too - it's done by means of the phone mouthpiece. A technological innovation brought in by Colonel Kiboko, the President's hatchet man.'

'You mean the phone is tapped and the mouthpiece picks up my conversations with callers?' Sue asked incredulously.

'No, worse than that. The mouthpiece acts like a microphone and its range picks up *all* sounds and conversations within a twenty yard radius. That means the whole of your office, the whole of your house. Suspicious stuff is reported to Kiboko's right-hand man, Major Nyoka, who is the local Public Safety Unit commander stationed here in Hekima. Behind his office, he has a personal monitoring room where he can select households to listen into as if tuning in a radio programme.'

'This is George Orwell stuff.'

'I'm sure you're aware that your professional and personal correspondence is steamed open and checked for subversion as well. You will have no trouble as long as you're careful.

95

Trust no-one. Suspect everyone - the bar staff at the Country Club, your house servant. Walls have ears. Be especially on your guard in lectures. Stay off politics and stick strictly to literature. Remember that some students will be taking down not only detailed notes but also every word you utter.'

'But that's what they're supposed to do, surely, professor?'

'But the students I'm thinking of are the Matata Youth Brigade spies taking notes as possible evidence to pass on to the Public Safety people. The harmless-looking, short-sighted youth who seems to be bored and sleepy may be weighing and memorising every thing you say in the hope of proving that you are a dissident, a Communist, or a Fascist. Weigh your acts and words with the utmost care. Make them clear. Make them unequivocal. Make them verifiable. These people are dangerous. Always keep relationships impersonal. If a student requests a private interview, beware. Give an interview by all means but take notes, leave your door open as though you expected a colleague within a few minutes. Best of all, try to have witnesses present. In your lectures, stay close to the text of the literature you are studying and there should be no problem. Shakespeare shouldn't present any problems but it has been reported to me already that you stirred things up in your first lecture this morning with many oblique references.'

'Stirred things up? Oblique references! I was simply giving background information to a Shakespearean play. I don't see how I'm to teach Elizabethan drama without putting it in context. I cannot keep it innocuous the whole time. Perhaps I should switch to nineteenth century romantic poetry! I'm sorry Professor Muli, I'm not prepared to spend this tour in Zambelia looking over my shoulder. I'm going to be true to myself and the literature I teach. If I'm deported for it, so be it!'

'Very well, Doctor Delamere. The choice is yours but it may not be a simple matter of deportation, however. You could end up in Gereza, the women's prison in Lundazi, just as Frank Johnson has been locked away in Tagooma. But at least I've done my job and made you aware of the true picture. Mind how you go! A copy of your first lecture on *Macbeth* is bound to be on Major Nyoka's desk by this afternoon. You can be sure that one or two of your students will see to that. Let us hope it's not passed on to Colonel Kiboko. And God forbid that any of it reaches Big Mama or you'll know what for!'

When Sue got to her office, she stared long and hard at the telephone. Now her dander was up. The Irish temper she had inherited from her Waterford grandmother all those years ago came to the fore and she felt a surge of cold anger go through her. She was bristling. That she should be told to be careful what she said in lectures! That her style and content in teaching Shakespeare should be dictated by a bunch of ignorant Keystone cops! She reached into her handbag and took out a pair of nail scissors.

'Like Alexander the Great,' she said aloud to the mouthpiece. 'This is how Sue Delamere cuts the Gordian knot. No-one is going to listen in to *this* lady's private conversations! And no-one is going to tell her what she should or shouldn't teach!'

She snipped the telephone wires and felt better immediately. After that, Sue went to lunch.

****

Chapter Eight

Major Nyoka interrogates Sue

Major Nyoka, Head of Public Safety Unit at the Hekima branch, was seated at his desk in his air-conditioned office talking on the phone.

'Yes, Colonel Kiboko,' he said, beads of sweat running down his forehead, 'the two student-informants you refer to have already told me about the provocative nature of the lecture given by the new member of staff, Doctor Sue Delamere. The two students are to be congratulated on their alertness in keeping you and me informed of possible threats to Zambelian security.'

'What's that you say, Colonel? Like her predecessor, Frank Johnson? Yes, I wholeheartedly agree; potentially dangerous and inciting. A possible trouble-maker? Yes, definitely. Must be nipped in the bud? Leave it with me, Colonel. I've already ordered her to attend for an interview this afternoon to explain to her that she must tone down her lectures. And yes, I shall have her house thoroughly searched first chance we get, that is, as soon as she is away from the premises for a reasonable period of time. Yes, sir. She lives in the house formerly occupied by Johnson and it's still bugged. The phone is also still tapped as was the phone in her office but she had the effrontery to cut the wire when she suspected the tap. I agree, colonel. That looks suspicious and we shall have to watch her closely. Vigilant at all times, sir? You can rely on me.'

Nyoka put the phone back in its cradle and mopped his

98

brow. 'Phew! Bastard Kiboko! I wish Mungu would hit him with one of his special thunderbolts!' he mumbled to himself, at the same moment pressing a button on the intercom to his secretary.

'Jessica,' he said, 'tell Sergeant Mboya that I want to see him. Send him in immediately he arrives.'

Five minutes later, Sergeant Mboya was standing in front of Nyoka's desk. 'You sent for me, Major?'

'Yes, Mboya. I have an important mission for you. Orders from the top. I want you to search the premises of a new teacher at the university, a Doctor Sue Delamere. I want you to make this absolutely thorough and leave no stone unturned. You understand?'

'Yes, Major. What exactly are we looking for, sir? Drugs, stolen goods, pornography, contraband?'

'You once worked in Zambelian customs, Mboya, so I don't need to tell you your job. Look for anything suspicious, such as subversive literature, tapes, videos, and so on. Look everywhere – in the living room cupboards; under the floorboards; in the bedrooms, under the beds and mattresses; in the kitchen cabinets, the fridge; in the roof space. Everywhere. She may have had prohibited material sent in her sea freight. The port authorities are less stringent than our own unit.'

'What about damage to the property? Can't be avoided if we are to do a thorough job. We may have to break things, cut things up, and so on.'

'Look Mboya. Just do it! Make it look like a burglary. If there's anything suspicious there, you'd better find it or *you'll* be for the chop!'

And so will you, Mboya muttered to himself as he left the office.

***

Around four o'clock that afternoon, as Sue was thinking of packing up her things and calling it a day, Professor Muli knocked and put his head round the door.

'Sorry to disturb you, Doctor Delamere, but I've had a call from Major Nyoka at the police station. He says he's been trying to ring you for some time but your phone doesn't seem to be working. He said he'd like you to call at his office this evening on your way home. Something about your temporary employment pass, I think. I do hope there's no problem.'

'There's none that I'm aware of,' replied Sue warily. 'Is this a request from Major Nyoka or an order?'

'A request. But I've found it's always best to treat it as an order,' he answered.

***

In Major Nyoka's office against one of the walls, there was a display cabinet filled with antique weapons - swords, poleaxes, bows and arrows, and a wide selection of firearms, from a Smith and Wesson .38 pistol to a Remington 12-bore pump action shotgun. On the opposite wall, there was an entire bookcase full of works on crime and punishment. Sue scanned the titles looking for Dostoyevsky's work on the subject but it was nowhere to be seen. She did note however works on subjects like: Methods of Interrogation, The Spanish Inquisition, Brain-washing, Psychology of Pain. Her eye alighted on one entitled "Torture of Heretics in the Sixteenth Century". She took the volume down and was thumbing through it seeing chapter headings like The Strappado, The Rack, The Thumbscrew, when the office door opened and Sue looked up into the glowering face of Major Nyoka. He glared at her with obvious hostility and without the slightest hint of recognition. Sue felt immediately afraid and ill at ease - especially since she was still holding one of his books. She felt like a little schoolgirl who had been

100

caught with jam on her face after raiding the pantry. The idea of waiting in Nyoka's inner sanctum had not been her idea but that of the desk sergeant who had insisted on it.

'Do you normally help yourself to other people's property and pry into their private affairs?' he snapped as he closed the door behind him.

'Sorry,' Sue faltered. 'It's just that I'm interested in the Elizabethan period and I couldn't resist....'

'Kindly make sure you put the book back in the correct place,' he barked as he settled behind his desk. He reached into a drawer, took out a large thick file and occupied himself in making a close study of it, ignoring Sue completely. He wrote several entries in the dossier.

Sue replaced the book and sat down again in the chair in front of his desk where she had begun her visit forty minutes earlier. She waited now for the Major to finish the task which appeared to have engrossed him. The sun was low in the sky and shone through the window at the back of the Major and into Sue's eyes. She wondered if his timing and his location for the interview were part of his interrogation technique. If so, it was certainly effective for she found she had to screw up her eyes to see him. Even then, she could make out only his silhouette. At last, he completed his business with the dossier, switched on his intercom and ordered the sergeant to come and collect the file. This done, he finally found time to address Sue who had been sitting patiently watching the man and studying his skilful 'put-down' ploys. First rule: get the victim into an inferior position. He was obviously a keen student of social psychology.

'You are new to our country, Doctor Delamere. I thought it would be in your interest if I gave you a little background information as to the way things are done around here. Also the way things are NOT done. Unfortunately, your predecessor, Frank Johnson, turned a deaf ear when I called him in to offer him good advice. Exactly as I'm doing with you today.'

The major leaned back in his chair. He was a blurred outline and Sue could not see his face clearly.

'What sort of good advice, Major?'

There was a long pause and his voice was wintry when he finally spoke.

'First, it is a criminal offence to tamper with the telephone system. I could have you arrested here and now for that alone. The Zambelia Post and Telegraph service have reported to us that the wire of the phone in your office has been deliberately cut. They are prepared to restore the service this time but, if there is a recurrence, I shall have no alternative but to place you under arrest.'

'Wait a moment,' Sue said defiantly 'I admit that I cut the wire but I have been informed that my telephone has been bugged and that the police are eavesdropping on private conversations. In my country, that is illegal.'

'Understand this, Doctor Delamere. This is Zambelia - not England. And this is Hekima - not Salford. Rumours that we listen in to phone conversations or any other conversations are unfounded. Do you think we are interested in boring conversations from a bunch of academics in their ivory towers? Don't believe everything you hear. Of course, we Zambelians must be vigilant at all times to root out rebels and agitators who threaten the stability and security of our country but that's a different matter. Which brings me to the next subject. One that worries us more than the business of the severed phone wire.'

'You mean my temporary employment permit?'

'No. That was merely a pretext to bring you here to this office. It has been reported to me that your first lecture at the university was bordering on the edge of sedition. That you stirred up the students and put ideas into their heads.'

'But that's what I'm paid to do - to put ideas into their heads.'

'I advise you not to be flippant, doctor, about this matter. The students are at an impressionable age and are easily roused. Take care how and what you teach them. We will not stand for any undermining of state authority. And most important, Doctor Delamere, and take care how you answer. Are you and have you ever been a member of the Communist Party?'

'Never. I have little or no interest in politics except in so far as they shed light on our understanding of literature. This morning, I gave a talk on Shakespeare and I tried to put the play *Macbeth* in historical context. Not once did I mention Zambelia or its authority.'

'We are not fools, doctor. We know full well it's possible to introduce rebellious thoughts by indirect references and subtle hints. Let our meeting today be a warning to you to take care lest you share the same fate as Frank Johnson. At present, you have a good job, a nice home and your stay in Zambelia could be a happy one. Enjoy your tour and stay out of trouble. You won't find the inside of Gereza Women's Prison so pleasant, believe me.'

For the first time since she came to Zambelia, Sue felt scared. If an innocent lecture on *Macbeth* could produce such strong reaction, God knows what would happen if she really preached insurrection.

'I apologise Major Nyoka, if I have broken some law or if I have clumsily violated Zambelian customs. If so, it was unintentional, I can assure you. But I shall find it difficult to teach Elizabethan drama without reference to the political and social background of the time. If I avoid mention of Zambelia and choose my examples from other societies, say the Marcos in the Philippines, would that be in order?'

'I can see no difficulty there. But students must be discouraged from associating your allusions to this country. We must not have a display like this morning's. I am

103

prepared to keep this little matter and this conversation strictly between ourselves. But if the subject reaches the ears of Colonel Kiboko, I cannot answer for the consequences. He is young and headstrong and he has risen through the ranks at frightening speed. So he may not be as accommodating or as sympathetic as we older officers. And pray that Big Mama doesn't get wind of any of it, that's all I have to say.'

He stood up signifying the discussion was at an end.

Sue left the Major's office bewildered. Zambelia was not Utopia after all that her friends, the Hallidays had described. Perhaps living and working in the rarefied atmosphere of the palace, they were not fully aware of what was going on at ground level outside in normal society. Ostrich-like perhaps they had their heads in the sand and didn't appreciate what life was like for the ordinary citizen. Zambelia was a police state. It was 1984 come true! She thought how naive she had been in accepting the contract appointment without researching further. She had fallen for it all right – "interesting, well-paid job, beautiful house, lovely climate, friendly people!" Huh! Phooey! What a fool she'd been! But what in God's name had she walked into? And what the hell was this stuff about hoping that Big Mama didn't get to hear about her lecture? And why was everyone so bloody scared of her?

****

Chapter Nine

We meet Big Mama

Big Mama was already awake sitting up in the big four-poster bed when she heard the gentle tap at the bedroom door. She'd had a bad night. Again. The same disturbing dream of being chased through the streets of Lundazi by a howling gang of men brandishing big sticks and clubs. She wasn't sure whether the weapons were phallic images symbolising her deep-seated fear of being raped or whether the men represented Nemesis pursuing her across the heavens. She still felt tired, heavy-eyed and she had a nasty taste in her mouth. What's more she had a hard, demanding day ahead of her and she could well do without the dark rings she would probably have under her eyes. Perhaps the tea and the fruit breakfast she had ordered might make her feel better.

'Yes, yes. Come in, Dora,' she called impatiently.

Dora, her lady-in-waiting, who had served her for over twenty years, came into the room carrying her breakfast on a bed tray. A dish of selected Zambelian fruits – peach, avocado, and mango.

'Good morning, Madame,' Dora said. 'I hope you slept well. It's a lovely day, the sun is shining and there's a clear blue sky.'

'Just put the tray on the bed, Dora, and pour the tea. There's no need for this forced gaiety and I can do without the weather report, thank you. As you well know, the sun is always shining and the sky is always blue here. Not only that. This is October, the suicide month, and later today, the

105

heat will be unbearable. Thank God, my office is air-conditioned. What we need now is not sunshine but a damned good downpour of rain.'

'Yes, Madame,' answered Dora. 'Sorry. I was only trying to be cheerful. I'll go and run your bath.'

'Very well. And don't forget a dash of oils in the water; lavender and sandalwood will do. They should help me relax.'

Twenty minutes later, she was lying back languidly in the soft, warm, fragrant water. She could feel the stress and the tension leaving her body. Stress and tension! She'd known them all her life - they were part of her destiny. Sometimes she felt as if she was carrying the whole world on her shoulders. Being born a woman in male-dominated African society had been bad enough but being the eldest of five girls was a calamity of the first order. Her father, Karanja, an important Chief in their village, had made no attempt to hide his displeasure - he'd wanted boys. Not only to help him rule the clan but to demonstrate his masculinity and ability to father men. Instead Mungu and his peasant wife had given him a household of women and he had never forgiven either of them for it. He'd consulted the local witch-doctor who, after throwing the bones of a hyena and examining the entrails of a chicken, had concluded that there was a *thahu* or curse on his house, put there no doubt by some vindictive enemy who bore him a grudge. Karanja decided to take no more chances fathering any more children but instead, sent his wife back to her family as a failure.

From that day on, he had found it impossible to accept that his first-born was a girl and had dressed her and treated her at all times as a male and a future leader of the clan. If she couldn't be a male, at least he could give her the name of a great queen, and, advised by a cousin who was a history lecturer at the university, had chosen her title from a list he'd supplied. Karanja had been particularly attracted to the name "Marie Antoinette", an eighteenth century Austrian

Archduchesse who, as the beautiful wife of King Louis XVI, had become Queen of France and Navarre. The grand title "Marie Antoinette" always seemed a bit of a mouthful for friends and the family and, within this closed circle, she was known simply as Marianne. No pounding the corn for Karanja's daughter, - no cooking the porridge - no trudging to the well for the daily water - no washing of clothes at the river. She'd been excused all those womanly duties. Instead, she'd learned to yoke the oxen, to tend the cattle, to climb, fight, and wrestle as well as any boy. Her father took her everywhere, even to the meetings of the *baraza* or village council there to listen to the headmen deliberating and settling the interminable local disputes. Later, he had encouraged her to participate in the debates, a most unusual thing in African society but such was her father's status, no-one dared dispute the arrangement.

When it came to her education, he had given her priority over her four sisters. Even though he was still disappointed that there were no boys, he had continued naming them after queens: Cleopatra, Zenobia, Guinevere, and finally Nefertiti. As a result of her father's insistence that she excel at all things, she had shone at everything at the Junior High School both in the classroom and on the sports field where she could out-run, out-throw, and out-jump any boy in the school. Nothing less than first would satisfy her father and that had become her chief pre-occupation in life. When she was fifteen, he arranged for her to attend an exclusive English traditional finishing school where she followed a two year curriculum which transformed her from being a "ladette" into a graceful, accomplished young lady. The course included such things as: deportment, etiquette, flower-arranging, appreciation of and preparation of gourmet meals, aromatherapy, personal presentation - in short how to pursue an elegant life style.

On her return to Zambelia, she devoted her time to putting what she had learned into practice insisting always on the highest standards in every department. Keeping him happy -

trying to make up for the lousy hand he felt life had dealt him. But, despite her best efforts, he had died a disillusioned and disappointed man. She only hoped that on the other side of the grave, he finally found out who it was that had cursed him so he could exact his revenge. She often thought how happy he would have been had he been alive today to see the exalted position she had come to occupy at the top of Zambelian aristocracy. How proud he would have been to see the way his ambitions for her had been realised in that chance encounter with the president of Zambelia, twenty-odd years ago.

In everyday family affairs, her four sisters had looked to her for advice and guidance and brought all their problems to her. In so many ways, she had become their substitute "Mama". Trouble with a bullying primary school-teacher? Ask Big Sister/Mama to sort it out. Squabbles between the girls as to whose turn it was to wash the cooking pots? Their "Big Mama" soon resolved it with a rapid, firm decision and it had not been unknown for her to knock their heads together. As for her own boyfriends, they were given short shrift and any hopeful youth looking for a quick grope was given a quick kneeing in a place which made him realise there were more important things in life. Other young men who tried pushing their luck or anything else in her direction soon found their manhood in jeopardy by one of Marianne's swift kicks administered with the skill of a professional footballer.

When it had come to choosing husbands for her siblings, it was Big Mama who gave the interview and decided Yea or Nay. She could spot the fakes and the phoneys from twenty paces. The losers from fifty. She had selected husbands for them all - young handsome men, not rich, but with lots of potential, and bright enough to recognise opportunity when it came a-knocking on the door. And she had made sure that it came knocking - often.

Only one of her selections had proved a disappointment. Fortunately, Kiboko, her nephew, had brought the affair to her attention. The man she had chosen for her youngest sister, Nefertiti, was named Idi, not the most propitious of names for a start, but he had turned out to be a regular Don Juan and had something going on with his office secretary. Marianne had had to call him into her office for one of her infamous royal reprimands. She'd warned him to stop tom-catting around and to mend his ways or else... She'd been perfectly willing to forget the matter, putting his lapse down to temptation and the fact he was a man and therefore lacking back-bone and will-power. But the one thing she could not forgive was his greed. For in reply, the arrogant fool had had the effrontery to accuse her of stealing from the presidential treasure chest. Had even gone on to threaten her with exposure unless she gave him a bigger house, a more generous personal allowance and a greater share of the fortune he was sure she was amassing. Sadly, he had died in a tragic car accident. Whilst returning with his secretary from a week-end at the Hekima Plateau Hotel, he had taken a hair-pin bend too fast and his Mercedes 500 SL Convertible had left the road landing in the ravine two hundred feet below where it had burst into flames. Ashes were all that had remained of the two bodies. A terrible tragedy and the family had been sorely distressed at the deaths. Her nephew, Kenneth, recently promoted to colonel, had done a fine job there, for a change. Of course, the five sisters had wept copiously at Idi's funeral - none more than Marianne. Later, they had been most upset by the malicious rumour that the car-brakes had been tampered with. That had been a year ago and now her young widowed sister and her two children were doing well. Nefertiti was once again eligible for marriage.

As time went by, Marianne had worked herself up to a position close to President Matata, leader of Zambelia and now that she was a person of influence, she had had her own private mansion built at Lake Zambelia and was having the most wonderful time embellishing it with lavish furnishings and ornamental works of art. In her new exalted status, she did not forget to look out as usual for her sisters' welfare. After all, she was still their big sister and they expected it of her. She had done them all proud and her younger siblings, along with their numerous progeny, were prospering in large country houses set in acres of the best Zambelian farmland. And, when it came to visiting the fashion houses of Europe, which she liked to do three or four times a year, she always took one or two of them to accompany her to help choose her own outfits and to select one or two for themselves – paid naturally from the government purse. Nothing but the best for the Makubwa girls. She had become so well-known in the fashion world that couturiers were in the habit of waiting around in the lobby of her hotel with their latest ranges, in the hope that she would favour them with her custom.

Once or twice, when pressed for time and there was no alternative, she had used one or two fashion boutiques in Lundazi to order the latest styles from Europe. On several occasions she had purchased dresses and *à la mode* outfits from Paris, Milan or London via the local suppliers who felt flattered by her patronage. When they had presented their bills to her and had received only half the amount due, they were canny enough to know that it would be unwise to press for full payment. On only one occasion had there been a misunderstanding and that was with a footwear specialist on First Street. Having registered her foot size with him, she had ordered a dozen pairs of the latest Italian styles from Milan and the shoes had been duly delivered along with the bill. As usual, Big Mama instructed the palace accountant to pay fifty percent of the sum requested. The shop owner, a Benjamin Bobozo, who was married with a family of three young children, had pointed out the discrepancy and had been told that he should consider himself privileged to have received her custom. The naïve man had then had the temerity to protest that he couldn't afford to give away his merchandise at half price, even to the President's official consort. A week later, a government inspector visited his

110

shop and, finding all kinds of fire safety hazards and health infringements, had the shop condemned as unsafe and closed it down. Hopefully, Bobozo tried several times to rent new premises but, for reasons not specified, had found himself rejected as unsuitable on each occasion. Now desperate, he applied for jobs as a salesman but when employers heard his history, they were unwilling after one or two phone calls to take him on. Gradually it dawned on him that he'd been black listed. At the end of his tether, he resorted to applying for more menial jobs which seemed to be the only ones open to him. He was finally taken on by the Lundazi Cleansing Department as street sweeper and, when they found he possessed an HGV licence and was an experienced driver, they put him in charge of a rubbish collection truck. And not any old rubbish truck but the heavy duty Mack Compactor that scooped up the commercial and industrial waste and crunched it into tiny pieces at the rear of the vehicle. Nobody else wanted to touch this particular branch of the work since compacting involved collecting the dirtiest, foulest-smelling debris from abattoirs as well as the fish and vegetable markets. The bilge was finally off-loaded into a vast container which provided a regular source of compost for Zambelian prison agricultural farms.

'A big comedown from running my own up-market footwear business,' Ben Bobozo thought, 'but it's better than nothing and at least I'm in work.' Nevertheless forever afterwards, he bore a particular loathing for, as he put it, "the spoiled brat of a woman who had engineered my downfall".

As the president's consort, Big Mama had helped and guided President Matata in his plans for two splendid palaces complete with luxurious residential suites, banqueting halls and soaring fountains. In gratitude, the President could deny her nothing and, over the years, she had grown to love and appreciate the finer things in life, so developing into a lady of refined tastes in *haute couture*, furnishings, works of art, and epicurean delights. Only top quality would do for Big Mama and she had come to understand the difference between the merely-good and the best. She learned how to organise state banquets that delighted the distinguished guests with gourmet delicacies and mouth-watering foods that gratified the most fastidious of diners: lobster tail, oysters, prime rib, filet mignon, smoked salmon and caviar. As for the wine list, only those with the rarest vintage would do: Bordeaux Haut Brion 1982 or Sauternes Chateau Yquem; and when it came to champagne, the sparkling Cava variety was never enough; it had to be Cristal, the finest and naturally the most expensive; though it must be said that when this was not available, she had no objection to going down market a little to say, pink champagne, the Hollywood movie stars' tipple. And if there was some aspect of the menu that was beyond her, she always had Peter and Helen Halliday to fall back on with their wide experience of catering for the high and mighty.

***

Big Mama got out of the bath and dried herself vigorously on the thick luxurious towel. She pulled her shoulders back, drew herself up to her full height and studied her Junoesque figure glistening like polished ebony in the six-foot mirror. She was pleased to see how high and firm her breasts had remained - incredible considering she was forty-three years old. She cupped her hands under them and examined them more closely. Large prominent nipples which had never been suckled by an infant though they had given pleasure to one or two supposedly grown-up men. She could never understand why men were turned on by women's breasts - to her they were simply mammary glands, lumps of subcutaneous tissue. She still had her slim waist and strong, shapely hips. Much of the credit went, of course, to the perpetual dieting and the never-ending Spartan regime of aerobic exercises. She had put on no more than seven pounds since the age of twenty.

Twenty! That was a long time ago. In those far-off early days, she had broken away from her father's early attempts to suppress her femininity by her success at the finishing school and by later entering the world of high fashion. Her sultry looks and her near-perfect figure had soon taken her to the top of high African couture. How proud she'd felt as she'd glided gracefully like a panther along the catwalk, showing off the latest African styles from the House of Frascati. At these shows she found that she was treated with great deference, especially if she arrived in a luxurious gown as she had on one occasion when she had appeared clad in gold from head to foot, the silk clinging to her figure like a second skin. She'd felt a sense of power over those fawning, slobbering men grovelling at her feet. Some of them had not been content though, merely to look - they'd wanted to feel and fondle everything with their hot, sweaty hands. She had treated them with contempt and given them a swift heave-ho.

Then one day – she'd been no more than twenty-two at the time - her eyes had alighted on Samson Matata and she had worshipped him and his strength from afar. Her first meeting and exchange of words with him came a short time later on the occasion of the public execution of three of his enemies - politicians who had been found guilty of plotting against him. In Lundazi's sports stadium, thousands of schoolchildren and students had been rounded up to watch the spectacle of Matata's enactment of justice and Marie Antoinette had attended the ceremony with her four younger sisters. The appropriate ambience had been created by the erection of gallows on the sports field and the condemned trio were forced to kneel in the middle of the stadium with their hands bound behind their backs. The event was carefully orchestrated with a procession, last prayers, bugle calls and a twenty minute interval between each hanging. Matata refused all calls for clemency. When the last of the accused had been left kicking and writhing on the end of the rope, Marie Antoinette had joined a line of admirers who

113

approached the President on his raised platfrom and placed a garland of roses round his neck.

'On behalf of the people of Zambelia, I thank you, our leader and our inspiration, for your wisdom and justice in enforcing law and order in our country. You have brought great happiness, safety and security to your people.'

So saying, she had backed away and joined her sisters in the crowd but she vowed that one day she would get to know this great demagogue on a more intimate level.

***

After uhuru had been achieved, the Zambelian leader had continued to inspire his people with the same fiery speeches that had won independence from their foreign rulers. For Marianne, he'd been like a lion among hyena. The people in their thousands, men in tattered shorts or smart suits, women with babies clinging to their backs, children with banners, placards, drums, and songs, had thronged the hillsides, climbed the trees, clung precariously to the windows of the buildings, stood on the tops of the buses, mud-spattered from their long dusty journeys, to catch a glimpse of their great redeemer and saviour to hear him when and whereverever he came to speak.

On these occasions, he would arrive dressed in his cheetah-skin cloak and toque, standing up in the open Land-Rover, decorated with the Massuyu Conference Party flag, to the tumultuous roars and thunderous applause of the great masses of people assembled there.

He would mount the platform packed with his party workers and three times he'd wave his fly whisk at the same time giving the staccato call, 'Zambelia!' Finally he would address the multitude:

'Our time has come. I, Samson Matata, have waited all my life for this moment of destiny. I have led you to independence and to freedom from the foreign tyrants. We have cast off our chains! Thrown off the colonial yoke! So now, let us go forward together! Those who still seek to dominate us must be struck down like vermin and trodden into the ground. You have followed me to victory and I have not failed your trust! We must continue the struggle! Death to our enemies! Zambelia! Uhuru!'

***

She had met him again by accident several years later when they had collided in the foyer of the Intercontinental Hotel in Lundazi one evening and he had invited her to dinner. She had been attending a fashion parade and was on her way out whilst he was on his way in and he'd helped her to her feet. Their eyes met. No words were needed. Perhaps it had been animal magnetism or simply remembrance of their brief meeting in the sports stadium. Or again, maybe it was an instinctive recognition of the potential power dormant in each others' hearts. Whatever it was, she was drawn to him by a strange, irresistible attraction as if by invisible witchcraft. She was in her early twenties and he in his mid-fifties but the thirty year age disparity didn't seem to matter and she soon found herself in his bed. The first man ever to dominate her and she had given herself to him with a hunger and a passion she had never before suspected in herself. When the Chamber of Deputies agreed to award him the title of Life President of Zambelia, she was there by his side as his consort and his mistress, organising his busy schedule, his finances, and his palace household. From that time on she had become celebrated throughout the nation as "Big Mama" a term of great honour and respect.

But that was in the past. Now, the President was a shadow of his former self. Five years ago, he had shown early signs of developing Alzheimer's Disease. Now, he sometimes had severe short-term memory loss and hardly knew what day it was. On one occasion she had found him looking perplexed and staring at a ten matunda note.

'Why is my picture on this piece of paper?' he asked.

'Because you are the president, Samson.'

'When did this happen, Marianne?'

'About thirty years ago, Samson.'

'I don't remember any of that happening,' he said plaintively.

Oddly enough, he had moments of unexpected lucidity and had almost total recall but on his rare public appearances, his speeches were often rambling and largely incoherent. Samson had become simply an amiable old man, which meant he was incapable of making most of the important decisions of state. For Marianne, it had been like the story of her own father and her family all over again. Once more she'd had to take charge of things; once more, she had to make the tough decisions - this time for the good of the whole country. She had become indispensable and in effect the Mother of the Nation.

****

Chapter Ten

We meet Nixon Makau, Senior Aide to the President.

She awoke from her day-dreaming, slipped on her long, silk dressing gown, and went into the bedroom where the ever-faithful Dora was waiting to dress her.

'Before we forget, Dora. There may be another suitcase for you to collect from my office in a week or so. You still remember what to do?'

'Of course, Madame. Like the last time I am to take the cash to the bank manager, Mr Fedha, and deposit it in the account that's in the name of the president and yourself at the Zambelia National Bank. Then I bring the receipt to you. Is that right, Madame?'

'Exactly right, Dora. We are also expecting shortly a payment of around half a million pounds sterling from one of our grateful Asian benefactors - a certain Tarak Tulshidas - but that will be in the form of a cheque.'

'I understand perfectly Madame. Shall we begin dressing now, Madame?'

'Certainly. Well, what's it to be today, Dora?'

Dora rolled back the long doors of the massive mahogany wardrobe which took up a whole wall of the large room.

'It's hard to make a decision, Madam, with so many dresses. Why, if we include the purchases you made last week in Johannesburg, there must be well over four hundred to choose from. And I don't know how many pairs of shoes from Italy.'

'Maybe we'll take the record away from Imelda Marcos. But come along, Dora. It's your job as lady-in-waiting and wardrobe mistress to advise and make the selection.'

'Very well, Madame, I think your black lace lingerie and the red-and-black kaftan with matching turban will suit you beautifully. You and your sister Guinevere, admired them when you saw them being modelled by Naomi Campbell at the Christian Dior fashion show in Paris last Spring.'

'Yes, I remember. Guinevere chose the black and green for herself but I preferred the red-and-black. So that's what I shall wear to-day.'

'What about shoes?'

'I've always liked the exquisite hand-made shoes you bought at Ferragamo's in Florence last summer, Madame; they look so elegant on *your* feet.'

'Sometimes, I think you take your flattery a little too far, Dora.'

Dora had slipped off her mistress's dressing gown and helped her on with the lace underwear when there came a gentle tap at the door.

'See who that is, Dora, will you?'

Dora went to the door and opened it a couple of inches. She spoke a few words to the visitor.

'It's Nixon Makau, the Chief Secretary, Madam,' she called over her shoulder. 'Come to discuss the day's schedule with you.'

'Ask him to come in, Dora.'

'Yes, Madame, but you're only half....'

'Yes, yes. I know "only half-dressed",' Big Mama snapped. 'But it's only the *Dudu*. He doesn't count.'

Nixon Makau who had overheard the remark lowered his head and came into the room.

'Sit down, Nixon,' Big Mama said. 'Tell me what's on your mind while I'm putting my clothes on,' she added with a faintly seductive smile on her lips, laying particular stress on the phrase "putting my clothes on".

She studied him as he sat tensely on the edge of the Georgian armchair. As usual, he was busy stroking the back of each hand in turn as if wiping away imaginary dirt. A small, musty, ageing civil servant - balding grey hair - steel-rimmed glasses balanced on a flat, ugly nose - hollow-chested - dressed in a shiny black coat with frayed white cuffs held together by cheap gold-plated cuff links, and striped trousers. He looked like an undertaker down on his luck. How repulsive she found him! She had only given him the job because he was remotely connected to her tribe and was distantly related to somebody or other in her father's family. And to think that this puny little creature, this little runt, had had the gall to ask for the hand of her widowed sister, Nefertiti, in marriage. At first, she had found it so droll that she had laughed to herself for a good half an hour. On reflection she'd found the idea so bizarre and so repugnant, it had sent a shiver down her spine. Later still, she had again seen how ludicrous the suggestion was and when she next saw him in a private consultation on some state matter or other, she had ended up laughing in his face and telling him to crawl back into the woodwork.

Now through compressed eye-lids, Nixon Makau watched Big Mama as she applied the lightest possible make-up to her flawless skin and the teeniest touch of crimson lipstick to her moist, sensuous lips. 'How I hate her at this moment,' he thought to himself. 'What's on your mind,' the slut had mocked. 'How I'd love to tell her the salacious ideas going through my mind as she tantalises me like this. 'How I loathe her when she taunts me like this applying her cosmetics so suggestively and so sensuously. How I detest her and that loathsome German doctor whom she seems to favour at the present time though I doubt he stands the faintest chance with her. But I know all about those so-called clinics of theirs and what they get up to in them. Blood donors indeed! Unknown to the poor victims, it was more than blood they were giving.

119

And, though I don't have the precise details as yet, I'm aware of the jiggery-pokery she gets up to with Paddy Reilly, the District Foreman, and the wheeler-dealing over big government contracts with people like Sir Percy Miles in England. I know too about the large cash deposits she makes in her personal bank account through her servant, Dora. Nothing escapes my eye and I'm noting everything down in my secret dossier. One day, this is going to pay off,' he told himself unable to suppress a satisfied smile.

He adjusted his glasses to the bridge of his nose, hunched forward in his chair and observed her from the corner of his eye. No wonder she made it a regular thing to visit the fashion houses of Europe and America to select the latest *haute couture* to grace her body And what a beautiful body it was! Broad, fleshy shoulders covered by a black lacy negligee with a plunging neckline; no bra needed to support those beautiful round breasts with the clear imprint of the nipples showing through the silk; the firm, flat belly; the wide strong hips where a man could bury himself. Long, shapely legs. He drank it all in.

The trollop knew full well what she was doing to him and was taking a sadistic pleasure in arousing him. Didn't she realise he was flesh and blood? If it weren't for his weekly session with one of the bar girls at the Lundazi Inn, he would have gone mad with frustrated desire long ago. And here she was flaunting her body and treating him like dirt. No, worse than that. Like a non-person. Like a common house servant, as if he weren't there. Just as she was doing right now - the cruel, spiteful bitch. He would never forgive her for the way she had sneered at his proposal of marriage to her widowed sister, Nefertiti. He'd not been considered good enough.

Big Mama watched him surreptitiously in her mirror. She didn't trust him an inch though he was privy to most of the deals she made with politicians and business men. But she'd had to buy his confidence by giving him a small cut of every secret contract. There was one scheme he did not know

120

about, however, - the bargain she had struck with Sir Percy Miles on the matter of the building of the new palace at Lake Zambelia. Sir Percy had won the tender from his German and French rivals with his bid of ten million pounds - the private arrangement he'd made with Big Mama had been the decisive factor in his success. For he had sweetened the transaction by agreeing to invoice the palace for twelve and a half, the extra two and a half million to be paid into a special London bank account operated by her. An immediate electronic transfer would move the sum to her personal account in a Swiss bank in Geneva. Furthermore the *Dudu* hadn't a clue about the large amounts she was depositing in her bank in Lundazi by her shake-downs of one or two Asian traders. But Big Mama knew full well the thoughts going through Nixon's head at this moment as he watched her dressing. That was obvious the way he held his clipboard close to his lap to cover his embarrassment - the lecherous, old goat. In a cruel way, she enjoyed leading him on and seeing his frustration.

'You seem unnaturally quiet today, Nixon. Do you have something on your mind?' Big Mama asked maliciously for the second time.

'No, ma'am,' he answered politely. 'I was merely thinking about the busy programme you have ahead of you today. I have the list of appointments here with me.'

'Well, come along. Let's hear them,' she said, hanging the thin gold chain with the twenty-thousand-matunda ruby around her neck. As Dora secured the clasp of the necklace, Nixon was hypnotised and could not take his eyes off the sparkling jewel which nestled in the deep cleft between her breasts.

'First, we have two petitioners who have come to ask favours, our head gardener - a Philip Thomas Gichuru, and a Washington Fundi, a labourer here in Lundazi,' he said hoarsely. 'Then there's the Asian trader, Tarak Tulshidas,

121

and after him, Paddy Reilly, The Ministry of Works District Foreman,. You asked to see them both this morning.'

'Good,' she said, slipping her body into the silk kaftan that Dora was now holding for her. Lustfully, Nixon watched her every move.

'Before we begin to see anybody,' she announced, 'We shall have a private interview with Colonel Kiboko. See that he's there waiting outside our office when we arrive. Then the two petitioners and after them Tarak Tulshidas; finally, Reilly.'

She slipped her finger into a huge fire-gleaming ruby ring and, as a finishing touch, clipped on two matching pendant ear-rings.

'Well, what do you think, Nixon? Do we pass?' she asked silkily through half-closed eyes.

'Oh, yes, ma'am. You certainly pass and with flying colours. You are very beautiful,' he stammered. It was the best he could manage.

****

Chapter Eleven

Big Mama's Court. She dispenses justice.

Promptly at nine o'clock, Big Mama, followed by a subservient Nixon Makau, swept imperiously through the supplicants waiting in the ante-room to her office. As one, they rose to their feet, the men doffing their hats, the female secretaries curtsying.

'We shall see you all in good time,' she announced to the assembly. 'But, you first!' she said, prodding Colonel Kiboko aggressively with her index finger. 'Nixon, please wait outside until we have finished.'

Trembling, the giant Kiboko followed her into the office. No sooner had he closed the door behind them than she turned on him furiously.

'If you cannot do the job I've given you,' she said striking the desk with her fist, 'You should go home and help your mother, Cleopatra, on the farm. You wantonly disobeyed my order that, under no circumstances, was the presidential motorcade to stop. There are mad dissidents everywhere waiting their chance to kill our leader.'

'But, Aunty, it was not my fault......'

'And how many times do I have to tell you that you must not call me 'Aunty' in this office? Are you determined to defy me? Call me "ma'am" like everyone else.'

'Sorry, ma'am. The trouble on the way to Hekima was not my fault. The two leading motor cyclists stopped because of some old man dying in the road despite me telling them a

123

thousand times that we must not stop, no matter what. Naturally, I've had the two disobedient soldiers executed. In the circumstances, though, I thought I acted quickly and did the right thing. I threw the old man's body into the ditch but, unfortunately, it was then that the mishap occurred.'

'Always the same story: "Not my fault!". I'm sick to death of hearing that same old excuse. You are an incompetent nincompoop! Are you going soft? You should have simply driven over the old wretch. He was probably only a Lugandan refugee anyway. As it is, you lost not only one of our valuable duplicate presidents but you went on to take out two university students. It wouldn't have been so bad if they'd been peasants as usual but to kill two educated types from the university is just asking for trouble. Let's hope there are no repercussions.'

'At least Doctor Schneider got himself two healthy bodies, ma'am. More money in the bank.'

'You fool, Kiboko. Two bodies aren't worth the storm of protest your rash actions may have unleashed. One of these days you will light a fuse to a bomb that'll blow up in our faces. If that ever happens, I'll make sure you're the first one to go.'

'Surely students are no different from Chamber Deputies who disappear from time to time?' he smirked.

'You dare to remind *me* of all people about those representatives disappearing. That was another of your idiotic blunders. I told you to dispatch the four Deputies Kasimu, Marango, Sithole, and Yabuku *judiciously* for daring to challenge the word of our Life President in the Legislative Council debate.'

'But I carried out your orders thoroughly and to the letter, Ma'am. I gave the commission to my Special Squad who arrested them, took them by night to the border, bashed their heads in and then pushed their Mercedes into a ravine to make it look like a road accident. It must have worked because the *Zambelia Herald* reported that it looked as if

124

they'd been trying to escape to the Congo. I couldn't have been more thorough than that.'

'You stupid, stupid man. You obviously don't know the meaning of the word "judiciously'. Don't you realise the problem you caused by killing them like that? The post-mortem found the corpses in such a terrible state we had to forbid the holding of an inquest. As for your attempt to stage it as a road accident, the post mortem found they had died from tent pins hammered in their heads. We could hardly maintain it was a road accident after that. When the relatives demanded the return of their bodies so as to arrange a ceremonial funeral, we had to have the corpses cremated quickly before anyone could see the state of the corpses. You act without thinking, Kiboko, as you have done with these two young men.'

'But they were only students, ma'am. If we can cover up the killing of government ministers, surely we can do the same with students? They're no different.'

'They *are* different, you idiot. We can always incriminate Deputies by getting our friends in Harare to write them one of their incriminating letters implicating them in a political plot. We can then claim that for reasons of security, we have to slap them in Tagooma gaol. Once we have them there, there's no problem disposing of them. We can do no such thing with students as their relatives are likely to come asking too many awkward questions.'

'No-one will ever know they were in the motorcade or at the State House in Hekima as I've covered up all traces, ma'am.'

'We only hope you have Kiboko, for your own sake. Now what about the two cabinet ministers who were sounding off against our President's plan to build the new palace at the Lake?'

'I arrested Deputies Chifunza and Chilolo intending to put them in Tagooma, ma'am. Unfortunately, Chilolo died in an accident on the way there when we were in the process of

125

questioning him but I think Chifunza will come to see sense. At this moment, my officers at the gaol are persuading him that it would be in his best interests to give the names of other troublemakers and dissidents. I shall keep you informed of our progress.'

'What exactly happened to Chilolo? How did he come to die so suddenly?'

'I thought it quickest to transfer them by helicopter. They were both shackled with leg irons, of course. We were over the Lake when we were interrogating them and unfortunately Chilolo slipped and fell from the aircraft. I trust I got this right, Ma'am, because there's no evidence of him now. The accident seemed to have a salutary effect on Chifunza for he seems inclined to talk to us now though I think he may perhaps need a little further persuasion.'

'Very well. But I warn you Kiboko. There'd better be no more slip-ups this time or it'll be your head on the chopping block. Now let's get down to business.'

Inwardly, Kiboko was fuming at the contemptuous and dismissive way his aunt had treated him. 'I deserve to be promoted to Brigadier,' he told himself, 'but instead I'm treated like a young boy. One day, the boot will be on the other foot and then we shall see whose head will be on the chopping block...'

'I shall require your presence in the office this morning to attend to the various matters that will probably arise,' Big Mama continued. 'Ask Nixon Makau to come back and bring in the first case, Philip Thomas Gichuru. We'll see what's bothering him and what he wants us to do.'

Big Mama settled behind her huge carved oak desk with the Colonel sitting by her side. Nixon Makau sat at his own little table close by ready to take notes.

***

126

Philip Thomas Gichuru, his head bowed humbly in submission, shuffled nervously into the room for he rarely came into Big Mama's presence. She held out her left hand. He took it gently and, going down on one knee, kissed her ruby ring.

'Thank you for seeing me, ma'am, and giving me some of your precious time.'

'You are one of our workers, Philip? Are you not?'

'Yes, ma'am. I have the honour to be your head gardener here at Lundazi and my brother, Samuel, is head gardener at Hekima State House.'

'Of course, you are a loyal family and you are also one of our beloved employees so we are pleased to give you of our time. We've heard many good things about you from Doctor Schneider. Not only do you keep the grounds in beautiful order but you have helped him by giving decent, civilised burials to those unfortunate few who die of terminal illnesses in the Medical Research Bureau.'

'Thank you, ma'am. I have sworn to devote my life to the service of you and the President.'

'Thank you for your loyalty, Philip. If we can be of assistance to you, you have only to tell us and we shall place our resources at your disposal.'

Philip began quietly and solemnly to tell his story and explain his grievance.

'I love my country, Ma'am, and I am a good citizen. I work hard at my job and obey my superiors. I pay my *kibanda* hut tax as the law demands. I have raised my six children firmly and punished them with a cane when they did wrong. I have brought them up to respect the old ways and Zambelian traditions. Because of the generous salary and the house you have given me, I have sent them to school where they have learned many clever things and many new ways.

'My eldest daughter, Charity, is an angel on earth and the light of my life. She is highly respected and honoured in our family and in the village. Though she can read and knows algebra, she has not forgotten her womanly duties. But evil students gave her *pombe* and her womb was impregnated by the seed of Daniel Chitanda, son of Joshua Chitanda. The boy says there is no proof that the womb is his. We cased the matter before the chief at Hekima and my daughter swore on the Githathi Stone that she has been with no other man. Daniel would not take an oath and refused to face up to his actions and restore honour to my daughter by marrying her. She wished to be a clerk but now her life is ruined. I come to you, ma'am, for help.'

'We are sorry to hear of your troubles, Philip,' Big Mama said. 'We must try to put things right for you. Have you any ideas, Colonel?'

'There are many things we can do,' said Kiboko. 'We can kill the goats of Daniel Chitanda's father. We can amputate this student, Daniel, in such a way that he will never impregnate another girl again. He will never want to. Or we could simply break his legs.'

'No, no,' protested Philip. 'Not those things. If you could persuade him and his father that it would be best for them if they did the right thing according to our custom and arranged a marriage to my daughter, I would be happy. Daniel is not evil; he is merely a thoughtless youth and must be made to do the manly thing and face up to his responsibilities.'

'If we frightened him a little,' Big Mama said, 'it would do the trick. Make a note, Colonel, and put one of your best men on it.'

'Very well,' Kiboko said, sounding a little disappointed. 'I think I know the very thing to frighten him.'

'Make sure that you don't overdo it, Colonel. I know what your men can be like once they get the smell of blood in their nostrils.'

Big Mama held out her left hand to Gicheru signifying that the interview was at an end. Philip took her hand a second time, kissed her ring and began backing his way out.

'Thank you, ma'am. I wish I had come to you first instead of the Chief's court. I pledge my life and that of my family in your service.'

'You have already done that with your work on our gardens, Philip, and your co-operation with the Medical Centre burials.'

Nixon got up from his table where he had been making notes and showed Philip to the door. He went to fetch Washington Fundi and his two sons.

***

Washington inspected his boys who were dressed immaculately in school uniform. He made a final adjustment to Franklin's tie and smoothed down the collar of Dwight's blazer.

'Shoulders back! Head up!' he commanded.

Washington himself had been up late the previous night ironing their white shirts and doing his best to make his own one-and-only pair of trousers presentable. Anxiously, they trooped into Big Mama's office and stood meekly before her huge desk. She held out her hand to each of them in turn and, one by one, they genuflected and touched her ring with their lips. Big Mama took one look at the gaunt, tense face of the man before her and guessed his problem before he'd uttered a word. A simple case and a simple solution.

'Washington Fundi,' she said. 'We seem to know that name from somewhere.'

'Yes, ma'am. My father, Noah, worked on your father's land many years ago. He was his farm manager, his *neopara*.'

'Why, of course. We remember now,' she lied. 'You must be from our village.'

'That's right, ma'am. Bakala - the same village. I can recall seeing you and your sisters going to school in the mornings carrying your schoolbooks. You dropped them once and I picked them up for you.'

'We hope we didn't forget to thank you, Washington. Now how can we be of service to you?'

'Well, ma'am,' Washington began sorrowfully. 'These are my two sons, Franklin and Dwight.'

'What splendid-looking, healthy boys,' she said, thinking how thin and underweight they looked. 'You must be proud of them.'

'Yes, I am, ma'am. But since my employer, Professor Oppenheim, went back to America, I have not been able to find work and I cannot pay their school fees. I have heard that it is possible to give blood and obtain a little money that way.'

'Yes, that is true. But you are from our village and we must try to give you extra assistance.'

She signalled to Nixon at his table. 'Give them two hundred matunda from the petty cash, Nixon. It's in a worthy cause.'

Shaking his head in disapproval, Nixon extracted twenty crisp notes and handed them over to Washington.

'You are right, Washington, about becoming a blood donor. Your two sons are over fourteen and so they too can give blood. We believe Doctor Schneider pays handsomely, especially if you are a rare group like AB. We shall write you a note for the doctor. Take it up to the receptionist in the Medical Centre and you'll get immediate attention. Best of luck to you and your boys. If ever they decide to become policemen, they should come and see Colonel Kiboko here. We're sure he'll find them something, won't you, Colonel?'

'You know I always look after anyone you recommend, ma'am,' the colonel smiled.

"I don't know how to thank you enough,' said Washington. 'You have a great reputation in Zambelia, ma'am, for kindness. You are loved by the people.'

'And why shouldn't we help a fellow-villager?' said Big Mama, as she proffered her ring to the trio.

As Washington departed with his sons, she turned to Nixon.

'Tell Dr Schneider that I recommend this man and his two sons be referred to his Medical Research Bureau. He can keep them in the hospital there and take blood and whatever else they have to offer as and when they need it, like milking cows in a way but it pays better. We can't have a precious commodity like their blood and their body parts going to waste. Now, fetch the Indian trader,' she commanded.

***

Tarak Tulshidas sat in the big armchair in Big Mama Makubwa's ante-room, waiting to be summoned. He had read the same page of *Drum* magazine over and over again without taking in a word. What did she want? he wondered. Could be good news? But that was doubtful since she wouldn't have called him in at such short notice. No, it had to be something bad. The currency deals and the cashing of cheques? The illegal purchase of electronic equipment? Anyway, he would find out soon enough when they called his name. If the worst came to the worst, he could always leave the country with his family - perhaps go to England. He had a cousin doing well there in Bedford. And there was his secret bank accounts in Geneva and the Bank of Commerce and Credit in Threadneedle Street. He could always start again using those as opening capital. His reflections were disturbed by the sound of someone calling his name. It was the presidential aide, Nixon Makau.

'Mr Tarak Tulshidas, please. Big Mama will see you now. Kindly come this way.'

His heart fluttering with fear and apprehension, Tarak followed him into the large office where he found the colonel and Big Mama seated at their big desk. Neither of them smiled - neither of them gave him so much as a glance. 'I've been found guilty without trial,' thought Tarak.

'Sit down, Mr Tulshidas,' said Big Mama without looking up from the thick file she was studying. 'We see you and your forebears have been resident in Zambelia for a long time.'

'Yes, Madam,' answered Tarak carefully. 'My great-grandfather came from India in 1900.'

'So there's absolutely no excuse for you breaking the law so blatantly,' she snapped angrily, suddenly looking up at him for the first time.

'Sorry, Madam. I don't understand.'

'Spare us the dramatic performance. Don't play the innocent with us. We know that you have been guilty of massive currency frauds for the last five years. Do you think we are fools? Furthermore, you have been purchasing the kinds of goods we allow our expatriates to import as a special concession. We did not pass that law so that people like you could take advantage of it. Do you have anything to say in your defence?'

'I apologise to you from the bottom of my heart, Madam. I confess my guilt. The only thing I can say in mitigation is that, for many years now, I have been trying to run my business under a severe handicap.'

'That is not good enough, Mr Tulshidas. You have systematically cheated the Zambelia Customs on a grand scale by doing deals with our District Foreman, Mr Paddy Reilly. We have had both you and him under close surveillance for some time now and we've been truly amazed at your audacity and the size of the consignments you have purchased from him. We shall be dealing with him shortly.'

'My only defence,' spluttered Tarak, 'is that my electrical business is for the good of the country and employs many workers in selling and distribution but I have been constantly short of foreign exchange with which to buy goods abroad. That is no excuse, however, for my despicable conduct and I offer you my profoundest, heartfelt regrets.'

'You claim you have been short of foreign exchange, Mr Tulshidas? How do you explain the half million pounds you have deposited in the Bank of Commerce & Credit in London?'

She consulted the fat file.

'Account No. 0043261.'

Tarak Tulshidas could only gaze at her in trepidation. And awe. How in Allah's name had she come in possession of such information? Why, even his own wife didn't know the number of the account nor the amount he had deposited.

'Once again, ma'am,' Mr Tulshidas wept. 'I am lost for words. But now you have brought these matters to my attention, I give you my solemn word on my mother's grave that I shall make amends and atone for my crimes.'

'If your only crimes had been irregularities with money transactions,' she said evenly, 'things would not be so bad but we have discovered much more serious matters which do not redound to your credit, I'm afraid. Colonel Kiboko, over to you.'

'Well,' said Kiboko. 'Thanks to the vigilance of our National Post Office, we have intercepted a number of letters written to you by a group of dissidents now hiding like rats in Harare. This correspondence which we now have in our possession points clearly to your involvement in arms deals with these insurgents. We intend to retain the letters as evidence at your trial.'

'But I know no-one in Harare. I would never plot against my own country,' Tulshidas protested sorrowfully.

'Of course, you would say that, wouldn't you?' said Kiboko.

'If we brought these matters to the attention of our president, we have no doubt whatsoever that he will have you executed forthwith. Fortunately, there may be a way out of this impasse,' Big Mama said.

'Only say the word,' whimpered Tarak, 'and it shall be done.'

'We have done a rough calculation, Mr Nixon Makau and I, and we reckon you owe the government something in the region of five hundred thousand pounds in back taxes and custom charges. However, we are merciful and do not want to empty your funds completely. A donation to our party funds will help matters. A cheque for four hundred and fifty thousand drawn on your London account and made payable to the President of Zambelia will exonerate you from all further charges.'

'But such a large sum will ruin me. May I have time to think the matter over?'

'But of course, you may,' said Big Mama warmly. 'In the meanwhile, whilst you are thinking it over and making up your mind, we shall be pleased to accommodate you in the cells of Tagooma Prison. Colonel Kiboko - your department again, I believe.'

Kiboko went to the door of the office and beckoned to the two Public Safety Unit officers standing guard outside.

'Come along,' he said. 'Another one for you.'

One of Kiboko's men came into the room and forced Tarak's hands behind his back snapping on handcuffs making sure that they were painfully tight. Tarak tried to speak but was slapped across the face and a black bag was placed over his head. A few minutes later a sobbing Tarak Tulshidas was escorted from Big Mama's office.

***

134

Paddy Reilly waited his turn. He had been supremely confident that the summons to see Big Mama held out the promise of yet another lucrative building contract. That is - until he saw the squat, podgy little figure of Tarak Tulshidas being taken away between two giant policemen. Something was up but he didn't know what. Still, no use jumping the gun and anticipating bad news. Always look on the bright side of life; that had been his philosophy to date and it had paid off – up to now. Nevertheless, he had a stomach full of butterflies, a bad headache, and a thumping heartbeat. Come to think of it, it was the first time she'd ever called him in.

The midget Nixon Makau appeared and signalled him to follow into the main office. Big Mama did not rise to her feet or offer her ring to be kissed. Instead, she regarded the giant Irishman coldly and with disapproval.

'Sit down, Reilly,' she commanded 'We have one or two things to discuss with you.'

'Thank you, ma'am,' said Paddy uneasily. 'I welcome this opportunity to talk things over with you.'

'We sincerely hope you feel the same way when this interview is concluded, Reilly. Now, how long have you been here in Zambelia as District Foreman?'

'About two years, ma'am.'

'Tell us Reilly, do you like it here? Do you wish to stay here as District Foreman?'

'Oh, yes, ma'am. I love it here. I've never been happier in my life.'

'Why have you been behaving in such an anti-social, criminal way?'

'I don't know what you mean, ma'am. I trust you have been happy with my building work here. I have insisted on the highest standard of workmanship at all times.'

'Including, I suppose, your own house and swimming pool which you built with palace materials and prison labour. But it isn't the standard of your work we have asked you here to discuss, Reilly. We shall come straight to the point. You have been systematically robbing us ever since you came here. You have been, as you put it to your companion in the bar of the Lundazi Inn last night, on the fiddle. "Like Nero in ancient Rome" I believe, were the actual words you used.'

'No, ma'am. It's not true,' protested Paddy, though not too convincingly. 'That was idle drunken talk in a bar.'

'Save us the beating-of-the-breast act, Reilly. Let's save time and admit it. Mr Makau, read out your findings.'

'Yes, ma'am,' said Nixon. 'First, Mr Reilly, you have been stealing construction materials by invoicing us for supplies that you used to build your own house in the Matata Park Estate. You have also been using our labour whose wages we have been paying. Secondly, ever since you came to this country, you have been filling your personal Volvo estate with petrol and oil from the palace garage where you have also had the vehicle serviced and repaired.'

Paddy Reilly's face had turned a deathly white and he felt sick. He was hoping for an earthquake or a cataclysmic opening of the earth.

'Wait,' said Big Mama, 'There's more. Please continue, Mr Makau.'

'According to our records, you have been importing electronic equipment on a huge scale without payment of customs charges by addressing them through diplomatic channels here at the palace. Last month, you imported twelve Canon Powershot digital cameras, twenty Toshiba laptops, fifteen Sony Camcorders, twenty-five Panasonic DVD players, and fifty Grundig radio sets, one hundred and twenty Baylis wind-up radios. In addition you bought one hundred illegal laptops meant for schoolchildren from the Minister of Education. You disposed of them all by selling them to Tarak Tulshidas and Ibrahim Suleman, the Asian dealers, at a considerable profit.'

Paddy Reilly realised the game was up and that it was no use arguing or objecting. They had done their research too well and they had his number.

'Colonel Kiboko,' said Big Mama. 'You said earlier that you wanted to add something.'

'Yes, thank you, ma'am,' the Colonel gushed. 'I have it on good authority, Reilly, that last night, in the Lundazi Inn you referred to our beloved president as "a bloody kaffir".'

'That last accusation is not true,' Paddy protested vehemently. 'On the contrary, I said he was the boss, - the bloody gaffer.'

'Furthermore,' Kiboko continued, 'the bartender says you called our glorious President a pig.'

'But when was that?' Paddy spluttered. 'I would never say such a thing – never in my life.'

'You said and I quote: "Working for the president is like riding on the pig's back. Does that not mean you think our president is a pig?'

'No, no. It's a figure of speech to indicate how happy I am working for the president.'

'No matter,' said Big Mama. 'The question is - what action we are to take. You realise, Reilly, that, if we report these matters to the president, he would either send you to prison for a long time or, at the very least, send you back to Belfast on the next plane. That would be the end of the Good Life for you, Mr Reilly. No more having your way with that young Zambelian maiden you have waiting at home.'

Paddy Reilly's world had fallen in. He could see himself back in Kelly's Cellar Bar and crying into his beer, that is *if he ever got back to Belfast.*

'However,' Big Mama continued, 'happily, there is a solution to all this if you agree to co-operate, Mr Reilly.'

'Anything, ma'am. You've only to say the word.'

'First. My four sisters have been talking about how they would like conservatories and swimming pools at their residences. Are you in a position to build them? We shall require the highest standards.'

'I shall build them conservatories fit for the queens whose names they bear, ma'am,' said a much-relieved Paddy Reilly. This sort of talk was more in his line. 'Is that all that will be required of me?'

'We believe Colonel Kiboko and our Senior Chief Secretary, Mr Makau, may also have some projects in mind. They will give you details of their plans. Naturally, you will send the invoices for this work to us. As for ourselves, we want little. Only that you transport a few small things from the palace to our private villa on the Hekima Plateau.' She opened a drawer in her desk and took out a manila folder. 'Here is the list.'

Paddy took the folder from her.

'Just the things on this list, Ma'am. Is that the lot?' Paddy asked happily.

'That's the lot,' she replied, 'and, in return for your co-operation, Mr Reilly, we shall have no objection to your present practices, provided you don't let the blood rush to your head and over-do it. We must point out, however, that you may have to do business with someone other than Tarak Tulshidas as he may be going away on an extended holiday. It depends on whether he sees good sense or not. We would suggest Ibrahim Suleman whom we, in the government, have always found very helpful. But I am sure your young lady will be happy to know you are remaining in Zambelia. Good morning, Mr Reilly.'

She stood up and offered Paddy her hand. He took it and kissed the ruby.

'Thank you, ma'am,' he said, genuflecting and backing out of the room.

When he got outside the office, he took a look at the list of things she wanted moving.

'Good God in heaven!' he exclaimed. ' "A few small things," she said.'

Now he truly understood why they called her "*Big* Mama".

****

Chapter Twelve

Tagooma Prison

Zambelia had six prisons in different parts of the country located five or six miles outside the main townships. Each accommodated around one thousand prisoners who had been incarcerated for the usual, one is tempted to say "ordinary" crimes like petty larceny, graft, burglary, shoplifting, brawling, car theft, public indecency, and the like. These "normal" prisons had farmlands attached and the inmates worked from dawn to dusk producing rich profits to add to the presidential coffers. There was also a woman's prison, Gereza, situated ten miles outside the capital, Lundazi.

The most notorious of the prisons was, however, that of Tagooma situated a little way outside Hekima and presided over by Captain Asa Gumbo. Its notoriety was because this establishment had a special section (Block P) reserved exclusively for malefactors who had committed crimes against the state, the so-called "political detainees" or PDs. It was to this block that the shackled Tarak Tulshidas was taken since his crimes, it was alleged, had involved cheating the state of its due revenue and was therefore political/fiscal in nature. The total number of inmates locked up in Block P fluctuated around ninety to one hundred and ten, depending on how many executions had been held recently. At the time of Tarak's arrest, there were ninety-two PDs housed in eight cells numbered 1 – 8 each holding eleven or twelve inmates, many with cases pending until such a time as they could raise enough money to buy their release. Twenty of these

140

prisoners were on death row because of extremely serious offences against the state, such as insulting the name of the President of Zambelia, giving public support to a banned political party, or passing confidential material to the foreign press, or organisations like Amnesty International.

The Police Land Rover bearing Tulshidas drew up outside the main gate of Tagooma and the wretched businessman was frogmarched into a scruffy interrogation office where a smartly-dressed officer made him remove his personal effects – belt, watch, and even shoelaces.

'In case you try to commit suicide,' the officer grinned by way of explanation as he chained Tarak by the handcuffs to the iron grille of the window.

After half an hour, the heavy iron gate of the office was swung open and a corpulent officer with three pips on his shoulder entered with two guards.

'My name is Captain Gumbo of the Public Safety Unit and I'm in charge of this prison. We welcome you to our establishment and hope you have a pleasant, comfortable stay with us. You have nothing to fear as long as you co-operate with my officers and answer their questions fully and honestly. Any attempt to hide the truth will be met with swift retribution, however, and it will be in your interests at all times to work with us and not against us. I shall be leaving you now but two of my best men will shortly be asking you one or two questions.'

So saying, Captain Gumbo left with the guards slamming the gate behind them.

Tulshidas was left to stew for an hour. Frozen in mortal fear, he was sure that his time was up and he resigned himself to death. But that was not the end that his captors had in mind for him. Not yet anyway. After what seemed like an interminable period of time, he heard the guards approaching and the door being unlocked. The handcuffs were released from the grille and re-fastened behind his back while shackles were fixed round his ankles. Grabbed roughly by the collar,

141

Tulshidas was dragged to a small office for interrogation. These were two different men whom he had not seen before: one was heavily built with a sallow face and narrow slit-like eyes which made him appear short-sighted; the other, a thin, sunken-eyed man with a pimply face that wore a permanent scowl giving the impression that it was taking him all his time to keep his anger in check.

The spotty one kicked off the proceedings by asking Tulshidas if he knew why he'd been arrested. When the answer came back as no, the slit-eyed, myopic one began a series of hard slaps across Tarak's face. The rest of the afternoon followed this pattern with the trader being accused of conspiring with unnamed fellow traders to undermine the economy of the country. A series of rapid-fire questions were directed at him and his "wrong" answers resulted in a flurry of yet more smacks and thumps which rained down on his head. In a fit of rage, the stocky one shoved his victim onto his back and began kicking him mercilessly in the crotch. As a screaming Tulshidas struggled against his shackles to regain his upright position, the pair roared with laughter at his helplessness. Hour after hour, the inquisition continued with the victim repeating the same statements and protestations of innocence. After what seemed to Tulshidas like an eternity, the inquisitors changed tack and removed the handcuffs and the shackles.

'Why do you think you were arrested?' Slit-eyes demanded.

'I don't know,' Tulshidas wept. 'I think this will become apparent when I am charged and there is a trial.'

'Charged! Charged!' the pimply skeleton guffawed. 'You won't be charged and this interview you're having right here and now is the only trial you're going to get! I ask you again. Why do you think you've been detained?'

'I think it may be a case of mistaken identity!' Tarak whimpered.

This reply earned him a punch in the face causing a purple bruise to come up in his cheek.

'But His Excellency Life President Matata is like the Pope; he is infallible and never makes mistakes. Are you saying our glorious President is stupid?'

'No, no. Our illustrious Life President is the most intelligent man on the planet.'

'Then why are you plotting against him with your crooked deals?'

Patiently Tulshidas mumbled his story of how he had always been loyal to the country and how his business activities had helped to make the country prosperous. But he was wasting his time and it was no good. They were determined to find him guilty, no matter what. While the spotty-one leaned against the wall to enjoy the entertainment, his heavy companion set about giving Tarak a thorough clobbering. He was clumped, kicked and thrown around the room like a rag doll. The inquisition and the violence only came to an end when the interrogators, wearied of asking the same questions and receiving the same old answers, gave it up as a bad job. The session had lasted over four hours.

'Very well,' Acne-face snorted at last, 'we have done with you for the present. But we shall be back. Of that you can be sure.' Turning to his corpulent companion, he asked, 'Where we gonna bung this one?'

'Room for one more in Cell Number 8, I think. Yeah, shove 'im in there.'

Tarak's hand-cuffs and shackles were put back and the shivering, terrified trader was left for another hour to lick his wounds and to think about his position. After what seemed like forever, the persecutors returned and released his chains once more. From there, he was prodded along dark corridors until they finally reached a cell with damp dripping walls where he was given a single foul-stinking blanket and flung on to the bare concrete floor. The stench of excreta and sweat was so fierce that Tarak seemed to *swallow* it as well as *smell*

143

it. After the guards had departed, Tulshidas tried to examine his surroundings through half-closed, bloodshot eyes. In his blurred vision, he saw that the room was a small dark cell, the only light coming from one tiny barred window high up on the wall. Out of the gloom a voice spoke.

'Welcome to this reeking hell-hole – Tagooma's very own health resort, and to Cell Number 8,' it said. 'Who are you and where are you from?'

'My name is Tarak Tulshidas,' he mumbled, 'and I am, or was, a trader in Lundazi township.'

'Greetings, Mr Tulshidas. We shall call you Tarak, if you don't mind, as we're on first-name terms here; we're a friendly crowd that likes to swap stories and maybe a few body lice as well. I'm Frank Johnson, formerly Reader in English Literature at the University of Hekima. What are you in for, Tarak?'

'I have been unjustly accused of profiteering but I am not guilty. I am sure that when I get access to my lawyer, the matter can be cleared up immediately and I'll be shown to be innocent and allowed to go home.'

'Innocent, you say. That applies to all of us here. So welcome to the club. As for seeing a lawyer, you can forget it. No-one gets to see a lawyer or goes to trial, not in Zambelia; no such thing as *habeas corpus* here, I'm afraid. We're all here for stepping on the wrong peoples' corns in one way or another. Our glorious president is rumoured to have said: "I will leave political prisoners behind bars until they rot. They'll be good meat for the crocodiles." So not much hope from that quarter, eh? I trust the guards haven't roughed you up too much.'

'I have managed to survive more or less,' Tarak said sorrowfully.

'At least you didn't have to run the gauntlet of warders with clubs, sticks and iron bars that I had as my introduction to this place,' Johnson said.

144

'At least I was spared that,' replied Tarak, 'but I'm not sure what they have in store for me tomorrow.'

'That too goes for the rest of us. There's one consolation, and it's the only one, - that we're not on death row because then it'd be all up with us. Pity the poor bastards awaiting execution; they're no more guilty than we are. Anyway, let me introduce some of your companions here who also don't know why they're here. It's like the old song soldiers used to sing in the trenches: "We're here because we're here", and so on *ad infinitum*.'

Through the murk, Tarak could just about discern the figures of ten or eleven naked men sitting back to back on the stone floor. Frank Johnson and another man were chained to the floor by leg irons. In turn, his host announced their names as if at a cocktail party.

'Let me introduce Government Deputy Chifunza; you will notice that like me, he is manacled to the iron rings on the floor.'

'Why only you two manacled?'

'Favouritism, I suppose,' Johnson retorted with a hollow laugh.

Tulshidas was amazed that anyone could take such punishment so lightly.

'To answer your question about the leg irons, the Deputy and I are reckoned to be the most dangerous kind of offender since we've dared to say we're not entirely happy at the way things are going in Zambelia. I was regarded as a subversive influence on my students though I was only trying to teach my students to think for themselves - a serious sin here in Zambelia. I suppose too that the fact that I had a couple of articles criticising the school system published in the British educational press didn't help matters. I thought I might have got away by being merely *Pee-Eyed.*'

'Pee-Eyed? What's that?' from Tulshidas.

'P.I.'d, that is classified as a Prohibited Immigrant due to be deported but no such luck, I'm afraid. Being P.I.'d has two advantages: one, the government has to pay your air fare home; and the other, I suppose, is that it would serve as a badge of merit and a good reference when applying for a job in certain U.K. universities. However, I was put down as a conspirator deserving of incarceration. So here I am.' Turning to his manacled companion, he said, 'Anyway, Deputy, would you like to say a few words about yourself?'

'Good evening, Mr Tulshidas,' said the Deputy taking his cue. 'Your name is well known and respected throughout Zambelia. I'm sure that, like the rest of us in here, you've been arrested on trumped-up charges. Deputy Chilulu and I were apprehended a few months ago by the Public Safety Unit in Lundazi for criticising the Life President for drawing multi-million dollar unsecured loans from state funds to build yet another presidential palace - his third – on the shore of Lake Zambelia. It's hard to overstate the level of corruption of the gang of boot-lickers close to the President.'

'Surely not all of them?' Tulshidas asked incredulously.

'Pretty well the lot of them. Except maybe for Nixon Makau, the presidential aide and private Secretary, who is perhaps the only one with sound commonsense but what can he do on his own? He's powerless and has to toe the line like the rest of them. Anyway, you can see why Deputy Chilulu and I were arrested for daring to voice our discontent at what was going on. Sadly, Chilulu slipped and fell in a so-called accident over the Lake when we were being flown here in the Kiboko's personal helicopter. Most unfortunate as he and I could have supported each other had we ever come to trial in one of our tribal courts. Not that those traditional courts ever dispense real justice anyway. It's all one because I think we've been judged guilty without *any* kind of trial. It's probably best to cooperate with the brutes who interrogate us here in Tagooma.'

'And I am Jacob Chimanga,' piped up another voice from the gloom. 'I was a teacher in Hekima and a member of the Zambelia Teachers' Union. In addressing the Union last year, I referred to our country's leader as "The President" instead of "His Excellency Life-President Professor Samson Matata". That omission is going to cost me at least five years in this hole. I was accused of lack of respect for the president and, in this country, that's a serious felony.'

Another voice piped up. 'I'm Gerald Mitinda and also a teacher and a victim of arbitrary arrest. In here for three years because I happened to say to my friends at a bar that I was not happy at being moved from my job and my home here in Hekima to a distant and isolated Northern province. It was taken as implied criticism of the government's educational policy.'

'Something similar happened to me,' said a man with a hoarse voice, 'I'm Barabbas Mbuzi and a cattle farmer. I came to Hekima to do business. I happen to be tone-deaf and can't tell one tune from another. I was having a drink in a noisy bar when the band on the floor above began playing at somebody's wedding. It struck up, or so they tell me, with the national anthem and I didn't notice when people stood up. So I'm in here for showing gross disrespect by not jumping to my feet when the others did.'

A young man who couldn't have been more than twenty years of age now told his story. 'I was thrown in here this morning and I'm here on the same charge. My name is Adlai Gwelo. I used to be cook/house-boy for a Canadian doctor who has gone back to Quebec and it's because of an old sea shanty that I learned from him that I've landed up in this terrible place. It's like this: I was at a party and when they asked me to do a turn, I gave them a coupla choruses of this Canadian ditty called 'Mary Anne' and I was arrested for it. The title of the song is too close to the popular name of the President's hostess Marie Antoinette, for their liking; it's

147

against the law, they said, to sing anything in public that even sounds like her name. I was accused of poking fun at her.'

'It's the most ridiculous thing I've ever heard,' bellowed Frank Johnson. 'It's a bloody mad world here in Zambelia because when it was her birthday not so long ago, we were all required by law to join in the chorus of that little birthday ditty that went: "Happy Birthday, Marie Antoinette. Let's Celebrate, Marie Antoinette. Call her Mama, Call her Mother. For there isn't any other quite like her. For she's Zambelia's Pride and Joy." How did your illicit song go, Adlai? Since you're here in prison anyway, you may as well be hung for a sheep as a lamb. Give us a sample of this Mary Anne song.'

'I can't remember the whole song,' Adlai replied, 'but, if I remember rightly, the last verses went like this. He sang:

Fare-you-well my own Mary Ann,
Fare-you-well for a while,
For the ship is ready and the wind it is fair,
And I am bound for the sea, Mary Ann, Mary Ann
And I am bound for the sea.

Don't you see that turtle dove
A sitting on yonder pile?
Lamenting the loss of her own true love,
And so am I for you, Mary Ann, Mary Ann,
And so am I for you

The listeners clapped as well as they were able, given their chains.

'Well done!' exclaimed Frank Johnson 'But that seems harmless enough,'

'Doesn't matter,' Adlai said. 'If the Safety Unit goons say it's seditious and making fun of the president's consort, there's no come-back. I tell you: if we ever get out of this

148

dump, the men to watch out for are those sitting around the place pretending to read newspapers through those dark, one-way wrap-around shades because most of them are undercover PSU police ready to snatch you, first chance they get.'

A man chained to the wall now offered a contribution. 'My name is Ishmael Masiku. I used to be manager of the National Bank of Zambelia in my home town of Njima. I am here accused of allowing the use of faxes and photocopiers to disseminate pro-multi-party literature. Needless to say, I have no knowledge of this being done by my employees. That didn't seem to matter and I have been put in here for an indeterminate period which probably means forever.'

'You will note,' Frank Johnson said, 'that we are mainly professional men from various walks of life: civil servants, teachers, business men except for my young friend from the university who'll tell you about himself.'

'I'm the young man Frank is referring to,' a voice said. 'My name is Geoff Shairi, and my offence was collaborating with him in writing poetry of the kind that doesn't meet with official approval. I suppose I come into the category of a prisoner of conscience.'

'Prisoner of conscience?' Tarak wondered. 'What's that?'

'That's anyone,' Geoff explained 'who is considered *persona non grata* or merely an inconvenience by holding the wrong opinions. You don't have to do or say anything seditious. Thought alone can be enough to get you detained as a potential threat. No charge. No trial. No open justice. Nothing. You're simply scooped up and slung in Tagooma for an undefined period. No-one is safe. You can be imprisoned merely for your religious beliefs, like the unfortunate Jehovah's Witnesses who have been recently persecuted.'

'I would add,' said Frank Johnson, 'that you can also be put away for having the wrong relatives if they happen to be

149

exiled or merely under suspicion because that means, of course, that you too are automatically a risk to the regime.'

'I find it hard to take this in,' exclaimed Tulshidas, shaking his head vigorously. 'People on the outside are hardly aware of what's going on under their noses. And conditions in here look pretty rough. Are things always like this? I mean, is it always as crowded as this? Twelve men in this room which can't be more than about twelve feet square.'

'Always like this,' Johnson answered. 'Conditions can be described in one word. Grim! As for crowding, this is nothing. Count your blessings. In the so-called "ordinary" prisons, there are often two hundred and fifty men in rooms meant for fifty. They are forced to spend the night standing crammed together because there's no space for them to sit down. As "pollies" - political prisoners - we are given special treatment in more ways than one.'

'But where do *we* sleep?' Tarak asked. 'Are beds and dormitories provided? And where are the toilets?'

'No dormitories, Tarak. We sleep on the floor - some of us chained back-to-back to keep warm, though if you bribe a guard, you may be given a space where you can sit against the wall. As for the toilet, that's the big bucket in the corner which some of us will have to empty tomorrow morning in the one and only flush lavatory outside. That is, if there's any water and the WC is working. The lavatory is only good as a breeding ground for mosquitoes, so the twelve inmates of this cell have only the use of the open latrine to relieve themselves.'

'But one toilet and only an open latrine for so many men!' Tarak gasped.! It's uncivilised,' Tarak gasped.

'Exactly,' Johnson said. 'Not easy to be civilised and maintain your pride and dignity when squatting over an open ditch with eleven fellow-inmates, I have to agree. But there's F.A. we can do about it.'

'I shall write to my lawyer first thing tomorrow,' Tulshidas said. 'We'll soon sort out this mess.'

'Sorry,' said Johnson, almost gleefully. 'Letters not allowed. Reading matter forbidden. Recreational material like chess or draughts: verboten. If you're caught with a book, newspaper, or paper and pencil, you'll be for it good and proper. The only literature permitted in here is the Bible and maybe a hymn book.'

'If I can't see my lawyer,' Tarak protested, 'I shall ask my wife to report matters when she comes to visit.'

'Visit! Visit!' Don't make us laugh!' roared Johnson. 'Us Pollies aren't allowed family visits! You'll be asking about conjugal visits next! Besides. most family members are too afraid to visit in case they're accused of something sinister simply by being associated with us. Your visitor may not get out after their visit. Maybe our poet, Geoff Shairi there, will have something to say about family visits. Geoff?'

'Too true I have,' Geoff said ruefully. 'I was imprisoned for over two years without a single visit from anybody.'

'Not even a member of a religious order like a priest or an imam?' Tarak asked.

'None,' Geoff said. 'I am a Catholic and no priest was allowed to come near me. Imagine that! Simply because I wrote the wrong sort of poetry.'

'I can add to that,' said a new voice. 'My name is Ely Karioki and I am a Presbyterian minister. I was arrested without charge by the Safety Unit Service on account of a sermon that was judged to be critical of the government though I made no reference whatsoever to anything remotely to do with the state.'

'So how on earth could they arrest you?' Tulshidas gasped.

'I quoted a biblical text from the book of Micah: "The godly have been swept from the land: not one upright man remains." The PSU thought I was getting at Zambelia and so accused me of making veiled references to our own

151

government in a critical way. That was enough for them to put me behind bars.'

'The more I hear, the more I believe that the Zambelian government has lost touch with reality,' Tulshidas said.

'Careful what you say,' the bank manager said in a hoarse whisper. 'That's enough to add a few years to whatever sentence they give you.'

'What about food?' Tarak asked, changing the subject hurriedly. 'From what you've said, I suppose that it would be asking the impossible to request that food be sent in.'

'You suppose right,' Johnson replied vehemently. 'We get three meals a day suitable mainly for our Bantu prisoners since it consists of maize. Breakfast is porridge, lunch is maize and beans; supper at 4 pm is the same as breakfast. Is it any wonder that prisoners are so skeletal, go blind and suffer from pellagra?'

Deputy Chifunza now spoke up, having been silent throughout the discourse. 'When I was a Minister in the Chamber of Deputies, I saw a government report to the American Embassy which claimed that prisoners were fed meat and fish. Complete lies! No-one here has seen such luxuries. Our diet is simply maize with beans infested with weevils and occasionally rotten vegetables or fruit that we can't eat and have to throw away. It is living hell in this prison. How I wish there was a way to get out.'

Tulshidas was shocked. 'People outside wouldn't believe this was happening and to think that Zambelia's University is only four miles away. Can this vile treatment be put down to the isolated excesses by individual prison staff?'

'I don't think so,' Deputy Chifunza said. 'I can vouch that these abuses and this cruelty are part of official policy.'

'Doesn't anyone ever complain?' Tulshidas protested. 'If I can only get to a telephone, I intend making the public aware of what's going on here.'

For some reason not clear to Tulshidas, this remark of his occasioned ribald laughter.

'What did I say that's so funny?' Tulshidas asked.

'I hope you never find out,' Frank Johnson said gravely.

'You try asking for a phone call in here,' the Deputy continued, 'and in double quick time, you'll find out exactly how rough this place can be. Let me explain. There are different kinds of punishment for anyone who has the temerity to speak out.'

'The mildest form,' said Jacob Chimanga, taking up the story, 'is probably the Balancing Board. I can tell you about that for I've had a taste. I was too slow in obeying an order one day and was awarded this as a penalty.'

'Balancing Board?' Tulshidas queried.

'It's a short plank placed over a large bottle which acts as a fulcrum like a see-saw. The punishment is being forced to stand upright on that for two hours or more. It doesn't sound like much but the pain it causes to the legs is indescribable.'

'And that's the mildest? I hardly like to ask what the next grade is,' Tulshidas said.

'The second level of punishment is usually reserved for semi-serious offences like answering back or deliberately disobeying an order. Arguably, this level is the strappado. It's a form of torture that was much favoured during the Spanish Inquisition. Your hands are tied behind your back and secured to a pulley. You're hoisted from the ground and released with a sudden jerk. This can almost wrench the arms from the sockets. Maybe in the sixteenth century, it did.'

'Surely,' said Tulshidas aghast, 'there can't be anything worse than that apart from whipping and birching.'

'It's a matter of opinion,' Deputy Chifunza answered, 'but I consider the Gumbo telephone caper to be the worst of the lot.'

''We'd better tell him the details,' said Frank Johnson. 'I've not suffered the strappado but I have had a short taste of the telephone call treatment described by the guards as a "local" call. How my heart goes out to those poor wretches who've had the "long-distance" type.'

'I shudder to ask for details,' Tulshidas remarked.

'A long distance phone call,' said the Deputy, taking up the account, 'means you are down to receive the top punishment of the prison. Here in Tagooma, our superintendent, urged on no doubt by that monster, Kiboko, has devised the worst torture you can imagine. It's known as the Gumbo Telephone in honour of the prison governor. The telephone consists of a generator taken from a crank-type phone and wired to two dry-cell batteries. Wires are attached to the big toe and the penis. When the crank is turned, it sends an electrical charge into the body. Victims say the pain is beyond imagination.'

'As I went about my daily business outside these walls,' Tulshidas said tremblingly, 'I never would have believed that such atrocities were taking place on my doorstep. If it's as painful as you say, I'm afraid to ask what is meant by "long-distance" phone call.'

'Long-distance,' said Johnson grimly to the half-question, 'means inflicting the pain short of the victim fainting. It's used both to punish and extract information. It's not unknown for a prisoner to die an excruciating death.'

'In my opinion,' Geoff Shairi said, joining in the macabre conversation. 'The worst punishment of all is *giza* the "dark cell treatment" or being shackled in solitary confinement with no human contact whatsoever for as long as thirty days in complete darkness. Food and water are given infrequently and buckets of cold water are thrown at you from time to time. Under these conditions, victims often die or simply go insane. No doubt in my mind. That's the punishment I fear most.'

***

Cold, hungry, and fearful, Tarak Tulshidas hardly slept a wink on that first night in Tagooma. As he tossed and turned on the concrete floor, only one question and only one thought revolved round and round in his brain. 'How in Allah's name, am I going to get out of here?'

****

Chapter Thirteen

Colonel Kenneth Kiboko.

Kenneth Kiboko was born on a Halloween, under the sign of Scorpio, to Kisio Kimathi and Cleopatra Makubwa, the second daughter of Karanja and sister of Marie Antoinette. Cleopatra was thirteen years of age when she gave birth to him. Village people later said that the child had been born with a knife between his teeth but that was only after they saw what a monster he became. While the knife story may have been simply superstitious nonsense, what *was* certain was that he'd been conceived out of wedlock and been given tribal respectability by a last-minute marriage forcibly arranged by his young eighteen-year old aunt, Marie Antoinette. Cleopatra herself claimed that she had been led astray by Kisio and had no desire whatsoever to marry him and had agreed to the ceremony only under duress and the threat of being banished and made an outcast from the tribe. As for the young Kenneth, he never got to know his father as the latter was killed in a knife-fight with a mysterious stranger in a local bar before he'd been born. His mother had never remarried though there had been several suitors offering themselves none of whom Big Mama, Marie Antoinette, had approved of. So that had been that. Kenneth sensed later that somehow his Aunt Marianne didn't approve of *him* either and, throughout his boyhood, he believed himself rejected and unwanted.

This feeling of rejection was confirmed when he was sent to live with his aged and sick paternal grandparents. As his

156

grandfather, a giant of a man, lay on his deathbed, he gave out word that Kenneth was to be brought to him. It was a bitter, misty morning. Kenneth, then twelve years of age, was ushered into the thatched mud hut where the old man lay, and was given the Massuyu blessing according to tradition. Though weak and well-nigh finished, the dying man put out a frail hand and laid it on Kenneth's head, croaking with his last dying breath:

'One day, this boy will be strong and powerful. He will be a leader - much feared and much respected. As my life comes to an end and the light begins to fade, Mungu has revealed this to me.'

He requested Kenneth stay with him until the end. He asked that a small quantity of goat's blood be brought to him in a goat's horn. He dipped his finger in the blood and made a sign of a dagger on the young man's forehead.

'May his friends love him! May his enemies fear him!' he pronounced.

Those were the last words his grandfather spoke. This benediction in blood made a deep impression on the boy and aroused the superstitious tendencies that lie buried deep in every Massuyu soul. Kenneth was convinced that Mungu had spoken to him through his grandfather's dying words. He was to be a powerful and dreaded chieftain in the Massuyu tribe. If he could not be liked, he would be feared and respected. The great African chiefs of the past would be his models - Mzilikazi, Shaka, Cetshwayo, Idi Amin, Mobutu, Emperor Bokassa. Men would quake in terror at his approach.

At night his dreams were filled with scenes of meadows of countless cattle, of great crowds of men dancing in adulation around him, of himself on a throne of gold, of a court where men prostrated themselves before him, of fierce battles with the warriors that he'd slain lying in great rivers of blood. Sword in hand, he beheaded the throngs of people all dressed in white who approached him endlessly, their hands

157

outstretched in supplication. On one occasion, he saw himself balanced on the top of a flagpole looking down at the miniscule people who swarmed below like ants. Even Mungu himself spoke in one of these fantasies and told him to be master in the land and rule with an iron fist. The old people in his grandfather's village refused to listen to his tales of nightly visions. They knew that such a dreamer was a man possessed by the devil.

As a child and a youth, Kenneth Kiboko was different from the others because of his sheer size and his cruel nature. He was called "The Shenzi" or "The Wild One" by his young companions, and he soon became a natural leader among the village youth, having discovered even at that early age how sensitive the testicles of his play-fellows were. He had no conscious feeling of cruelty. At seven, he used his bow and arrow to bring down many multi-coloured touraco birds for the sake of their feathers which he plucked from their living flesh, leaving the creatures to die a slow, painful death. He caught small baby vervet monkeys and tried to sell the half-starved animals in the market, taking it out on the tiny beasts with torture when he failed to do so. At his mother's home, he refused to help in any way; he would not carry water from the well, he refused to join in the battle against the great hordes of army worms which came one year in their zillions to devour the maize crops. Once, in anger, he pushed a young playmate into a swarm of soldier ants. His mother punished him by ordering the headman on the farm to tie him to the fence of the kraal and flog him. The whipping served to strengthen his hatred of the human race. Not long after his grandfather's death, he revenged himself on the headman by killing some of his goats and cutting off the nose of one of his cows. Later he had sneaked into the headman's hut and, whilst the adults were talking and drinking *pombe*, he had tied a pillow case over his baby son's head and, had the muffled cries of the infant not reached the ears of the mother in the next hut, the child would most certainly have died.

158

At school, he proved to be intelligent and bright but education did not appear to have the chastening effect his mother had hoped for. At the time, bitter conflict raged between missionary and tribal schools on the subject of female circumcision - the missions regarding the practice as an evil throwback to the Massuyu primitive past. But many Massuyu saw it as a quasi-religious ritual and an essential part of tribal custom. As a result, many traditional tribal schools broke away from the missions to preach a strong anti-Christian message. At fifteen, Kiboko became a student at one of these break-away institutions. The headmaster there was so impressed by his quick mind that he took him into his home to inculcate the old ways of thought and to help him progress faster in learning traditional ways of doing things. Kiboko rewarded his kindness by stealing his money and even going so far as to sell some of his goats and pocketing the proceeds. Disgusted, the Head eventually saw the light and chased him away. It was a mistake because, many years later, when Kiboko had become chief of the Public Safety Unit police, he had the Head arrested, tortured, and executed in Tagooma prison. Like the true Scorpio he was, Kiboko was willing to bide his time until he was in a position to settle old scores. He bore grudges heavily and he never forgot and he never forgave.

Kiboko was a stickler for Massuyu traditional practices but was not beyond changing them to suit his own convenience. At seventeen, he was circumcised at the Hekima Medical Centre. When it became known to other youths in the district that he had not undergone the normal public ritual performed by the witch doctor, he was mocked and ridiculed. Kiboko reacted furiously and challenged each one to a wrestling match in the village square - three at a time, if necessary. The whole village assembled to witness the sport but unfortunately, all the youths went down with mysterious illnesses at the time appointed for the contest. The fixture had to be cancelled and Kiboko was the victor by default.

He tried his hand at many jobs. He started his own night school and gave private lessons on the basic subjects of reading and writing, and taking as payment paraffin or soap which he sold in the local market. He was at various times a lumberjack in the Forestry Department, a clerk in the timber office, a parking attendant; he sometimes supplemented his wage by winning prize money for boxing and wrestling. As usual, his life was irregular and unsettled. He stole a bicycle in the north of the country; he beat up a Chunzani shepherd and took the little money he had. He was always on the move and was a law unto himself.

By this time, his Aunt Marie Antoinette had become an important personage in the presidential palace. Cleopatra, Kiboko's mother, appealed to her older sister for help with her wayward son. A lowly position in the state police was found for him. Here he caused trouble yet again. In the first week at the police college, he threw lumps of *posho* at the Principal complaining that the porridge had been prepared with stale maize. A month later, he received his first pay which he spent on extra-strong *pombe*. A drunken brawl blew up and he was arrested by his Public Safety colleagues and thrown into the cells to cool off. While there he made the acquaintance of the only being who ever showed him any affection. It had only one eye and was the mangiest, ugliest thing he had ever set eyes on - the prison cat. It appeared one morning as he lay on his hard, wooden bunk thinking murderous thoughts as to what he would like to do to his captors when the animal jumped on to his chest and began to nuzzle into his face. It was love at first sight. Kiboko picked up the little monstrosity tenderly and stroked it gently. Little Nelson, he'd called it and the two had struck up an immediate bond of mutual sympathy. From that moment, they were inseparable. His attachment to the cat was the only love in his life.

As an adolescent, Kiboko had found no attraction towards the opposite sex but was strangely drawn to the company of other boys, especially those whom he felt were inferior to him and he could easily manipulate. So draconian were the laws of Zambelia with regard to homosexual relationships however, he found it advisable to avoid the slightest display of affection in case it was misunderstood. While sodomy was punishable by imprisonment or even death, sadism seemed preferable being not only acceptable but approved and rewarded.

Along with his new feline friend, Kiboko was rescued from his chaotic life style by the intervention of Aunt Marie Antoinette who called him into the presidential palace one day and told him the facts of life. Whatever it was she said to him, he was a changed man forever afterwards. His rise through the ranks was meteoric, which caused a good deal of resentment amongst long-serving officers – including Major Nyoka though the latter had long since learned wisely that survival in Zambelia involved disguising one's true feelings. Some of his colleagues, however, were less canny and had been unable to contain their fury. They paid the price in front of a firing squad. They had seemed naively unaware that Kiboko had the precise qualities required for advancement in independent Zambelia. He was big, strong, and ruthless. And most important of all, he was related to Big Mama.

***

Today, Kiboko was bristling. For a start, today's assignment was not the kind he normally did himself. It was one he would have left to underlings but Big Mama had been so furious about the motorcade fiasco, he felt it wise to supervise it personally so as to make sure there was no cock-up this time. It was coming to something when he could no longer trust his own men to do a simple job. Always they seemed to overstep the mark and overdo it. He'd had to leave his Little Nelson in his comfortable office back at the Lundazi palace and come down yet once again to this provincial, one-horse town. The day had begun badly. First of all, the official Land Rover had refused to start and he'd

161

had to send for a new battery making him late for his meeting with Major Nyoka in his crummy Hekima police station. The hordes of refugees clogging up the road hadn't helped matters either. Furthermore, since he'd arrived, everything had gone wrong. That stupid bastard, Nyoka, had the wrong date in his diary and wasn't expecting him and so had failed to carry out the preliminary investigations of the student they had come to interview. Finally, the coffee he'd been offered tasted like horse-piss. When things went well, Kiboko was a mellow individual full of mirth and bawdy stories. But when things went against his wishes, he was a firebrand of the most venomous kind, a seething cauldron of invective. Now, puffing impatiently on his cheroot, he waited in the front of the Land-Rover with Major Nyoka. In the back seat sat two big constables awaiting their orders.

The one he was waiting for emerged at last from the student hostel. He was with a group of other young people - a couple of boys and three girls. They were laughing together at something or other as they walked over towards the college dining hall. The spoiled bastards, he thought. He hadn't had the chance to go to university like these molly-coddled whelps; he'd been too busy patrolling the beat and learning police business.

'It was you, Daniel, wasn't it?' one of the girls was tittering. 'Trying to get into our room last night.'

'That's not the only thing he was trying to get into,' snickered one of her companions. 'It's time you got that thing of yours under control, Daniel.'

'And it's time you girls unlocked those chastity belts of yours,' Daniel laughed.

'That's him,' Kiboko muttered. 'The tall one with the stupid grin. Take him when they get near to us.'

The unsuspecting students continued their bantering as they drew alongside the police vehicle. The two big constables got out. If we get this right, they thought, we'll be in Kiboko's good books, and who knows, there may be a spot of promotion in it. They were anxious to please for they knew only too well the price of a foul-up.

'Daniel Chitanda?' asked one of the policemen gently.

'Yes, that's me,' replied Daniel politely. 'Anything wrong, officer?'

Daniel found both his arms suddenly pinned back in a grip of iron.

'Nothing to worry about,' the constable answered. 'We want you to come down to the station to answer a few routine questions, that's all. It shouldn't take too long.'

Puzzled, Daniel Chitanda got into the back of the Land Rover. 'Take the notes for me at the History lecture, Eliud,' he called to one of his friends. 'I'll see you shortly.'

Major Nyoka started the motor and the little party drove off. A short time later, they arrived at the Hekima police headquarters. Daniel was hustled into the building and thrust roughly into the interrogation room where he was left alone to ponder as to what crime he could have committed to merit such treatment. He didn't have long to wait. The four men who had picked him up came into the room – including the monocled colonel still smoking his cigar. Daniel leapt to his feet.

The two big constables stood behind him and grabbed both his arms twisting them up his back. The colonel approached him and blew smoke into his face.

'You know a girl called Charity Gichuru?' he snarled.

'Why, yes,' stuttered Daniel. 'She's a student on the English course, I believe.'

'You know her all right,' Kiboko snapped. 'In the fullest biblical sense of the word, you bastard. You have been a naughty boy and a busy boy. With these!'

As he spoke, he seized Daniel's testicles in a vice-like grip and squeezed them in a massive fist. Daniel let out a piercing scream. He struggled to break free but the two constables held him firmly. The colonel, having vented his anger, released his grip. He laughed, his huge body shaking with mirth. He always laughed when someone squirmed. It was the height of amusement to see someone in pain.

'If I'd had my way, you young bastard, I'd have cut these off so that you would never be able to use them again on innocent young virgins. I was told I had to go easy on you but today you must be taught a lesson you'll never forget.'

Once more, he grasped Daniel's genitals in his huge hand and crushed the life out of them. Daniel went limp and fell to the ground.

'Bring him round,' he barked. 'We're not finished yet.'

Water was splashed in Daniel's agonised face. The two big men held Daniel up. With cold deliberation, Kiboko balled-up his fist and landed a heavy blow on Daniel's right eye raising an ugly purple bruise. Daniel collapsed in his captors' arms and was close to passing out.

'Now,' said Kiboko, poking him in the ribs with his baton and stamping on his right foot with his heavy boots. 'You are a Chunzani bastard and you're lucky I've not killed you. You will arrange with your father to marry the girl Charity Gichuru who bears your brat. It will be done with due courtesy and respect for Zambelian customs and traditions. You will love and honour her to the day you die. If I hear even the slightest hint of anything to the contrary, you will find yourself singing soprano in the Hekima Cathedral choir. Do you understand?'

'I understand,' whispered Daniel weakly.

'Good. Now I have to make sure you remember our little meeting today. I don't want you going away from here forgetting all that I have said. Which hand do you write with?'

'My right,' mumbled Daniel through his pain. 'Why do you want to know?'

The two men placed two bricks on the table and stretched Daniel's left arm across them. At lightning speed, the colonel

164

smashed his heavy truncheon down on the extended arm. There was a cracking sound and Daniel's primeval howl of agony was heard throughout the station. Then he fainted and collapsed in a heap on the stone floor.

'Time for lunch now, I think,' murmured the Colonel.

'I can recommend the menu at the Hekima Inn - it's especially good on a Monday,' said Major Nyoka. 'And afterwards, we can visit Tagooma Prison for a flying court martial and a spot of entertainment, if you're so minded.'

'Sounds like a reasonable programme,' said Kiboko as they strolled together out of the interview room.

***

On a Sunday morning a week later, a haunted-looking Daniel - his right eye badly contused, his left arm in a sling - accompanied his father, Joshua, on the two-mile walk to keep an appointment at Philip Thomas Gichuru's house near Lundazi palace. Daniel withdrew some distance off whilst the two old men sat together under the sacred fig-tree - talking, talking, talking. Occasionally a voice was raised in argument and disagreement but things died down again and the parley continued. Four hours later, the two rose to their feet and shook hands.

'It is agreed then,' said Philip Thomas . 'The bride-price will be fifty goats on the contract being signed. Twenty more if the offspring is a healthy boy. None if it's a girl. Twins or a child born the wrong-way round to be killed at birth.'

'Agreed,' said Joshua Chitanda, pouring out the home-brewed *pombe* from the gourd. 'After all, a baby is not a person until it's one year old. Let us now call in the young betrothed.'

Joshua waved to his son. Daniel got to his feet and hobbled over to join them. Charity who had been watching anxiously from a distance did the same.

'We have agreed the marriage settlement, daughter,' said Philip Thomas. 'The choice is now yours. I have Chitanda's beer in my hand. Shall I drink it or pour it on to the ground.'

'Drink, father,' Charity said, placing a hand on her father's arm.

'Drink, father,' echoed Daniel.

Two days later, the couple took their Massuyu oaths before a *mundumugu* witch-doctor. A goat was ritually slaughtered to appease their ancestral gods, to invoke their blessing, and to ward off evil spirits. Later that week, they were formally married with nuptial Mass celebrated by Monsignor Gerry McGinn in the university chapel of St Thomas Aquinas. Daniel's friend, Eliud Chumvi, was best man.

****

Chapter Fourteen

Party Games

Three hours after Daniel Chitanda's chastisement, Kiboko and Nyoka emerged from the cool shade of the restaurant into the bright afternoon sunshine, the Colonel trapping a loud belch with the back of his hand. So Nyoka had got it right for once. It had been a particularly good lunch of Lake Zambelia fish plus a wide selection of fresh vegetables. The Chef had given him a couple of fish heads for Little Nelson, his cat.

As the two officers strolled from the Inn, Kiboko was in a happier frame of mind.

'A good meal, Nyoka,' he said. 'We must do it again next time I'm in Hekima.'

His earlier anger had subsided and he looked forward to an afternoon of amusement. The Major raised his finger and the police Land Rover came forward to meet them.

'Tagooma,' he said to the driver.

It was but a short drive to their destination. As the car swung through the massive iron gates of the jail, the Colonel adjusted his monocle and lit up a large Havana.

***

They were met by the superintendent of the prison, Captain Gumbo, a simpering, fawning individual who was so overawed by the presence of such august personages that he bowed several times and practically genuflected. Finally he clicked his heels, saluted smartly, and said, 'May I say, sirs, how deeply honoured we are that you have graced us with your presence this afternoon and...'

'Yah, yah, we know all about that,' Kiboko snapped, cutting him short and poking him in the ribs with his swagger stick. 'I find the need for strong cigar smoke whenever I visit this god-forsaken dump. You should do something about the stench, Gumbo. It reeks as if a bunch of hyenas have been through the bloody place.'

'In a way I suppose they have, Colonel,' chuckled Major Nyoka.

'Sorry, sir. I'll look into it immediately, Colonel sir,' Gumbo said. 'I'll make sure that the place is thoroughly cleaned and fumigated the next time you visit us. Leave it with me. If there's even the smallest hint of unpleasant smells, someone will pay for it, I can assure you, Colonel, sir.'

Kiboko puffed impatiently on his cigar. 'See that you do, Gumbo, or you'll answer to me personally.'

'Yes, sir! Yes, sir! Thank you, sir. How may we serve you this afternoon, Colonel?'

Nyoka thought he'd better join in and establish his authority with this underling, Gumbo. 'Yes, you make sure you do what the colonel asks.' Tongue in cheek, and looking to Kiboko for approval, he continued, 'Clean this pig-sty up and make it a fit place for us to hold our esteemed prisoners. We don't want any complaints from them, do we now?'

Kiboko joined in the sarcastic guffaws.

Encouraged that Kiboko had appreciated his sarcasm, Nyoka turned to him and asked, 'What do you have in mind for this afternoon, Colonel?'

'I thought we might organise a little entertainment,' Kiboko said. 'After that excellent lunch, I feel in need of a little amusement to aid the digestion.'

Turning to Gumbo, he barked: 'Have a dozen political prisoners you are holding brought to the large interrogation room – on the double! Make sure that Tarak Tulshidas, and that university lecturer, Frank Johnson, are included in the group. They are to be given their release on the president's orders.'

'Right away, colonel sir,' Gumbo replied, giving one of his mechanical robotic salutes. 'At the moment, Deputy Chifunza is in the S.I.R. - the Special Interrogation Room where he is receiving a long distance phone call.'

'Ah, yes,' Kiboko guffawed. 'One of your famous long distance phone calls, Gumbo. I've heard about 'em. Your reputation and your generosity for permitting these phone calls is legendary and well known throughout the land. After these calls, prisoners seem most anxious to co-operate. Most innovative of you. Why, I couldn't have thought of anything as creative myself.'

'Thank you, Colonel,' Gumbo said, preening himself, 'but to be perfectly honest, the idea came from a prison in America. I read about it and thought how appropriate it would be here.'

'All the same, Gumbo. It was enterprising of you to import it into our country. Now, let's get to the business on hand. Has Deputy Chifunza finally seen the light of day? He seemed more than willing to be helpful after his trip over Lake Zambelia in the helicopter.'

'Yes, he's been most co-operative and he'll soon be ready to supply us with the names of fellow-conspirators. A little more time on Gumbo's telephone should do the trick.'

'When he does,' Kiboko said, 'I am sure President Matata will be more than willing to grant him his release.'

'Release, colonel? I don't understand,' Gumbo said with a puzzled frown.

Kiboko gave a Cheshire cat grin. 'I saw the word on a gravestone in a cemetery somewhere. "Release at last!" the tombstone said. I'm sure these gentlemen guests will be truly grateful to hear the good news. I will give it myself to the lucky ones who are chosen a little later. Now please take me to the S.I.R. to see this telephone machine in action. After that, I have a number of other requirements. Do we have a piano and a decent pianist in the prison?'

Captain Gumbo was puzzled. He was aware, as everybody in Zambelia was, that Kiboko was eccentric and unpredictable but this was a new one.

'A piano? I'm sure there's one somewhere on the premises, Colonel. But, I believe it's an old battered one dating from the time when our colonial masters ran the place with their liberal views on penology. And I feel sure there must be a pianist amongst our thousand inmates.'

'Sounds intriguing, Colonel,' Major Nyoka said. 'What's your plan?'

'That's my little surprise party. I shall also require twelve straight-backed chairs and, oh, have your pistol ready and fully loaded. We shall need your services. You, Major Nyoka, are an important part of the game but when I call on you to do your part, try not to damage the body, especially the eyes. I don't want Big Mama and that quack, Schneider, complaining to me again that we have ruined the merchandise.'

Gumbo shouted orders for the unusual items demanded by Kiboko to be assembled in the large interrogation chamber and various prison officers scurried in all directions to find them. Meanwhile, he conducted Nyoka and the colonel to a small ante-room off the Special Interrogation Room where they found the wretched Deputy Chifunza stretched out and handcuffed to a long wooden table. Metal rings and wires were attached to his body and he was bleeding from the mouth and nose. Three prison officers were supervising the procedure. Chifunza now followed the three visitors with his agonised eyes, wincing in anticipation of the pain he associated with visitors.

'Good news, Deputy Chifunza,' shouted the colonel. 'You have been so cooperative up to now that soon the

170

President will be ordering your release. Are you sure you have given us all the information we require?'

'Everything! I've told you everything,' the Deputy sobbed.

'Better make sure, major,' said Kiboko. 'A little inducement, I think.'

At a nod from Gumbo, one of the supervising prison officers threw a switch and operated a sliding control as if raising the volume on a record-player. The Deputy's mouth opened as if taken by surprise and it was a good half second before the agonised scream that came out of his throat filled the room.

'Everything! Everything! I've told you everything!' he howled through his torment.

'Very well,' the colonel chuckled, puffing on his cigar. 'You understand we have to be sure. A few more names from you and you will have earned your release, Deputy. To celebrate, you are invited to take part in my little farewell party in the main hall. Party games, Deputy, to relieve the boredom. Won't that be nice?'

At a signal from Gumbo, one of his subordinates unlocked the handcuffs and helped the crippled Deputy to his feet. He summoned two warders who propped the victim up and escorted him to the main interrogation centre - a spacious room with a stone-flagged floor and high windows. The walls were of white glazed brick - the kind that are easily hosed down. When all was ready, the colonel strolled in and, fixing his monocle securely into place, examined the twelve ragged wretches who stood, shoulders slumped, in front of the chairs.

'Do sit down and make yourselves comfortable, gentlemen,' he smiled. 'No doubt you must find prison life tedious and so to give you a break this afternoon, we're going to have party games. First of all, we're going to play musical chairs. I'm sure you all know the rules. You walk round the chairs in time to the music after I've removed one chair.

171

Then when it stops, you must run to a chair and sit down quickly. Naturally, there is a forfeit to be paid for the poor unlucky fellow who fails to find a seat. All good fun. Now, Mr Pianist, I'm sure you know the tune 'Here We Go Round The Mulberry Bush' - the familiar nursery rhyme we learned at Infants School. Stand up now and let's begin the fun. Right, Mr Pianist.'

Puffing happily on his cigar, the colonel began to sing in a loud voice,

'Here We Go round the Mulberry Bush, the Mulberry Bush......Come on, all of you. Sing! Sing!'

The stricken prisoners began to stumble around the chairs singing in their cracked voices as Kiboko, now thoroughly enjoying himself, roared with laughter. Suddenly, he tapped the pianist on the shoulder with his stick.

'Stop! Now run! Find a chair! Find a chair! Ah, you sir! Too late! Too late! What is your name?'

The tortured prisoner stood slouched in the middle of the room as his fellow prisoners occupied all eleven seats. 'My name is Adlai Gwelo,' the losing competitor moaned.

'Ah, yes. The young man who insulted our official hostess, Marianne, by singing bawdy songs about her!' Kiboko chuckled. 'A forfeit! A forfeit! Now you must pay the price for your slowness, Mr Singer. Take him out into the courtyard, Major, for his forfeit.'

The major gestured to the pitiable loser of the game.

'Outside,' he said. 'Now you have to pay the forfeit like the Colonel said.'

Young Adlai Gwelo tottered through the door into the open yard. A few moments later, there was the sound of two gun shots.

'Ah, he's paid his fine,' laughed Kiboko, happily clapping his hands. 'I enjoyed that. Reminded me of my childhood. Now, let's have another round.'

172

The gruesome game was repeated with another chair removed. This time it was Frank Johnson who was not quick enough and had to pay the price. The same routine as for the young Adlai Gwelo. Outside for the forfeit and the double crack of a pistol.

'This *is* good fun,' chortled Kiboko, blowing cigar smoke in all directions. 'I don't know when I've enjoyed nursery games so much.'

Tarak Tulshidas approached him.

'I've thought the matter over, Colonel,' he said meekly, 'and I've decided to make a contribution of 450,000 pounds to the president's charity fund.'

'Ah, but the price has gone up since you came into prison. It's now half a million.'

'But that would take all my capital and leave me nothing.'

'Take it or leave it,' said Kiboko, blowing smoke into his face.

'I'll take it,' Tarak whimpered. 'Please arrange for my wife to bring my cheque book when she's allowed to come and see me.'

***

'Altogether, a most satisfactory visit,' the colonel observed as he departed with the major. 'Return the others to their cells. We shall think up more games for my next visit. Let Tulshidas see his wife and I shall return some time later to collect his cheque personally. The fool doesn't seem to realise that, when he signs over his money to us, it's as good as signing his death warrant. But Big Mama will be pleased when she sees the cheque. She'll be even more pleased that I got two more bodies for Schneider's Medical Research Bureau.'

Kiboko and Nyoka took their leave of Captain Gumbo.

'Thank you for a most entertaining afternoon,' Kiboko said. 'Remember what I said about the stench of this place. I shall expect an improvement on my next visit.'

'Yes, Colonel, sir,' Gumbo fawned. 'It'll be done according to your wishes. I shall see to it myself. Thank you for your visit and for a most educational afternoon. I have learned a great deal from your imaginative methods.'

'I must say,' Kiboko said preening himself. 'I am rather proud of my musical chairs variation. However, I still think that the accolade must go to Idi Amin of Uganda for his fertile imagination. I thought his idea of giving prisoners sixteen pound sledgehammers to bash each other to death set the benchmark for us all, especially when he promised the winners their freedom and gave the sledge hammer to the next prisoner and told him to do the same so as to continue the process. Brilliant.'

'I agree wholeheartedly,' Gumbo gushed.

Kiboko turned to the major. 'I shall see you on my next visit, Nyoka. We'll have lunch again at the Inn and perhaps we can arrange another visit to the prison. Be sure to enter the appointment in your diary this time, if it is not beyond your ability and it's not too much to ask.'

Even Nyoka - the master of simulation - found great difficulty in hiding his loathing and contempt for this pathological killer.

****

Chapter Fifteen

Dr Max Schneider (aka Dracula)

At ten-thirty, Washington Fundi accompanied by his two sons climbed the stairs leading to the Lundazi Palace Medical Centre. The usual daily crowd was there and every seat taken. Some individuals were simply standing around, others leaning against walls. There were patients of every age and condition, stoically waiting their turn. Nobody talked, nobody smiled. There seemed to be an inordinate number of mentally-handicapped young people. A baby started to howl and instantaneously all the other infants began to wail in sympathy until the mothers, appearing to respond to some invisible command, put them to the breast. Washington found the reception window and presented his letter signed by Big Mama herself to the appointments clerk.

'I see you are volunteering to give blood,' the clerk said mechanically. 'Your ages, please.'

'I am thirty-eight. Franklin is sixteen and Dwight is fifteen,' replied Washington.

'Before you are accepted, there are some important questions you must answer. I must warn you that false declaration can result in a long prison sentence. Have you or your sons ever suffered from any of the following diseases: Aids, hepatitis, glandular or undulant fever, malaria, syphilis, or any other serious disease?'

'No to all of them,' Washington answered confidently.

'Have you or your sons ever been addicted to drugs such as heroin, cocaine, or marijuana, or any other drug?'

'No, once again to all those things.'

'Very well. Please take a seat and remain there until a nurse calls your name.'

It was over an hour before a nurse appeared and reading from a long list announced their names as if inviting them to a prize presentation. Washington Fundi! Franklin Fundi! Dwight Fundi!'

'Here! We're all here!' Washington called back, awakening from his reverie.

'Follow me!' she commanded, conducting them into an inner consulting room where she took a small sample of blood from each of them by pricking the ear lobe and squeezing a tiny drop on to a slide. Washington and his sons returned to their waiting.

Twenty minutes later, the nurse burst excitedly into Dr Schneider's office.

'Sorry to disturb you, Doctor, but I thought you might be interested in this,' she said breathlessly. 'We have three people in the waiting room with blood type AB Negative. Isn't that the blood type you've been waiting for?'

Dr Schneider looked up from the file he was studying. His nervous tic was twitching more than usual.

'In the waiting room, you say?'

***

Dr Max Schneider had a giant chip on his shoulder. All his life, he had tried to help people and where had it got him? Wormwood Scrubs Prison, that's where. As far back as he could remember, he'd wanted to be a doctor like his German father and grandfather before him. His father had emigrated to England in 1960 and practised medicine in Appledore,

Kent. At the secondary school, Max had been a model pupil and worked hard - his favourite subjects being German (naturally, as he was bilingual) and on the science side, physics, chemistry but especially biology. That last subject had got him into trouble for the first time at the age of fourteen. He'd been caught in a deserted school store room exploring a female classmate's body. In the interests of biological studies, of course. He claimed he'd wanted to check on the accuracy of the text-books, that's all. So what was the problem? But nobody would believe him and it was at that early stage in his career that he came to know that the world was a nasty, suspicious place filled with malicious, perverted people.

For three years he had tried his luck in the United States studying anthropology at Berkeley College in California. He had enjoyed his sojourn there, dating and making out with the glamorous co-eds who were only too willing to participate in his corporeal experiments. Occasionally he devoted some of his energies to studying the subject of his choice whenever he could find the time away from the more licentious sports. He was eventually fired off the course when one of his so-called girl-friends reported him to the authorities for attempted rape. All nonsense of course because hadn't she been the one to force *her* attentions on him? And this accusation was simply her way of getting revenge after he'd jilted her. Or so he told the disciplinary sub-committee when they investigated the affair. His abysmal failure in his chosen subjects hadn't helped matters either and he was asked to remove himself from the course forthwith.

He returned first to England and to his grandparents in Munich where he got down to serious study at the University there, his father's and grandfather's *alma mater*. He worked obsessively at his medical studies to such an extent that he'd had little or no time for anything outside medicine and so, after six years of resolute application to his field, Max became a qualified medical practitioner with the highest grades of his year: 99 per cent for surgery, 99.5 for gynaecology, 90 for orthopaedics, 89 for pathology and preventive medicine and 88 for applied anatomy, so setting records for the university's Faculty of Medicine. The final feather in his cap was being recognised as a fully-professional doctor by the German Medical Association.

Encouraged by his father to extend his academic career by gaining further qualifications, he secured a place at the University College of London where he specialised in a field which had always held a fascination for him - gynaecology. From the beginning of his medical studies, he'd been deeply interested in the care of women during pregnancy and with the diagnosis and treatment of disorders of the female reproductive tract. Whilst pursuing his advanced studies, Max had the opportunity to observe demonstrations by and work with some of the great gynaecologists of the day. The techniques of men like Sir Douglas McDougall inspired him and he became more and more captivated by his chosen specialist field with a passion that one usually associates with religious fervour. As at Munich, Max kept his nose clean and devoted his boundless energies to his chosen field. His British professors were deeply impressed and predicted a glittering future for him. It was around this time that he became so uptight worrying about his academic work that he acquired the convulsive nervous tic which contorted his face whenever his nerves were on edge.

There was only one notable deviation from this single-minded dedication and it was this that set him on the road to perdition. In his final year, he had carried out an abortion on a cocktail waitress as a special favour to an old school pal who had come to him begging for his help to get him and the girl out of a jam. But Max had felt no guilt about this aberration from the straight and narrow, considering it to be merely part of his medical studies and no problem at all.

What he found difficult in gynaecology was overcoming the coyness, even the prudery, amongst female patients about exposing their sexual organs to a male doctor. Most of his patients were extremely shy when it came to initial pelvic examination involving investigation of the external genitalia, the vagina, and the cervix. There was even difficulty in using a simple instrument like the culdoscope to view internal organs. He found the task was invariably made easier if he first administered a mild anaesthetic.

Eventually, he came to the end of the long and arduous road to consultancy and, with his father's financial help, set up his practice in Harley Street where, as a young, handsome doctor, he quickly gained a reputation amongst the rich social set for his gentle, sympathetic bedside manner. It wasn't long before he had to hire a secretary and a receptionist. He was kept so busy that there was little time for any social life which might go some way to explain why he was still a bachelor.

One of his first patients was a famous star in a West-end hit musical. After a quick examination - no shyness there! - and a few simple tests, he gave her the "good" news.

'You're pregnant,' he told her, 'About nine or ten weeks, I'd say.'

'But I can't sing and dance with a bun in the oven,' she'd protested. 'You'll have to take it away or the show'll be ruined. It'll close the theatre and maybe put a hundred people out of a job.'

That was the beginning of the slide down the slippery slope. It wasn't long before it became known among the female Thespian set that he was available. Pretty soon, he found himself doing around twenty abortions a week and his reputation spread far and wide, not only in Britain but also in Europe. Cases came to him from all over the continent and not merely from the "luvvies" but young *au-pairs* and married women alike, all in trouble, and seeking his medical skills. Nice, easy work with the money rolling in and everybody happy; like doing the spring-cleaning, clearing out the basement of the unwanted things that had accumulated there.

From there it had been but a small step into the sex therapy business and, before long, he'd found himself having to deal with all kinds of problems of psychosexual dysfunctions - from impotence to frigidity. The difficulty in most of his cases appeared to be psychological in origin and connected with their extreme primness and their puritanical upbringing. He saw as his first task that of releasing their inhibitions and freeing them from their deep-seated repressions. Why, some of his female patients had never experienced an orgasm! For his work of liberation, he needed free-thinking staff around him - people who were not strait-laced and easily shocked. And that's what led to his ultimate downfall and to his stay as a guest of Her Majesty's Prison Service. He'd been merely doing his job and the world had misunderstood him and his motives which were strictly altruistic. Now, as he sat at his desk in the Lundazi Medical Centre, with a grim smile, he played out the court scene yet once again in his mind, enjoying in a masochistic way, re-living the experience.

In Number 2 court at the Old Bailey, the prosecuting attorney, Mr Robert Broach, QC, was addressing the jury.

'The gynaecologist, Dr Max Schneider, has an extraordinary hyper-sex drive needing repeated sexual release. He has a need for high risk sexual activity, the higher the risk the more excitement and the greater the sexual turn-on. The defence has claimed that his extraordinary behaviour is due to excessive secretion of testosterone - the hormone governing the virility of the male. It won't wash. It's a flimsy excuse indeed to explain rape in terms of hormone production. Otherwise, eighty per cent of the male population would be in the dock. No, Max Schneider seriously abused his position as a doctor in assaulting the ten women you now see in court. Some of the women attended his surgery as patients; others were invited to visit either for social reasons or in connection with employment. His purpose in inviting them was for his own sexual gratification. He used two methods. He either used a strong tranquilliser or hypnotic drug to remove his guests' inhibitions about

agreeing to sexual intercourse. Or he persuaded his guests, on quite improper grounds, that they needed to be examined and in the course of that examination, assaulted the female concerned.'

Now Dr Schneider sat at his desk in Lundazi seeing and experiencing these traumatic events in his mind's eye. What a rotten, unjust world it was that could condemn an innocent doctor like himself who was simply carrying out his duties to the best of his abilities. The evidence that the prosecution put forward was nothing but a tissue of lies from beginning to end. One lady had been unable to resist his attractions and had agreed to have sexual relations with him in the shower after he had assured her that the douching was no more than symbolic and his aim was merely to cleanse her of her hang-ups. Was it his fault when she came on to him? The second one had dabbled in prostitution, and the third, a German student of biology - the one to whom he had introduced the vibrator - was a naturist with a reputation for easy sex. As for the seventeen-year old who had come to him about the word-processing job, she'd enjoyed stripping naked and participating in oral sex. The other six women had only come forward after the wide publicity the case had received. Their evidence had been rigged by the Metropolitan police who were keen to add yet another conviction to their files.

As for that rot about spiked drinks which the alleged victims said tasted "funny"! He'd taken a bottle of the actual wine he'd given them -1986 Gerwuztraminer - into court for the jury to taste. And they had admitted while it did taste unusual, it did not induce lewd thoughts. That had caused no little laughter in court. But despite that amusing episode during the trial, he was convicted, struck off, and sentenced to five years' hard labour. The world had come to something when an upstanding professional man like himself could be sent down on the flimsy evidence of a bunch of confused females.

Doing time as a "Rule 43" prisoner had been the toughest period of his life and there had been several situations where his life had been in danger from ignorant, perverted prisoners. They'd called him 'The Rapist' which was their idea of a joke playing on the word 'the-rapist'. With time off for good behaviour, however, he had mercifully been released after thirty months inside. His self-confidence had been shattered and he had lost faith in British justice. It was blind indeed. It had failed to see that the task of a psychosexual therapist involved the emancipation of patients from their qualms and anxieties!

***

After his release, he had looked around for a job but there had been little hope. He'd been struck off not only by the British General Medical Council but the German also – his father's home country! He was ruined and the capital he'd managed to accumulate during the prosperous Harley Street years had evaporated in legal costs.

Then out of the blue had come the offer of an appointment as palace physician in Zambelia. He had not even applied for the job, had never heard of Zambelia, didn't even know where it was! Couldn't even find it on the map! The offer had come through his letterbox one day along with the bills and the usual junk mail. His few remaining loyal friends had supplied him with glowing references and, before he knew where he was, he was en route to Lundazi. The one thing that he had never been able to understand, though, was why the Zambelia Special Branch had not managed to unearth his prison record. They were reputed to be thorough and hyper-efficient. After he had worked in Lundazi for a few months, he found out why. Big Mama called him into her office one day and introduced herself.

'I am Marie Antoinette Makubwa though Zambelians prefer to refer to me as Big Mama. Since you are European, I have no objection to you calling me "ma'am". Now through our Special Branch investigations, we have been aware, Dr Schneider, from the beginning, of your unfortunate experiences in Harley Street and that you have been struck off by the GMC. We have ignored these things and decided to employ you because we know that, besides being an outstanding doctor, you are also short of capital. We think we may have the answer to your problems. We have here in the Lundazi Medical Centre a blood transfusion service which collects, stores and sells blood plasma abroad. We have found these transactions to be profitable.'

'Blood *from* Africa! It's usually the other way round!' Schneider protested. 'For a start, the British Blood Transfusion Service would never allow it because it goes against all their strictest rules and regulations.'

'Don't begin by making problems, Dr Schneider,' she replied. 'First, who said anything about sending blood to Britain. Secondly, once the blood has been mixed with other plasma, who is to know its source?'

'And you want me to operate a blood donor centre, is that it?' he said. 'Well, that shouldn't present too many problems. Provided, of course, we can guarantee the blood is not contaminated, especially with the Aids virus.'

'Whether the blood is contaminated or not is no concern of ours. It's up to the receiving organisations to investigate that end of the business. The only thing we know is that there is a world-wide shortage of plasma and there is great demand for donors.'

'That's certainly true. I read somewhere that in Germany, where donation is still voluntary, the selling of blood has become big business. The Baden-Baden authorities used to organise so-called "Dracula Parties" in discos, with coffins, spiders' webs and fancy dress to encourage students to give blood. Last year, Germany exported 133 tons of blood which earned it £4.5 million in foreign currency.'

'Quite right, Dr Schneider - blood has become big business. Why should we let the Germans and others have all the profits? The volume of blood traded internationally last year was 6.3 million litres. I don't see why we shouldn't get a piece of the action. But the big profits are not in the sale of plasma, however.'

'Where?' asked Schneider, his interest now fully aroused.

'In organs for transplants, she said. 'Our Medical Research Bureau has many wealthy clients in the Middle East and the Far East on its waiting list. Most of the merchandise is sent to Moscow, however, where the organisation distributes world-wide.'

'Organ donation is quite ethical,' he replied. 'In the UK, the medical authorities are trying to encourage the carrying of donor cards. There's even been talk of enforced donation when a person dies through "presumed consent" programmes, so-called opt-out systems. Admittedly, the campaign has not been a success except in a few countries, like Spain and Austria.'

'It's this lack of success in encouraging voluntary donations that has led to the world-wide shortage,' Big Mama said. 'That's where we come in. It's a matter of supply and demand.'

'Surely, you're not suggesting we sell organs for transplants?'

'And why not? Blood in one sense is an organ. Why, there has even been commerce in the buying and selling of semen! Look, Doctor Schneider. May I call you Max? Out there in the big bad world, there are thousands of people waiting for kidneys and corneas because, as you know, these organs are transplanted so successfully. I feel so sorry for those poor, desperate people who are hoping for auto accidents and the like to yield a fresh supply.'

'I've had experience of this, ma'am, in my London clinic. The sad thing is that when these accidents occur, we are reluctant to approach the relatives of the victims. We think it's too sensitive an issue and the result is that sound, healthy organs are consigned to the flames of the crematorium or given to the worms.'

'That is why, Max, in our compassion, we must do something to help these wretched souls crying out for help. That is why we have set up our Medical Research Bureau to supply the world with desperately needed organs. Naturally we must charge them for the service.'

'The sale of human organs? Why that would be a breach of medical ethics. One could be struck off for such ......'

He paused. He remembered. Big Mama was looking at him steadily with a knowing smile.

'Precisely,' she said. 'That's why you are the ideal man for the job.'

***

'Bring in the three AB Negatives.,' Dr Schneider said, rubbing his hands together. 'I take it they're all healthy specimens?'

The nurse went out to fetch Washington and his sons.

'Washington Fundi and his two sons,' she called loftily above the hubbub of the waiting-room. 'This way. The doctor will see you now.'

Nervously the three followed her into the surgery and stood humbly in front of the doctor's desk awaiting his first move.

Dr Schneider ignored them and, tapping his pencil on his writing pad, continued studying the documents before him. Finally, looking up over his thick-rimmed spectacles, his facial tic working overtime, he examined the trio intently as if they were medical specimens in one of his jars.

'Good news for you,' he announced at last. 'The three of you are rare blood types and you will be paid an extra premium. Fifty matunda each. So a total of 150 matunda simply for giving a little blood. Not bad for a morning's work, eh?'

'But that's wonderful news, sir,' exclaimed Washington, thinking to himself that with the fifty Big Mama had given him, he'd raised the school fees for the year. 'What do we have to do?'

'It's a simple matter of lying on a bed for half-an-hour and relaxing. No pain. Nothing to it. The easiest money you've ever earned.'

'My prayers to Mungu have been answered,' Washington said. 'Please show us what we do next, sir.'

'There is a way in which you can earn an even higher fee,' Schneider murmured. 'Your blood group is so rare that we could take bone marrow from you and your sons. It's a simple operation and you could be back home by tomorrow afternoon. For this service, we could pay you one hundred matunda each in addition to the fifty for the blood.'

Washington could scarcely believe his ears. Three hundred matunda plus two hundred already promised. That came to five hundred. This was better than having a post office family allowance book in England. His dreams had come true. Not only could he pay the school fees in full, he would have a nest-egg of three hundred to put by. After so much bad luck, Mungu had smiled on him at last. So there was light at the end of the tunnel after all.

'This operation, sir. Is it dangerous?'

'Not in the least. A routine operation and as simple as giving blood. It's only because of the rarity of your blood type that I am able to make you this offer. This is your lucky day, Washington.'

'An extra three hundred and we'll be home by tomorrow you say, sir. Then we'll do it.'

'I'll make arrangements for this afternoon,' said Dr Schneider. 'The two boys first and then you, Washington, last. I'm sure you've made the right decision.'

***

186

Later that afternoon, Washington lay back in the bed in the small ward. He had been ordered to put on a hospital gown - the kind that tied behind the neck and only just covered his lower regions. The back was open. He hated and dreaded the hospital at that moment. He felt nervous about being there. He knew little about medical matters and he associated hospitals with disease, illness, and death. It was hard to explain his irrational fear as his two sons had already undergone their operations and were now sleeping peacefully like babes in their cots. He'd watched the nurse giving them their injections and the orderly wheeling them out on the trolleys. They had looked so vulnerable, so helpless. Within twenty minutes, they were back from the operating theatre. 'Theatre' - that was another strange thing about these white men - the way they used words to stand for the opposite.

He had always understood the English word "theatre" to mean a place of entertainment. It was hardly that this afternoon. Since the doctor had announced that he would do it 'this afternoon', he had spent the time in a continuous cold sweat, wishing his turn would come quickly and yet dreading it at the same time. The time had dragged slowly yet relentlessly towards the hour when the orderly would come for him. The doctor had said it was only a routine operation. So why was he, Washington - the Zambelian warrior - so worried about it? It was a good job he wasn't going into the theatre for something serious. But suppose something went wrong! Suppose the drug they gave him was not strong enough and he felt the pain! He told himself to stop being such a coward. His sons had braved the ordeal and were now back safe and sound. He himself was still young and healthy and there was absolutely no danger. He trusted that nice, yellow-haired doctor with the jerky face. And when all was said and done, giving blood and marrow meant his boys could complete their education and things would be easier after this afternoon. Downhill all the way. His anxiety was for nothing and he chided himself for being so chicken-hearted.

His thoughts were disturbed by the door of the ward opening and the sudden entry of the orderly with his tray of instruments.

'Time for your first shot, Washington Roll over on to your front,' said the kindly orderly.

He did as he was bid and the orderly bared Washington's backside and grabbed a handful of buttock. The needle darted in and out before he knew what had happened.

Ten minutes later, when the orderly wheeled him along the corridor, he was happily intoxicated as if he had drunk extra-strong *pombe* in the beer hall. By the time they had reached the theatre, he was chuckling blissfully to himself. He had lost track of time and he was no longer concerned whether he lived or died. His brain ceased to make sense of anything. He looked up at the great arc-shaped lights and could barely make out the distorted face of Doctor Schneider smiling down at him.

'Good afternoon, Washington,' he said. 'It'll soon be over. I'm going to give you your last shot and then you can take a little nap.'

Dr Schneider injected Washington intravenously.

'Start counting to thirty, Washington.'

'One - two - three....' began Washington in a slurred voice. He did not get past the number seven. That was the last word he spoke. Washington finally fell asleep.

'He's under,' Schneider said.

He checked the eyelid reflex and observed that Washington had already achieved a deep level of unconsciousness.   A further injection of Pentothal and Washington's anaesthesia deepened to a state of oblivion. There were one or two muscle twitches and complete relaxation followed. His breathing was barely discernible. Schneider checked blood pressure, pulse, temperature - all normal. Next, he tested response to light by lifting his eyelid.

The pupils were enormous. He shone his penlight into Washington's eye. No response. The pupil stayed big.

'Excellent. He's in a coma,' he said to the nurse assisting him. 'Now, tell the orderly to wheel him into the Intensive Care Unit. We'll keep him deeply sedated until it's time to put him in the Research Bureau along with the other coma patients awaiting the next stage. We can leave Big Mama to organise the details of when and where to send the organs.'

****

Chapter Sixteen

Big Mama and President Samson Matata.

Big Mama was busy with President Matata. She was feeling tired as she had spent the previous hour rehearsing the Ngoma dancing women on the spacious terrace. It had been a particularly trying session as the stupid ladies did not seem to understand that the main purpose of the exercise was to protect the president from would-be assassins, not to provide entertainment. The music and the choreography came a good second. Several times in the make-believe rehearsal, the substitute president had been exposed to a potential bullet or spear, and several times she had blown her top. All very exhausting.

That was behind her and now, she got down to the serious business of giving the president his daily aromatherapy session. It was the highlight of his day and he waited impatiently each afternoon for her to appear. For Big Mama, it was the most important activity in her schedule for it gave her the opportunity to brief the president on the latest developments and to secure his signature on Orders-in-Council and other significant documents.

When Big Mama entered the palace health studio, the president had anticipated her arrival and was already robed in boxer shorts and silk dressing gown. As soon as she walked through the door, he removed the gown and lay front-down on the massage couch.

'Good afternoon, Mr President,' she said affectionately. 'I see you are ready and waiting.'

'Good afternoon to you, Marianne. As you know I always look forward to our meeting. Sometimes, I think this daily massage session is the one thing that is keeping me alive. I know that when you have finished, I feel like a new man.'

'I'm glad to hear that, Samson. You and I have been together for a long time. I'm only too happy to do anything I can to keep you in the best of health.'

She looked down at the leathery face of this pitiful old man stretched out on the couch before her - the man she still loved and respected. He'd been so different at the start. She remembered what a fearless, idealistic young man he had been when she'd first met him and, as she began mixing the oils, her mind travelled backward over the great man's career.

Samson Matata was born in the southern region of Zambelia, the youngest son of Solomon Matata, a poor peasant with a small holding on which his large Catholic family barely subsisted. As a young child, Samson was a quiet, serious and withdrawn little boy, happiest in his own company with his head in a book. At school, he proved to be very intelligent and at the age of ten, supported by his village, he was sent to a Jesuit mission boarding school where he showed a distinct aptitude in spoken English. While there, Samson suffered a personal trauma when his father abandoned the family and ran off with another woman leaving his mother with six children to care for. As far as Samson was concerned, his father no longer existed and he never made further reference to him throughout his long career. At sixteen, having achieved high marks in all eight subjects at the Cambridge Overseas School Certificate, he secured a place as pupil teacher at a missionary school. His principal, Father O'Shea, later commented on how impressed he had been by Samson's intellectual ability.

When the first African political protest movement in Zambelia began against a white-settler dominated government, Samson joined the movement and it wasn't long before his exceptional talents took him to the top and he became leader of the new Umoja (Unity) Party which aimed at winning – by armed insurrection, if necessary - independence from Britain. Seeing him among others as a dangerous threat, the colonial government thought the wisest thing to do was to remove him from the scene by arranging a scholarship for him to study at a British university hoping that this might also tone down his extremist views. It was a big mistake because at the Department of Government at the University of Manchester, he organised a Pan-African Congress which demanded immediate *uhuru* from colonial rule. Later, he told party members, 'When I returned to Zambelia after studying for a degree in economic and social studies, I was completely hostile to the white-dominated system. The only language the British Imperialists seem to understand was the language of extreme conflict.'

After many long and bitter struggles, he eventually found himself at the head of the movement. In Zambelia his name became venerated and people referred to him as the promised Messiah who would deliver the people from bondage. It was at this time that for public occasions he adopted the mottled cloak of the cheetah.

Just as a term in a colonial prison was a recommended qualification for an aspiring African dictator, so a story or a myth surrounding his early boyhood gave him a distinct advantage. Samson Matata was no exception. He claimed that one day as a youngster, he was walking through grasslands with his grandfather when they espied impala grazing. Suddenly a King Cheetah cat emerged from the grass and gave chase to the impala which leapt, bounced and swerved in a desperate attempt to escape the predator. 'Observe the poor, helpless impala,' the grandfather said. 'Run beside the cheetah and save that innocent, defenceless animal by throwing your arms around the big cat and bringing it down.' 'But the cheetah is the fastest animal in the forest. I cannot catch it, grandfather.' 'Yes, you can,' said the old man. 'Never say "cannot" because you are blessed by the Gods and nothing is beyond you.' Samson did as he was told and, running at full pelt, caught up with the cheetah and, throwing his arms around it, wrestled it to the ground. 'You are right, grandfather,' he said. 'There's nothing in this world that I cannot do.' After that incident, he adopted the cheetah as his insignia and a symbol of his divine powers. He used the King Cheetah skin as his cloak and made the cheetah hat his personal image, always having a reserve stock of half a dozen designed by a London furrier. 'The King Cheetah or the Duma in our language,' he told visiting dignitaries, 'besides being the most beautiful animal in the world is also the fastest and can equal the speed of a racing car.' He told them how he liked to be known as *King Duma*.

***

Came the day when he was due to address a crowd of Zambelians assembled in the main square of Lundazi to hear his speech which was also broadcast on national radio. Early in the morning, a heaving, braying throng marched through the town out to the airport, its ranks swelling to over twenty thousand. A forest of placards, banners, and streamers declared their devotion and loyalty to their leader: 'Samson Our Saviour!' 'Samson Free Us From The Oppressors!' and 'Welcome Our Great Liberator!'

Ragged-trousered urchins jostling with men in tattered shirts mingled with the joyful, ululating women in their colourful David-Whitehead dresses. Smartly-dressed businessmen, dark-suited civil servants and shopkeepers still in aprons, rubbed shoulders together. Mothers with babies bouncing on their backs, danced ecstatic jigs of welcome.

At midday, the figure of Samson Matata, his King Duma cloak flung over his beautifully tailored safari suit, appeared on the rostrum in the main square. As he made his way to the podium, he was surrounded by ululating, prancing women who danced to the accompaniment of whistles and drums. The crowd began its rhythmic chant of 'Samson! Samson! Samson!'

Most political leaders in the public eye have developed a symbol giving them a distinctive look by which they are instantly recognized. Roosevelt had his ceramic cigarette holder; Chamberlain, his umbrella; Churchill, his Cuban cigar; Hitler, his toothbrush moustache - all of which were a gift to cartoonists everywhere. For many African leaders, it was the fly whisk based on the horse's tail which that animal employed to flick off troublesome insects. Fly whisks came in a wide variety: some adorned with elaborate handles of expensive materials, such as ivory or ebony; others plainer and more utilitarian in their decoration but few of them were used for their stated purpose, that of swatting irritating flies. Instead they were brandished as symbols of power. A sweeping movement could mean: "Off with his head!" or again, it could indicate: "Bang him up in jail and throw away the key!" A poke in the ribs with the base of the handle could signify the displeasure of the president and it was usually all up with the victim. The instrument and the way it was wiggled and waggled were enough to reduce the recipient to a quivering jelly.

When at last Matata spoke out, he gesticulated furiously with his ornate ebony fly-whisk as he harangued the mob as if it were a pantomime performance with playful bantering: "Oh no, you're not! Oh, yes you are!" - a routine which they adored him for.

'Whose Zambelia is it?'

Roar: 'OURS!'

'Oh, no, it's not!'

Roar: 'OH, YES, IT IS!'

'What do you fight for?'

Roar: 'UHURU!'

'Will you ever stop fighting for freedom?'

Roar. 'NEVER!' from the twenty thousand hysterical throats.

'*Uhuru*! I say again. That is what I have come to offer you! Let them put me in prison or even kill me! I am King Cheetah and I fear nothing. I will fight for your freedom even from my coffin. My ghost will come back to haunt the oppressors. We are done with tea-parties and polite speeches! We must resist with all our might and main in the struggle to win our freedom and shake off the imperial chains. You must be ready for self-sacrifice. If European industries in our country make guns to be used against us, we must destroy them by ruinous strikes and walk-outs.'

As his convoy of Land Rovers departed, men waved their hats, youths tussled with each other to touch his car, young women flung themselves on the vehicle covering it with kisses.

When these speeches were reported in the *Zambelia Herald*, there was panic amongst the non-African sections of the community with rumours of threatened bloodbaths, the slaughter of the white and Asian populations as had happened in the Congo.

Samson, along with a number of other leaders was accused of fomenting violence and unrest; he was sentenced to two years in Tagooma. On arriving at the detention centre, Samson warned his imprisoned colleagues not to expect early release as it was only the beginning of a long nationalist struggle. He also urged them not to squander their time in prison but to use it productively by studying as he did. While behind bars, he gained two external degrees in economics and law from London University. Apart from the degrees, he now had the further status of being an "Ex-Colonial Convict" – an indispensable qualification for an aspiring African leader.

He was right too about not expecting early release for nationalist prisoners because for the next eleven years, he found himself in and out of prison, mostly in. The more the white supremacist government tried to consolidate its entrenched position, the more fiery and provocative his speeches became.

'We shall work with those whites who want to work with us. But the rest must get out and find a new home.' Reverting to Massuyu language, he added 'We will kill those snakes among us, and crush them completely.'

This last speech was enough to earn him yet another term of two years in clink. There was strong reaction among the people to this last imprisonment of their "redeemer".

Riots and rebellion throughout the country flared up and the government declared a State of Emergency. A mob of one thousand marched on Tagooma demanding their leader's release. The Police Commissioner read the Riot Act and the police made a baton charge. Tear gas grenades were fired and the crowd began to retreat, throwing bricks, rocks, and a variety of other missiles including Molotov cocktails. The police opened fire and twenty protestors were shot dead. Mayhem followed and in London, a panic-stricken government hurriedly arranged a constitutional conference at Lancaster House and Samson was released, this time for good. Independence followed.

Next, elections were organised and Samson Matata became Zambelia's first Prime Minister and, later, President. Though a young lady at the time, Marie Antoinette could recall word for word his first speech to the people and the Zambelian Chamber of Deputies.

'You have chosen me to be your leader and I am moved to the depths of my heart for the confidence you have shown in me. I will devote my whole life for the good of this country of my birth and I will suffer death if that is what is required of me. I am an angel and messenger sent from Mungu. Every morning He speaks to me in dreams and orders me to pass His message to you, my beloved people of Zambelia.'

'What I am going to say today may not be popular but it is Mungu's message not mine. He continued looking pointedly

at his fellow politicians on the platform, but I don't give a damn for popularity. I am not here to be liked. I am here to rule and to rule firmly and wisely.'

A few Deputies sitting behind him shuffled uncomfortably in their seats, pursed their lips and shook their heads in doubt. The new president glowered at them.

'People must stop fighting and hating each other with one tribe trying to kill the other. People must stop feeling that only their own tribe matters. They go to the polls to vote and who do they vote for? The best candidate? No! Instead, they vote for their own tribe even if he's the village idiot. It happens all over Africa and our people are starving because they spend so much time trying to kill each other in inter-tribal warfare. This will now stop! Racism, tribalism, regionalism whether practised by whites or blacks, are evils. Zambelia cannot be a country of only blacks. It is and will remain our country, all of us together: black, brown, white.'

'Don't talk to me about democracy. It's a foreign idea and our people are not educated enough for it – they don't understand it. When everyone has a say, it's the Tower of Babel. We can't have everyone talking at once and deciding policy. Our people need to be guided by one strong leader and I am that leader! So, as from today, no more elections! They're done with, finished! From this day forward, it's going to be: One Party, One Leader, One Government, and no more nonsense. I shall draw up a list of names and the people can choose their Deputies from that. If any of my ministers don't like it, let them resign now. This is no game. It is about survival and, when our country is dying from famine, ignorance and disease, swift and decisive action is needed. Like a cheetah, I shall leap on these evils and destroy them.

From now on, I, Samson Matata, will make the decisions round here. Today the Chamber of Deputies has voted me

President for Life, so I shall rule you and guide you until the day I die.'

Some of the Deputies behind Matata engaged in urgent whispered conversations but they soon ceased when the president awarded them one of his famous scowls and a flick of the fly whisk. They knew what that could mean.

Many of our people think it is clever to copy the ways of the Western world where they now have The Permissive Society. Women going about half-naked in public and doing immoral things on the stage, and calling it art and civilisation! If that is civilisation, let them keep it in the West! Here in Zambelia, we must recover our true African identity and stop copying our colonial oppressors. From now on, I strongly recommend men to dress like African men; no more collars and ties and European suits which are unsuitable anyway for our tropical climate; they will wear safari suits or loose fitting 'T' shirts and adopt correct male hair styles. Women will dress as African women should and not as prostitutes or in men's clothing. No more wigs or short skirts; they will wear the traditional wrap. I call my new policy "Authenticity". From now on, we will go back to simple tribal values and reject the sinful ways of the corrupt western world.'

***

When Matata said "I strongly recommend", it had the force of irrefutable law. At first, the people thought he was merely against drunkenness and drug-taking but the ban extended to personal behaviour and dress including mini-skirts and women's trouser suits.

'Remember this, my beloved people' he said, rounding off his speech, *'anything I do, I do for Zambelia. If anyone tries to get in my way, I shall cut them down like poisonous weeds!'*

There was a howl of protest from some fellow Africans including his own cabinet ministers who spoke out fiercely against his autocratic rule. They plotted against him not only for his removal but his assassination. Samson came down on them like several tons of bricks and ordered their arrest and execution. Eight government Deputies were arrested; five were executed by firing squad in Tagooma prison; three were accorded the honour of public hanging in the Lundazi Sports stadium. After that there were no more protests and Samson ruled with a rod of iron.

After the failed *coup d'état*, he gave greater attention to his own security by creating an elite special Praetorian guard, the Special Presidential Division, with the duty of protecting him from enemies and potential conspirators. He formed also a Matata Youth Brigade based on Germany's Hitler Youth with the job of rooting out would-be traitors by infiltrating other youth and student organizations at colleges and university. Samson became increasingly contemptuous of advisers and experts whose advice did not coincide with his own. They were dismissed as 'talking through their backsides'. Law courts inherited from the colonial power were replaced by traditional tribal courts and even there, any decisions he didn't like were simply over-ruled.

'We must identify those who threaten us and liquidate them immediately. Forget that stuff about legal formalities from the liberal sheep bleating about habeus corpus rubbish which allows the guilty to get off scot free. Not here in Zambelia!

Samson's tyranny dated from that period. For Marie Antoinette in those far-off days President Matata was a god on a pedestal to be worshipped and venerated.

***

'The Chuzuni tribe,' he told her one afternoon during an aromatherapy session, 'are a sly, cunning set of bastards and must be eradicated.'

She began kneading his back and applying lavender oil. 'What makes you say that, Samson?'

'Because all our troubles arise from them, Marianne. We must cleanse Zambelia and exterminate them like vermin.'

Being such a controversial and unusual figure, Samson soon found himself on the covers of weekly news magazines, even topping the two George Bushes and Robert Mugabe. The churches loved him for his austerity and piety; foreign union leaders poured in the money; the world of entertainment lionised him for his celebrity status and the lecture agents begged him to accept speaking engagements. Samson, polished, handsome and always impeccably dressed with a wardrobe of safari suits, a wide range of silk cravats, and a selection of cheetah-skin hats and cloaks became the darling of the celebrity lecture circuit.

***

Today however, Big Mama reflected, he was a mere shadow of the young, dynamic Matata and given to rambling without making much sense though occasionally there were rare shafts of intelligence. He had entered on that life phase that was sometimes referred to as "the long goodbye". On these occasions, if sufficiently rehearsed, he could still manage a coherent speech and even order a miscreant's execution. His physical condition however had deteriorated severely over the previous five years. His left arm was subject to sudden spasms and he felt dizzy and sick for hours at a time. His eyesight had become so bad that the documents presented to him had to be in extra large print. Max Schneider filled him full of all sorts of quack medicines but the immediate people around him had the impression he was a burnt-out shell. Despite this, he was still adulated by his loyal entourage who hoped he would grant them favours and help them to prosper.

Marie Antoinette still loved and admired him. In the early days of their association, she had been the President's lover but that was in the past. Her job today was to look after his interests and act as the official consort and hostess on public occasions.

'I have been lucky to have found you, Marianne,' he said suddenly. 'Today I am old but still a warrior and I still love all women, especially you, Marianne. And the women of Zambelia love me, their warrior. *They* love me and *I* love them. Wherever I go in Zambelia the women sing and dance for me!'

***

Deep in thought, Marie Antoinette continued mixing up the essential oils. First a tablespoon of grape-seed to which she added drops of fragrant flower oils - lavender, rose, and geranium plus the spices, coriander, ginger and nutmeg. Next she began to massage the mixture into his body beginning with his back, working towards his legs and feet.

'This is so relaxing, Marianne. Did you know that massage was used more than three thousand years ago by the Chinese? Later the Greek physician, Hippocrates, used friction in the treatment of sprains and dislocations and kneading to treat constipation. So it's not entirely new.'

'That's most interesting, Mr President. As old as that?'

'What is, Marianne?'

'What you said about massage.'

'But what did I say?'

'You were talking about the Chinese and Hippocrates,' she said, now working on his arms and shoulders.

'Was I?' he said. 'Did you know that the bath was a recognised feature of Roman life? By the fourth century, there were over a thousand in Rome alone. The Stabian Baths at Pompeii are the best examples we have today.'

'I see, Mr President.   And massage parlours too, I presume.'

'Not only that - the hot baths were called thermae and they attracted the great thinkers of the day, poets, orators, philosophers. People gathered to hear them speak. It is said Julius Caesar always had his personal masseur with him when he went into battle.'

'Please turn over on to your back now, Samson,' she said, 'and I'll massage your chest and abdomen. I agree with everything you say.   Which reminds me.   I've ordered the arrest of Dr Frank Johnson who was publishing vicious lies about us in the British press and preaching anarchy to his students. No doubt Colonel Kiboko will have dealt with him by now. We may also have another dissident at the university, I'm told, in the person of his replacement, a Dr Susan Delamere, who has been reported to me as a possible future troublemaker and we may have to arrest her too if she continues to stir up the students. Then there are the two Deputies Chifunza and Chilulu who have spoken out in the Chamber of Deputies so strongly against our plans to build the new palace at the Lake. I have had them both thrown into prison.'

'Good.   I approve. Johnson is an anarchist and deserves everything he gets. Any other academics like this Delamere woman with the seditious ideas should receive the same treatment and be thrown into Gereza prison and left to rot. As for those two Deputies opposing my will, I won't have it. They are both active members of the Justice and Peace Commission of the Catholic Church. Notice how our rebels seem to stem from these same two sources. Academics at the university and Catholic members of the Chuzuni tribe. Always the Chuzuni tribe! Occasionally I'm tempted to order the execution of all Zambelian citizens whose names begin with 'CH'. Sometimes I think the country's coming apart at the seams and being run by a set of gangsters. I cannot have people opposing my will.   As for the two

Deputies, so be it. If we allow tribalism and Catholicism to rear their ugly heads once again, there's no telling where it will end. It was the same in ancient Rome when Caesar allowed factions to flourish. He should have nipped them in the bud.'

'In anticipation of your decisions, Mr President, I have brought their execution warrants for you to sign.'

'Whose execution?'

'The two Deputies Chifunza and Chilulu and also Frank Johnson, the university lecturer guilty of inciting students to revolt. The ones we've spoken about.'

'Oh, them! Did you tell me what it was for? Surely not for opposing my decrees? Let Chifunza live a little longer until he gives us the names of the other rebellious deputies; we must root them all out - no exceptions.'

'As I said a moment ago, Mr President. They have rebelled against your orders but if you think we should let Chifunza live a little longer, it shall be so,' she replied, massaging his scalp. 'Have you ever thought of having the mole behind your ear removed, Mr President? It would be a small operation.'

'I am too old to worry about a small mole behind my ear, Marianne. I suppose we must execute that lecturer fellow. We cannot tolerate conspirators who incite the students. I will sign the warrant for Johnson today.'

'I have a number of other arrest orders requiring your signature, Mr President, including one for the Asian trader, Tarak Tulshidas, who has been defrauding the customs on a grand scale. He must repay what he has stolen.'

'I knew his father, a good man and a clever trader.' Samson said pensively. 'Zambelia needs good businessmen for economic development. They generate wealth and provide employment. I am puzzled that his son has committed crimes against the state.'

'Shall I tell you the full story, Mr President?' she said, kneading his neck muscles.

'Spare me the details, Marianne. I trust your judgement. Show me where to sign.'

She had now completed the aromatherapy treatment and she assisted the President to his feet and helped him on with his robe. There was a healthy glow in his cheeks and a more relaxed look about him.

'I feel as light as a feather - as if I'm walking on a cloud,' he said gaily. 'I feel ten years younger. Now, Marianne, where are those documents you want me to sign?'

Sadly, she studied the stooped, forlorn figure of the once-great leader giving presidential assent to her Orders-in-Council. As she left the health studio, she looked back and smiled wistfully at the sight of him relaxing on his couch, with the glass of white wine containing the tiny pinch of medicine she always insisted on 'to clear the system'. When it came to her own personal view of life, she loved her sisters, she loved the president, she loved Zambelia. In that order. He was still mumbling to himself about the glories of ancient Rome as she closed the door behind her.

****

Chapter Seventeen

Schneider is oversexed.

It has been claimed - though the precise authority is never quoted - that men have a brief sexual thought every six seconds. This means, of course, that there must be at least five seconds when they're not having a sexual thought. For Doctor Max Schneider - not so. He thought about sex all the time. And did it! Constantly. He could not resist a shapely woman. How did that lawyer at the Old Bailey describe it? 'An over-active sex drive'. That was putting it mildly. Why, even when carrying out routine examinations or minor operations, it was sex, if only at the back of his mind. And when it came to his gynaecological and contraceptive work amongst the young married ladies in middle-class Zambelian society, the subject leapt into the foreground. For him, the ladies were like toys to be played with.

As in Harley Street, he had taken it upon himself to liberate these lovely creatures from the bondage of ministering to male pleasure without the slightest thought for their own enjoyment. Altruistically, he had introduced them to their own erogenous zones by demonstrating how enjoyable sex could be either with the use of external appliances such as vibrators - specially imported under medical supplies - or, if the patient was attractive enough, by unselfishly using his own body for the purpose. It had begun to look as if the emancipation of women in this way was his mission in life but to be truly fulfilling, two conditions were necessary. First, his patients had to be not only pretty but inexperienced and naive about love techniques since his professional fulfilment lay in giving them their first sexual thrill and seeing their eyes light up when they realised the possibility of ecstasy in sexual experience. Secondly, it was essential that he remain in control of the procedure and the experiments at all times. Occasionally, a patient released from her deep-seated inhibitions, had been carried away and had tried to take charge of the situation. He could never allow that of course since it was unethical for a patient to give orders to her doctor.

**

Now, in Big Mama's boudoir, Max Schneider kicked off his shoes, dropped his trousers before he took off his white coat, shirt and tie. He removed his boxer shorts and vest and folded the lot into a neat pile which he placed on the *Louis Quatorze* cabinet. He opened the large drawer in the cabinet and considered the various sarongs stacked there. He chose one which he thought appropriate - one with a picture of President Matata breaking links in a large chain, and wrapped it tightly round his loins. Naked to the waist, he sighed and sat down in the period French armchair, peeled off his socks, wiggled his toes, and waited. Big Mama was still in the shower and no doubt thinking up the latest fantasy for tonight's session. Three times a week, they played dressing-up games, or games of seduction and pretend. The rules usually meant he had to do whatever he was commanded and she rewarded him with sex having made him wait for it. She seemed to find it a real turn-on and she never failed to come up with something new. He wondered what it would be to-night. They must have worked their way through all the possibilities - doctors and nurses, butlers and maids, vicars and tarts, and so on. Last time, she had emerged from the bathroom dressed as a slave girl (complete with transparent pantaloons, etc) and he had to play the part of a turbaned slave-driver; the time before that, she had been a school-girl in gymslip and woollen stockings and he, the schoolmaster. Her games always had the same conclusion. She ended up on top and he was the underling (in more ways than one) in the encounter. Not really his scene since he liked to call the shots.

After what seemed eternity to him, Big Mama appeared. Wrapped around her exquisite body was a bright crimson cloak and her head was encased in a red, fur-lined hood. Her radiant features were lightly made-up and her moist, sensual lips were tinted to match her garment. She smiled alluringly.

'What do you think, Max? Do you fancy me as Empress of Zambelia?'

'By heavens, Marianne,' he replied, ready to join in the game. 'You are the most exquisite thing I've ever set eyes on. If you are the Empress, I am your loyal, adoring subject and ready to do as you command. Be it to climb mountains, swim oceans, go through fire, to die for you. Only give the word.'

'Pretend I'm Red Riding Hood and you are the wicked wolf,' she said opening up the robe to reveal her naked body.

The doctor had seen a thousand female forms but never one like this.

'Marianne, I am lost for words. Your beauty is so dazzling, it takes my breath away. I must have you.'

'First, the game, Max. The game! Red Riding Hood, remember?'

She gazed deeply into his eyes.

'Oh, Gran'ma what big eyes you have!' she whispered seductively.

'All the better to see you,' he said cooperatively.

'Oh, Gran'ma, what big ears you have!'

'All the better to hear you!'

'Oh, Gran'ma, what big hands you have!'

'All the better to touch you!' he said reaching for her.

She playfully avoided his hands and stretched over and, in one deft movement, flicked the sarong off his thighs.

She pushed him roughly back on to the bed.

'Enough talking!' she said throatily as she mounted him and began to kiss him slowly on the ears, gradually making her way down his neck towards the hollow where his throat joined his body. Max stretched out, placed both arms behind his head, and let it happen.

***

'You were a superb gran'ma,' she said later as they lay back on her bed. 'And an even better wolf.' She was gleaming with sweat after her vigorous exertions. 'We could perhaps work our way through the whole of Grimm's Fairy Tales. Maybe Cinderella or Rapunzel next time.'

'You have the imagination of a poet, Marianne,' he said, 'as well as the wisdom of a statesman and the shrewdness of an entrepreneur.'

'Why, thank you, Max. Talking of entrepreneurship, did you deal with the three transfusion cases I sent up to you?'

'I did indeed, Marianne. They were rare blood types and should bring us a pretty tidy profit. I have the three bodies in a coma already in storage in our Research Bureau; the two sons have already unknowingly given a kidney each but there are more parts we can harvest when the time comes. Given the rarity of their blood groups, they could fetch us around 36,000 dollars. Not a bad profit margin when you consider they will cost us no more than a couple of thousand matunda.'

'But what about the relatives?' she asked. 'Doesn't Washington Fundi have any family making inquiries about him?'

'He has two brothers still living in their home village and I have told them that Washington's operation went wrong and

208

his body is still in a coma if they want to come and see him. They think the sons are still at school and so I told them the hospital will be paying the boys five hundred matunda in compensation for the hospital's error and that should cover their boarding school fees. They seemed more than happy about that since it freed them from any obligation.'

'Good work, Max. The big problem with the organ donor business is always dealing with troublesome relatives wanting to take the body home.'

'I think I've solved that difficulty, Marianne. If there is a sudden demand for an organ, I simply tell Kiboko to shoot a couple of prisoners. Then there are the occasional executions in Tagooma prison. I've told Kiboko, though, to take care not to mutilate the bodies, especially the eyes, as one or two have arrived in a mess lately and it wasn't possible to extract the corneas.'

'Impressive, Max, and I know you have to work fast if you are to extract the organs before they atrophy. I believe you said they were good for just under forty hours. How do you ensure a constant supply of live donors? Where do you find them?'

'Mainly from homes for the mentally handicapped who are usually readily available and relatives are not usually as inquisitive. In some ways, we are relieving them of a burden. Then there are the beggars on the street. Sometimes we simply send out the ambulance to collect a few healthy looking specimens, grab them and drug them. As you know there are lots of waifs and strays on the streets and we take those if there is a call for children's organs. I don't think street rag-a-muffins are missed by anybody in particular.'

'Excellent, Max. At this rate, you'll soon be a millionaire. Your share of the three I sent you should come to around 12,000 dollars. Not bad for a morning's work. The demand for kidneys and livers seems endless.'

'Thank you, Marianne. I have read somewhere in the medical press that it might be possible one day for scientists to grow miniature livers and kidneys in the laboratory but I think that day is a long way off. So looking at the long-term, I can see even greater opportunities in this business.'

'Tell me more, Max.'

'There are experiments taking place at the University of Edinburgh which hold out the promise of human eggs from the ovaries of aborted female foetuses. The later the abortion, the better the chance of developing the eggs.'

'You mean we could farm the eggs and sell them in our organ transplant enterprise?'

'Exactly. And, as you know, given the difficulties of finding husbands for their daughters, families here in Africa prefer male offspring. If we had the latest electronic equipment to determine the sex of children still in the womb, we'd be able to reap a fortune. There'd be no problem in persuading pregnant mothers with unborn female children to have abortions. It's already being done in India and I'm sure they'll be quick there to spot the commercial opportunities.'

'Bringing you to Zambelia was one of the shrewdest things I ever did, Max. On the subject of pregnancy, I hear good reports of your Family Planning Centre. You seem to have hit it off with the young married ladies of the district. While on this subject, you remind me that you can be of assistance to my own family in this matter of family planning. One of my younger sisters, Guinevere, is only twenty-five and already has five children. Something should be done about it. She is an attractive young woman and that's her problem. Her husband, Albert, doesn't seem to be able to leave her alone and he refuses to use condoms. Says it's like poking the fire with your gloves on. I've never heard such rubbish. But, as you know, the trouble with contraceptives such as the pill is that they can have nasty side-effects, like high blood pressure or palpitations. What would be your recommendation?'

'She could wear a Dutch cap, I suppose.'

'That sounds like one of our sex games, Max. I hope you

won't try anything on with her. I should be a trifle displeased if you did.'

She made that word "trifle" sound like anything but "trifle".

'Not a chance of that. You know me, Marianne.'

'Only too well, Max. So what would you recommend?

'We could try an IUD, an Inter-uterine device, I suppose, but I think I may have exactly the right thing for Guinevere. State of the art - the latest development in the field. It consists of six tiny rods which are implanted under the skin of the upper arm. Effective for up to five years and no side effects. Takes ten minutes to implant. Send Guinevere round to my surgery and we'll see what can be done.'

'You're a good man, Max. A good friend and a good lover. Now what about another Nursery Rhyme game. I'd suggest The Frog Prince this time.'

A month had passed since Schneider's meeting with Big Mama and Nixon Makau was reporting his monthly financial returns to her. Reading from his notes, he said: 'Summing up, ma'am, we have dispatched twelve bodies in prime condition to our Medical Research Bureau, which should produce a net profit of around twenty-four thousand dollars, thanks to Kiboko's executions in Tagooma prison; Schneider's organ transplant business showed a net gain of ten thousand, and the deportation of twenty-five young virgins to the Middle East showed the greatest return of all with a net balance of thirty two thousand dollars. In total these three businesses alone have shown a healthy contribution to the state treasury of sixty-six thousand. These are sound returns to add to our other state enterprises, which I am sure will be a source of great satisfaction for our illustrious Life President.'

'We are most grateful to you, Nixon, for the accurate way you have kept state records. I don't know what we'd do without you. You are the most trusted member of the palace staff. Why don't you call me Marianne as the people closest to me do?'

Nixon's heart swelled with pride when he heard these words.

'I shall be honoured to do so…Marianne,' he said hesitantly.

He had been equally touched when she referred to him as Nixon which was a more intimate way of addressing him than his formal title, Mr Makau. At that moment, he would have done anything to please her, walk through fire, jump off a cliff. She'd only to name it.

'I'm aware too,' she said, continuing the flattery, 'that you keep your ear close to the ground and know the latest goings-on here in State House and the palaces. You hear the latest gossip. Who's sleeping with whom and who has fallen out with whom and so on. I expect you to keep me informed on these matters as part of your duty as presidential aide. I shall be angry with you if ever I discover that you have been holding anything back from me. In my capacity as the president's consort and counsellor. I need to know everything. Everything, do you hear?'

'Yes, I hear you, Marianne, and I always try to give complete satisfaction.'

'Well, what's the latest chit-chat in the back offices?'

'You are the most important member of the president's staff and I hesitate to waste your valuable time, Marianne, with tittle-tattle to which there is no substance. Much of it is unsubstantiated and without foundation.'

'Did you not hear what I said, Nixon?   I said EVERYTHING! That means holding nothing back.'

He noted the anger in her voice and he knew that he couldn't afford to get on her wrong side. Not yet anyway, he told himself. If he wasn't careful, she'd be referring to him again by that hated nickname "Dudu".

'Very well, Marianne. On the jungle telegraph, I have heard that your brother-in-law, Albert, is going round the palace cursing and vowing that he is going to murder your doctor-friend Schneider.'

'Murder Max? But what in heaven's name for? I only sent him to the family to help them overcome Guinevere's problems with birth control.'

Big Mama's features had hardened and she was no longer the sweet-tempered lady he had been dealing with. In a matter of seconds she had transformed from the Fairy Queen to the Witch.

'What's Dr Schneider supposed to have done?' she snapped, though she already had an inkling of what Schneider might be up to.

'As I said, Marianne,' Nixon said in his most oleaginous tone of voice, 'it's only tongue-wagging among the lower echelons in the palace and I shouldn't attach too much importance to it.'

Too late. Big Mama was no longer a gentle Good Queen Bess. She was Boadicea and ready to strike and decapitate her Teutonic target, Max Schneider!

'Tell me what the word is, Dudu,' she snarled, 'or it will be the worse for you.'

'I hardly like to say, as it is no more than gossip and rumour but people are sneering and jesting that Dr Schneider insisted on giving Guinevere practical demonstrations of efficacy of his birth control methods by indulging in the sexual act in order to show her how best to avoid impregnation.'

Big Mama had now turned pale and was trembling with rage. 'No-one crosses me and gets away with it,' she ranted. 'Max Schneider will learn that if he crosses me, there will be a high price to pay.'

The next time Schneider approached in her office, she told him in no uncertain terms exactly what she thought of him.

'Get out of my sight,' she hissed venomously. 'You are a loathsome, lecherous animal and I cannot bear to see you any further in my presence. I can no longer tolerate your nauseating white-man's odour nor the sight of your sickly-pale, corpse-like body. You are hideous in my sight, with your bloodless, colourless skin like that of a dead fish and there is about you a nauseating, cloyingly sweet smell that repels me in the extreme.'

She stormed out of the office, slamming the door behind her. Nixon who had witnessed the encounter returned to his own domain and sat down at his desk with the satisfied smile of a crocodile that had just digested a large bullock. 'My God!' he muttered to himself. 'I hope I never cross Big Mama as Schneider has done. Now, how did that line of Congreve's poetry go?

"Heaven has no rage like love to hatred turned,
Nor hell a fury like a woman scorned".'

****

214

Chapter Eighteen

Security at the Palace

In another part of the palace, Peter Halliday was preparing his weekly returns in his little store-room when Paddy Reilly knocked on his door.

'I hope it's important, Paddy,' he said irritably. 'Only I'm due to meet Nixon Makau in a few minutes to give him my 'Stores-and-Security' Report.'

'It's important all right,' Paddy answered. 'A helluva sight more important than your meeting with the Dudu. I have here a requisition for some small items Big Mama wishes to have transferred from State House to a place of greater safety. The document is signed by her and the president himself.'

He placed the list on the desk. Peter looked it over.

'Good God!' he exlaimed. 'This is like asking for the Crown Jewels. I'll have to check this out with Nixon first.'

'Do what you like,' Paddy said. 'But I'll be back in an hour to collect them. If they're not ready, watch out. Big Mama'll play merry hell.'

***

Nixon's office at the rear of the palace was sparsely furnished. There was a plain wooden desk with chairs for visitors, a small bookcase containing a few tatty, out-of-date

215

volumes on accounting and management, and two strong, metal filing cabinets secured with padlocked iron bars running through their handles.

Nixon sat at the desk up-dating his notes and records. He prided himself on his memory. He could remember who said what to whom and where and when going back for many years. Furthermore, he had kept detailed records of all the events and decisions made in the palace. He wrote up full accounts of the cases Big Mama had dealt with that morning - the people, the time, the decisions: Philip Thomas Gichuru's problem with his daughter's pregnancy and the assignment of the case to Kiboko who had undertaken to put matters right 'without over-doing it'; Washington Fundi and his sons who had been sent over to Schneider's Research Bureau - that'll be the last we see of *them*, he thought. There was the trader, Tulshidas locked up in Tagooma clink until such a time as he saw the light and coughed up more money; next, came the tasks given to Reilly as recompense and absolution from his crimes of misappropriation and customs fraud; lastly, came the decisions on the fate of the Tagooma prisoners, Deputies Chifunza and Chilulu and the lecturer, Frank Johnson. Nothing escaped Nixon's all-seeing eye. He knew precisely who'd been locked up in Tagooma and why; also how many had since disappeared plus the vast amounts of money that had been extorted from the victims. He had tabulated a complete dossier on the career of the despicable, psychopathic monster, Kiboko. He had watched him descend from wanton acts of cruelty to gross inhumanity until he had become the brutal, callous killer he was today, who derived perverted pleasure from torture and murder. Clearly, as insane as Uganda's Idi Amin.

As for Schneider, he had been most careful to log accurate lists of the organs and bodies and their prices that the perverted practitioner had stored in his Research Bureau "coma wards" before exporting them by presidential jet to sundry addresses in the Middle East and Russia. Neither Big Mama nor Schneider realised that payments for these evil transactions came via the Private Secretary's office thus giving him access to the details of their nefarious traffic. To date, he calculated that the pair had earned well over a million American dollars from the trade. He knew that Big Mama took seventy-five per cent of the proceeds and Schneider the balance. What's more, he had watched and counted the number of times Schneider had visited Big Mama in her boudoir at night. He was amazed at their sexual appetites. Why, they seemed to be at it every night! People who did it as often as that must be depraved. God knows what they got up to behind that closed bedroom door! He'd wondered for a time if he could have got away with installing a hidden TV camera in there but decided against it as too risky.

'The Dudu' they'd nicknamed him in the palace. The little bug. How he resented and abhorred being called that! It had been the same at school when he was a kid. The butt of everyone's mockery – "half-pint, midget, peewee, pipsqueak, shrimp". He'd heard 'em all. Even the teachers who should have known better had joined in the sarcastic jibes with remarks like 'Come on Mister Microbe.' He'd been pushed around and bullied all his life because of his small stature. Was it his fault that he came from a family of small people? After all, he wasn't exactly a pigmy being almost five feet tall. Was it his fault that he'd inherited a particular set of tribal genes? The psychology books claimed that it was the tall, strong people who took the popular leadership roles and to whom the glittering prizes went. They couldn't have been more wrong. They had forgotten about Napoleon Bonaparte and Adolph Hitler. In his wildest fantasies, he had visions of watching the scene where Kiboko and Schneider got their come-uppance. How he relished the thought! 'Only pipe-dreams,' he sighed

After finishing the chore of making up his records, he took a key from the chain he wore round his neck and unfastened the padlocks on his filing cabinets. He pulled open the bottom sliding drawer and deposited the folders amongst the many files stored there. It was his intention whenever he got the chance to send them to the British authorities such as the Commonwealth Secretariat or the Commission for Justice and Peace. He was finding it difficult however to smuggle the dossier out of the country under the ever-watchful eyes of Big Mama's secret police. He locked up the cabinet and returned the key to the chain under his shirt. At that moment, the Hallidays appeared at his door for their weekly meeting.

He was always glad to see the Hallidays. They were the only people in the palace who treated him with the respect his position deserved and referred to him using his full and proper name, Mr Nixon Makau, though they were on first term names when talking together. He appreciated and liked them for that. It showed sensitivity and understanding. In addition, the Hallidays and he shared a mutual esteem. Nixon admired Helen Halliday's culinary skills and her ability to estimate costs and catering requirements for the numerous grand social occasions the palace had to organise for visiting diplomats and ambassadors. Her husband, Peter, had demonstrated shrewd judgment not only when it came to accounting for palace stores and equipment but also in advising on security arrangements. The Halliday's expertise in costing and estimating helped Nixon enormously when it came to budgeting and allocating palace funds.

On their side, the Hallidays thought highly of Nixon's organising and management skills along with his elephantine memory for details. His instructions were always firm, clear and unequivocal though he did have a tendency to sneer and scoff at the shortcomings of other palace workers. They forgave him this fault. Nobody's perfect, they thought.

'Good afternoon, Nixon,' said the Hallidays warmly. 'Are we on time?'

'As always. Nice to see you again,' Nixon said earnestly. 'Do come in and sit down. I must say, you're looking nice today, Helen. Also pleased with yourself.'

'Why, thank you Nixon. It's true I'm pleased with things at the moment. A close family friend of ours, Sue Delamere, has arrived to take up a post at the university. Peter and I are fond of her and we're over the moon about it, aren't we, Peter?'

'We certainly are. We've known Sue since she was a little girl and it's so good to see she's got on so well, now a PhD and a senior lecturer at the university.'

'I sincerely hope she's happy here in Zambelia. Hekima is a lovely place to live. If ever I can be of help to her, don't hesitate to let me know. Now, what have you got to report to me?'

'Not much, Nixon. Here are the monthly accounts for costs of the various social events last month. I think you'll find the necessary receipts are included for your records. I've also enclosed estimates for next month's activities.'

'Excellent, Helen. As usual, you are a model of efficiency. What about you, Peter? Anything of note to report?'

'Two things, Nixon, sir. First, the new rear gate you requested has now been installed.'

'Ah, yes. It's always been a nuisance having to go through the formalities at the front gate. All those sentries insisting on identification when they know damned well who I am. And what was worse were all those hangers-on waiting to accost me to ask for favours and privileged treatment. It's going to be so much more convenient to be able to slip away through the small gate at the back of the palace.'

'The electronic locks on the inner palace doors are the latest, state-of-the-art technology,' said Peter.

'Excellent,' Nixon said, always intrigued by security devices. 'How do they work?'

'We have examined a number of security systems, Nixon, and the one we liked best was a combination of biometrics and a smart card.'

'Sorry, Peter, you've lost me. You'll have to tell me a little more if I'm to understand it.'

'One of the highest levels of security uses two-factor identification, namely: something you have like a key or a smart card plus something biological like a fingerprint, retina scan, facial feature, or voice pattern. We liked the combination of smart card with voice pattern.'

'Sounds perfect to me, Peter. Go on. So that's what you decided on in the end? Explain it to me, please.'

'We chose the double system: smart card plus voice recognition. It works like a car's electronic locking system. The locks are activated by the card together with the voiceprint ID and they have been programmed to respond to voices of senior palace staff only. The President's of course, Big Mama's, Colonel Kiboko's, Doctor Schneider's, mine and Mrs Halliday's, plus some supervisory staff, and last, but certainly not least, your own.'

'What happens if someone else tries to use my card?'

'The card won't work, Nixon, without the biometric factor; in this case your voice pattern.'

'Ingenious, Peter. The routine is as we agreed?'

'Yes. The gate locks automatically but to open it, you must insert your identification chip into the slot and speak your name in full into the built-in microphone. "Nixon Makau speaking!" Same routine when you leave the grounds and when you come back.'

'Is it foolproof? I mean, couldn't someone get through the gate with my card and a tape-recording of my voice?'

'Impossible. The lock reacts only to the actual voice with its subtle intonations and inflections. It's foolproof all right.'

'Well done, Peter! A stroke of genius that's going to make life a lot easier. I shouldn't mind having something like this installed on the gate of my little private domain as I keep many important documents in the basement of my home. Could you arrange to install a combination of smart card with

220

finger print? There's lots of confidential stuff over at my place and I shouldn't like any unauthorized person going through my things.'

'No problem,' Peter said. 'Only say the word and I'll get the same company to install a triple set of devices for you. Once you check in with the sentry on the gate, you will need a smart card and voice recognition to get into the villa complex and finally a finger print check for access to your home.'

'Why, thank you Peter. I'd like to see any prowler get past those! Both you and your wife are first-class professionals. Now, what was the other thing you wished to tell me about?'

'Thank you, sir. The other matter was simply a list of items Paddy Reilly wants to remove from the palace to Big Mama's mansion on Lake Zambelia. The requisition document is in order and has been signed by President Matata.'

'If it's been signed by the president, there's no problem. Do you have the list?'

Peter handed over a copy of the list. Nixon took it and examined it. He whistled in amazement. He said, 'If it's been authorised by the president, Peter, there's no argument. But leave this with me and I'll have it photo-copied for the records.'

Their business finished, Helen and Peter shook his hand and departed. Nixon sat chin in hand and stared at the requisition list before him. It read:

a. Paintings by Pablo Picasso.(All in frames):-*La Source*; *Le Peintre; La Femme aux Yeux Noirs; La Femme a la Colerette Bleue; La Demoiselle.*

b. Bronze Sculpture by Picasso: *Femme Boisgeloup*

c.. Paintings by Georges Braque (in frames):-*Le Chateau de Roche-Guyon; Nature Morte*

d. Paintings (in frames) by George Stubbs of lion, giraffe, monkey, rhinoceros.

e.. *William & Mary* walnut half-circular card table;

f.. *Queen Anne* walnut fall-front bureau with well.

It was a good ten minutes before Nixon Makau was able to move again.

'Big Mama,' he said quietly to himself, 'does nothing by halves.'

He recognized all the works of art on the list. They were stolen works that had never been recovered.

'How shrewd our Marianne is,' he said to himself admiringly. 'Precious works of art but not so famous as to be unsaleable. She knows what she's doing all right.'

****

Chapter Nineteen

On the road to Mombo Island

Early on Friday afternoon, Mike Goodman accompanied by Jack Zulu drove the bright red ambulance with the legend 'Gift of the World Health Organisation' emboldened on its side, up the steep roadway leading to Sue's house. He brought the vehicle to a halt outside her kitchen door. She appeared immediately, carrying her small week-end valise and a large art portfolio.

'Very impressive, Mike,' she said. 'Is this to be our transport to the refugee camp?'

'It is, Sue. Sorry, if you find it an unconventional vehicle for taking a lady out for the week-end. But Jack and I are to take a leper from the camp over to Mombo Island. I hope that's OK.'

'Fine with me,' she said. 'Before we set off, how about a coffee?'

'Love one,' Mike said. 'We've a long way to go but there's always time for a coffee, eh, Jack? Make it strong and one sugar for Jack. Same for me but no sugar.'

'Coming right up,' Sue said. You're a man after my heart, Mike. Without coffee, I think I'd die.'

'That bit about me being a man after your heart is absolutely right.'

'Very funny,' Sue laughed. 'Now, what about you, Jack?'

'I'm not after your heart, Doctor Delamere, but I'd love a coffee,' said Jack joining in the banter. 'Coffee the same as Mike's, but don't forget one sugar, please.'

'Sikio!' Sue called. 'You probably heard all that. Three coffees.'

'Yes, memsahib. Rightaway. The coffee's already percolating.'

'Well, how have you found life here so far, Sue?' Mike asked.

'Love the town of Hekima and its quaint shopping centre but I've run into trouble already in my work in the Department, I'm afraid. I was called in to see Major Nyoka about a lecture I gave on *Macbeth* and for cutting the telephone cord in my office. He said my talk was too political and bordering on the seditious since it made veiled reference to Zambelia's leaders. Of course it was nothing of the sort; it was merely an attempt to put the play into its historical setting. As for the telephone business, he threatened to arrest me if I cut the cord again. But I object most strongly to police listening into my private conversations.'

'Sounds as if you've been having an exciting time, Sue. But, it doesn't pay to provoke these people. My policy is to keep my head down, maintain a low profile and get on with my work quietly.'

'I don't agree with being a *status quo*, don't-rock-the-boat, type of person, Mike. When you see something wrong, you can't just bury your head in the sand and ignore it. I believe in confronting it and having it out once and for all even if it means a rebellion.'

'In that case, you won't last long in Zambelia, Sue. You'll get yourself deported or worse still, slapped into Gereza Women's Prison and then it'd be God help you. What could you do from there? Our first object is survival if we are to do any good in this country. Look, I could have spoken out many times whenever I saw something wicked. And where would that have got me, may I ask? Behind bars in double quick time. If you're to help the people here, you have to learn to turn a blind eye to many things. Bend with the wind. Otherwise you're removed from the scene and your effect on the situation is nil. It's called pragmatism.'

Sue's temper flared. 'I'd call it expediency. But there's an even stronger expression for it. Appeasement or "Peace at any Price" - the kind favoured by Neville Chamberlain at Munich in 1939. 'Anything for a Quiet Life'. That's moral treason and it's not for me, thank you very much, Mike. Bullies, whether Nazis or Zambelians, have to be beaten. If the authorities here in Zambelia are so dictatorial as to object to my lecture on the Elizabethan political system, they're no better than Hitler's Germany or Stalinist Russia. Surely you're not trying to tell me that if you were faced with downright wickedness, with blatant evil that you would simply turn a blind eye?'

'That'd be different, I suppose,' Mike replied equably. 'So far I haven't met such an extreme situation. I'll wait until it arises before I throw away all that I have been trying to achieve here in Zambelia. We'll see what your views are after you've seen the refugee camp and the leper village.'

'Hey, you two,' said Jack. 'Cut out the squabbling. Typical English people getting all worked up over a hypothetical situation. No-one can say how they would react until they're actually faced with it. So let's calm down. Now we'd better be on our way if we're to get to Mombo before dark. We've got the whole weekend ahead of us to argue and debate, for Pete's sake.'

'OK, Jack,' said Sue. 'Point taken. Forget that there was a quick-tempered Irish lady in the cab here with you a minute ago.'

She climbed aboard the Land Rover and, and sitting next to Jack, said, 'To change the subject, I've brought my art stuff. Thought I might get a chance to do a spot of sketching

225

and painting. But I'm also looking forward to seeing you both in action.'

'I'm not sure "looking forward" is the right expression, Doctor Delamere,' said a solemn-faced Jack. 'You might find some of it pretty horrific.'

***

The ambulance soon left Hekima behind as it sped along the two-laned dusty, corrugated M1 heading to the north of Zambelia.

'You don't seem your cheerful self, Jack,' remarked Sue. 'Anything the matter?'

'He's worried about his brothers,' said Mike, answering for him. 'They've failed to turn up to register for the beginning of the term. Most unlike them.'

'Perhaps they're taking an extended holiday at home. They won't be the first students to do that,' Sue said.

Jack grimaced. 'No, it must be something more serious than that. I know for certain that they left home last week to come to Hekima. I'm puzzled and worried about them. I can't imagine where they've got to.'

'I'm sure they'll turn up and there'll be a rational explanation for their late appearance. Imagined fears are always worse than reality or as Shakespeare put it: "in the night, how easy a bush becomes a bear!" Or words to that effect.'

'I hope you and Shakespeare are right, Doctor.'

They drove along for a while in silence. Mike began to sing in his tuneless voice "When Irish Eyes Are Smiling" and Sue and Jack laughingly joined in. After a short while, they came to the main gate of the refugee camp and the adjoining sentry box where Mike stopped the ambulance. He nodded to the guard who gave him a smart military salute and handed over a flat exercise book. Mike filled in the details of the

226

vehicle and the names of the passengers. The sentry raised the zebra-painted barrier pole and Mike drove into the camp and up to the main office.

As they disembarked, they were met by a dark-haired, middle-aged European woman who greeted them affectionately.

'Hello, Mike. Jack,' she said taking their hands in a firm handshake and kissing them both on the cheek. 'So nice to see you both again.'

'Sue,' said Mike. 'I'd like to introduce Dr Regina Benvenuto. She's in charge of this operation.'

The two ladies shook hands warmly.

'Look, Gina,' said Mike. 'While Jack and I are attending to the paper work, etcetera for our new leper patient, I wonder if you would show Sue around the camp and tell her a little about your work here. We'll collect our new patient and take Sue across to Mombo Island. See you later.'

'Be glad to show Sue around, Mike, ' his colleague said.

Dr Benvenuto and Sue began their tour of the wards.

'Lambara Camp caters for over twenty thousand refugees but in this particular section, we are responsible for feeding over one thousand adults and children,' the doctor said.

'That must cost a lot of money,' said Sue.

'I spend about four hundred matunda a day – that's about two hundred pounds - on rice and fish in the town market but I have to spend more cash on buying back my own looted drugs from thieves who stole them three months ago. We have a staff of about forty orderlies and medical workers. One of our difficulties is that we have no electricity supply and have to work by the light of kerosene lamps after dark. But that doesn't compare with the problems some of the other sections have.'

'For instance?'

'Lugandans who fled the civil war to find sanctuary are living in fear from a wave of rapes, robberies and murders

227

which have swept through some of the camps. There have been reports of over a hundred rapes in the last month, mostly by State security forces acting brutally and with impunity. There is little that can be done as we're completely at their mercy. We have complained to Colonel Kiboko many times but in vain.'

'I'm sorry to hear that,' Sue said. 'Thank God, it's not happening in your section.'

'The main reason is that our little people are too ill to be of interest to them. There is much sickness here. There is the ever-present danger of dysentery and cholera from infected water supplies. I've worked in India and Liberia but I have never seen anything as bad as this. Children have been seriously damaged by the civil war that has ravaged their country. It has forced whole families to walk hundreds of miles with no shoes or clothes through semi-desert in search of food and safety. When they arrive here, they are often unable to respond to the food and medical care we give them. I have been shocked by the total collapse of their immune system even after treatment.'

'Could that be Aids?' asked Sue.

'Perhaps. But often when you look at these little people's eyes, you often see no life behind them. Sometimes they have seen too much and they seem to have given up the will to live. They have been witnesses to a kind of holocaust.'

They entered the first ward - an abandoned Catholic church. A girl, aged thirteen, but looking about nine years old, lay dying from hepatitis although she had been treated with drugs that should have defeated the disease. She moaned loudly and appeared to have vomited on her pillow.

'It is not hunger in her case,' said the doctor. 'She has totally lost her grip and her mind is wandering all over the place. She came here after seeing her family wiped out with all their livestock.'

Sitting on the edge of her bed was a forlorn little girl hugging herself and rocking to and fro.

'The children here need some affection to give them the feeling that their lives are worth living,' she said, sweeping the tiny starving child into her arms. 'This one has no obvious physical ailments but she will probably die. She was found abandoned and will not eat. She is an advanced state of starvation.'

'Sorry, Doctor Benvenuto,' said Sue. 'I don't understand. What does that mean? An *advanced* state of starvation?'

'Well, when you starve to death, this is what happens. At first, there is hunger and a craving which turns into pain after two or three days. Then the pains subside and the stomach shrinks. Next, your body begins to live off its fat reserves and, perhaps with a meagre amount of food, the process lasts for a month or two. Eventually your body runs out of fat and you begin to live off the muscle in your thighs, buttocks, and upper arms. In a desperate bid to stay alive, you start to consume your own body. Soon your limbs look like broomsticks and you're literally 'skin and bone'. As starvation takes its final grip, you lose interest in everything and a seductive apathy seeps through every fibre of your body. That's what has happened to this little girl. But as for the girl in the last bed, something worse than starvation happened to her. She was forcibly mutilated with the approval of her parents.'

'What in heaven's name happened?'

'Her parents, following ancient African tradition, told her she could only remain pure by cutting out the unclean parts of her body. They said that if she was not circumcised, the impure parts of her body would grow until they reached her thighs. She would develop a male sexual organ and no man would be able to mate with her. Furthermore, no man would want to. She was forced to submit to mutilation of the genitalia. Result - severe blood poisoning. Her aunt, who carried out the operation, was none too fussy about the kinds of instruments she used nor how clean they were.'

229

'My God! How awful! Africa needs more doctors like you,' said Sue. 'And more medicines.'

'No,' Gina Benvenuto replied. 'What the people are dying of is poverty. It's not doctors and medicines that are needed so much as peace, economic development, clean water, improved food production, and most important - improved education. That's where you and your university colleagues come in. You must train the teachers who can go out and educate the people in the villages.'

***

Later that day, Sue met up with Mike and Jack and the new leper patient. As they left the camp, she was strangely silent. After a while, she said:

'You know, Mike. I've been thinking. Maybe you're right about keeping a low profile if we are to be of any help in alleviating the terrible suffering in this country.'

****

Chapter Twenty
Mombo Island

Towards six thirty, before dusk descended, they reached the edge of Lake Zambelia from where they could make out the lights and outline of Mombo Island. A large wooden ferry was already waiting with six leprous boatmen at the ready, their job being to move the craft across the half-mile of water by pulling on a rope attached to a pulley on the opposite bank. Mike and Jack carried their male leper patient on the stretcher and placed him carefully on board. Sue joined them in the unsteady, swaying craft. Ever so slowly and gently, the boatmen propelled the ferry across.

After a little while, they began to chant and dance to a rhythmic, polyphonic song, as they changed places in line in time to their heaving and pulling on the rope. Their singing became louder as they got nearer to the island, to indicate to the men on the opposite bank that they were approaching. Someone on the shore began ringing a bell, the boatmen stopped their heaving, and the ferry drifted noiselessly on to the beach where a small crowd had gathered.

Wide-eyed children were playing games in the sand, a few convalescent patients were leaning on their wooden staffs like characters out of the Old Testament as they watched the boat dock. Some wore only cotton trousers, others the traditional dress of gaily-coloured-material, hung casually and fastened around the neck and falling loosely like a toga. Mothers sat around on the steps of the hospital, breast-feeding their infants; an old man with skin as dark and withered as the bark of a tree marched about in a tattered military tunic, peaked helmet askew; a middle aged man with leprous, leonine features and dressed only in ragged shorts and a yellow pith helmet walked by with upright, dignified bearing.

Mike and Jack were out first. Tenderly they lifted the leper patient off the ferry and carried him ashore in the direction of the hospital reception room.

'We'll see you later at supper, Sue,' Mike called over his shoulder. 'Joseph there will look after you till then.'

Sue stepped gingerly off the ferryboat and was helped ashore with her luggage by a tall, particularly dark-skinned African in his mid-twenties. At first sight, his face appeared to be the grotesque kind one would expect in a horror film. Most of his nose was missing, the forehead deformed by leprous growths, the eyes yellow and bulging, his feet toeless and his hands merely a collection of stumps. But there was something strangely beautiful in his Calibanesque appearance.

'My name is Joseph. I am a medical orderly here at the hospital,' he said courteously. 'Greetings, Doctor Delamere. We are happy to see you on Mombo Island. We have been waiting for you. Doctor Goodman phoned to tell us earlier this week that you would be coming. He has asked me to show you to your room as he and Jack will be occupied with patients for most of the evening.'

Sue felt welcome and happy at this warm reception.

The heat that night was intense and a storm was brewing. She lay back in her bed, feeling secure and protected by the gauze tent that was her mosquito net. She watched fascinated as myriads of sausage flies swarmed under her door and flung themselves suicidally at the pressure lamp, after which they fell to the wooden floor where they shed their wings, running to and fro bewildered at suddenly finding themselves earth-bound creatures. She turned off her lamp and was lulled to

232

sleep by a symphony of bullfrogs and the endless chatter of countless cicadas sounding she thought like a million miniature electric drills in a goblin's workshop. During the night, there was torrential rainfall but Sue was so exhausted she slept through it all.

Next morning, she awoke and rubbing the sleep from her eyes, stared at the unfamiliar little room not unlike a monk's cell. Though it was early morning, it was already hot and humid. She pulled back the mosquito net and turned on her side, the bed springs squeaking as she did so. She looked round the cabin. Apart from the narrow, iron bed in which she lay, there was a table with a Tilley lamp, a washstand with a jug, basin and glass, a chair and a bottle of boiled water on the floor now covered in a thick carpet of insect wings. She poured out the water and washed with the tablet of Lifebuoy which had been thoughtfully provided. She rinsed out her mouth with the boiled water after which she slipped on her slacks and loose white shirt and went to the dining-room for breakfast.

'You see, Sue,' said Mike a little later as they sat with Jack in the tiny surgery. 'Leprosy, or Hansen's disease, is one of the least contagious of communicable diseases and only five per cent of the world's population is susceptible to it but the subject has always been shrouded in fear and ignorance. People associate it with the ill-defined disease of the Bible and the bell-ringing outcasts of the Middle Ages calling out "Unclean! Unclean!" But since the early 1940's, effective drugs, the sulfones, have rendered the disease medically controllable. At the end of the nineteenth century, there were over a thousand lepers on Mombo Isle. They were simply abandoned there by their relatives; that's why it used to be called the "Lonely Isle". In the fifties, there were over five hundred residents. Today, we have only about a hundred - adults and children - and hardly any of them are contagious.'

'How are they supported, Mike? Do you get help from outside agencies?'

233

'We get considerable support from the World Health Organisation but the village is a self-contained unit with its own workshops and its own little farms complete with livestock. It's kept spotless by the collective work of the patients and their children. Its orderlies are inmates and when a patient is cured, he is given work in the community since their home villages will not have them back. Someone like Joseph is a good example. He works hard all day, dressing wounds, giving injections, and nursing children. He has been a leper from boyhood. Once you get used to the sick joke that life has played upon him, to your surprise you'll see a serene beauty in him. Nature has made a travesty of his face but his warm humanity shines through in his smile, his compassion, and his tranquillity.'

'I think I may have said this before, Mike, but you do have a beautiful way of putting things. You and Jack must find this work rewarding.'

'We do indeed and that's why I try to avoid stirring it on the political front. It would only prevent us from carrying on.'

'I can well understand that now, Mike. But if the disease is under control, why do these people live here? I notice a few healthy-looking children here.'

'Some are patients who have not responded normally to sulfones and some have mutilations which developed before the advent of effective drugs. Some of them are helpless and need our support. Besides that, they have been thrown out of their villages and treated like pariahs because their fellows retain the traditional dread of the disease. They associate it with the curse of the devil. As for the children, about half are leprous. The rest are here because their parents are infected. It's been found that children's chances of survival are best when they are left with their parents and the risk of infection is negligible. It is my dearest hope, my greatest wish, that one day we shall have eliminated leprosy completely from the face of the earth, as we have done with smallpox. Anyway,

234

enough of this lecturing. There's work to do. Let's have the first patient in.'

Jack opened the surgery door to admit a tall African. He was minus all his fingers and toes. Mike consulted the man's case notes.

'Good news, for you, Lucky Strike,' he said at last. The last series of tests have proved negative. You are now free of infection.'

Jack translated into Massuyu.

The man beamed happily.

Mike took the man's right hand in his own and examined it. He shook the hand warmly, even affectionately. He knew that his touch was of enormous importance.

'Leprosy is not only a physical disease, Sue,' he explained. 'It's also psychological. The leper feels that he is repellent and untouchable and touching his hand like this helps restore some of his lost confidence.'

'You mean like this,' said Sue, taking the leper's other hand in both her own.'

The African's eyes lit up in gratitude.

'*Asante daktari. Asante memsahib*,' he murmured. 'Thank you.'

Mike looked at Sue approvingly and with a new admiration. He addressed the patient.

'You will be able to go on working in the craft workshop. Today, you truly have the right name, Lucky Strike.'

The maimed hands seemed useless but in the craft workshops, the lepers had succeeded in creating the most beautiful artefacts. Some lepers worked on a simple loom making brightly-coloured rugs and tapestries, some on a hand-operated lathe producing wood-turned ornaments, others carved in ebony figures, still others hand-weaved intricate basket work.

Next in line was a leper with both feet badly mutilated. He carried his small son in his arms and stood him before Mike, his fingerless hand placed on the child's head to guide and console him. The boy had had one leprous foot amputated and he seemed to be covered in tiny festering cuts.

Jack Zulu spoke furiously in Massuyu to the father.

'What's that all about?' Sue asked.

'This young lad has already lost a foot because of an ill-conceived treatment by a native quack in his local village. Now the father has taken him to the local *mganga*, witch-doctor. This so-called traditional healer has inflicted yet more pain on the little fellow with his misguided, superstitious practices. He has made these small cuts in his body and introduced maggots into each wound. The idea is that the maggots will eat up the disease and so effect a cure. We have told that father if he does it again, we shall refuse to treat them. If only he had brought the child to us early enough, we could have cured him completely. This job sometimes has its frustrations.'

Mike Goodman dealt with patient after patient that morning. Sue watched him at work with a growing sense of wonder and admiration not only for his skill but, also for his goodness and tenderness in dealing with the most difficult of cases. The morning's observations had given her real insight not only into his professionalism but also into his character. He was gentle, kind, sympathetic and she knew she was falling in love with him. She wondered what she could do to help in his work. Then she had an idea.

'You said earlier, Mike, that there is a flourishing craft workshop. That's fine for the adults. But what about the children? How do they spend their time?'

'There's not much provided for them, Sue. We haven't thought about it. Why, do you have something in mind?'

'Maybe. Do you have lots of paints in the workshop?'

'I believe so. What's the plan?'

'I was thinking that in Northern Ireland, people often paint huge murals on the sides of houses, usually partisan slogans, in their case, I'm afraid. But I thought we might try something similar, only less provocative of course, here with the children. That is, if there is no objection to our decorating the side of one of the buildings.'

'That's a wonderful idea, the best I've heard all day,' said Jack eagerly. 'It would give them a real purpose and make them feel useful. Let's do it.'

In the afternoon, Sue gathered the children of the village together and they decided on the buildings which were to receive their attention. Jack divided the walls up into sections and, according to age and talent, allotted spaces to be filled by anyone who wanted to join in. Soon, a group of children were bent on the task of filling their allocated portions with technicolour images. The smaller ones painted the lower sections while the taller ones operated above their heads. One or two reached the highest sections by standing on ladders and stools. The subjects for treatment varied from birds and wild animals to representations of Jack in his white coat and Mike with his stethoscope. One small boy had even executed a simple matchstick drawing of Sue. Work on the project continued into the next day. Sue skipped and danced from building to building giving encouragement and praise.

'She is like a ballet dancer the way she bounds from one painting to another,' said one adolescent girl. 'She's like the Waltzing Matilda we sing in our concerts.'

The children took up the theme and began to chant the Australian folk song as they worked on their pictures. When the murals were completed, a great cheer went up and the adults of the village gathered round to applaud and praise the finished masterpieces.

When Sunday afternoon came, her work with the children and the close rapport she had built up with them made it difficult for Sue to leave Mombo Island. After tea, the visiting trio walked down to the beach to board the canoe which would take them back to the mainland. A little crowd of lepers - adults and children - had gathered to say goodbye. As they embarked, the group suddenly struck up with the song forever linked with Sue, 'Waltzing Matilda' The canoe pulled away from the shore and, as it drew further away, Sue was glad the children could not see her face or the tears in her eyes.

***

The drive back to Hekima was quiet and sad. Hardly a word was spoken the whole of the way. As they came to the outskirts of Hekima, they were waved down by two policemen.

'Put up the sign, Jack,' Mike said. 'This might amuse you, Sue.'

Jack put the printed board on the windscreen where it could be read clearly by the two officers.

"ANGALIA - UKOMA" it read. **"BEWARE – LEPROSY"**

They brought the ambulance to a halt close by the policemen.

'Anything wrong, officer?' asked Mike, smiling broadly.

'We wish to check your road tax and your insurance documents,' barked one of them.

He saw the sign.

'Never mind,' he said hurriedly, waving them on. 'Please proceed.'

'Works like a charm, every time,' Mike grinned.

***

It was turning dark when the ambulance finally pulled up outside Sue's house. She heaved a sigh of relief. 'After such a hectic week-end, it'll be so good to get inside and put my feet up. Come in and I'll make you both a cup of tea. It's

238

Sunday and Sikio's day off but I reckon I can still remember how it's done.'

'Thank you but not for me,' said Jack. 'I'd better get the ambulance back to the university garage before everyone has gone home. I'd also like to check if my brothers have arrived yet.'

'Tea would go down well, Sue,' said Mike. 'You go on, Jack. I'll phone one of our colleagues to pick me up later.'

They collected their belongings and watched Jack drive off down the pathway in the direction of the university workshops. Sue inserted the key into the lock and opened the kitchen door. She was not prepared for the sight which met her.

**

'Oh, my God!' she exclaimed as she entered the lounge. 'It looks as if a herd of elephants has stampeded through the place.'

There was chaos everywhere. Tables had been overturned; cushions ripped to shreds and the stuffing strewn across the floor; curtains torn down and left in a heap where they fell; books and tapes pulled off the shelves and flung across the room; photographs scattered everywhere; lamps upset and smashed; cupboards emptied and the contents ditched on the carpet; floorboards lifted and abandoned. Even the kitchen had been ransacked: the fridge emptied and the rotting food dumped on the floor. The intruders had not forgotten the bedrooms: sheets and blankets had been torn to ribbons and thrown higgledy-piggledy across the place; pillows sliced open; wardrobes eviscerated and Sue's clothes that had once hung there so tidily had been cut to ribbons; her chest of drawers had been up-ended and her lingerie ripped apart; her dressing table voided and the perfumes and cosmetics hurled around the room.

'Well,' said Sue surveying the destruction, the tears

239

sparkling in her eyes, 'I'll say one thing for the blackguards who did this. They were thorough. They've missed nothing.'

'Oh, Sue, Sue,' Mike exclaimed, putting his arms around her and kissing her on the forehead. 'I'm so sorry that this should happen to you. Thank God that you were not here when these hoodlums arrived to do their dirty work or it might have been you who'd have been damaged.'

'But what did they want, Mike? Why did they trash my place? Were they looking for something? Did they think I'd smuggled in valuable contraband? Or maybe they imagined I'd come to Zambelia in order to cause a revolution or something and they were looking for incriminating evidence. Though what they expected to find is beyond me.'

'My guess is that it has something to do with Nyoka and the Public Safety Unit. Perhaps it was a warning from his office to watch your step after what he'd heard was a provocative lecture. This vandalism is a shot across your bows.'

'Some shot! Well whatever it was, maybe we could try to tidy the place up a little and establish a little order though I'm afraid most of the things are damaged beyond repair. Tomorrow, I'll contact my British insurance company and see what is and what isn't covered. I didn't pay those exorbitant premiums for nothing, I hope.'

'And what about you, Sue,' Mike asked letting his gaze wander round the room. 'Doesn't this make you want to run back to England?'

'On the contrary, Mike. I want to find out who these bastards are and give them a taste of their own medicine. We peasants carrying a combination of Lancashire and Irish genes don't give in that easily. Now how about giving me a hand to re-establish some semblance of civilisation around here.'

'OK. Include me in,' said Mike.

***

For two hours they worked, frantically tidying, sweeping, washing down the floors, walls, curtains, and furniture, as if the place had suffered a fire. Finally, the battle against the chaos the wreckers had left behind was over and the place took on a more orderly appearance though much more required to be done and many of the damaged items would need to be replaced.

'All that has been like something out of a crime movie,' she said with a rueful smile. 'I never thought we'd restore normality. As far as I can tell, nothing valuable has been taken though I do seem to be missing a few books I know I had shipped out in my advance luggage. I don't know which ones as yet. I shall only be able to tell that after I've taken a full inventory. Oh, Mike, I'm so relieved that you were here to help. I can't tell you how grateful I am.'

He took her in his arms and held her close. He kissed her, gently at first. Their lips met more passionately.

'You are the most beautiful, wonderful creature I have ever met,' he said softly. 'Most people would have been overwhelmed at coming back and seeing the havoc that met our eyes when you opened the front door. Not you! "Where are they? Let me get at 'em'!" you said. Ever since I met you on the flight out here, I've not been able to get you out of my mind. I'm in love with you, Sue.'

Their eyes met. He looked at her wonderingly, his expression asking the unspoken question.

'Yes, Mike,' she whispered. 'The answer's yes.'

****

241

Chapter Twenty-One

Sue and the Censorship Board

It was the morning after their return from Mombo Island and Sue was sitting up in bed enjoying her first coffee which the faithful Sikio had brought her at eight o'clock. How she always relished that first cup! Her mind and body did not start to function fully until she'd replenished her caffeine intake to the required level of efficiency and this was a Zambelian blend which made it extra good and extra special. As she sat there savouring the flavour, her thoughts went back to the events of the previous day and their return from Mombo Island. What an awful shock it'd been to find her living room so ravaged! What on earth could they have been looking for? Why, she was an absolute newcomer to Zambelia and had been in the country just over a month! Damn it all, there hadn't been time for her to have done anything that deserved being house-searched unless giving a lecture on *Macbeth* and a visit to a leper colony were in some mysterious way against the law. Her puzzled thoughts were suddenly interrupted by the ringing of the phone in her study. Who could that be at this time? she wondered. Possibly Mike, though most unlikely at that early hour, to ask how she was feeling after the week-end on Mombo and if she'd recovered from the horror of finding her house so vandalised. Feeling a little miffed at having her thoughts and her coffee disturbed, she got out of bed, slipped on her dressing gown and went into the study to answer the call.

'Hello,' she said. 'Sue Delamere here. Who's speaking, please?'

'Good morning, Doctor Delamere,' a mellifluous voice replied. 'I am Major Kwanini and in charge of the Zambelia Censorship Board. I wonder if I could trouble you a little this morning.'

'Sorry. How do you mean "trouble me a little"?'

'We should appreciate, Doctor, if you could call and see us at the Board this morning.'

Sue's heart skipped a couple of beats. Censorship Board? What had she to do with censorship boards?

'But what's it all about, Major? I'm sure you know that I'm a recent arrival in Zambelia and know nothing about censorship.'

'Nothing to worry about. Only a couple of matters we'd like to clear up that's all. Shall we say eleven o'clock?'

The major managed to make the way he said "eleven o'clock" sound ominous as if he would brook no argument on the matter and his words were less of a suggestion than a command. Sue was completely baffled as to why but she had the strangest presentiment that she'd better obey or else...

'Very well, Major. I'll be there at eleven though I must say I haven't a clue as to why you should want to see me and at such short notice.'

***

Worried out of her mind, Sue phoned Mike for advice.

'I've had this call from a Major Kwanini at the Censorship Board and I have to confess, Mike, it's got me nervous and on edge. Could you please come over this morning as I'm in great need of some moral support, especially as I haven't a clue as to what they want me for?'

Mike didn't hesitate. 'I have a tutorial, Sue, until ten o'clock and then I'll be right over.'

'Good old Mike,' she thought. 'So dependable and ready to help as soon as he's needed.'

***

At ten-thirty, they drove over together to the office of the Zambelia Censorship Board in downtown Hekima.

'I can't imagine why I've been summoned, Mike,' she fretted. 'I've given only one talk and that was on *Macbeth*. Surely, they can't want to see me on the basis of a single lecture. Unless they found something incriminating when they raided my home. Perhaps the books that were missing have something to do with it?'

'Can you remember the titles of any of the missing books?'

'Not entirely sure, Mike, as I have so many books and I haven't had time to carry out a thorough check but off the top of my head, I seem to recall that one of them had the unusual title of "Shakespeare the Iconoclast".'

'I should think you'd be safe with that one. These Censorship boys wouldn't know the meaning of "iconoclast".'

For over an hour they sat together in a small ante-room waiting for someone in the Board offices to recognise their existence. The longer they waited, the more anxious Sue became.

'Making you wait is part of the process,' Mike said. 'Relax. You'll be OK, I'm sure.'

At last a female secretary emerged from the inner office. 'The Major will see you now.'

Both Sue and Mike stood up, ready to go into the inner office.

'Sorry,' the secretary said, 'Not you, Doctor Goodman. The Major wants to interview Doctor Delamere alone.'

Mike gave Sue a thumbs-up. 'You'll be all right now Sue. I know you'll get through this without any problems. You stick to your guns.'

At the mention of the word "guns" the secretary looked up in alarm.

'No, not real guns,' Mike said quickly. 'It's merely a figure of speech.'

**

In the inner office, Major Kwanini sat with two smartly dressed men in tailor-made safari suits with silk cravats at the neck, both wearing the standard dark wrap-around glasses. Kwanini himself was courtesy personified, first standing up and offering Sue a chair before his desk.

'The two gentlemen here present,' the Major said, 'are from the Zambelian PSU, that is the Public Safety Unit, and they are here simply as observers. They will take no part in our discussion. First, let me say how sorry I am to have interrupted your university work, Doctor Delamere, but I want to discuss with you one or two matters that have come to our attention and are of some concern to us.'

Sue noted that, although the two strangers sitting at the desk may not have been participants in the discussion, that certainly didn't stop them from taking notes of everything that was said even though she was sure the proceedings were being tape-recorded as well.

'Why am I here? And why am I being interviewed like this?' Sue demanded. 'You say "matters that have come to your attention" but since I have been here such a short time, what can these matters possibly be? As far as I know I have broken no law.'

'Maybe so. Maybe so,' Kwanini said in his most unctuous tone of voice and forming a steeple with his hands, 'but we have been apprised of the fact that you gave a lecture, your first, that was incendiary in nature and likely to stir up the students against the established government.'

'But my lecture was on Shakespeare's *Macbeth* and had nothing to do with the Zambelian government about which I know practically nothing.'

'You must think we are naïve and stupid, Doctor Delamere. There is such a thing as a veiled reference. The students are not slow to grasp hidden meanings and, by all accounts, were not slow to do so on this occasion even if it *was* your first lecture.'

'I can only say that my intentions,' Sue said angrily, 'were to further knowledge, understanding and appreciation of Shakespeare and are in no way connected with Zambelian politics or government policies.'

'Your predecessor said much the same thing when we interviewed him only six or seven months ago. He too was stirring up the students with his anti-authority, anti-government speeches. Look where that's landed him! But let's forget the lecture for a moment. I must tell you now that our investigations into your background have revealed that you were once a member of the British Communist Party and were a regular attender at their meetings.'

Sue was nonplussed. Where on earth had he got such misinformation? Me, a communist, she thought? I've never heard of anything so crazy! For some unknown reason, these people are determined to castigate me. This situation is not unlike those Senator McCarthy pogroms in the USA that we used to read about years ago.

'I haven't the faintest idea of what you're talking about,' she protested at last. 'I am *not* and have *never* been a member of such an organisation. I have no interest in politics or joining any political party whatsoever. My field is English Literature and that is what I have been appointed to teach.'

One of the silent men sitting by Kwanini's side handed him a note which the major quickly scanned. According to our research, you were a member of...' he recited, reading from the note, "both the Left Tea Party Group, an ultra red debating society, and also the Manchester Marxist Discussion group whose stated aims were to hold discussions based on the works of Karl Marx and other left wing thinkers". What do you have to say about that?'

Sue could not believe what she was hearing. 'But that must be well over twenty years ago!' she exploded. 'I was a young eighteen year old student and I took part in many different Student Union Societies. Everyone did. We joined various societies when we first became students. If I remember correctly, I joined the Sirens Choir as well but that doesn't make me a Lesbian also the Flat Earth Debating Group and that doesn't make me a medievalist.'

'Maybe so, but having been a member of a Marxist group does make you out to be a liar for when you entered our country, you declared to the Immigration Officer at the airport that you had never been a member of the Communist Party which is patently untrue and you have just told the same lie to us. Let's change the subject for a moment. How do you explain the seditious literature we found on your premises?'

'Seditious literature! Found on my premises! What does that word "found" mean? My house was ransacked and trashed during my absence. What right do you have to break into a person's home and go through personal belongings. Did you have a search warrant?'

'In this country, madam, we don't need a search warrant if we suspect someone pursuing anti-government activities. State security takes precedence over private inconvenience. But let's get down, as you English people put it, to brass tacks. On your book shelves, we found a wide selection of provocative and anarchistic literature. We cannot understand how these got past the censor unless you used cunning, underhand methods to sneak them into the country.'

'I cannot begin to imagine what you are getting at,' a bewildered Sue objected. 'I have no such literature since politics and government are not my particular interests. Which books are you alluding to?'

'How about these?' he said reading from a list.

Mutiny on the Bounty by Charles Nordoff and James Norman Hall;

Literature and Revolution by Leon Trotsky;

The French Revolution by Thomas Carlyle;

Love and Revolution: An Elizabethan Anthology;

Radicalism in the Arts: the Elizabethan Renaissance;

Civil War and Literature;

The Reformation: Authority under attack;

Shakespeare the Iconoclast;

The Biological Time-Bomb

Sue was aghast. 'Some of those books are great works of literature for God's sake,' she almost screamed. 'They have nothing whatsoever to do with overthrowing governments, especially Zambelia's. Can't you see that?'

'Please, madam,' Kwanini said, now the epitome of tranquillity. 'You will please stay calm and refrain from taking the name of God in vain. Do you realize on the evidence we have before us, we could have you arrested or at the very least deported. Why do you need books on these subjects?'

Sue realised it was useless taking part in an argument she could never win. Kwanini was a philistine and determined to find her guilty no matter what.

'You must have strange laws,' she said defiantly, 'if you can arrest a person for possessing books which are meant to stimulate and inform. What possible precedent can there be for such blatant injustice?'

'Perhaps a couple of letters on our files might convince you,' Kwanini now said taking some papers from the middle drawer of his desk. 'Here is a case I dealt with only last week. Let me read from this letter to His Excellency, Life President. I quote:

"Your excellency, I have the honour to report that police have arrested Mr Aaron Chipoka for subversion. Police searched his house and found three suspicious books:

"Marxism today"; "Spy Counter Spy"; "What is to be done"? by Lenin

Mr Chipoka graduated BA at Zambelia University, joined government service as a teacher and became a District Commissioner. May I be directed by your Excellency in this matter?"

'Let me read now the answer from His Excellency:

"Have this man arrested, imprisoned and after whatever sentence he serves, he must be detained indefinitely..."

'So you can see, my dear Doctor Delamere, how seriously this government takes such matters. Chipoka's case is similar to your own, is it not? You can see now how my hands are tied and the books which you have illegally imported by means of advance baggage are much more dangerous than Mr Chipoka's. Why are you so interested in subjects like, Radicalism, Civil War, attacks on Authority, Time Bombs, Iconoclasm? Yes, madam, we are not ignorant here in Zambelia and we know what Iconoclasm means.'

'I think the case of Chipoka is extreme,' Sue replied. 'I can't see how you can think me subversive. I've been in Zambelia only a short time.'

'So you think Chipoka's case extreme, do you. Here is another and this one was treated in the same way but involved far less subversion than in your own case. Let me read it to you:

"Your Excellency, I have the honour to report a request to issue a passport to Michael Mbira to go to the USA for studies. May I have the formal approval of your Excellency

before Immigration issues the passport? I am, sir, your Excellency's most obedient servant."

'This is what His Excellency replied: *"Pick this man up right away and lock him away for ever."*

One of the two taciturn men now handed Kwanini a second note which Kwanini examined. He was a slow reader because it was a full ten minutes before he looked up, now with a triumphant and malicious smile on his lips.

'According to a report which has reached our ears, you did in a conversation with a university student and colleague utter the following, and once again I quote verbatim:

"The authorities here in Zambelia are so dictatorial that they're no better than Hitler's Germany or Stalinist Russia. We must do something about it; we simply cannot turn a blind eye?"

Sikio, her house servant! And to think she imagined she could trust him when all the time he'd been in the pocket of the government and probably reporting everything she did and said. The scales fell from her eyes in that instant and she realised she was being set up.

She heard Kwanini's voice again. 'Doctor Delamere, I must ask you point blank. Did you or did you not say these words?'

'What you have quoted,' she protested vehemently, 'has been taken completely out of context and given a particular slant. I did not say those words in that particular order and therefore I have to say that the accusation is a despicable and downright lie.'

'You can see, Doctor Delamere,' Kwanini said, 'that, given the information we have about you, your own case is much more serious than those I have quoted to you and I have no alternative but to send a full report of your behaviour to the Life President for his evaluation. I think that concludes this morning's interview. I shall communicate His Excellency's decision to you as soon as I receive it. It shouldn't take more than a day or two. Meanwhile you should stay in your house and hold yourself ready for a visit from a government representative. Thank you for attending and good morning to you. Give our regards to Doctor Goodman who, I am informed, is waiting for you outside.'

Sue realised that not only was the interview terminated but that there was little point in trying to argue her case. Like banging her head against a brick wall. She walked out of the room not only angry but scared. Maybe Mike would be able to advise her as to what to do next.

On the way back to her house, Sue gave Mike a full account of the interview describing angrily how they had accused her of being a Communist as she had joined a student's Marxist Society twenty odd years ago..

'It's utterly mad,' she wept. 'I was a teenager when I went to university and I only joined because my boyfriend, who was a student of philosophy, had joined and I wanted to be with him. I hadn't the slightest interest in Marxism then and I still don't.'

Mike said nothing throughout her account but simply pursed his lips in dismay as she outlined all that Kwanini had said. When she'd finally finished telling him about the two cases Kwanini had quoted, they had reached her home. Before going inside, Mike put his finger on his lips, pointed to the house and shook his head indicating that there should be no further talk inside the house. Before they went in, he took her in his arms to reassure her.

'Don't worry, Sue,' he whispered, 'we'll get through this somehow.'

She noticed the way he had said "we". So quick to accept *her* problem as *his* problem too.

When outside and clear of the house, he spoke again. 'Remember your house and telephone are bugged. It looks too as if you can't trust your house servant, Sikio, either.'

'Point taken, Mike. I hadn't forgotten about the bugging and the wire tap.'

'OK Sue. It's best always to confine our conversation until we are on the outside in the garden and right away from the house. It's clear to me what is going to happen next. You will be either P.I.'d and deported or worse - arrested. You have no alternative now, my darling, but to pack up a few things and get the hell out of here ASAP. Either the police or Immigration Officers will soon be paying you a visit and we must make sure you're not around when they do. It's uncertain as to how long it'll take the Public Safety guys to swing into action but it's probably best to err on the safe side. Advisable to avoid trying to flee via the only airport and it's most likely that the borders will be watched too. Is there any place here in Zambelia where you could be securely hidden away? Do you know anyone who could help? What about those friends you mentioned to me on the flight here?'

'Peter and Helen Halliday? They're old family friends but they live in State House right next to the palace in Lundazi! Hardly the place to run to! Right under the nose of the president.'

'On the contrary,' Mike said thoughtfully, 'right under their noses might be the last place they'll look if you can persuade your friends to hide you. It's a lot to ask of them as they'd be risking their own necks.'

'They're friends of long standing, Mike and there's no reason why I shouldn't at least *ask* them but, Mike, how do I phone them? The lines are bugged and the police would be on to me like a shot.'

'I have a secure private line at the university for use in hospital emergencies. As far as I know, the authorities don't have access to it as yet. We don't have any alternative but to try it. I'll phone them early this evening, give them a brief run-down on the situation and I'll be back as soon as I can, certainly before it gets dark. Provided they agree to give you sanctuary, I'll have the Ambulance Land Rover fully fuelled and we'll make a run for it to Lundazi using secondary roads. Meanwhile, pack a small bag of essentials and hold yourself ready to do a bunk. Also get your servant, Sikio, out of the house on some pretext.'

***

After Mike had gone, Sue went back into the house only to find Sikio waiting. He had assumed a deadpan, poker-faced expression as if he had pulled down all the shutters in front of his eyes and there was no way of knowing what was going on in his mind. Sue looked at him steadily for a few moments before he dropped his eyes. She in turn gave no hint that she was aware of his perfidy in reporting her private conversations to the authorities. Instead she gave him an unusually long errand which would require him to go into town to shop at several dukas for sundry provisions.

'Sorry I can't give you a lift into town, Sikio, but I have a great deal of work to prepare for my lectures this week. I hope you don't mind going on foot.'

'Not at all, memsahib. The walk will do me good.' He seemed relieved at the excuse to escape from the house and from under her searching gaze.

At least, Sue thought, the errand will get him out of the way for a couple of hours and, if he meets friends and any of his innumerable relatives, as he invariably does, maybe longer.

The moment Sikio had left, Sue went to work in a frenzy packing an overnight bag. What should she take? She had no idea how long she'd be away or even if she'd be coming back at all, but the important thing was to be ready when Mike returned with the Land Rover. Hurriedly she went round the house collecting essentials for a possible longish absence: toiletries, underclothes, day and night wear, two pairs of comfortable shoes; a few items of stationery like pens, pencils and writing paper. She also thought it might be advisable to take a novel to while away any long periods of waiting she might be forced to endure. She searched the bookshelves for a long one and chose one of the innocuous kind - if such a book existed in Zambelia. Finally selected Steinbeck's "The Grapes of Wrath" thinking that should keep her going for a while even though she had read it several times before. Lastly, and most important, she collected together all the spare money she could lay her hands on. In emergency situations such as the present one, she thought, ready cash is always an invaluable commodity to have at one's disposal. She sat down and did something that was unusual for her. She poured herself a stiff gin and tonic to steady her nerves.

She thought, 'What a crazy, crazy situation I've found myself in. I came to Zambelia in good faith with the hope of opening students' eyes to the beauty of English literature. Talk of innocent abroad! I walked right into a bear trap and now I'm beside myself with fear and apprehension. Oh, Mike, do hurry back and bring me good news. Tell me Peter and Helen Halliday will take me because I have nowhere else to run. If they turn me down, I don't know what will become of me.'

She eyed the bottle of Gordon's and was tempted to have a second drink but resisted, knowing from past experience, that another drink, far from cheering her up, was likely to have the opposite effect and make her feel maudlin and depressed.

****

Chapter Twenty-Two

Flight

It was a good two hours before Mike came back and Sue had almost given up hope when there he was striding up the path with a broad smile on his face and she knew right away that he was bringing good tidings. How she needed that, the way she was feeling! And what a relief that he had made it back before Sikio returned from the shopping expedition! Once again, Mike placed a finger on lip and beckoned her to come out to the car. Grabbing her hold-all, she ran out into the garden and straight into his arms.

'Good news, Sue!' he said, hugging her for all he was worth. 'Your friends have agreed to help you. We have arranged to meet the Hallidays outside the Lundazi Inn at ten o'clock tonight. Peter warned us though not to go into the Inn as it is the haunt of many government officials and it would simply be asking for trouble. We simply have to wait outside in the Land Rover until he comes to tell us our next move.'

'Oh, Mike,' she said. 'I'm so relieved that I have somewhere to run! If they'd said "No", I don't know what I'd have done.'

'Well, my girl, we'd better be on our way. It's seven o'clock now and I reckon it'll be a good two and half hours' drive to Lundazi taking the back roads. That should put us in time to meet the Hallidays. You'll notice that I've brought the 'Leprosy' ambulance in case we are stopped by the police, though we shouldn't have any trouble with them on the way as I doubt if Major Kwanini will have had an answer yet from President Matata as to what to do with you. So that should give us a day's grace, maybe two if we're lucky, to organise something.'

Sue didn't like the use of that word "something". What did that mean? Going into permanent hiding? Making a run for it to Mombasa or Dar-es-Salaam or over the mountains and across Lake Victoria? It didn't bear thinking about.

'Nevertheless,' Mike continued, 'I think we should err on the safe side in case there's a search party already out looking for you. I think it'd be best if you travelled in the back of the ambulance and talked to me through the little communication window. In the unlikely event that we're stopped by the police, it'd be best if you got into the bed and got under the sheets. Pretend you're a leper.'

'How on earth do I do that, Mike?'

'Here, wear this beret to cover up your hair and put on these sun glasses. But if any dare-devil policeman is rash enough to look in the back, I doubt he'll come anywhere near you.'

'I'm scared, Mike. Really scared.'

'You don't look it, Sue. On the contrary, you look quite calm under the circumstances.'

'Fear manifests itself in different ways, Mike. Some tremble, others make jokes to cover up. Me, I simply try to put on a brave face.'

***

It was turning dark when they set out. A screen of thick cloud hid the moon and the stars. For the first half hour of the drive, neither said anything. Mike's concentration was focussed on negotiating the dusty murram roads in the dark while Sue was too pre-occupied thinking about how the Hallidays would react when she dumped herself in their lap, and what her long-term future plans were going to be. It was Mike who broke the silence by sliding back the dividing window.

'Well, Sue, that's Hekima left well behind; we should reach Lundazi in about forty-five minutes or so. I'm glad we managed to clear the township without meeting any inquisitive neighbours or the police. The leprosy sign on the windscreen would probably have done the trick though; it's usually enough to frighten off nosy-parkers.'

They had made better time than Mike had expected and he was rejoicing in their good fortune because so many things could have gone wrong. The road had become steeper as they reached the hills approaching the Zambelian capital and he had been concentrating on negotiating a series of bumps and hair-pin bends for quite a few miles when their luck ran out. The car engine began to splutter and to lurch. Finally, it stopped.

'Bugger it!' Mike cursed. 'That would have to happen now and at this god-forsaken place in the middle of nowhere! I'm damned if I know what's happened! The car's only recently been serviced in the university workshop.'

'I hope you know something about car mechanics, Mike, or we're in big trouble.'

'Don't I know it! I'm not much good fixing engines unless it's something simple. Keep your fingers crossed, Sue. And we'd better be prepared to bluff our way out of it if any snoopy policeman comes along to investigate; though I can't see that happening in such a remote spot as this.'

Mike pulled the bonnet catch and armed with a Hunter torch and a set of spanners, went out to investigate the trouble. It took no more than five minutes for him to find the problem.

'Good news, Sue. The lead had come adrift from the battery; no doubt caused by this badly corrugated road we've been driving on. Wait till I see that careless mechanic back at the university! Anyway it's a simple matter of replacing it and tightening it up and we can be on our way.'

Mike got back into the cab and turned the ignition key. There was a healthy roar as the engine fired.

'So there *is* a God after all,' Sue said. 'I was saying my prayers like mad just now, I can tell you.'

'Yes, I heard your prayers, Sue,' Mike laughed, 'and I decided to grant your wish.'

'Huh! Very funny!'

***

The Land Rover picked up speed and they were soon rolling along at a healthy fifty miles an hour.

'I'm beginning to feel like a burglar,' Sue said suddenly, 'like a fugitive from justice.'

'In a way, Sue, that's what you are, though on the contrary, you're a fugitive from *in*justice.'

'Maybe so, Mike, but as we drove out of Hekima, I couldn't help wondering if I hadn't got things out of proportion. It's like something out of Hollywood movie. I know I was being monitored in my office at the university but I'd no idea that my home had been wired as well. As for having a few books that have harmlessly revolutionary titles, surely the censorship people are intelligent enough to see they're not dangerous. They couldn't be after me only for that? Come to think of it, there's no definite evidence that they're actually chasing me, is there? Maybe it'll die down and I can get on with my teaching, which is why I came to this country in the first place. Are we being paranoid about it all? I mean, the notion of the Zambelian police and Public Safety officers accusing me of seditious behaviour because I gave what they saw as a provocative lecture on *Macbeth;* well, it's beginning to seem a trifle far-fetched, don't you think, Mike?'

258

'Paranoid, Sue? Us! Surely it's the other way round. It's this bloody Zambelian government that's paranoid; they suspect everyone of plotting against them. They believe there are anarchists and revolutionaries behind every bush. As for your house being monitored, you can take it from me that it was well and truly wired; your telephone was tapped and the house was bugged.'

'I've been meaning to ask you about that, Mike. What's the difference between "tapped" and "bugged"? Or are they the same thing?'

'Not the same thing, Sue. Tapping is used to describe a hardware link anywhere along a telephone line. The tap can then be connected to a tape recorder. A bug is a form of radio transmitter used to intercept a conversation.'

'I am surprised you think that a third world country such as Zambelia could be capable of such electronic wizardry, Mike.'

'No wizardry involved, Sue. It's now possible by means of a cheap transformer, to convert an ordinary loudspeaker into an incredibly sensitive mike which can amplify and record conversations. People are not aware of what goes on in today's world of micro-technology. You can put a pin-sized camera or microphone anywhere – in a button-hole, or in a lady's earring. I've even heard of a toothpick microphone, whatever that is, but you don't need anything as sophisticated as that.'

'Surely Mike, this "Big-Brother-Is-Watching-You" stuff is an exaggeration?'

'Take my word for it, Sue. It's no exaggeration. Electronic surveillance has developed beyond imagination. At the present time, there is a satellite rotating round the earth about 150 miles up and it's surveying the whole world twenty-four/seven. The resolution of these cameras is such that they can read the number on a car registration plate, and can recognize a face anywhere in the world. Thank God, Zambelia is not as advanced as the Western world but even

259

here, their listening devices are pretty sophisticated. If you think the suspicions about the dangers attached to your own position are unfounded, you've only to consider the fate of your predecessor, Frank Johnson. We know he's in Tagooma prison but no-one has had any news about him for some time.'

'I'm sure you're right, Mike. My talk of things being exaggerated here is probably wishful thinking. It's like a nightmare and I'm praying that it'll all go away.'

'Anyway, we're here, Sue! The Lundazi Inn and it's ten o'clock! Here's hoping the Hallidays are not too late as I am driving straight back to Hekima to allay any suspicions the Public Safety police might have when they come to investigate me as I'm sure they will. They are bound to have learned that you and I have been seen together. I shall of course swear blind that I haven't seen you after your visit to the Censorship Board. I can well understand that....'

Suddenly, he slammed the window shut. 'Sue!' he yelled. 'Quickly into the bed! Put on the beret and the glasses! Cover yourself up! Two PSU Officers are coming out of the Inn! They're looking at us suspiciously! Pray they don't decide to carry out a thorough check.'

Sue didn't argue. She obeyed and got under the blanket, asking herself stupidly, 'How does one make oneself look like a leper? Please God, don't let them look inside.'

She could hear Mike talking to the officers outside.

'I'm here from Mombo Island, officer. Just collected a patient to take back to the leproserie. Then, next to Lundazi Hospital to pick up two more. The case I have in the back is a particularly bad case. Would you like to take a look?'

She could hear the buzz of conversation but could not make out what they were saying.

After what seemed like an eternity, she heard Mike call to her. 'It's OK now, Sue. For some reason, after they had checked our 'Leper-on-Board' sign they decided not to investigate further but seemed in a hurry to get away.'

'Thank the Lord for that,' she sighed.

'So your prayer worked once again, Sue.'

'Mike, you too are taking a big risk on my behalf. How can I ever thank you?'

'I'm sure, we'll think of something,' he grinned, kissing her on the lips. 'And now I see your friends, the Hallidays, have pulled up in a BMW over the road. If you get out of the back, we can walk across and greet them. But we'd better make it snappy before any more inquisitive types decide to come a-looking. I shall stay long enough to say hello and I'll be on my way.'

***

Sue and Mike got out of the Land Rover and walked swiftly across the road to meet their friends who were now standing outside their car. Helen was the first to move.

'Sue, Sue,' she exclaimed, embracing her, 'we were so devastated to hear your news. What a crazy misunderstanding! Peter and I are sure it'll be cleared up in good time.'

'I echo Helen's sentiments,' Peter said. 'We were taken aback by the notion that our friend Sue could be anything but an excellent teacher. As for her being a dissident, we've never heard of anything so barmy in all our lives. We're sure that madman Kiboko is somewhere at the back of it.' He turned to Mike. 'And thanks Mike for looking after Sue and driving her up here.'

Sue said, 'I'm only sorry for having got you, my friends, so embroiled in this rubbish. Let's hope it's cleared up pronto so that we can all get back to work.'

'I second that,' Mike said. 'So what's the score here in Lundazi? Will you be able to hide Sue until this thing blows over?'

'We've got some excellent news in this regard,' Peter said. 'The Senior Aide to the President is a certain Nixon Makau and he's agreed to provide Sue with secret accommodation until this difficult situation is resolved. At the moment, I can't say any more than that since we don't know what he has in mind but rest assured, Sue will be safe in his hands as he is a mighty powerful person at State House. And two other pieces of good news: Colonel Kiboko is away visiting Tagooma Prison, Schneider is busy in his medical centre and Big Mama Marianne, is away with her sisters, Zenobia and Nefertiti, attending a fashion show in Milan. On her way back she is also hoping to buy furnishings and works of art in Rome for the new palace and her own mansion at the Lake.'

'Again!' Mike said. 'She must have visited Europe a dozen times shopping this year.'

'Yes, again!' Peter continued. 'She has a credit card giving her access to state Treasury funds and several foreign bank accounts. God knows how much she spends on clothes, furnishings and works of art for herself and her family. I wouldn't be surprised if we had to raise yet more taxes to fund these shopping trips.'

Sue said, 'I can't begin to tell you how grateful I am to all of you for the risks you're taking on my behalf but at the same time, I'm extremely worried about what's going to happen. You say things like "when this thing blows over" and "when this situation is resolved" but I don't know what any of these things mean. It sounds like Wilkins Mickawber's waiting for "something to turn up". I only know that I've walked into a minefield and I don't know how the heck I'm going to get out of it.'

'At this moment,' Mike said, 'we don't know the answer to that either but trust us, Sue. We'll do anything, even start a

262

revolution, if necessary, to see that you're safe. Now, I'm going to have to rush back to Hekima before I'm missed and before Major Nyoka and his P.S.Unit gang come to pay me a visit, which I know for certain they will. Be sure of this, Sue, my love, I'll be back within a day or two as soon as I can shake them off.'

'In that regard,' Helen said, smiling mysteriously, 'we have devised a little scheme to get you past the guard at the gate. His name is Jason and I have told him that I am suffering from chronic pain in the lower back and that I shall be receiving regular visits from my chiropractor.'

'I'm so sorry to hear that,' Mike said. 'I suppose it's a result of all the bending and stretching you do working in the palace. Who's the chiropractor? I might know him.'

'I believe you know him well,' Peter chuckled. 'It's you. We've given you the fictitious name of Dr Alan Finlay after the well-known TV character. We've cleared your name with the guard and you will be coming to give Helen "treatment" every week-end.'

'You two are a devious pair,' Sue laughed. 'So much intrigue! You belong in a John Le Carre spy story and come to think of it, so do I!'

'Well, it sounds great to me,' Mike said enthusiastically. 'I don't mind being Doctor Finlay as long as there's no gruff, grumpy old Dr Cameron bossing me about. So expect me over every Friday night and I shall stay until Sunday night, if that's OK. Now I must be on my way if I'm to avoid suspicion in Hekima.'

Sue and Mike embraced and Mike ran across the road to the Land Rover. There was a revving of the engine and his red tail-lights disappeared into the dust kicked up from his tyres.

****

263

Chapter Twenty-Three
Jack Zulu looking for his brothers

Jack Zulu crouched at the edge of the bush outside the main entrance of Hekima's State House, and waited. He was trembling with apprehension for he felt in his bones that to-night, he was going to find out for sure - one way or the other. He looked at the sky. The sun was low over the Plateau. It wouldn't be long before the man he was expecting came through the big iron gate.

For five long weeks, ever since his younger brothers had failed to turn up for the beginning of term, Jack had been racked by fear and anxiety. At first, he'd been merely concerned and puzzled at their absence. It was most unlike them not to be there on the opening day for he knew how keen they were on their studies and how much they enjoyed life in college. He did not believe in anticipating trouble, however, and had put their non-appearance down to some minor illness. Perhaps somebody in the family had suffered a bout of malaria or a dose of flu. But in that case, he asked himself, why had they not got in touch with him to let him know what was happening? No, it had to be something more serious. He had decided to put a hold on his imagination and his fears until he heard something definite. The trouble was that communication in Zambelia was extremely difficult. He had tried several times to contact Dr Mike Goodman at the week-end but unusually for him the latter had been away from campus for a good many days. As for his own relatives, his parents were both dead and his two uncles were difficult to reach, one being a medical orderly in a refugee camp in the extreme south of the country whilst the other one lived in their Chunzani village where there was no telephone. Perhaps his two younger brothers were still with them for some unknown reason. The only way of reaching the uncles was by means of an agonizingly slow passing of messages along the jungle telegraph. Using a combination of long-distance bus-drivers and various other travellers, he'd managed to send off an inquiry to his relatives. He'd had to wait an anguished ten days for an answer via a fish-seller who had brought his merchandise to Hekima market.

The reply did nothing to allay his fears. On the contrary, it filled him with doubt and foreboding. The twins, the return message had said, had set off in the normal way on the Saturday before the opening of college; they had been in the company of Daniel Chitanda and Eliud Chumvi - students in the English Department.

Hurriedly, he had found his way to the hostel where the students lived only to be told by one of their fellows that the two young men were away at a wedding. 'A shot-gun wedding' the friend had added with a wry grin. On tenterhooks, Jack had had to wait yet another week, his anxiety growing by the day. His twin brothers, Andrew and Bernard, had been missing now for over three weeks and still no word had been heard. There must be some serious reason for this; they couldn't simply have vanished into thin air.

'Yes. Your brothers were with us for part of the way,' Daniel had told him when he finally came back, 'but we split up into pairs, thinking it would be easier to pick up a lift that way. We were amazed to see them go riding past in a Land Rover which was part of the motorcade carrying the President and Colonel Kiboko. Yes, the very same Kiboko who broke my toes, fractured my arm, blacked my eye and is loathed and feared by all Zambelia.'

Daniel's news had sent cold shivers down Jack's spine as the truth began to unfold. The only solution was to confront the local police and demand an explanation. But Major Nyoka had been unable to shed any light on the matter and had hinted that Kiboko was something of a homicidal lunatic and a law unto himself.

'Why not,' he'd suggested - somewhat maliciously Jack had thought at the time - 'ask someone from Hekima State House? The old chef there is of your tribe and comes from the same district as yourself. If your brothers were ever in State House, he's the one who should be able to tell you something.'

Filled with despair and dismay, Jack had arranged a secret meeting with Maurice Mpishi, the chef. Waiting now outside State House, he was on edge and overwrought for deep down, he had a hunch that he already knew what the chef was going to tell him. How he wished and prayed that he was wrong in his supposition. Within the hour, he was going to hear the news he dreaded and he would gladly have given his life and career for it not to be true. He climbed into the thick bush near the wall and waited. It was gradually becoming dark and in a couple of hours, the sun would be gone and night would fall.

Maurice Mpishi signed the 'pass-out' book at the sentry's lodge and passed through the gate into the main road which led into Hekima township. He had walked no more than fifty yards when he heard from the voice from the bush.

'Psst. Over here,' Jack whispered.

The old cook looked nervously about him to make sure he'd not been followed, and stepped off the road into the undergrowth.

'This way,' said Jack in his native Chunzani dialect. 'We'll walk in the wood. No-one will see or hear us there. If any of Kiboko's men spotted us talking together, it would be the end of the line for us.'

'I pray to God that no-one did see us,' the chef answered, trembling in fear. 'Colonel Kiboko is dining with Major Nyoka at the Hekima Inn today and if he knew about the

266

subject of this meeting, he'd have us both in the cells and have us shot.'

'They walked a while in silence until they were deep in the darkest part of the forest.

''Now, tell me, Mr Mpishi, for God's sake,' Jack asked. 'Did you see my brothers at any time in State House?'

Despite the isolation of the spot, the cook was still on edge.

'I did not see them with my own eyes but there are stories of two young men who arrived with the motorcade a few weeks ago.'

'Stories? What stories?'

'That two young men arrived with Colonel Kiboko and the stand-in President. I myself cooked two meals which were taken to them by the soldiers. I even washed the two empty plates later but I had no sight of the visitors.'

Jack's heart skipped a beat when he asked. 'So you cannot confirm that they were my brothers and you do not know what happened to these "visitors"?'

The old man's answer made Jack's flesh creep. 'I don't know for sure that they were your brothers,' the chef whispered anxiously. 'but later that night, the head gardener – Philip Thomas Gichuru - was told there were two bodies but they were not to be buried; instead he was to put them in the Land Rover as they were to be taken immediately to the Matata Medical Research Bureau in Lundazi.'

'Oh, my God!' exclaimed Jack now grief-stricken. 'Was there no trace left to establish the identity of the victims?'

'Nothing. Kiboko ordered his soldiers to destroy their clothes and belongings. But, when I swept the refectory floor later, I found they had missed something. This small badge must have fallen from a coat lapel.'

When he saw the pin, Jack knew for sure. He felt a twisting of his stomach muscles and a freezing paralysis enveloped his whole body. He struck a match and examined the badge more closely. He shuddered and went white to the lips.

'Bernard's,' he said, horror-struck.

'All his fears, all his nightmares had come true. His two young brothers were gone along with their hopes and their dreams. He had not been there to protect them and now there was nothing he could do for them. Suddenly he was filled with despair. His plans to become a doctor one day were irrelevant. What was the point in anything? He would give up the university and the need to study; he would free himself of duties and obligations, abandon life itself. He felt a raging and impotent fury and a desire to retaliate blindly against not only Kiboko but all those involved in the cold-hearted murder of his twin brothers.

Kiboko has brought darkness and death to Zambelia and now he brings it into my life, he thought. He has destroyed all hope. Everyone in Zambelia knows that he is devoid of humane feeling and cares not whose life he ruins in his perverted lust for power. With the deaths of Andrew and Bernard, I have nothing more to lose; I have lost all because Kiboko has destroyed my *raison d'etre*. Today, I vow that my chief purpose in life will be to destroy him for the good of Zambelia. He must be stopped no matter what the cost.

'Tell me, *mzee*, dear old man, where is Kiboko now?' he asked of the chef.

'He has come to Hekima to see Major Nyoka. I know they planned to go to dinner at the Inn as they usually do on these visits because I was instructed not to prepare food for them. I heard that they will be going over to Tagooma to inspect the prisoners later. I know Kiboko wishes to be back in Lundazi later tonight.'

There was only one thing left for Jack Zulu to do. He thanked the frightened chef for his courage and, in a trance-like state, returned to the university. He let himself into the surgical wing and went into the empty operating theatre. There, he unlocked the cupboard where the instruments were kept. Selecting the largest scalpel he could find, he left the department. He could hear Mike Goodman lecturing to the first year group - the one his brothers should have been attending. He crept out quietly as he didn't wish to see or talk to anyone. He wanted only to leave and complete the desperate mission he had set himself. Since he could see no point in carrying on, he cared not what they did to him after that.

Grimly, he strode towards Tagooma. The sun was beginning to slip behind the Plateau when he arrived there and the light was gradually fading but there would be sufficient for him to do the job he had in mind.

He found a vacant seat at the open-air café outside the prison. The waiter approached him nervously, could he have sensed in Jack's strange smiling expression that something serious was amiss? Jack ordered a Fanta and a cheese sandwich, suddenly remembering how hungry he was. He gazed around him. Most of the tables were occupied by young male students - and the bar girls - laughing and drinking and enjoying their sundowners.

The waiter returned with his order and Jack paid up immediately. After all, it wouldn't be fair to saddle the man with an unpaid bill. The Fanta was over-sweet and the sandwich tasteless but no matter. Jack glanced at his watch, a cheap watch but fairly accurate. It registered seven thirty. His quarry would emerge any moment now. Jack pulled his chair to the right to give himself a better view of the road leading out of Hekima. Then he saw it. The police Land-Rover with full headlights blazing; it had come to collect Kiboko from the prison. Jack watched the car getting nearer - his Fanta half-finished, the sandwich half-eaten. He put his hand in his pocket and gripped the handle of the knife; it felt good and reassuring as he held it securely against his thigh.

The Public Safety soldiers parked the vehicle in front of the prison gate and waited for the colonel to appear. Kiboko was pleased with himself today after an afternoon's entertainment killing and baiting the prisoners. He was feeling smug and content with good reason for in his pocket, he had a cheque from Tulshidas for half-a-million pounds. His own share would be well over a hundred thousand. Not bad for a poor village kid who was living rough only a few years ago. Not only that, he might win back some of the kudos he had lost with Big Mama over the motorcade fiasco. What a fool Tulshidas had been though to write the cheque so readily. Once the money was cleared, he thought, I'll go back to the prison and enjoy a few more party games with the inmates. Tulshidas would be like a milch cow and he'd be milked until he was dry and then it would be goodbye to him. He made a mental note to see if he could think up a few more amusements equal to the party games that had gone down so well that day. There must be one or two new ones they could try. What about Blind Man's Buff or Hide and Seek? They'd be great fun as the prisoners were sure to give of their best with the stakes so high. Usual rules, of course. Losers get the chop.

He stepped out of the main prison gate and stretched his arms. It felt good to be alive. He could hardly wait to get back to Lundazi and to his comfortable home with Little Nelson there waiting for him. As he waited on the pavement for the major to join him to say his farewells, a young man at one of the tables at the café opposite suddenly stood up and strode determinedly towards him. The youth was smartly dressed in a light-blue safari suit – almost the standard dress of university students. He had a strange smile on his face as he approached. Happy though he was, the colonel was in no mood for socialising. Not another one seeking favours for some stupid relative who's got himself into some fix or other, he thought.

'Colonel Kiboko?' the young one asked. 'I wonder if I might have a quick word with you.'

'No time now,' Kiboko replied brusquely, trying to brush the young man aside.

'My name is Jack Zulu,' the youth persisted. 'I'm the brother of the two young men you had strangled a few weeks ago.'

'Stand aside,' Kiboko snapped and then his expression changed for the youth had suddenly pulled a large blade from his tunic pocket and was aiming it at Kiboko's neck. The action was swift but the colonel was swifter. Instinctively, he raised his left arm in protection and the scalpel plunged deeply into his forearm. With his free hand, he slammed a fist into Jack's face knocking him to the ground. Next he kicked him in the groin.

'Blast and damn you to hell,' he bellowed. 'You'll pay for that..... with your life, you stupid young bastard.'

Bleeding profusely, he withdrew his revolver and pointed it at Jack. At that moment, Nyoka joined them.

'No, Colonel,' he shouted. 'Not here. Not in front of the prison and that café with all those witnesses.'

'Very well,' gasped the colonel. 'Later. For now, this will have to do.'

'He struck Jack on the head with the butt of his revolver knocking him unconscious.

'Take the stupid young imbecile to the cells, Nyoka. I'll deal with him when I come for Tulshidas which shouldn't be too long. He'll be top of my list for party games. In the meanwhile, you'd better get me to hospital to stem this bleeding.'

****

Chapter Twenty-Four

Sue meets Nixon Makau

'Now what?' Sue said as soon as Mike's ambulance was out of sight. 'Helen and Peter, I'm worried sick about all this. I feel trapped in my worst nightmare and at this moment, I can't see any solution.'

'Trust in God,' Helen said. 'He'll find the answer.'

'And also in Nixon Makau,' added Peter.

They piled into the car and Peter drove quickly through the deserted streets until they reached the extensive villa complex of the state palace on the outskirts of Lundazi. The area was bounded by a dense, impenetrable, twelve-foot high thicket of razor-sharp Mauritius thorn.

Peter drove to the rear of the property and stopped the car several hundred yards away from the palace gate.

'I'm amazed that the grounds of the palace are so extensive,' Sue murmured from the back seat. 'There must be at least five hundred acres of woodland behind that hedge.'

'Probably more,' Helen said. 'Yes, the president likes space and lots of it and it's one of the most beautiful areas you can imagine; the rocky outcrops around us are clothed with cedar and pine forests all the year round, and, in season, with fields of wild orchids and gladioli. The palace complex itself is located in its own private thirty-acre site, an inner sanctum with numerous landscaped gardens kept in superb condition by twelve skilled gardeners. The president also believes in security because, not only does he have guards at the front and rear entrances to the outer woodland, he allows only eleven trusted people to have access to this inner villa where we each have our own private rondavel cottages.'

'Only eleven trusted people!' exclaimed Sue. 'They must be a highly privileged group of employees.'

'Not all the employees have access, Sue. The eleven people are: the President himself of course, Big Mama, Nixon Makau, Colonel Kiboko, Doctor Schneider, ourselves – how many's that?'

'That's seven,' Sue replied.

'Ah yes, the other four are the Head of Domestic Staff, Head Chef, Head Gardener, and finally the president's personal nurse, Florence, an Umbuka, same tribe as Nixon Makau. She not only attends to Matata's medical care but takes him for his daily constitutional, if you can call a ride in a wheel-chair a "constitutional".'

'So, apart from the eleven trustees who reside in the villa, what about the great army of staff the palace must need if it's to operate smoothly?'

'You do have a lot of questions, Sue. The army of staff, as you put it, are allowed on to the park and into the inner sanctum each morning. That's one of the jobs Peter and I are employed to do – to vet and supervise the staff when they arrive. I suppose we can be called Household Managers or Major Domos if you want a fancy title.'

'Most impressive security,' Sue said.

'Not only that, Sue,' rejoined Helen. 'This inner world is surrounded by a thick wall two miles long so, as you can well imagine, the place is like a fortress. Sometimes I think we could withstand the force of an invading army, not that we want to try such a thing. It's the ideal hideout. You'll be perfectly safe here, Sue.'

'Talking of security,' Peter added, 'I've parked here some distance away from the rear gate so that Sue can get in the back section of the car and hide under the blanket I've left there. I shall report our return to the guard. Sorry to ask this of you, Sue, but whatever happens, no-one must see you arrive here.'

'Don't worry, Peter,' Sue replied. 'I'm getting used to living under a blanket. It's like playing a star role in a Hitchcock thriller.'

Peter drove on a little further and stopped again outside a staunch iron gate manned by a member of the presidential guard.

'Be on the alert,' Peter called back. 'I have to speak to the sentry as I always do when coming in late. Mustn't arouse his suspicions, whatever we do.'

'Good evening, Jason,' he called to the officer who had now approached and was peering into the car. 'How's it going?'

'Good evening, Mr and Mrs Halliday,' the guard replied giving a smart salute. 'Everything's fine. No problems to report.'

'That's what we like to hear,' Peter said jovially.

'And good evening to you, Jason,' Helen said, joining in. 'How's your wife and daughter? Have they recovered from that bout of flu you were telling me about last week?'

'Oh, yes, Mrs Halliday. Both are feeling much better, thank you. Mr Halliday tells me you've been having back problems. I hope they're not too painful.'

'They are just about bearable, Jason. No doubt they're due to all the bending and stretching my job involves. I'm hoping that the chiropractor, Doctor Finlay will be able to help me when he comes to visit on Friday.'

'Hope so too, Mrs Halliday,' Jason said, opening the gate to let the car through.

Peter drove into the grounds along a gravelled road for about a mile until he reached a second gate set in a ten foot high stone wall where he got out, and after inserting his smart card into the slot, announced his name clearly into the built-in

274

microphone on one of the upright stanchions. 'Peter Halliday here.' The gate swung open.

'We are now in the inner sanctum,' Peter announced.

'I'm impressed,' Sue said emerging from the blanket. 'I never expected state-of-the-art technology here in Zambelia.'

'You'd be surprised how up-to-date things are here at the palace,' Peter said. 'Now before we do anything, I have been instructed to take you without delay to meet Nixon Makau.'

The three of them got out of the car and walked along a labyrinth of paths until they reached a cottage with its own private entrance where they stopped and waited.

'Now what?' Sue asked. 'Surely not yet another gate and another piece of wizardry!'

Helen said, 'I'm afraid so. We have to stay here until someone opens up.'

'What, no secret code to go through the door?'

'Not this time, Sue,' Peter replied. 'This one's really special. It's Nixon's own private arrangement; he insisted on extra precautions and secrecy for himself for some reason or other. I suspect he keeps secret state files hidden in his basement but I'm not sure. There's certainly no chance of strangers or intruders gaining access to *his* place. Whereas the last gate required two things for entry - card plus voice recognition, this one needs a third input, namely, a thumbprint and that has to be that of Nixon himself. He'll be aware that we are here and so we must now stand in front of the hidden TV camera and wait to be recognized. As you can see there's no chance of strangers or intruders gaining access to the palace and certainly not to our private residences.'

While they were waiting, Helen said, 'I think I should warn you, Sue, to take whatever Nixon tells you with a pinch of salt. He has his own personal agenda and hopes one day to further his power by marrying into her family. Rumour has it that he's got his eyes on Big Mama's youngest widowed sister, Nefertiti, but I don't think he stands a cat in hell's chance as she's twenty-three and he's about fifty. He'll also probably say lots of complimentary things about Big Mama and how she's aloof from the political shenanigans that go on in this country but don't believe a word of it. Peter and I have gradually reached the conclusion that Big Mama's just as much involved in the corruption and wickedness that go on in Zambelia as anyone else. If anything, she's the chief influence over the people around her and not the other way round. Mind you, her nephew, Kenneth, is probably the worst of the whole bunch when it comes to evil for he has the reputation of being a pathological killer. One story that went around was that the president was once worried about Chunzani rebel tribesmen acquiring guns and ordered Kiboko to go into the tribal area to collect their arms. He returned with several baskets of severed limbs. I don't know how true it is; maybe it's only hearsay.'

A few moments later the gate was opened and there stood before her one of the smallest men she'd ever laid eyes on except maybe for the Bushmen of the Kalahari she'd once seen on a holiday visit there. He hardly came up to her shoulder and couldn't have been much more than five feet, maybe even a little less. He had a high forehead, and a lively, intelligent face.

Peter said, 'Let me introduce Mr Nixon Makau, Senior Aide and personal adviser to the President and Marie Antoinette Makubwa. This is Doctor Susan Delamere.'

'Pleased to make your acquaintance,' her host said in a quiet, gentle tone of voice taking her hand. As he spoke, he looked over Sue's shoulder as if someone he feared were approaching. He continued to glance nervously in every direction checking that there was no-one else apart from the Hallidays in the vicinity.

Sue noticed how his eyes seemed to dance and sparkle as he spoke; his handshake was firm and reassuring.

'First,' he said, addressing Sue, 'let's dispense with formalities. May I call you Sue? And since we shall be working together, please call me Nixon; it'll be a little less formal than our full titles.'

'That's fine by me,' Sue returned happily.

'I'm so relieved that you got here safely. It must have been a hair-raising journey getting here on those dark roads. These are dangerous times.'

Then addressing Peter and Helen, he said, 'I trust that no-one saw her come into the palace grounds.'

'No-one,' Peter said. 'I made absolutely sure of that. Jason, the guard on the rear gate, saw nothing. I guarantee it one hundred per cent.'

'Thank heavens for that,' Nixon Makau said. 'Everything depends on Sue here not being seen by anyone outside our little group. That's crucial to my plans. It's been most fortunate that she has come here today of all days because, as you know, Kiboko and Schneider are away whilst Big Mama is abroad with her sisters. It's a good omen that they're absent because it means we can formulate our plans in secret. Now, may I invite the three of you to my home? Perhaps you'd like some tea.'

'Sorry, Nixon,' Peter said, 'but I think it best if Helen and I return to the palace as soon as possible in case anyone is wondering where we've got to. We don't want to arouse suspicions, whatever we do.'

Helen nodded her agreement, 'Peter's right. Besides, we've already discussed this matter with you, Nixon, and we are in complete agreement. We'll leave it to you to explain things to Sue. So we'll take our leave of you as we know that she is now in safe hands.'

'Very well,' Nixon replied. 'It's always best to be on your guard at all times. Tomorrow, I'll give you details of anything we may decide.'

***

Inside, the cottage was deceptively more spacious than was apparent from the exterior. The drawing-room they entered was well furnished and comfortable with a luxurious three piece suite, mirrors and gilt-framed pictures on the wall, a polished tile floor and an Indian rug before a large fireplace.

'Not exactly a mansion,' Nixon said, ringing a small hand bell, 'but it suits my purposes well enough. Most important, it affords me the privacy which I value highly. Please sit down, Sue, and I'll organise some tea while I explain the situation.'

He called to the diminutive manservant who had now appeared from the kitchen. 'Rafiki, prepare tea and bring a few biscuits for our visitor, there's a good man.'

'Yes, sir. Right away.'

'Now, let's get down to business, Sue.'

'Agreed,' Sue answered, still puzzled as to where all this was going.

'Let me tell you why you are here.'

'Before you say anything, Nixon, are you not concerned that we might be overheard by your servant? My own experience with my cook in Hekima has made me wary indeed.'

'Good point,' he smiled. 'There's no problem on that score, I can assure you. I am of the Umbuka tribe as are my servants, Rafiki, the cook and, Mlima, my gardener. There is also another Umbuka on the site and that's Florence, the president's personal nurse. In both senses of the word we are the smallest, tribe in Zambelia and are bound together by ancient and sacred family ties. I would entrust my life to any one of them. So we can speak freely and without fear.'

'May I say first of all, Nixon, that the thing I do not understand is why an important person like you, being so close to the seat of power, would be willing to help me, a mere teacher at the University? Isn't it a dangerous thing for you to do?'

278

'I'm glad you are an open and frank person. Peter and Helen are already well aware of my views on developments here at the palace. So they will confirm what I am to reveal to you when you speak to them later. I am greatly concerned about what is happening here in Lundazi at the centre of government. Marie Antoinette, the president's consort, is a good friend of mine and she confides in me a great deal. I can't help thinking sometimes though that she and the president are too easily swayed by those two wicked men, Kiboko and Schneider. They are both devious and manipulative men. The former is a cruel psychopath who enjoys both murder and torturing his victims, and is capable of the most unspeakable atrocities while his partner in crime, Schneider, is a corrupt and perverted physician, guilty of practices that I cannot bring myself to describe to you. Perhaps it is enough to say that among the staff he is referred to as Count Dracula.

'Marie Antoinette's problem has been that, from early youth, she's had to look out for her four younger sisters. As a result, she's become so obsessed with furthering their interests that she's lost the plot to certain extent and allowed those two malicious men to exert undue influence over her. It could be said too that she has too strong a penchant for designer clothes and the good life in general, which may distract her and prevent her from seeing some of the evil things taking place under her very nose. Apart from those shortcomings, however, there's much to admire about her and President Matata relies heavily on her for advice in formulating policy. My dearest wish is that one day we can remove the evil duo, Kiboko and Schneider, and have a fair, just and democratic society here in Zambelia. Then President Matata and Marie Antoinette together could rule the country wisely and we'd have a happy and prosperous society.'

'These are weighty matters that you're telling me about, Nixon, but how do I come into all this? I'm not in the least involved in high politics or power struggles. It's way over my head.'

'Very well, straight down to business. I have a plan to expose these two wicked men to the British Government and have them removed from power.'

Sue was still puzzled as to how she could fit into any such scheme.

'There's a good chance,' Nixon continued, 'that if you fell into the hands of this evil pair, they'd have you thrown into the women's prison at Gereza and that'd be the last we'd see of you. My plan is to help you escape back to Britain through an East African port such as Mombasa, Dar-es-Salaam, Beira, or even Durban.'

'But why are you doing this? Apart from our mutual contact through the Hallidays, I don't know you. What would you get out of it?'

'I can see you are a shrewd lady and no mistake. Over the years I have built up a dossier on the evil practices perpetrated by these two homicidal maniacs; the documents in question provide details of their crimes along with dates, bank account numbers and so on. My plan is for you to carry it to England on my behalf. It may take me from four to six weeks to put the final touches by gathering together the last pieces of evidence which will certainly condemn the pair of them. In my basement office, I store my archives with dates of every important event, both good and bad, that has happened here in Zambelia during the past ten years. The problem for me is getting these details out of the country and into the hands of the British Foreign and Commonwealth Office and possibly Amnesty International. And that's where you come in, Sue. I could have tried sending it in the diplomatic bag but I don't trust the couriers; I think someone like you would be infinitely more reliable.'

'I still don't see how, Nixon, since I am a virtual prisoner here in Zambelia and it will be no easy job to spirit me out of the country. However, there may be another answer to your problem. You may or may not be aware that a Doctor Moroney, an entomologist at the University, will be attending a scientific conference in London a little later this year. It might be worth considering him as a possible courier.'

'Thanks for the suggestion, Sue, though I think I'd prefer you, as a friend of the Hallidays, to do the job. I don't know this Doctor Moroney and am not sure how reliable he'd be.'

Sue replied: 'Dr Moroney has the advantage of being completely beyond suspicion. He's got to be in London anyway to attend this symposium. Perhaps my colleagues Mike Goodman can find the precise date. Doctor Moroney could hide your dossier among his own papers and deliver it to the Commonwealth Secretary in Whitehall without any problem. Far less risk than sending me out with such important files. If I were caught at the border, all your efforts would have been in vain.'

Nixon narrowed his eyes and pursed his lips as he considered the idea. 'I think you may be right, Sue. I must admit that this Dr Moroney would be less of a risk if we can trust him. He leaves later this year, you say. When I know the date precisely, I shall try to have my dossier ready for him. But how could we get the material to him? I can't travel down to Hekima to see him and we certainly don't want him seen here at State House.'

'My good friend, Dr Mike Goodman at the university, will be here next week-end and regularly each Friday after that. He's completely reliable and could pass your files on to Moroney with strict instructions to deliver them to the Commonwealth Office.'

'I think this is the answer, Sue. If I burn the midnight oil for the next week or two, I could have everything ready to pass on to this Dr Moroney. Very well, Sue, let's do it. I shall pass the dossier on to your colleague, Dr Goodman, so that he can take it to this entomology academic. When this information reaches London, watch the sparks fly. Now I am sure you must be tired and you have done enough for one day. Be assured that no matter what happens, I shall make arrangements for your escape. Meanwhile I have arranged a self-contained and comfortable rondavel cottage for you on my little private estate here. You'll be well looked after and will have the services of both my servants, Rafiki and Mlima.'

'I'm so deeply grateful to you, Nixon, that I hardly know what to say. However, about my possible escape, I'm not sure that I want to leave Zambelia so quickly because I came here to teach and I've not been given much of a chance so far. If I left the country in such a hurry, I would consider that to be something of a defeat.'

'At the moment, Sue, I don't see that you have much choice but to remain here on my little compound until things are resolved and we can make the best decision for you. If you leave here too soon you may find yourself in prison and I shudder to think what that may entail. Perhaps when our country achieves democratic law and order, you'll be able to return to Hekima and take up your post again.'

'That seems a distant prospect, Nixon. At present though, as you say, I have no alternative but to go along with your scheme. It's my fervent hope that I shall be able to stay in Hekima and go back to my job of teaching at the university.'

'That's settled then for the time being. Your stay on my property won't be too bad, Sue; I'll see to that. You'll see your friends the Hallidays every day and your doctor friend from Hekima may be able to visit you each week-end provided we can maintain the strictest secrecy. Meanwhile I suggest you let Rafiki here take you across to the cottage I have reserved for you. You will be comfortable there and you'll not be disturbed. I guarantee it.'

***

Encouraged but still heartbroken, Sue spent that first night weeping in the little cottage. What have I done to deserve this? she asked herself. Why didn't someone warn me that I was coming to a mad Orwellian country like this? Why didn't the Hallidays tell me about it? But perhaps they didn't know that my lectures would be so misconstrued and would result in my being hounded out of job and home.

After a troubled night with thoughts like this buzzing around her brain, Doctor Susan Meredith finally fell asleep.

****

Chapter Twenty-Five

Major Nyoka is looking for Sue

Major Nyoka was depressed. Not only did his mouth taste like the proverbial parrot droppings but he also had a throbbing headache from chain-smoking too many cheap Zambelian cigarettes. The couple of tots of whisky he'd drunk earlier hadn't helped either. He had a problem and at that moment, he couldn't see any solution. It was two days since the lecturer, Delamere, had disappeared without trace and he had that mad bastard Kiboko breathing down his neck demanding that he find her. And quick. All right for him, he thought, sitting up there in Lundazi giving his orders but he'd exhausted every avenue without result.

On the day he had received the call from the colonel instructing him to go round to her house and arrest her, he had done exactly that. To no avail.

'The warrant for her arrest has come straight from the President,' Kiboko had bellowed down the line, 'so get round there and handcuff her and send her up by the Black Maria to Gereza Prison. I'll attend to Madame Delamere myself.'

Sounded so easy but when he'd called round to her house, there had been nobody there but the servant Sikio and he didn't know a thing.

'The last time I saw her,' he'd claimed, 'was when she returned from her interview at the Censorship Board.'

'Did she return alone or did someone bring her home?'

'Doctor Goodman from the university brought her back in a Land Rover but he didn't stay.'

'Did he not enter the house for tea?'

'No, he didn't come in. He seemed in a hurry to get back to his home at the university.'

'Did you overhear anything that was said?'

'No, sir. They spoke outside in the garden. I tried to catch what they were saying but they spoke too quietly and were too far away. The memsahib gave me a huge shopping order and I had to walk into the township to about five or six dukas to collect the groceries and then to the market for the vegetables. When I came back, she'd gone.'

'And nobody saw her go?

'No, sir. Nobody.'

'Have you checked her things to see what she took with her?'

'Yes, sir. I have looked through her belongings and, as far as I can tell, she took hardly anything. Only a hold-all is missing and a few clothes.'

'In that case, she can't be far away? Did she take her money and her documents? Her passport and her work permit?'

'She normally kept such things in a drawer of her dressing table, sir, and they are no longer there. So she must have taken them with her.'

The major along with his Sergeant Mboya made a thorough search of the house and, what Sikio had reported appeared to be true. Most of her clothes were still hanging up in the wardrobe and her books seemed to be intact on the shelves. There was no trace of her personal documents without which she couldn't have got far. They left the house no wiser than before.

He sent Sergeant Mboya round to the bus depot and the railway station with a photograph of Sue Delamere, though commonsense told him it would be a wild goose chase. As expected, no-one could recall having seen her. In any case, a white woman would never get through such places without being obvious.

Next port of call was Mike Goodman at the university. He had been the last one to see her after the Censorship Board interview.

'Sorry, Major Nyoka,' Mike replied in answer to his questions. 'I dropped Doctor Delamere off after the Censorship Board meeting and I haven't laid eyes on her since.'

'I suspect you're lying, Goodman,' the major snapped, thinking direct confrontation might pay off. It didn't.

'I wish I could help you,' Mike protested angrily, 'but the truth is that we are so busy here at the university, we are run off our feet with students and supervising at the hospital. We don't have time to keep checks on the movement of our colleagues on the staff especially in other faculties. Who knows where she is? Perhaps she's managed to flee the country before the alert was out and you and your men came looking for her. Some of your borders are as leaky as a sieve.'

'Impossible,' the Major barked. 'She couldn't get through any of our borders without the necessary documents.'

'Perhaps she got through one of your loosely guarded frontiers in a secluded part of the country.'

'Out of the question. How could she find transport to any of these isolated places?'

'Maybe she departed on a scheduled flight.'

'Even more unlikely. Zambelian customs and immigration are the most efficient in the world. She'd never get past our officers.'

'She could have greased a palm or two. That usually does the trick in this country.'

'That's a despicable thing to say, Goodman. Our government officers are beyond reproach and not open to corruption and bribery. Everyone knows that.'

Mike smiled. 'If you say so. I'm truly sorry I can't help you, Nyoka, but we are so rushed off our feet here that we haven't time to be thinking about problems that your Safety Unit men and the Censorship Board may have. Caused no doubt because of their inefficiency.'

'We could have you arrested and questioned at our police headquarters, Goodman. That would soon loosen your tongue and you wouldn't find them so inefficient in that department.'

'Threats like that won't get you anywhere, Major. If you take me away, who's going to look after the two hundred patients we have here in Hekima hospital? You and your sergeant here? I think the death rate would go up exponentially if you adopted that tactic. Why not admit that Doctor Delamere has got one over on you and has done a bunk, a disappearing act. At this moment, she's probably having dinner at the Waldorf and planning a visit to the London Palladium to round off the evening.'

The major strode off furiously. He knew he was stymied. Now he would have to face the wrath of Colonel Kiboko but it wouldn't be the first time nor probably the last. If the woman Delamere had escaped via one of the lax border posts, there was nothing he could do about it. Let Kiboko deal with that, it wasn't his pigeon. Big Mama would soon sort the colonel out. With luck, he might get the boot or better still, be shoved into one of his own dungeons. That'll be the day, he murmured to himself.

****

Chapter Twenty-Six
Monsignor and the Bishops have a problem

The chaplaincy of Hekima University was a popular and much used source of advice for students with personal problems and they often came away remarking on how peaceful they had found the atmosphere there. Perhaps it was the highly polished wainscoting, the fine leather of the chairs, the smell of beeswax, the faint aroma of incense from the early morning Mass, or simply the quietude that induced tranquillity. Again, perhaps students were put at ease by the soothing notion that somewhere within the chaplaincy lay the answers to life's problems. Whatever it was, it was not working that Monday afternoon for the chaplain himself, because at that moment Monsignor Gerry McGinn was sitting at his desk, his right hand cradling his chin, not unlike a worried clerical version of Rodin's "The Thinker". He was in a quandary as to what his next move should be. The problem had arrived in the person of a young curate who had flown in from London the previous day bringing with him a letter from the Commission for Justice and Peace. The document was still lying on his desk and, though he had read it several times over, he could not make up his mind as to what to do about it. He took off his horn-rimmed glasses and polished them carefully with his large pocket handkerchief. He turned his attention to the letter and began studying it once more though he could have recited it from memory.

"Dear Monsignor McGinn," it began

"We have recently been receiving deeply disturbing reports from the International Secretariat of Amnesty International about the deteriorating political situation in Zambelia. The Organisation has brought our attention to the continued denial of human rights of people alleged to be opponents of the Government. Several prisoners of conscience, as well as a large number of alleged opponents of the government, are being held without charge or trial in the most dreadful conditions in prisons throughout the country. Four Deputies who challenged the existing order were killed in a suspicious car accident while other politicians have simply disappeared. Amnesty has also continued to receive harrowing accounts of torture and inhuman treatment of both political detainees and prisoners convicted of criminal offences which have often resulted in their being either seriously maimed or even executed.

The Commission for Justice and Peace feels that it is the duty of the indigenous Church to encourage the laity as Christians to express their revulsion at such savagery and to demand that government cease this inhuman and evil treatment of its citizens forthwith. The local Church should also insist that the authorities devote more resources to improving the lot of its poorest people and to spend less on enriching the privileged few.

For many years, the Church in Zambelia has been censured for remaining silent under the oppressive rule of President Samson Matata. There is a danger that the world will see such silence as complicity and we at the CCJP believe it is a primary obligation of the local church and its members to take positive action to persuade the government of the day to enact just civil laws and to administer them impartially. A call to all citizens – possibly by a pastoral letter - should be made as soon as possible to encourage them to become fully involved in the pursuit of justice for all.

Our aims must be to make people aware of their rights and duties and to encourage love, understanding and harmony through the promotion of the Church's social teaching.

I remain, Yours in the love of Christ, Very Reverend James Corcoran, General Secretary CCJP (Zambelia)

The monsignor looked up from the letter and sighed, thinking to himself. What a nasty, intractable problem to land on my desk! It was the sort of enigma suffered by all priests working under oppressive regimes. Here in Hekima, I follow my daily priestly routine but is it enough? I do my best to provide the students with spiritual help and services but all the time knowing that the elephant in the room, as the saying goes, is the brutish tyranny going on all around us. It's all very well for the CCJP in London to advocate direct action against the government here but such efforts will certainly be self-defeating and can only result in further oppressive measures and persecution. Attempts to oppose the blatant injustices in this country usually result in imprisonment, deportation or even death for the protestors, thus defeating the object of the exercise. It's a problem being faced every day in so many places like Libya, Ivory Coast, Zimbabwe or Burma and God knows where else.

What to do next was the big question facing him. Should he pass on the letter to the Zambelian bishops? As Apostolic Administrator of Zambelia and a monsignor of the Church, did he have a choice? He could let sleeping dogs lie of course by ignoring the letter and carrying on regardless, much as he had been doing for the past three years but that would remain on his conscience as it still did. Besides it would be a dereliction of his duty. On the other hand, if he passed on the letter, he knew precisely what would happen. Archbishop Kazembe would have to call a Special Conference of the seven Zambelian bishops to discuss what action the local Catholic Church should take in response to the CCJP letter. Who knows what they would decide and what the consequences might be? The Archbishop himself was a mild-mannered man and would probably take the line of issuing a pastoral letter offering understanding and sympathy to the impoverished peasants who suffered under President Matata's yoke. His Excellency, the Archbishop, was wise enough to realize that discretion was the better part of valour and that speaking out was likely to result in Matata taking violent revenge against his subject people. Was speaking out worth it if it resulted in imprisonment or death of innocent people? Was the price too high? On the other hand there was the firebrand Bishop of Lubutu, Mica Mambo, who would no doubt advocate a strongly worded pastoral letter that might stir the peasantry to revolt and then there would follow vicious government reprisals. And what a can of nasty worms that was likely to open! All hell would be let loose. Hence the dilemma; hence his chin in his hands.

What was it my old mother and grandmother used to say, he asked himself, when you were in a pickle? Sleep on it and the answer will be there the next day. Perhaps our old folk saw that, by letting the matter rest, you got a clearer grasp of priorities. That's fine, he thought, but what if you can't sleep? He had the answer for that too: one of the mild sleeping pills his doctor had prescribed last time he'd had to make a difficult decision. Before turning in that night, he popped one of the pills and was asleep within the hour having put the question to the back of his mind.

Next morning he awoke at six am and he knew what he had to do. After a light breakfast of fruits, he booked a phone call to the archbishop in Lundazi. It was ten a.m. before he was finally put through.

'Good morning, your Excellency,' he began. 'This is Monsignor McGinn in Hekima. I hope it's a convenient time to speak with you. It's an important matter I think I should bring to your attention.'

'But of course, Gerry. It's always good to hear your voice. Not bad news, I hope. How would you classify your news on our five point scale?'

Knowing that there was every chance that their phone calls would be monitored by the government's Public Safety Unit, the bishops had developed a private classification of their communications with each other. A1 being "important"; A2 very important, up to A5 being urgent.

'I would put it down as an A5, Your Excellency.'

'Very well, Gerry. Say no more. I trust your judgment implicitly. I shall call a meeting of the seven diocesan bishops for the end of this week. Expect details before this day is out.'

Archbishop Pius Kazembe was as good as his word and a meeting of the bishops was called for the afternoon of the Friday of the same week.

***

For Gerry McGinn, the rest of the week seemed to fly by. After the usual formalities of greetings and good wishes, the conference was opened by the Archbishop.

'I am happy to see you all present this afternoon, my fellow bishops. It is rare for one of these extraordinary meetings to be called but it has been done at the request of our fellow cleric, Monsignor McGinn and we know him well enough to know that he would have only requested a meeting like this under extreme circumstances. We are faced with a difficult dilemma here in Zambelia. Everywhere we see cruelty, corruption and injustice. What we in the church should be doing about it is the question before us this morning. One thing is clear: neutrality is not an option for us men of the cloth. Moral decisions must be made. I hand the chair over to Monsignor for clarification.'

Some of the bishops lit up cigarettes in order to aid concentration, or perhaps to hide their nervousness; others

292

leaned forward and looked in Gerry McGinn's direction anxiously.

'I know,' Gerry began, 'that many of you have made long and difficult journeys to be here and so I shall come to the point immediately. The Commission for Justice and Peace in London has been in touch with me recently and has expressed serious concern about the deteriorating political situation here in Zambelia. They refer specifically to persecution, corruption, denial of human rights, false imprisonments, torture and the execution of citizens without trial. The world, they claim, is largely unaware of these matters and the Commission raises the question of what we in the Catholic Church should be doing to bear witness to these wicked injustices. To outsiders, it would appear that the Church has been doing nothing and, by so doing, has given the impression that they are resigned to the state of affairs here. Have we here in Zambelia shoved these vital issues under the table and adopted a policy of "let sleeping dogs lie"? That is why this conference has been called to consider what actions we should take to express our condemnation of these evil and immoral acts of the government. I shall say no more but leave the matter open for discussion.'

Gerry sat down and awaited reaction.

There followed heated debate with several bishops denying the assertion that nothing had been done.

'There may apparently have been silence and acceptance,' said Barak Pandule, Bishop of Zamani, 'but at the local level, the Church has constantly niggled the government and expressed its opposition to the wrongs being perpetrated but in many ways, the church is powerless and would only make matters worse by interference.'

The Archbishop nodded in agreement but said: 'This is not a time however for silence. Remember the words of the philosopher, Edmund Burke, and repeated by the holocaust survivor, Simon Wiesenthal: "In order for evil to flourish, all that is required is for good men to do nothing".'

293

'Wise words and I fully agree with them,' Micah Mambo, Bishop of Luburu said passionately. 'I believe we should issue a strongly worded letter to our parishioners urging them to rise up and take action in their locality. It is the only thing this government understands and the only way that true justice will ever be achieved in this country.'

'I cannot agree with the Bishop of Luburu,' said Lazarus Simba, Bishop of Falajani. 'His suggestion can only result in mayhem. We should continue as we have been doing, that is, harrying the government in small ways and, whilst our actions may not be earth-shattering, we have made things inconvenient for our rulers.'

'Not enough!' declared Japeth Jenga, the Bishop of Monila, 'but the difficulty is that we are caught up on a web of deceit, fear, and mistrust on which Matata's henchmen depend. If we speak out and become involved in the defence of justice and morality, our parishioners are likely to suffer the consequences. So how do we justify our boldness in speaking out?'

'I only know,' the Bishop of Lubutu proclaimed, 'that I feel helpless when faced by the enormity of the evil before us. We have only to remember the four Deputies whose bodies were found at the bottom of a ravine in that fake car accident. Their corpses were returned to their families in a dreadful state. We should take some action regardless of the consequences, but what? That is the question.'

The Archbishop now spoke up. 'Since hearing from Monsignor McGinn, I have given the matter much thought and I think we should publish a pastoral letter bringing the attention of our parishioners to the things that are wrong in our society and at the same time calling on the government to take some positive action to relieve the lives of our people.'

'We can expect a major brutish reaction from President Matata,' said the Bishop of Sandoa who had not spoken so far. 'Are we ready to face it?'

When I learned of the subject of this meeting,' said Micah Mambo, nicknamed "the Firebrand Bishop" by his fellow bishops, 'I took the liberty of composing a possible pastoral letter and with your permission, I should like to read it. Here it is:

The government has given undertakings of land reforms and control of the Public Safety Unit police and the Matata Youth Brigade but nothing has come of these promises. This government is an obstacle to the reign of God. It only knows how to crush the people and defend the interests of the rich. I call upon the United Kingdom and the international community to stop all aid to this country until such a time as it satisfactorily resolves the problems of the many "disappeared" citizens, including children, and submits itself to the judgment of the United Nations control. When a cruel dictatorship like that of this country seriously violates human rights and attacks the common good of the nation; when it becomes intolerable and shuts off all avenues of dialogue, the Church has no alternative but to declare the people's legitimate right to rebel with insurrectional violence.

'Zambelia is a country of poor peasants while those of the United Kingdom are wealthy. Why can they not see our plight? My dear brethren it is up to us, you and me, to throw off the yoke and defy the injustices which oppress us. I appeal also to the officers of the Public Safety Unit and to remind them that they too are part of the people. Yet they kill and torture their own kith and kin. Let them remember the fifth commandment of God: Thou Shalt Not Kill. No member of the police is forced to obey any law that violates the law of God. Rise up all you people and oppose the unjust government that oppresses us.'

The bishop of Lubutu sat down breathless after the exertion of reading his impassioned speech. There was a long pause as the conference considered the import of these words.

It was the Archbishop who finally broke the silence. Solemnly he said: 'Of one thing, we can be sure. If we wish to bait the bear and sign our own death warrants and those of a great number of our parishioners, there is no surer way of achieving it than circulating such a provocative letter. It is my view that we should aim at something much less bellicose. And if you approve, I think we can safely leave it to the good sense of Monsignor McGinn. If he would kindly work on a draft this week-end, I shall study his effort and circulate it to the rest of you. Pending approval it will be read in all Catholic churches in a fortnight's time.'

There was a general murmur of approval and it was left to the luckless monsignor to compose a final version.

'So be it,' the Archbishop announced. 'I hereby request our monsignor to compose such a pastoral letter on our behalf.'

Gerry McGinn heaved a long sigh: 'Very well. I shall do as requested, but in some ways, I feel like the mouse that was chosen to bell the cat.'

****

Chapter Twenty-Seven
The Pastoral letter: Living the Faith

After consulting the archbishop and winning general approval of the other bishops, a milder form of pastoral letter was agreed on.

'Let us hope,' the Archbishop concluded, 'that we have toned-down the letter sufficiently to avoid stirring up a whirlwind.'

The final version of the pastoral letter entitled "*Living the Faith*" became:

My dear people,

"The Bishops of Zambelia and I have agreed to circulate this pastoral letter to all parishes. It is true to say that there is a deep crisis in our country and there has been a loss of confidence in our hopes regarding the future for ourselves and our children. A first step in the restoration of the climate of confidence should be taken by recognising the pitiful state of the nation, remembering the saying that "the truth will set you free." People will not be scandalised to hear these things; they know them already. They will be grateful only when their true needs are recognised and efforts are made to answer them. Feeding the people with slogans and half-truths – or untruths – only increases cynicism and mistrust of government representatives. It gives rise to a culture of rumour mongering. Real progress can only be attained when the true problems and our country's real needs are identified and resources channelled towards solving them.

"What are these problems with which the people of Zambelia are faced? They are: poverty, hunger, disease (most notably HIV/AIDS), illiteracy, human rights abuses, and political corruption. Until these problems are recognised and dealt with, our country can make no progress in the betterment of our people.

"People in positions of responsibility have an obligation to know the actual conditions in which their people live and to work tirelessly for their improvement. So far, the present government has responded with ever harsher oppression through arrests, detentions, banning orders, beatings, and torture. Our government should be willing to allow their performance to be judged by the people they serve. Accountability is a quality of any good government and is sadly lacking in Zambelia today.

In their agony, our people of Zambelia are asking (in those words from the Book of Isaiah), 'Watchman, how much longer the night?'

Yours devotedly in the love of Christ,

Archbishop Pius Kazembe."

The following Sunday, the letter was read out at all Masses in the country's Catholic Churches. As the priests read out the words, there was a shocked silence in every congregation as the words gradually sank in. After the services, parishioners stood around outside the church gossiping and wondering what they were supposed to do. Was their bishop asking them to go on strike? Write letters to their local Deputy? Not that he could do much since he was under the heel of President Matata? Start a revolution? What chance would we, unarmed ordinary people, stand against the police and the army? they asked themselves. We are only farm-workers, clerks, teachers and we can't take on the might of the militia. They felt lost and uncertain as to what action to take.

Not so, Matata's government. Response was swift. And it was vitriolic.

***

At three o'clock on the Sunday afternoon, Private Secretary, Nixon Makau, received an order to place a copy of the pastoral letter on the President's desk. He did as commanded, stood back as if he had lit a fuse to a time bomb and awaited reaction. As the President read through the document slowly absorbing its content, his blood pressure rose to boiling point. By the time he had finished, he was beside himself with rage. He thumped his desk and made all the objects rattle, then he picked up his ubiquitous fly whisk and began flicking it in every direction, a most ominous sign of the extent of his fury.

Finally thumping the desk again angrily, he fumed, 'This letter is treasonable and someone will answer for it with his life. Now, call an immediate meeting of the inner executive council. Tell them to drop everything that they're doing and be in my office by 4 pm. We must waste no time in rooting out this evil.'

By four o'clock, the executive council of the Zambelian Government was in place sitting round the long table in the President's office. In addition to the presidential aide, Nixon Makau, also present were Kiboko, Schneider, Big Mama, and the President himself.

'I take it that you have all read the disgusting and seditious pastoral letter that was read out this morning in Catholic churches,' Matata seethed, glowering round the table. 'I want to hear your immediate reactions and your suggestions as to what we must do about it. You first, Kiboko.'

The committee had no difficulty in recognizing what their reactions were expected to be. The angry flicking of the fly whisk had sent a clear message.

'There is no doubt in my mind as to what we must do in response to this malicious piece of treachery,' Kiboko said immediately. 'The criminals who composed this letter must be put to death. We should round them up, bang them up in Tagooma and arrange a public hanging immediately as a lesson to other potential dissidents. Meanwhile, we should pass a law making it illegal for anyone to read or possess the letter which has been put out as a booklet. Any person found with it in his possession will be arrested forthwith.'

'I agree entirely with Kiboko,' Schneider said silkily. 'We cannot allow such treasonable activity to go by without an appropriate response. We have shot people in the past for far less.'

'This document,' Big Mama now added, 'is one of the most blatant examples of perfidy I have seen in many a long year. We have only to consider some of the cases we now have in prison awaiting execution. They have been justly imprisoned for insulting the good name of Zambelia by showing gross disrespect to the president or for cheating the government out of taxes but this letter from the Catholic clergy is infinitely worse than any of these. We cannot allow things like this to go on. My vote goes to whatever our President decides to do with them.'

President Matata was beginning to look a little less threatening now that he had received approval of the policy he had already decided beforehand.

'What about you, Makau,' he now demanded. 'Do you agree with the majority view? Shouldn't we execute these mutineers, these anarchists, for this high treason, this stab in the back?'

Nixon Makau knew he had to tread warily and that it was like walking on eggs and, so measuring his words carefully, he said: 'Of course, Your Excellency, the committee

300

members are right in their analysis. Agitators and seditionists like these bishops must be justly punished but I should be failing in my duty as Aide and Counsellor if I did not warn you that execution of these dissident clerics is likely to have repercussions on the world stage. The British Government, the USA, the United Nations, not to mention the Church of Rome, may try to cut or even cancel international aid on which our economic survival depends.'

'Leave the international stuff to me,' President Matata snorted. 'I shall defend our right to act independently in matters like this which involve our national security. So we are agreed? We call the Bishops to a meeting and ask for an explanation and we arrange for their execution.'

There was a murmur of agreement, not that the committee, given Matata's rage, had any other choice but to accept his decision.

'Very well, that concludes the meeting,' the President said, getting to his feet. 'I shall leave it to you Kiboko as Head of the Public Safety Unit to phone the malefactors concerned and order them to be present at Lundazi Central Police Station at 4 pm tomorrow. Meanwhile I shall give statements to *The Zambelia Herald* and Radio Zambelia.'

Later that afternoon Colonel Kiboko phoned round the six bishops and Monsignor McGinn. The clerics were left in no doubt as to what to expect.

'This is Colonel Kiboko speaking from State House,' he snarled down the telephone. 'As Head of the Public Safety Unit of Zambelia, I command you to present yourself at the Lundazi Central Police Station at four o'clock tomorrow afternoon to meet with the President and his executive committee to explain the meaning and purpose of the pastoral letter which was read out at Catholic churches last Sunday. I shall make no personal comment at the moment except to say that the President is seething that you, as leaders in the Catholic Church, should take it upon yourself to advocate civil disobedience against the constitutional and legal

301

authority of this country. Prepare for a long stay away from your diocese and make sure you are there and on time.'

There was only one protest and that was from Bishop Mambo of Luburu.

'As you know, Colonel, we in Luburu live in the extreme south of the country and I doubt it's possible to make it to Lunduzi in so short a time.'

'Look, Mambo, if the president orders it, be there even if you have to hire a private plane. And don't be late or the President won't like it.'

***

On Monday morning both the *Zambelia Herald* and Radio Zambelia included comments on the pastoral letter problem in their features.

The *Herald* branded the booklet as seditious and described it as the work of Mafia-style crooks. "Archbishop Kazembe is a known illiterate," the article declared, "and it is doubtful he is able to write decent English. The brains behind the letter is an Irish Catholic cleric, Monsignor Gerry McGinn. It is a calculated international campaign to use ignorant bishops to import IRA terrorism into our country and spread the chaotic situation of Northern Ireland and so discredit the good name of our country by inciting innocent Zambelians into open rebellion against our Redeemer and Saviour, Life President Matata. Any traitor on the payroll of foreign governments hoping to disturb the existing peace and calm in this country must face the clenched fist of our laws without mercy.'

Radio Zambelia warned in its news bulletin that "anyone who procured the episcopal letter should immediately take it to the nearest police station. Possession of the letter is in itself sedition and will result in immediate criminal prosecution."

Later that Sunday afternoon, a huge gang of the Matata Youth Brigade marched on to the printing company that had published the document and torched the building housing the presses. The police were called but were slow in arriving at the scene. One youth was killed and several people were seriously injured in the ensuing mêlée.

***

Colonel Kiboko had stressed to the seven clerics that under no circumstances should they be late for the meeting with the executive council. Such a warning was superfluous for having seen and heard the featured articles published, they were well aware how dangerous it would have been to provoke Matata further by not being punctual. By half past three, they were all present and checked off by the police superintendent in charge who handcuffed them and escorted them into the main interview room, a large panelled office with a long table, several hard wooden benches and one huge, throne-like seat. There they were left quivering anxiously to await the next development. Two hours later, several officers of the Public Safety Unit marched in and ordered the bishops to be taken into separate interview rooms where for eight solid hours, the clerics were subjected to fierce interrogation as to their political affiliation and their intentions in publishing such an extremely subversive document.

Were they communists trying to take over the government?

Were they acting on behalf of some international organisation?

Was it part of a papal plot to usurp the President?

Who were the brains behind the conspiracy?

Did they belong to a dissident group plotting a coup d' état?

Name the treacherous Deputies behind the scheme.

Were they hoping to foment a revolution and destroy the President?

Were they in league with the devil?

In the early hours, they were each thrown into a cell and left for the rest of the morning to watch and pray until the next gruelling part of the proceedings. Later that morning after a skimpy meal of gruel, they were hustled back by the police superintendent to the main interview room for the next stage of the investigation. By this time, their nerves were shot to pieces and they had been reduced to the proverbial quivering jellies. It was another hour before any of the executive committee put in an appearance and this was in the person of Nixon Makau who came as a harbinger of what was to follow. He looked as nervous as they were when he addressed them.

'Good morning. My name is Nixon Makau and, as you may know, I am Senior Aide and Counsellor to the President. His schedule is running late as he has many affairs to attend to,' he explained. 'I should tell you in advance that he is in a titanic rage at the pastoral letter that was read out in churches yesterday. I must also warn you that if he is wearing his dark glasses, be on your guard for it means he is in a particularly vicious mood and anything can happen. If he flicks his fly whisk in your direction, it signifies that he is dangerously on edge and would like to have you flogged or even beheaded. So be careful in what you say to him because one wrong word can send him into a towering frenzy.'

***

At eleven o'clock, President Matata swept in with his entourage ready to do battle. In addition to Nixon Makau, also present were the other four members of the inner circle: Matata went immediately to the raised throne and sat down scowling menacingly at them. He was wearing his dark glasses and he flicked the fly whisk aggressively in their direction.

'How dare a bunch of clerical pipsqueaks like you lot think you can instruct me the Life President, in how I should run my country!' he bellowed, striking the table with his shoe

304

which he had removed for the purpose. 'In Zambelia there is one leader and one party only. Otherwise there is disorder and confusion. You are the Church and I am the State and we are separate as has been the case in England since the time of Henry the Second. Keep your clerical noses out of my business! I am tempted to ban Christianity in my country and close down all Christian schools as Mobutu once did in Zaire. I am fuming that you should have the effrontery to urge my people to revolt and plunge the country into chaos. You will receive the punishment you so richly deserve. The executive council agreed yesterday that all of you shall be executed as an example to other potential rebels against the legitimate authority of this country. People must learn that they cannot go about opposing the government as the mood takes them. I shall call on each member of the council to confirm the decision.

'Colonel Kiboko?'

'Hang them! It is what they deserve for their treachery.'

'Schneider?'

'Definitely. I'm for execution!' he pronounced, at the same weighing up the relative health of their bodies and what price he might possibly get for their organs.

'Marianne?'

'The President's decision is final. Execute!'

'Chief Secretary?'

'Agree with Madame Marie Antoinette!'

'It's settled then,' the President bristled. 'The nine of you will be taken from here to Tagooma Prison and early next week, you will be taken to Marie Antoinette Square and there you will hanged by the neck until you are dead. And...'

He was about to say, 'may the Lord have mercy on your soul' when he was interrupted by the Archbishop who had flung himself to the floor and prostrated himself before him.

'Your excellency, Life President Matata,' the Archbishop pleaded in a strained and hoarse voice. 'I beg you with all

305

my heart to reconsider your verdict. We have been guilty of opposing your will and I beg your forgiveness and ask for mercy. As the most senior cleric present, the fault has been mine and not that of Monsignor McGinn or any of my other colleagues here today.'

The stern features of the President did not alter and he continued to scowl at the clerics. It was apparent to everyone there that there would be no mercy shown as Matata was livid that any of his subjects had had the temerity to go against his authority in Zambelia. Then Archbishop Pius Kazembe played a master stroke. He knew from listening to the many speeches delivered by the President that he saw himself as a person of elite status and also as one of great wisdom in the mould of a philosopher like Plato or Socrates. Shrewdly, the Archbishop now exploited this vanity.

'You will know, sir, from the words of the medieval philosopher, Francis Bacon, that it is the mark of a great prince, such as yourself, to grant mercy and forgiveness. Such a prince shows his power and his wisdom by his clemency. May I quote from my lowly position his words with which I know you are familiar. "In taking revenge," the philosopher says, "a man is but even with his enemy; but in passing it over, he is superior; for it is a prince's part to pardon. And Solomon saith that it is the glory of a man to pass by an offence".'

The words obviously hit home for on the President's face there appeared the glimmerings of a smile. He was flattered that he should have been referred to as "a prince". He turned to his fellow committee members who beamed and nodded in approval at this suggestion of royalty and wisdom. It looked as if Matata might be relenting.

'We cannot allow you to go against the legitimate authority of the country but I shall ask my colleagues for their views. Superintendent, remove the prisoners while we confer on the matter.'

***

With the prisoners gone from the room, President Matata turned to the committee. 'Well, what are your views?'

'I still say, no mercy. Hang them!' snapped Colonel Kiboko.

Schneider hesitated. Mealy-mouthed, he knew it was dangerous to say or even second-guess anything that was contrary to what the President was contemplating. 'I say, let the President himself in his wisdom decide on the fate of the accused. We know that the Life-President will make the right and just decision.'

Big Mama said: 'In my opinion, we should punish them but in some less extreme way. We must take into account what international reaction might be if we hang them.'

'Marie Antoinette has hit the nail on the head,' Nixon Makau said warmly, nodding in her direction. 'We cannot afford to alienate Western nations who donate so much needed financial aid. A Presbyterian missionary in America has already expressed sympathy with our bishops. It would be disastrous if America cut off its aid, especially as there is a critical food shortage and severe drought in the northern region of Zambelia. I would dare to suggest that we put the bishops under house arrest for six months and we deport the Irish monsignor who after all is the culprit who wrote the letter.'

Big Mama smiled her agreement and nodded towards the President who now appeared mollified. He was still thinking about that Francis Bacon's medieval prince and he rather fancied himself in the role.

'Very well,' he said at last. 'Thank you, Marianne, for your usual invaluable contribution. You always seem to know what's best in these difficult situations though we cannot simply allow foreign governments to dictate policy by taking away our money but in this case, perhaps we might allow an exception. Superintendent, bring the prisoners back!'

307

The Bishops were brought back crestfallen, fearful and resigned to their fate.

'We have re-considered the matter,' the President pronounced sternly, 'and while we do not for a moment condone your wicked pastoral letter, we have decided after deliberation to be merciful and commute your sentences. The seven of you Zambelian Bishops, plus the Archbishop, are hereby placed under house arrest for one year. You will be confined to the immediate vicinity around your cathedrals and will not be allowed under any circumstances (not for church dedications, ordinations, funerals, or anything else you may claim as exceptional) to leave the area. If any of you write seditious documents anything like the one that has brought you here, the sentence of death will be reinstated. As for you, Monsignor McGinn, as the perpetrator of the letter, you are hereby declared a Prohibited Immigrant and you have forty-eight hours to gather your belongings and get out of my country. If you are ever tempted to return, you should remember that the death sentence will be re-imposed and carried out immediately. Our Aide and Counsellor, Makau, will issue you with your final documents: air ticket, tax clearance, and so on, to be presented at the airport as you leave. Now all of you, get out of my sight. I am offended and disgusted by your presence. Though the sentences have been commuted, your treachery will be recorded forever in the annals of our country.'

****

Chapter Twenty-Eight
Sue and Mike declare their love

Sue had been living in Nixon's rondavel cottage for three weeks and she was bored and frustrated waiting for something to happen. While the rondavel was situated in a particularly beautiful part of the forested plateau, she was missing her job. She loved teaching and she felt bitter about the fact that she had been forced to leave her post for what seemed, to her at least, crazy political reasons. What had she done wrong? What had Elizabethan literature got to do with Zambelian state affairs, for heaven's sake? By what twisted logic could she be accused of seditious teaching by helping students to understand and appreciate the genius of Shakespearean drama?

On week days, she was confined to the immediate area around the cottage and had to be wary about being seen by anyone outside the little circle of confidantes who were aware of her presence. But the little group of five consisting of Nixon, his two servants and the Hallidays hardly satisfied her need for wide social contact. Peter and Helen did their best to keep her entertained by inviting her across to their house for one of their delightful dinners when the coast was clear and it was safe to do so but charming though they were, she still felt bereft. She filled in the time by reading but she had soon exhausted their little library of light airport novels and technical books on cooking and entertaining. They had also provided her with a few household items they had to spare like a mantelpiece clock that chimed the hours, a radio, a CD player, though it must be said the Hallidays' taste in music did not coincide with her own. Whilst she was reasonably keen on Gilbert and Sullivan light opera, there was a limit to the number she could take. Her one great joy during the day when she felt most isolated was the ability to tune into the BBC by short wave radio, which naturally was against the law though there was not the remotest possibility that anyone would detect this illegal activity so close to the president's palace. How she looked forward to listening to the afternoon play! All the same, time dragged and she found herself constantly checking the time on her clock and watching the hours and the minutes tick oh so slowly by. During these long hours, her mind sometimes went back to her life in Salford and, while she did not miss her frustrating job at the Polytechnic, she became nostalgic recalling the good things that she had once taken for granted; things that she had not thought about for years and which she now discovered she missed so much: the community spirit, the friendliness, simplicity, and genuineness of Northern people; her two brothers and their young families; her friends and the happy nights they used to have in The Crescent pub on Friday nights when the week's work was done and they let off steam laughing at some of the bizarre things that happened at work, like the occasion when the Principal had addressed the staff on the need to dress smartly at all times, but being unaware that his own trouser zip was unfastened; she recalled her membership of the Irish Club choir and their performance at the Free Trade Hall one March 17th when Mary O'Hara and her traditional harp had been among the star performers. Strange that it was only now in her loneliness that these warm and sentimental thoughts came floating to the surface. It's funny, she thought, how we become homesick and wistful about people and things only when they're no longer available.

The high point of her life came at week-ends when Mike drove up from Hekima and stayed with her in the cottage. He had no trouble with the guard at the gate as the Hallidays had

310

made him aware of the impending visit of Mike who came posing as Dr Alan Finlay the "chiropractor", and he was simply waved through. He came on the pretext of treating Helen for lumbago and sciatica but it was Sue who needed his attention. They made love, they explored the area walking through cool glades, he even tried fly fishing without much success. How the time between Mike's week-end visits dragged and how it seemed like an eternity between them though, in reality, it was no more than a few days.

On his third visit. he brought some books of poetry that she'd requested from the University library. They'd been like manna from heaven and so welcome after she'd finished reading the umpteenth "Who Dunnit?".

He picked out one of the books from the pile and said: 'As you know, Sue, I'm no great lover of classical literary works as I'm usually up to my eyes in blood and guts in the hospital but, by accident, I came across this poem and I found it very moving. I've been longing for this visit so you could read it aloud to me.'

The poem was from the works of Robert Bridges and the title was: "I Will Not Let Thee Go."

'Your wish is my command, sir,' Sue said with a bow. 'The poem you have chosen happens to be among my favourites.'

She began reading. When she reached the fourth stanza, she could not help the catch in her voice.

"I will not let thee go.
The stars that crowd the summer skies
Have watched us so below
With all their million eyes,
I dare not let thee go."

By the time Sue reached the seventh and final verse, both she and her audience of one were in tears.

I will not let thee go
I hold thee by too many bands:
Thou sayest farewell, and lo!
I have thee by the hands,
And will not let thee go.

They made passionate love that afternoon and as they lay naked together, Mike suddenly said: 'You know, Sue, that I love you dearly. You are the loveliest, most desirable woman in the whole wide world.'

For the second time that day, the tears rolled down Sue's cheeks. 'But you're weeping, Sue,' Mike said. 'Why?'

'Because I'm so happy now you're by my side, Mike, and I do love you from the depths of my being.'

'Sue, my darling, ever since I first saw you on the flight out here I have been mesmerized by your beauty. I am under your spell and yours to command.'

'Then, Mike, my dearest love, please do everything in your power to get me out of here and back to civilisation, so we can be together. When you're not here by my side, my whole existence seems so dull and pointless. You are my inspiration and my hope.'

'The same goes for me, Sue. Nothing as beautiful as the love I feel for you has ever happened to me before. You are the shining light in my life and I long for the day when we'll be back together again in Hekima. As you know, wheels have begun to turn and I know, deep in my heart, that we are going to come through this and we can be together forever.'

'But these wheels you speak of, Mike. They turn agonisingly slowly and sometimes I'm tempted to throw in the towel and try to go back to England. But a little voice within me says, "No, Susan. Nothing doing. You're a Delamere and we Delameres don't give in so easily. It'll come right in the end." I think it's all very well for this little voice to say that but I'm the one who has to sit here day after

312

day listening to Gilbert and Sullivan CDs and reading out-of-date novels.'

'Just be patient, Sue. It'll come out right in the end, I promise you. You can rely on that. Meanwhile, we must relish every precious moment that we get together. For me, this little rondavel in the middle of the presidential estate has become heaven for a few days. That's because you are here, my love. It's our little private, secret world for the time being.'

'Let's hope it remains secret, Mike. If it ever leaked out beyond our little circle, it'd be the end of both of us. At the drop of a hat, Colonel Kiboko would have me whipped into Gereza and you into Tagooma.'

For Sue and Mike, Fridays were the happiest days for they were together even if only for a few golden hours. Sunday was the saddest day for it was the day they had to part. On Sunday afternoon, they made love once again to round off their brief week-end of romance together. As they lay there once again exchanging kisses and words of endearment, the mantelpiece clock chimed the hour reminding them it was time to say goodbye.

'I shall have to think about going, my darling,' Mike whispered sadly.

'Oh, no, Mike. Not yet. Can't you stay a little longer, say another day?'

'I'd give anything to do that, Sue, my dearest love, but you know I have to be back in Hekima by early evening. Otherwise people there might become suspicious. I think Major Nyoka already has his doubts about me and my story.'

'I've begun to hate that clock, Mike. Sometimes, I'm tempted to fling it against the wall but I know it won't do any good. I can't make time stand still.'

***

After Mike had gone, Sue was left with the same question every week-end. When is something going to happen? Obviously she couldn't spend the rest of her days cooped up in this little cottage. She could have taken up Nixon's offer to smuggle her out of the country via one of the ports he'd mentioned but to her that would have been admitting defeat. And she wasn't prepared to give in to the bullying tactics of Major Nyoka or the Censorship Board.

At the end of the month, Nixon came to see her.

'Sorry, Sue, I haven't been able to visit you and keep you up to date as to developments,' but I have been extremely busy preparing the dossier I spoke to you about. Now I think it's ready to be passed on to the British authorities for action. I have listed with full details and dates, the nefarious deeds of Kiboko and Schneider. I have traced back and logged their corrupt practices over several years: their murders, their torturing, illegal imprisonments, embezzlement of state funds, and so on. It's all there with proof for everyone to see. And most important, I have drawn up the long list of political detainees who have mysteriously disappeared over the years as well as those still languishing in Tagooma Prison plus details of their supposed crimes. If we can get the dossier to the British Commonwealth Secretary, Sir Hugh Baxter, with a copy to Amnesty International, I think we may soon see some action.'

'I am so relieved to hear this,' Sue said. 'Despite the wonderful accommodation you have provided, Nixon, I was beginning to feel that I too am in a Zambelian gaol. How I long to get back to the university and return to my job of teaching which is why I came to this country in the first place. Your dossier may be the first step along the road but it seems like a very, very long road sometimes. I pray with all my heart that my enforced stay here will come to an end soon.'

'Let us hope so, Sue. Re. getting my dossier out of the country, I've thought the matter over carefully and I agree

314

that perhaps the safest and most efficient way of getting the files across to the British Government is through your colleague at the University. I believe you said his name was Doctor Bugsy Moroney and he will be attending a scientific conference in London at the end of this month.'

'That's right, Nixon. My friend, Mike Goodman, will be here this coming Friday and we can absolutely rely on him to pass the documents on to Doctor Moroney as they see each other every day.'

'Then, Sue, that's what we shall do. I shall put the finishing touches to the dossier and address it to the Head of the Commonwealth Secretariat with a copy to Amnesty International, to be delivered in person by this Dr Moroney. After that, there is nothing we can do but await developments. It's my guess that we shan't have to wait too long as I think the Commonwealth Secretary is going to be shocked to the core when he hears the details of what has been going on in this country.'

***

The following Friday, as Sue had said, Mike Goodman, alias Dr Alan Finlay the "chiropractor", came to visit Helen Halliday for her usual "treatment" after which he made his way to Sue's cottage. She immediately sent the gardener, Mlima, over to Nixon inviting him to tea. After the usual formalities and polite exchange of greetings, Nixon said, 'Right, Dr Goodman, let's get down to serious business. I have brought with me the dossier to which I have been putting the final touches during the past fortnight. It is probably the most important document I've ever produced because it is going to take the lid off the injustices that have been weighing so heavily on Zambelia and its people for such a long time. It is vital that we get the information across to the British Government authorities safely and as soon as possible. I can't stress enough how important these data are. Exposure of the dossier in London could lead ultimately to a welter of prosecutions that will expose the extent of corruption in this country. Tell me about this Doctor Moroney fellow. Can we trust him?'

'Oh, yes, we can trust him,' Mike replied. 'He's trustworthy, has a first-class mind, perhaps a little scatty at times, but if he places your report among his own academic papers on symbiosis, he'll have no trouble getting past the checks at the airport.'

'You say, Mike, that he is a little scatty. He may be a trustworthy man morally and so on but suppose he loses the documents. Why, we'd be sunk!'

'I have to admit,' Mike said, 'that Moroney is sometimes distracted but he values his own academic work so highly that he will guard his files as if they were the crown jewels. If he includes your material among his own stuff, I am sure he can be relied on to deliver it to the right people.'

'Here's hoping you're right,' Sue added, 'though I have to admit to certain misgivings in placing such a vital piece of evidence in his hands but what choice do we have? We simply have to hope that Bugsy keeps his wits about him in London. After all it's a fairly simple job delivering a couple of packets.'

'Very well,' Nixon said. 'My mind is made up. We'll take a chance on this Moroney fellow and hope for the best. I shall have the papers ready for you to take back to Hekima by Sunday afternoon before you leave. So much depends on their reaching the right offices. Let's hope that Dr Moroney overcomes his forgetful tendencies and proves equal to the task.'

***

When Nixon had left, Sue turned to Mike and said, 'Are you confident about Bugsy, Mike? He's well-known at the university for his grasshopper mind.'

'I'm as confident as anyone can be, Sue. Remember Bugsy will be carrying the files among his own precious entomological papers and you can bet your life he'll watch

316

over them like a hawk because he is presenting the first paper at the conference. We must have faith. I'm going to have to return to Hekima a little earlier than usual in order to catch Bugsy before he catches the London flight later to-night.'

****

Chapter Twenty-Nine

Bugsy Goes to London

That same Sunday evening, Bugsy was preparing for his trip to London. Observed by his eagle-eyed wife, he had packed and repacked his main suitcase with his clothes and personal belongings that morning. Now all that remained was his precious brief case with his travel documents, conference papers and the sealed dossiers which Mike Goodman had entrusted to him an hour earlier.

'Remember, Bugsy,' Mike had said, 'we're depending on you to get these crucially important materials to the right people in London. There's a lot riding on them and so, for God's sake, don't lose them.'

'Don't worry, Mike. I am attaching the dossiers to my own papers on the African parasitical tick and I'm certainly not going to lose *them*. Otherwise, there'd be no point in my going to London.'

Reassured, Mike had left him to his packing.

'How I wish I were going with you!' Betty-Jo exclaimed. 'Can I trust you to get there in one piece? Do you know what you have to do?'

'Aw, c'mon, Betty-Jo, I'm not a kid. Of course I know the routine. Of course I know how vitally important Mike's file is! Do you think I'm dumb or something? Remember I'm the one who'll be kick-starting the conference with the first reading and all the notes I'm taking are as safe as Fort Knox.

Not that I need notes anyway as I know my subject inside out and can recite it in my sleep.'

'Yeah, yeah, I know that, Bugsy. Do you think I've been married to you for thirty years without knowing a thing or two about you. So, now, let's go over it once again. What are you carrying in your personal hand grip?'

'For Pete's sake, Betty-Jo, I've been through it a dozen times. I have my air tickets, my passport, my American Express card, traveller's cheques for £200, and thirty pounds in sterling for petty expenses such as a cab or a newspaper.'

'Yeah, and..and..and..'

'Oh yah. My T.E.P. my Temporary Employment Permit.'

'Whatever you do, Bugsy, don't lose that or they won't let you back into Zambelia! And I'll be left on my "ownio". Also don't forget to ask each cab-driver for a receipt so you can claim it back on expenses. Now once again, what do you do when you leave here?'

'First I fly to Heathrow. I take the bus to Victoria. From there, I take a cab to the hotel.'

'Right so far, Bugsy. Now what's the name of the hotel?'

'Do you think I don't know, Betty-Jo. It's named after a famous American writer who killed himself, the guy who wrote "A Farewell to Arms" and "For Whom the Bell tolls". Say, wasn't that a swell movie with Ingrid Bergman and Gary Cooper?'

'OK, Bugsy. Don't change the subject. What was the writer's name? C'mon. Began with "H".

'Hemingway. It's the Hemingway Hotel in Russell Square. I knew all along. Don't worry, Betty-Jo, I'll be OK. You'll see.'

'I hope so, Bugsy. Without me, you always seem to land up in that famous creek without a paddle. I don't see why I can't accompany you.'

'You know only too damn well, Bee Jay. This is an academic conference and you'd be bored out of your skull. Trust me. I'm gonna be fine, you'll see.'

***

Monday evening, Betty Jo Moroney drove her husband to Lundazi's Matata International Airport to catch the British Airways overnight flight to London Heathrow.

'Now remember everything that I told you,' Betty Jo said as she kissed him goodbye. 'I wrote it all down on a list of things you have to do. You haven't lost the list already, have you?'

'No, honey, I got it right here in my inside pocket. Now quit worrying, and relax will ya. I got everything under control.'

'OK Bugsy. But I've got my fingers crossed. And on both hands.'

That Sunday night, Bugsy flew out from Lundazi on the ten-o'clock flight. Betty-Jo was tempted to call at the church on the way back home to say a few prayers to St Jude that Bugsy managed the trip without his usual foul-up.

***

Next morning, Bugsy arrived at Heathrow without any mishaps. He had slept most of the way and he felt relaxed and alert as he collected his suitcase from the carousel and passed through the green channel at the customs exit. He caught the airport bus to Victoria and arrived after an hour's drive through London's heavy traffic.

'So far, so good,' he thought. 'Don't know what Betty Jo was getting so steamed up about. She doesn't have any faith in me but I'll show her how I can operate smoothly without her breathing down my neck. Now, the next stage is to take a cab to my hotel. What was the name of it again? The Gary Cooper Hotel. Wait a minute. That don't sound right.'

320

He consulted the list he carried in his inside pocket. 'What am I talking about? The Gary Cooper Hotel for Pete's sake! He was the actor in that film about the bell. The hotel is the Hemingway Hotel in Russell Square!'

He waited in the taxi queue and gave the name and location of the hotel to the cab-driver when it came his turn.

'Right, Guv,' the driver said. I'll have you there in a jiffy.'

'How much is that?' Bugsy asked when they arrived at the hotel.

'That'll be nine pounds, guv.'

Bugsy handed over a ten-pound note.

'Keep the change. And oh, I nearly forgot. Could I please have a receipt?'

'Thanks, guv. Receipt? No problem.'

***

It was early evening on the Monday when Bugsy finally registered at the small but comfortable private hotel and he soon settled in his room with his luggage around him.

'I'll show Betty-Jo that I can manage travelling without her,' he said aloud to himself. 'That wife of mine worries too much. Must admit though. I almost forgot to ask that cab-driver for a receipt. But there are no flies on me. Now let me go over my routine for tomorrow. Tonight, I pack my things ready for tomorrow morning. I get up bright and early at seven and breakfast at seven-thirty. I check my effects ready to leave the hotel at around 8.30 and take a cab to the Royal Linnean Society of Natural History.

'Now for the order of packing.'

He recited aloud as he organised his programme:

'In my brief case I pack my conference lecture notes and Mike's dossier; next, my traveller's cheques and passport. I put small change for the cab fare in my trouser pocket and I put my American Express card in the inside pocket of my jacket. In the suitcase back at the hotel, I leave behind my

321

change of clothes and my Zambelian Employment permit since I shan't need it until I go back. So much for the packing.'

'It was lucky that we were given the first afternoon free to "find our bearings" the invitation had said. This gives me the chance to do those "crucial" jobs for Mike.'

Still talking to himself, he went through the morrow's routine reading through the list which Betty Jo had prepared for him.

'1. Cab to the Royal Linnean Society Lecture Theatre in Piccadilly; get cab receipt.

2.   Attend the inaugural meeting of conference and read my paper.

3.   Go for lunch with colleagues.

After lunch:

4.   Take cab to Bank with my passport and cash traveller's cheques.

5.   Take cab to Foreign and Commonwealth Office, Westminster and hand over Mike's dossier to senior officer there. Get receipt for this.

6.   Cab to Amnesty International, Easton Street, London WC1. Hand over dossier to a senior official. Get receipt.

7.   Return to Conference in time for tea (hopefully).

8.   Evening Session of Conference 5 pm.'

***

In the knowledge that he was organised right down to the last detail, Bugsy slept like a top that first night in London. Next morning, he was up bright and early and the routine he had so carefully planned went like clockwork. At 8.30 he called at the reception of the hotel and asked the clerk to call him a cab.

'I can try, sir, if you like, but the taxi service is usually busy at this time of the morning and it can take as long as twenty-five minutes before one comes.   Here in Russell Square there are dozens of taxis passing the door all the time.

It'd be much quicker if you simply stepped outside and hailed one at the hotel entrance.'

Bugsy took his advice and found he was right because, within two or three minutes, he was able to wave down a cruising mini-cab. The driver was of middle eastern appearance and he gave Bugsy a broad smile as he asked: 'Where to, sir?'

'Burlington House, Piccadilly. Do you know it?'

'Yes, sir. It's in Old Bond Street. Not far from Fortnum and Masons. Hop in, sir.'

'That's great,' Bugsy said. 'Let's go.'

The driver may not have been a Londoner but he certainly knew the streets because he weaved his way through the heavy traffic skilfully and had Bugsy at his destination within twenty minutes.'

Bugsy got out of the car and went round to the left hand side of the car to pay the nine pound fare with a ten pound note, thinking nine pounds seems to be the going rate for these London cabs. Then he remembered.

'And could you let me have a receipt, please.'

'Sure thing, sir,' the driver said. 'I don't have official receipts printed. Will my signature on a pad be OK.?'

''Fine by me,' Bugsy replied.

The driver scrawled a receipt on a lined notepad and handed it over, saying, 'Burlington House is right opposite, sir.'

So saying, the taxi-driver was away back into the swirl of London traffic.

Bugsy looked around him and had no difficulty in locating Burlington House and saw within the entrance a big notice with the sign: "Linnean Society Lecture Theatre: Meeting of the Natural History Society: Ground Floor."

With a sigh of relief, Bugsy went into the theatre where he found a number of colleagues standing around enjoying refreshments. He ordered a coffee and helped himself to a couple of biscuits. There were many new faces at the conference but he was happy to see one or two familiar ones. There was the usual chit-chat and the Chairman of the Meeting rang a little bell and asked everyone to find their places as the proceedings were about to begin. Bugsy found his place near the front and thought he'd better get out his notes as he would soon be called upon to deliver the first lecture. It was then that he discovered he could not find his brief case. Horror! Panic stations! He remembered clearly having the case in his hand when he'd left the hotel. But where was it now? It came to him in a flash. He slapped his forehead with the back of his hand. He'd left the damned thing on the back seat of the mini-cab! He'd been so distracted thinking about getting a receipt, he'd clean forgotten the thing. Surely there'd be no problem in tracing the cab company and getting his belongings back. He rooted out the receipt the driver had given him but there was no name and no address. In a scribbled hand, it said simply:

"Received £10 for fare. Russell Square to Piccadilly." With an illegible signature. No address. No phone number. No nothing.

He could hear his name being announced as the Chairman introduced him as the first speaker. He had no choice but to go to the front of the class and give his lecture without his file. Fortunately, he knew his material so well that he didn't need notes but his delivery was halting and distracted as he thought about the enormity of the loss he'd sustained that morning. There were no slides and no cam-corder recordings which he had so carefully prepared back in Zambelia but no-one seemed to notice. How could they be aware that there were no visual aids if they didn't know about them in the first place, he thought.

At lunchtime, Bugsy tried frantically to trace the name of the taxi firm that had brought him to the convention. The receptionist back at the hotel could offer no help since Bugsy didn't have a name he could check.

'It was probably one of those unlicensed taxi companies,' the clerk told him. 'There are many illegal immigrants running these illegal cabs. They certainly won't come forward voluntarily as they'd be afraid they'd be prosecuted and deported. Always go for a registered black cab, sir.'

'Huh, now he tells me,' Bugsy thought.

It was a white-faced Bugsy that rang Betty-Jo in Zambelia that afternoon to give her a full report of the disaster.

'Oh, my God!' she squealed. 'I knew it! I just knew it! I should've come with you. Now Bugsy, this is what you gotta do. First you gotta go immediately to the American Consul in Grosvenor Square and report the loss of your passport. Tell 'em you must have new travel documents so you can come back to Zambelia on Saturday. Next go to American Express and ask 'em to cancel the travel cheques. I'll phone them from here and give 'em the numbers as I have them copied into my diary. Meanwhile, I'll phone Mike Goodman and tell him he can kiss goodbye to that precious dossier of his. Too bad. He and his girlfriend Sue will have to think of something else.'

***

The news of the loss shook Mike Goodman to the core when he got it from Betty Jo. He could have kicked himself for hadn't Sue warned him a hundred times that Bugsy was something of a nitwit and he'd pooh-poohed her. Most frustrating of all was that he had no way of telling her and Nixon until his visit on Friday as even his secure phone-line had probably been tapped after Sue's disappearance. If he rang her, no doubt, Nyoka and Kiboko would be on to them. How devastated they would be after Nixon's careful work in amassing that crucial evidence to reveal to the British authorities just what was going on in Zambelia! No doubt, Nixon could do the job again but that would take time and meanwhile poor old Sue was stuck up there in that rondavel, going mad with frustration and unable to make a move. How he could have kicked himself for trusting Bugsy when it was obvious to everyone that he would make a pig's ear of it. But there was nothing he could do but wait until his next visit to Lundazi when he'd pass on the disastrous news.

***

Mike thought Friday would never come. Not that he was looking forward to being the bearer of the such bad tidings. He wasn't sure either how Sue would take it. Maybe she'd blame him for the snafu because he'd been blind to the obvious fact that Bugsy was hare-brained. Would she ever forgive him?

Though seemingly calm and unruffled when he told her, deep down Sue was traumatised by the news.

Crestfallen she said resignedly, 'That's the last straw! I give up! I've become so used to receiving bad news since I came to this country that it's become simply par for the course. I'm really desperate, Mike, and I don't think I can wait until Nixon can gather the data again. Maybe I'll just have to take his offer to smuggle me out of the country through one of the East African ports.'

'I can well understand, Sue, how bitterly disappointed you must be. I know how much hope you'd pinned on Nixon's dossier reaching the right quarters in London.'

'Now, we must give Nixon the bad news,' she said solemnly. 'I don't know how he's going to take it after all his hard work in keeping those detailed records and now seeing his efforts go down the drain. He'll blame us for recommending a scatterbrain like Bugsy.'

They called Nixon's shamba servant in from the garden and sent him over to ask Nixon to come across so they could tell him of the disastrous turn of events. When Nixon appeared, they gave it to him straight.

'Sorry to be the bearer of bad news, Nixon,' Mike began, 'but our Dr Moroney lost the dossier in a London taxi and it looks as if we're back to square one.'

Mike and Sue studied Nixon's expression and waited for the explosion. But it never came. Instead, Nixon's face lit up with a smile.

'I thought something like this might happen. You see my investigations as to what is happening in Zambelia extend to university staff and I was aware that this Moroney man was something of a dreamer but I decided to take a chance. However, I am a cautious man and I believe in hedging my bets. What you call "belt-and-braces" prudence. You'll be happy to know that my dossier reached the intended targets and both the Commonwealth Office and Amnesty International received the evidence which I have so painstakingly put together over the past ten years.'

'But how?' Mike and Sue chorussed.

'Unbeknown to everyone, I gave copies of the dossier to Monsignor Gerry McGinn when I was ordered to brief him about the procedures involved in his deportation. It was the ideal opportunity to have my report delivered by hand. Who better than a senior cleric of the Catholic Church? And one last important consideration as far as I was concerned: I knew I could trust him to be meticulous in covering up the origin of his information for, as you well know, if the president or Big Mama suspected even for a moment that I was the source of the leak, they'd have me locked up so quick, my feet wouldn't touch the ground.'

'Well. I'll be bugg...blowed!' Mike exclaimed. 'But how could you be sure that the Monsignor would deliver the files to the right places?'

'Because I knew that it would be in his own best interests to ensure that the dossier reached the right people and for three good reasons. First, in the interests of justice because, as a priest, he's as deeply concerned as we are about the corruption in Zambelia; secondly, he'd be anxious to rescue the bishops from the wrath of Matata; and thirdly in the hope that his action might ultimately lead to big changes at the top of our government and give him the chance to come back to his post as chaplain at the university.'

'Life here in Zambelia has been like living on a roller coaster,' Sue laughed hysterically. 'First, I'm in seventh heaven about my job and my home; along came the censorship board and the escape to Lundazi and I'm down in the dumps. Next my hopes are raised when Bugsy takes the dossier to London. Down again when I learn that he's lost the stuff in a taxi. Now up again with the news that Monsignor McGinn has got the papers through. At the moment, I'm riding on cloud nine and hoping I don't fall back to earth again.'

'I don't think you will,' Nixon said with a broad smile. 'You see that's not all the good news I have for you. We heard only this afternoon that the British Government is proposing to send a delegation to this country to investigate various matters to do with violations against human rights. There are some long faces here in State House, I can tell you. Kiboko and Schneider are, to put it at its politest, quaking in their boots because a full inquiry is likely to reveal their heinous crimes and then it's "Goodnight Vienna" for them. Big Mama is bewildered and is not sure how to react and the President is blowing steam as usual. He has already called an emergency meeting of our inner circle for tomorrow morning to discuss our reaction to the proposal. So hang on to your hats until the next news bulletin.'

****

Chapter Thirty

British Delegation offer to visit Zambelia

As Chief Secretary to the President, Nixon Makau was first to receive the official communication that the British Commonwealth Secretary had indicated a wish to visit Zambelia with a delegation in order to investigate reports of human rights violations. Hardly able to hide his glee, he passed the word to Big Mama who in her turn, passed it on to the President knowing full well it was more than likely to cause that gentleman to froth at the mouth with uncontrolled fury.

It was a common belief in medieval times that the body's health depended on the balance between four vital fluids: blood, phlegm, yellow bile, and black bile. It was reckoned that those prone to fits of anger suffered from an excess of the last two. If there was any basis for this theory, President Matata was a prime example of one who must have had gallons of the fluids flowing from his liver since no-one could remember ever seeing him other than being in a foul temper. His moods varied on a ten-point scale, all the way up from number one, irritation, on a good day; then climbing to number ten, fury, in a particularly black period. Survival in the life of the palace depended to a large extent on being able to assess his mood on a given day. Nixon often wondered why the skin of the president's knuckles wasn't pared to the bone, given the amount of time he spent thumping the table.

Early on the morning after receiving the communiqué from the British Commonwealth Office, the inner circle was summoned to an emergency meeting in the presidential office. It wasn't hard to estimate the level of Matata's anger – somewhere between an eight and a nine. It might be wondered why not "a ten" but that level could only have meant apoplexy and madness.

The meeting was set for ten o'clock but the four subordinate members were in their seats at the committee table a good half an hour before it was due to start. It wouldn't have done to have poured fuel on to the fire of Matata's fury by being late even by a second.

On the stroke of ten, Matata stormed into the office, the Commonwealth letter in his hand. He sat at the head of the table and slapped the letter on the table-top and thumped it hard with his fist. He was his usual fuming self.

'I suspect that someone in the know has blown the gaffe and revealed state secrets to the British government,' he bellowed. 'How else would they have taken it into their heads to come here to carry out an investigation?'

Nixon's heart skipped a beat when he heard this; he hoped his consternation was not apparent on his face. Had Matata heard something? Was he, Nixon, under suspicion? If so, the game was up and he could expect to be arrested and banged up in Tagooma any time now. Execution would certainly follow.

He decided it was best to allay the president's suspicions right away by diverting the spotlight away from himself and on to somebody else. 'I think there can be no doubt,' Nixon proclaimed, 'that the source of our trouble has come through Monsignor McGinn. I'm sure he has gone immediately to the British Commonwealth Office and told them all he knew and suspected. I am positive that that is what has triggered this sudden desire on the part of the British Commonwealth Office to look into our affairs.'

'Whatever the reason,' Matata exploded, thumping the table for the second time, 'how dare these guttersnipes in London order us to receive a delegation to investigate supposed violations of human rights! Who is running this country? Have they forgotten that we are an independent nation? Was our fight for freedom from our colonial masters in vain? Yet here they are having the effrontery to demand that we accept a mission to look into our policies and procedures! It's an insult to Zambelia!' he bellowed, banging the table several times with his knuckles. 'I propose we send them a reply telling them in no uncertain terms that, on no account, shall we agree to such an investigation! Now let me hear what the rest of you think!'

Nixon looked around at the faces of the other members and knew that it was going to take every ounce of his diplomacy, tact and guile to persuade them to change their minds. The best route to Matata's heart, he thought, is through Big Mama. If she's opposed to the delegation, that's the end of my big plan and it's back to the drawing board to devise a different scheme. But if she agrees that the investigation should take place, there's hope. However, it was Colonel Kiboko who spoke first as Nixon knew he would.

'I think we should tell the British Government to go to hell. They have no right to investigate anything in this country. What we do here is our own business and we should call in the British Ambassador immediately and tell him that under no circumstances can we allow such a delegation to trespass on our soil and on our independent status. I should like to know definitely where the British got hold of such detailed information about our affairs. It's by no means certain that Monsignor McGinn was the source of the leak. I have my own suspicions but I shall keep them to myself until I have more evidence.'

This last observation worried Nixon for a moment and he wondered how much Kiboko knew. Then he dismissed this stab of concern because he was sure Kiboko wasn't bright enough to work things out for himself. I can see what's worrying him though, he thought. He has all those murdered bodies buried in the grounds of Tagooma and it certainly wouldn't be in his best interests to have them dug up and have to explain how and why they got there. For him that would mean curtains and no mistake.

Next to speak was Schneider. 'I agree with our Life President. 'We don't want a bunch of strangers traipsing through our hospital wards infecting our patients with their foul germs. We should reply in the strongest possible terms that we object to such a mission as that proposed.'

Nixon thought: there's another one with a lot to hide. Schneider would have to account for the numerous blood donors who mysteriously vanished and the patients who inexplicably suffered brain death on the operating table following minor operations. He would have great difficulty too in covering up the hideous activities that took place under the euphemistic title of research.

It's time for me to speak up, Nixon thought. It's going to be uphill work to bring them round to a sensible decision for the good of the country.

'We have every right to tell the British Government to go and jump in a lake,' he said carefully, 'and I sympathise with the sentiments so far expressed. But stop and think for a moment. If we turn down the request of the Commonwealth Office, consider the consequences. We shall undoubtedly lose the financial aid, not only from our mother country but from other countries as well, including the USA and a few other European countries. Our treasury is already in a parlous state and we are broke. Without international aid, we are in really serious trouble and we should have to cancel many major projects, like schools, roads, hospitals and...' Here Nixon paused and took a sly look in Big Mama's direction, 'our new palace complex at the lake.'

The ploy worked for she frowned and looked distinctly worried. She could see her ambitious plans for the palace with her own adjoining personal mansion, plus the regular shopping trips abroad, being sucked down the plug hole.

It was Matata however who uttered the next contribution. 'WE are an independent country and we've had to fight hard to win this recognition. I accept what our Aide, Mr Makau, has said and we should tell the British to jump in a lake, preferably their own.'

It was Big Mama's turn to offer an opinion. 'It is easy to tell the British government to take a running jump and we should feel the better for having said it but I think on this occasion we should swallow our pride and accept the delegation.'

The President was looking wonderingly in her direction. He relied so much on her and her therapeutic ministrations, he would do anything for her. He was completely under her spell.

'Yes,' Big Mama continued, 'our country would be left in dire straits if we were to lose international aid. There would be great hardship and suffering without those external funds. I vote that we accept the delegation but take measures to reduce its effectiveness. Surely we in Zambelia are astute enough to draw the delegation's teeth by making sure that the investigators get to see only those things we want them to see, hear only those things we want them to hear. We can manipulate things by insisting on choosing who the delegation will be allowed to interview. Whatever we do, we must keep our visitors away from troublemakers among the prisoners or the citizens in the street. Think of the United Nations delegation to investigate the WMDs of Saddam Hussein in Iraq. He succeeded in pulling the wool over *their* eyes. If he could it, so can we!'

Matata was now smiling approvingly in Big Mama's direction. 'As usual, Marianne, we have to come to you for wisdom. Refresh our memory. What were those WMDs you speak of?'

'They were the Weapons of Mass Destruction that Saddam Hussein was supposed to be hiding in Iraq. The UN team carried out a thorough investigation and found nothing.

Hussein somehow managed to conceal his facilities for manufacturing poison gas and nuclear weapons. Iraqis are surely not cleverer than Zambelians! We could adopt techniques to hide our facilities too. Kiboko could give better food, clean up the prisons, issue mattresses, remove evidence of torture machines, give special attention to prison records. Schneider could do a similar job on his medical facilities. All of us must be on our toes so the delegates suspect nothing and we must seem to be as innocent as new born babes. Put on expressions as mild as milk. The same precautions in the hospitals. Clean them up! Make sure the medical records are in order. Dr Schneider knows what I mean by "in order".

By this time the President was nodding vigorously in approval. Taking the cue from him, the others began to fall in line. Nixon knew that her arguments had prevailed.

Kiboko said: 'I could instruct my subordinates to clean up their act, I suppose. In Tagooma, I could order Nyoka and Gumbo to fumigate the place – God knows, it certainly needs it. They could improve conditions for the prisoners by adding a little meat and fish to their diet, providing new mattresses, a few extra blankets and so on. As for the prison records, they'll be dumped into Lake Zambelia. I'll get on to it right away.'

Schneider invariably followed Kiboko when it came to speaking. 'I could do the same in the medical facilities, the hospitals, the mortuary, and the research unit. The delegation will get to see nothing unless I have approved of it first. However whatever happens, we must keep them away from the Research Bureau. It wouldn't do for them to start inspecting our comatose cases. If it means we continue to receive overseas money, I'm in favour of it. I shall crack down on all medical staff and see that a thorough sanitation programme is instigated.'

Big Mama felt it was time to press home her viewpoint. 'Apart from the question of international aid, Mr President, I don't think we need have fear about overseas funds being cut off because the West is in mortal fear that we shall go over to the East for aid. We have only to suggest that we shall be approaching Russia or China and the West becomes neurotic and paranoid. They fear that we shall go over to Russian Communism and, worse still from their point of view, that we shall become Maoists. We can rest assured that financial aid will continue to flow from London and Washington.'

The President said, 'As usual, it is our wonderful First Lady who puts our minds at rest. We have given our opinions and it is time to vote on it. Having listened to Marianne's persuasive arguments, I, for one, am in favour of allowing the delegation. Let us now have a show of hands.'

Naturally all five members were in favour and Nixon duly noted the decision in the minutes. By early afternoon of the same day, he had typed up the account of the meeting and the decision that had been reached. Before taking it into the President for final signature, he met Big Mama in her office so that she could vet what he had written as a true and accurate record.

'Well done, my dear Nixon,' she exclaimed. 'As usual, a model of efficiency. I shall take the minutes into the President for his approval after his nap later today. Then you can communicate our agreement to Sir Hugh Baxter, the British Commonwealth Secretary.'

'Very well, ma'am, it shall be done as soon as I get the signed document back. On another matter, I should like to alert you to what I suspect has been taking place behind our backs. As you know there is no love lost between Colonel Kiboko and Doctor Schneider but I have heard on the palace grapevine that it was the German doctor who wrote to the British Commonwealth about the violations of human rights at the colonel's prisons at Tagooma and Gereza. Schneider would dearly love to see Kiboko brought down and his face trampled in the mud.'

'But, Nixon, wouldn't a British investigation land Schneider himself in the soup as well? He too has a lot to hide.'

'I believe he thinks he has hidden his hospital records and activities so well that he will be in the clear. Of course, he may be mistaken if the British delegation is sharp-eyed but Schneider believes himself too clever and so will be above suspicion. As I said earlier, this is the rumour going round the palace and I'm not certain how much significance we should attach to it.'

'Best to leave it for the present, Nixon, because if the President gets wind of it, he will order their immediate arrest and possible execution of either one or even both.'

'Yes, ma'am. You can rely on me to keep such rumours under my hat but in the past you have insisted that I make you fully aware of what people are thinking and saying. I felt it was my duty to keep you so informed.'

'You are absolutely right, Nixon, and I am grateful to you for it. Fore-warned is fore-armed.'

****

Chapter Thirty-One
Sir Hugh Baxter and his delegation

The Right Honourable Sir Hugh Baxter looked at the massive map of the world that dominated the main wall of his superbly furnished office.

'Where in hell's bells *is* this damned place Zambelia?' he grumbled to Sir Nigel Eddington, his Permanent Secretary, who was seated before the huge mahogany desk taking notes.

'As the Commonwealth Secretary,' Sir Hugh continued, 'I suppose I ought to know but damn it, there are fifty-four countries in our family of nations and I can't be expected to remember the exact locations of every single one of them. Not only that, the bloody names are so confusing as they all sound the same to me. Mali, Malawi and Malaya, and I'm damned if I can remember which ones are members and which are not. If I remember rightly, Malawi is in the Commonwealth, isn't that right?'

'Yes, sir, and Mali comes under the French umbrella,' Sir Nigel replied evenly. 'Malaya joined the Commonwealth in 1957, dissolved in 1963 and came back as a part of Malaysia.'

'As for Nigeria,' Sir Hugh complained, 'it's been in and out like a bloody jack-in-the-box. And then there are all those damned Zam countries like Zimbabwe, Zambia (and not to be confused with The Gambia), Mozambique, and Zambelia.'

The Permanent Secretary approached and examined the map closely. 'There it is, Sir Hugh, wedged between those other Zambesi nations.'

'So that's the place I'm to visit with the Human Rights delegation. Thank the Lord it's only for a couple of days until I've got the investigations started and well under way. It isn't strictly necessary for me to make the visit but, given the condemnatory secret reports we've been receiving from the Justice and Peace Commission and that clandestine document smuggled out from that mole in the Zambelian government, it wouldn't have looked good if I'd pleaded that I was too busy to accompany the mission. I must say though, Nigel, it's a damned nuisance having to go with the delegation since I shall have to forgo my nightly visits to the Athenaeum. The trip has one saving grace however since it'll give me a chance to practise my Kiswahili in which I was once fluent. And who knows? I might be able to fit in the odd round of golf as I hear they have some fine courses out there.'

'I believe so, sir,' Sir Nigel agreed.

'We've also been given the job of choosing members to serve on the delegation and liaising with the Zambelians about their itinerary. I'm damned if I know anybody who is able and willing to serve. The P.M. suggested a team of five and we've been told to put a good representative group together. How I was expected to make the selection, God only knows, since I'm new to this game. Good thing I can leave the business to a chap like you, eh Nigel! And now whom did you and your civil service chappies nominate? Refresh my memory?'

The Permanent Secretary consulted a file marked Zambelia Investigation. 'Head of the team is to be Sir Michael Mowbray QC for his extensive experience of dealing with human rights cases; Richard Sutherland, M.P. from the Home Office for his wide knowledge of the British prison system.'

338

'Gained, it's to be hoped, from the outside and not from experience within, eh what! Nigel!' Sir Hugh guffawed.

Sir Nigel responded with a pained smile. 'Yes, quite so, sir. To continue: there's Margaret Donaldson from the EHRC, the Equality and Human Rights Commission; Doctor Robert Lovell, a hospital administrator with supposedly a deep understanding of the British National Health Service; and finally another woman, Professor Jane Radcliffe from the Justice and Peace Commission.

'All splendid choices, Nigel. I congratulate you. Together they should have the gumption to ferret out any serious violations of human rights.'

'A good team, sir. The P.M. reckons five days should be enough to assess the situation there. He suggests that you yourself accompany the team for the first two days to introduce our people to the Zambelian executive committee, their so-called inner gang of five, who will organise their detailed itinerary.'

'Sounds fine to me, Nigel. I certainly don't want to spend more time out there than I have to. Thank you, Nigel. 'You're absolutely top-notch as usual. Thank God we have people like you to do these administrative chores for us.'

***

Sir Hugh was a big man – in every sense of the word. He weighed around twenty-five stone and had a finger in every pie, "literally", his rivals joked, as well as referring to him as the Billy Bunter of the Commons. Sir Hugh put it down to professional jealousy because his true friends, being more intelligent and perceptive, described him as sturdy and strong, a view confirmed by his doting mother who regarded him as being "well-built and a fine figure of a man". He'd tried every diet under the sun but nothing had worked and he had finally come to the conclusion that it was in his genes and there was nothing to be done about them. Laugh and grow fat, he told himself reassuringly.

Ten days after receiving acceptance of the proposed visit by the Zambelian authorities, Sir Hugh called the five members of the British delegation to a meeting in his office in King Charles Street, Westminster. The meeting began with coffee and the usual cordial chit-chat, those present using first names with each other as they were well acquainted having served together on previous committees. The atmosphere was relaxed and Sir Hugh maintained that more work was done face to face than could have been achieved by a blizzard of written memoranda posted out to them.

'Thank you for making the effort to attend here today,' Sir Hugh told them when opening the formal proceedings. 'I shall hand you over to my Permanent Secretary, Sir Nigel Eddington, who has called this meeting on my behalf and is much more *au fait* with procedures and protocol etcetera.'

'Thank you, Sir Hugh,' the Permanent Secretary began. 'I know how difficult it must have been for you to postpone your busy schedules to be here this morning but I am sure you are aware how vitally important this delegation is. I take it you have read and studied the top secret and distressing dossier written and sent to us by the private secretary to the president of the country. I cannot stress enough the need to keep the identity of the presidential aide who drew up the dossier a secret because, were his name to become public, it would almost certainly mean not only his imprisonment but also his torture and death. I must say that government circles were somewhat surprised that the Zambelian government agreed to this delegation. We can only assume that they are a little afraid that international aid may be discontinued if they do not accede to our request for this investigative mission.'

Sir Michael Mowbray who was to head the delegation replied. 'Thank you, Sir Hugh and Sir Nigel. I think I can speak for the rest of us here when I say how deeply honoured

340

and touched we feel to have been invited to join this important delegation. We fully appreciate the need to keep the name of the Zambelian aide a secret and you can rely on our complete and absolute discretion. Perhaps we could put it about in Zambelia government that it was a disaffected civil servant who had been recently deported who was our main source and compiler of the dossier. I know from preliminary discussion with members how deeply shocked we have been by its revelations. Perhaps I could ask Sir Nigel to brief us now as to the details of the programme envisaged for this mission.'

'Certainly, Sir Michael,' the Permanent Secretary replied. 'It will entail flying out to Lundazi early next week where you will meet the executive committee of the government there. Unfortunately, President Matata himself will be unable to attend this initial meeting because of indisposition. Confidentially I should tell you that the President is now quite old and rumour has it that he is senile and extremely forgetful and so not in a fit state to preside over an investigative delegation such as this. There will be an opportunity however to discuss findings with him after completion of your various enquiries. Meanwhile, you will liaise with the other four members of the Zambelian executive committee: namely Marie Antoinette Makubwa the official and confidential presidential consort; Nixon Makau, Senior Presidential Aide; Colonel Kenneth Kiboko, Head of State Security; and Doctor Max Schneider, Head of Medical Services. With this so-called inner circle, you will be able to discuss how best to deploy members of the delegation so as to make best use of your various specialisations. One last point and an important one is that I am requesting that a Major Fisher from MI6 accompanies you to check out the security arrangements for your visit. By security, I mean not only your safety but the privacy of your deliberations because Zambelia is well-known for the ubiquitous listening devices it has installed in private and public rooms.'

Throughout the proceedings, the Commonwealth Secretary, Sir Hugh, who had been nodding approvingly like one of the little dolls one sometimes sees on the back shelf of a car, felt it was time he explained his own part in the arrangements. 'I'm only sorry,' he said plaintively, 'that I cannot be with you for the whole period of your investigations. I have been asked however in the absence of President Matata, to open a new model farm, built with British funds, at the Odongo College of Agriculture on our arrival. So I shall be with you for the first two days only and will then have to return to London for an important conference with another Commonwealth member.'

'Thank you, Sir Hugh,' the Permanent Secretary said, 'no-one understands more than I the pressures you are under and I am sure the delegation quite understands your predicament. I shall now hand over the chair to Sir Michael as head of the delegation to tell us how he proposes to ploy his team.'

'Thank you,' Sir Michael Mowbray replied. 'We have read the dossier referred to and so we are aware of the seriousness of the situation in Zambelia. I propose to ask Richard Sullivan because of his expertise of Home Office Prisons to concentrate his attention to conditions at Tagooma Prison; Margaret Donaldson from the Equality Commission to look at the women's prison at Gereza; Dr Robert Lovell to investigate the Lundazi Hospital, the morgue and especially the so-called Matata Medical Research Bureau there; Professor Jane Radcliffe will talk to the university people – both student and academic staff; I myself will try to meet and talk with ordinary members of the public - the so-called man in the street. At the end of four days, we should be in a position to assess the general situation in the country and so we shall meet in Lundazi to have a preliminary discussion of our findings. By that time we should be able to assess the accuracy of the picture painted in the secret dossier. On the fifth day, we shall meet with President Matata himself and discuss any concerns we may have. Finally we shall return to Britain and write up our reports and submit our

342

recommendations to both the British and the Zambelian governments. May I take it that these arrangements meet with your agreement?'

There was a general murmur of approval from the other members. Richard Sullivan said: 'I think the arrangements proposed are admirable and will be welcomed by everyone here. I'd like to sound one note of caution, however; one that we should perhaps keep in mind, namely that the various supervisors of these institutions we shall be visiting will try every trick in the book to pull the wool over our eyes. So we need to be alert. Remember too that many of the interviewing rooms we shall use will be bugged. Our Major Fisher can only be in one place at a given time. Remember that walls have ears and we must try to interview our subjects in the open air whenever possible. Insist on it if necessary.'

'You are right, Richard, of course' Margaret Donaldson said. 'No doubt, frenzied steps will be taken to hide evidence by providing such things as new mattresses and improving the food in the prisons and the hospitals. Inmates may also be intimidated and may be nervous about telling us about the true state of affairs in their institution if they think for a moment that there is any chance of their confidences being betrayed.'

'That's why it is so important,' Jane Radcliffe added, 'that we interview our subjects without the presence of their guards or supervisors. In that way we have a better chance at getting at the truth.'

'Point taken,' Dr Robert Lovell said, 'which brings me to the subject of talking with President Matata who may be suffering from dementia and the fact that his evidence may not make much sense.'

'I think we must take that into account when assessing its worth,' Sir Michael said.

The discussion of these points continued for a couple of hours and when the meeting finally broke up, the members had a clear idea of what to expect during their visit to

343

Zambelia. It would not be true to say they were looking forward to their trip but they were hoping that their findings and proposals might at least lead to an improvement in the lives of Zambelia's citizens.

***

The following week, the delegation and Sir Hugh Baxter flew out to Zambelia to launch the investigation. Sir Hugh had had a busy demanding schedule in the week preceding the trip, having presided over more than a dozen conferences involving many different Commonwealth members. By the time he was due to fly out to Zambelia, he had forgotten not only what day it was but the name of the country he was going to. This might explain why the mission began inauspiciously with his first speech at the opening of the model farm at which there were present staff, students, local farmers and their workers. Sir Hugh had been brushing up his Swahili and had been hoping to try out one or two choice phrases in a little speech but he put his foot in it in his first few words.

'Academics and fellow farmers,' Sir Hugh proclaimed, 'let me begin by saying what a great pleasure it is to be here today in this beautiful country of yours, Zimbabwe...'

On the platform Sir Michael tugged at his sleeve and whispered urgently, 'No, Sir Hugh, not Zimbabwe – Zambelia!'

Sir Hugh didn't quite catch what he'd said and corrected himself with, 'Sorry, sorry. Not Zimbabwe. My mistake. I'm happy to be here with you here in Zambia.'

Now the presiding Professor of Agriculture, David Waithaka, stood up and rasped angrily, 'Not Zimbabwe! Not Zambia! But Zambelia! Zambelia!'

'Zambelia! Zambelia!' Sir Hugh gasped, correcting himself for the second time. 'I thought that's what I'd said. But to continue. *Watu wote* ("My dear people") *Ni me kuja hapa leo* (I've come here today) from the great Mama Queen Lithabet in Buckingham Palace, London.'

344

'Mavi! Mavi!' the crowd roared back.

Several senior officers of the Public Safety Unit who were supervising the event looked most unhappy at this response and scowled menacingly at the crowd.

What a lovely warm welcome, Sir Hugh thought. Despite the obvious disapproval of the supervising militia, the audience evidently thinks my speech is Mave –Marvellous! At least I've made up for that initial *faux pas*. What a blunder to make getting the name of the country wrong! He went on with his speech.

'I have come from the British Government and we can promise you great improvements in your lives here.'

'Mavi! Mavi!' the audience screamed.

Mavi, Sir Hugh thought. That's a new Swahili word but its meaning is pretty obvious. Encouraged, he continued with his address. 'Yes, improvements in your lives. Better sewage! Better health care!'

'Mavi! Mavi!' from the crowd.

'Better educational facilities! Better roads and a better transport system!'

'Mavi! Mavi! Mavi!' the yells reached fever pitch.

I cannot remember ever being received by such enthusiasm, Sir Hugh said to himself. They evidently approve of the promises I'm making. He continued with his speech by enumerating the various things that the Westminster Government could do for them. He finally rounded off his speech with a final promise.

'We shall build more schools and more colleges for you. As a British statesman, I give you my word. You can rely on it! My word is my bond!'

These final words were greeted with clamorous shouts.

'Mavi! Mavi! Mavi!' and one last acclamation that rose into the heavens. 'MAAAVI!'

At the end of the speech, Sir Hugh turned to the Professor of Agriculture and exclaimed, 'My dear Professor. I am most touched by the heartiness of their response. I think my little speech went down well judging by the ardour of that reception.'

'I'll give you that,' Professor Waithaka replied evenly. 'Your speech certainly evoked deep emotions. Now, may I invite you and your visiting team to my house for tea? It's just across this field. Take care how you go. This field has been grazed by a large herd of bulls recently so do be careful that you don't step into the mavi.'

Sir Hugh Baxter's misreading of his map of Africa may explain the "mavi" response of the audience but that was not the end of the matter. Zambelians exacted their revenge for his confusing their country Zambelia with Zambia when that same evening, the Radio Zambelia news bulletin announced that the country had given a warm welcome to the arrival of Sir Huge Backside, the British Common Secretary.

****

Chapter Thirty-Two
Delegation prepares report

After the Commonwealth Secretary had returned to London, the delegation settled down to the serious business of checking the veracity of the condemnatory dossier. The five delegates dispersed to their various destinations: Sir Richard Sullivan to Tagooma Men's Prison; Margaret Donaldson to Gereza Women's Prison; Dr Robert Lovell to Lundazi Hospital; Professor Jane Radcliffe to Hekima University; and Sir Michael Mowbray to interview "the man in the street".

***

After four days of intensive visits and interrogations, the delegates finally met up again in a large interview room provided by the Hotel Sanduku which they had been using as the base for their headquarters. The five of them looked exhausted after their whirlwind tour.

'Welcome back,' Sir Michael Mowbray said. 'Before we begin our deliberations, let me assure you that Major Fisher has done a complete sweep of this room and it is free of bugs and so you may speak freely. I hope you have had a chance to wind down after the ordeal of the last four days. I'm sure you've found it gruelling but I look forward to receiving your reports. The question before us is: how far is the secret dossier we received from the Zambelian mole an accurate picture of the political situation here at the present time. I shall call first on Richard Sullivan for his contribution. Sir Richard?'

'Thank you, Sir Michael. I have spent three harrowing days talking to prisoners at Tagooma prison. The superintendent in charge is a Captain Gumbo but also present were Major Nyoka and Colonel Kiboko of the Public Safety Unit. I must confess that I had some difficulty in persuading these gentlemen to leave me so that I could interview the prisoners in private. In the end I had to resort to interviewing the inmates singly out in the open. Let me say right away that I think the dossier is accurate in the description of the place despite the futile and obvious attempts to cover up the dreadful conditions that exist there by providing new mattresses and a recent improvement in diet by the provision of a little meat and fish. There is severe overcrowding of ordinary prisons and I found two hundred and eighty-five (285) prisoners in one cell measuring five metres by four metres with one prisoner dying on average every two nights. Political prisoners and prisoners of conscience who have been incarcerated without charge or trial suffer particularly harsh conditions, which in many cases amount to cruel, inhuman and degrading treatment. Prisoners are kept naked and chained to the floor, given minimal food, denied medical care and severely beaten. Many prisoners have died because of these terrible conditions. One of the detainees, Deputy Chifunza, a former Minister in the government, is kept chained to a wall; he told me how his colleague Deputy Chilulu was disposed of by being thrown from a helicopter on the way to the prison. One young medical student, a Jack Zulu, has been beaten up several times; he is there because he made accusations concerning his two young twin brothers who have now become additional names on the list of "the disappeared". An Asian trader by the name of Tulshidas says he is being tortured and has been threatened with execution even though he has already paid a ransom of half a million dollars. Many prisoners have been simply shot on the whim of Colonel Kiboko whom many described as a homicidal maniac. There is perhaps a little hope in Tagooma Prison in the persons of Captain Gumbo and Major Nyoka and I believe both these men could be turned given the right circumstances. Both of them say - and I believe them - they are forced under the threat of their own execution to participate in the barbaric activities taking place at this prison. If we can guarantee him protection, Captain Gumbo has volunteered to show us where the bodies of many prisoners who met with sudden and unexpected deaths are buried. Things are desperate in Tagooma Prison and the sooner we come to the aid of the inmates there, the better. Colonel Kiboko, Head of the Public Safety Unit has a lot to answer for.'

'Thank you, Richard, for that frank and comprehensive account,' Sir Michael said. 'Let us hope that this evil man Kiboko will get his comeuppance. Right, now let's hear from Margaret Donaldson who has been gauging the situation at the women's prison. Margaret.'

'Thank you, Sir Michael. The conditions I found at Gereza Prison are pretty much the same as those Richard has observed at Tagooma. Women prisoners sleep on the floor and the number of blankets provided depends on the whim of the prison warders. There have been cases of rape and sexual favours being the price some women have to pay for an extra blanket. Many female prisoners have received severe beatings and electric shocks, and one woman I spoke to had been stripped naked, beaten and poked with an electric cattle prod. There are so many distressing cases in the women's prison that it is difficult to single out any cases worse than those at the men's prison. Perhaps one or two cases may be sufficient to give a general idea of how desperate things are in Gereza. One lady, a Dr Sadie Mazoe of the university law department, is at present serving an indefinite sentence (since there was no trial) for having written a letter to the Roman Catholic magazine *Leo* criticising the arrest of women for wearing or selling culottes – under Zambelian law, women are not allowed to wear trousers. The most depressing case is perhaps that of Veronica Wichira a university lecturer in law who was imprisoned along with her late husband, Joshua, for the "crime" of opposing the government's foreign policy. They were both tried before a "traditional court" which refused them a defence lawyer or the right to call witnesses. Both were sentenced to death for treason but because of an international outcry, this was commuted by President Matata to life. When Joshua died in prison, Veronica was not even permitted to attend his funeral. She remains chained up as a prisoner of conscience.

'There are many similar cases but these will illustrate the profound injustice that prevails in Zambelia at the present time. I would close by saying that conditions are indeed as those described in the secret dossier; if anything it is an understatement.'

'Thank you, Margaret, for that superb summary. The political situation in this country is every bit as bad as we feared. I turn now to Professor Jane Radcliffe who has been visiting the university at Hegima to talk to students and academic staff to gauge the situation there. I hand the chair over to you, now, Jane.'

'Thank you, Sir Michael,' Jane replied. 'I managed to talk to students and staff at the University and the only thing I have to report is that the prevailing mood there is one of extreme anger at the political repression in the country and the way human lives have simply been snuffed out or forced to endure years of detention without trial. They feel too that intellectual life is being stifled by the dead hand of the strict censorship laws. The people I spoke to are seething too because of the disappearance of both students and staff. In particular, they feel furious and frustrated at the treatment they have received. Two highly regarded members of the academic staff have simply disappeared, both from the English Department. The first was a Dr Frank Johnson who is believed to have been arrested with one of his students, Geoffrey Shairi, both of them accused of writing seditious poetry and literature. Nothing has been heard of them since they were taken away by the Public Safety police. The other missing lecturer is a Dr Sue Delamere who recently arrived in the country and has not been seen since giving her first lecture on Shakespeare. No-one knows what has happened to her and her disappearance is a complete mystery. In the matter of students, three brothers from the Zulu family have also vanished without trace. The two youngest, twin brothers, Andrew and Bernard, were last seen on the way back to the university for the start of the term. Two friends of the twins think they saw them being driven towards Hegima in the presidential motorcade though they are not one hundred per cent sure since the cars drove by so quickly. At a meeting of the Student Union, I had the impression that the more radical students among them are so incensed by what is happening in their country that they are ready to revolt and march on the government. The atmosphere when I was there was like a time bomb waiting to be primed and about ready to explode. The only thing that's stopping them at the moment is the influence of the more thoughtful students among them who hope that our delegation may help produce some positive results.'

'Thank you Jane for that clear but distressing picture,' Sir Michael said. 'It is to be hoped that things improve soon in Zambelia or we may witness extreme violence if the students take it into their heads to riot and march on Lundazi. I too have been trying to sound out opinion but I have not been as successful as the rest of you in getting people to talk openly. I got the impression that the ban on free speech has been so effective, it has resulted in extreme fear and the ordinary citizen is too frightened to say openly what's in his mind. Typical was the man who would only talk to me if it were in secret. When I asked him why, he replied: 'Because in this country, there is no freedom of expression whatsoever. If we were seen talking in full view, I would face prison or even hanging.' 'Is it that bad?' I asked. He replied and I quote: "It's so bad that nobody dares to come out and say what they feel and think. Matata's Youth "Gestapo" Brigade could kill us as easily as you would crush an insect." Similar views were repeated to me many times over. We can see now why this country has been described as "The Country Where Silence Rules." I turn now to Dr Robert Lovell who has been visiting the Lundazi Medical facilities. Robert, your report, please?'

'Thank you, Sir Michael. I have listened with profound shock to the reports which have gone before but I regret to say that my own findings at the medical facilities are much worse than anything so far described. In thirty years of medical experience, I've seen many terrible things but I've never been as sickened as I was by what I saw here at the ominous-sounding Matata Medical Research Bureau. The Medical facilities are divided into four sections: the General Hospital, the Intensive Care Unit, The Mortuary, and the Matata Research Bureau. I cannot remember coming across anything as frightening and as horrifying as what I found at this so-called Bureau. The hospital and the morgue are bad enough but what upset me to the core was what went on in this division presided over by Dr Max Schneider. In the wards of the Bureau there are approximately forty comatose bodies lying in beds and awaiting attention. What caught my eye was the fact that none of these patients appeared to be very old being mainly youths or children. I asked to see the medical records but was told that unfortunately they had been "lost" in a recent fire. Some of these young people are there having barely survived routine operations, like an appendectomy or gall bladder removal while some were simply blood donors; but all came out of the operating theatre like zombies. Most shocking is that some of these helpless patients were simply snatched off the street. We have all heard of the kidnapping of street children taken for illegal adoption agencies but this is a more sinister development; it's a case of children being kidnapped for organ transplants. I would never have been able to unearth this information had it not been for a practitioner named Dr Simon Timothy who has observed the evil routines being conducted and supervised by Max Schneider. This Dr

352

Timothy came clean only when I promised him immunity from prosecution and I think we should honour that pledge. For some time, this man has been under great stress because of what he has been compelled to do and he seemed relieved to be able to open up and tell me exactly what had been going on. Had he tried earlier to expose these corrupt and evil practices, he would most certainly have become one of the coma patients himself.

'The Research Bureau is a clearing house for the sale of illicit black-market organs for transplant. Patients are first tissue typed and then during the operations on these young people, a touch of carbon monoxide is introduced into the anaesthesia; just enough to destroy the upper brain and induce a state of coma; from that point on, he or she becomes a living corpse. Though the victim is brain dead, the vital organs are still healthy and functioning normally. The patient remains in the ward until the organs can be extracted and sold on the black market, kidneys and corneas being most valuable and much in demand. Dr Timothy showed me examples of organs about to be flown out to addresses in the Middle East and South Africa; they were to be sent in insulated boxes clearly labelled "HUMAN ORGANS. EXTREMELY URGENT. FRAGILE AND PERISHABLE". Speed is of the essence as the organs last for only about forty hours. This Research Bureau is nothing more than a holding unit for the sale of human organs and body parts.'

'Dr Timothy described many heart-breaking cases among the victims. For example, there was a whole family of father and two sons who came to the hospital to donate blood and instead gave their vital body parts. One young orphan boy slipped and banged his head at school and was admitted with slight concussion. He never came out again. There also seems to be some evidence that sometimes organs have been extracted before the patient was clinically dead. Dr Timothy told me that in some cases, there was still evidence of response in their encephalograms when the parts were taken.'

Sir Michael was aghast. 'What you have told us, Robert, is so horrifying as to be beyond belief,' he said, visibly moved. 'We should be able to corroborate everything you have told us if ever we get to dig up the bodies now interred in the hospital cemetery. The corpses would have body parts missing and there are the relatives who'd be missing their loved ones.'

'Schneider appears to have thought of that,' Robert Lovell replied, 'by having many of the bodies cremated but fortunately not all. As for relatives, he chose his victims carefully from street children, patients from psychiatric hospitals or simply down-and-outs whose relatives, if any, would not miss them.'

'Nevertheless, this man Schneider, like Kiboko, is a criminal of the first order and when we finally get things moving, we must make sure these men are brought to justice and get what they deserve, if it's the last thing we do.'

****

Chapter Thirty-Three
Delegation meets President Matata

For more than three weeks, the members of the British Human Rights Delegation had been waiting, with a certain amount of trepidation, for D Day. This was to be the day they were to meet the great man himself, President Samson Matata. A British journalist who had once interviewed him had told them how at one meeting, the president had become incensed at something said and had slammed his fist so hard on the desk that dishes and a water jug had flown into the air showering the aides with peanuts, crisps and soda water. 'He was like a cabaret act,' the journalist had laughed, 'and we were entertained whenever he threw a wobbly' the accepted expression meaning "blew his top".

At eleven o'clock on the morning of the fateful day, delegation members arrived at State House in Lundazi and were ushered into a large, comfortable, panelled interview room and provided with coffee and biscuits and left to await the appearance of the Chief. Sir Michael lit his pipe and Richard Sullivan one of his foul-smelling Abdullah cigarettes. The place that had been reserved for the President himself was a throne-like gilt chair set on a dais two feet above floor level. The arrangement was deliberate, the delegates thought, since they would have to look up to him whenever they addressed him. First to meet them was Mr Nixon Makau, Private presidential secretary. Members of the delegation realized that although he was small in stature, he

355

was the second most powerful influence after Marie Antoinette who undoubtedly was number one.

'Good morning, ladies and gentlemen,' Nixon began. 'Welcome to State House and to this audience with our Life President who will be with us soon. Please put out your cigarette and pipe as they are likely to throw the Life President into a foul mood.' He signalled to a servant to open the windows and switch on the ceiling fan.

The use of the word "audience" put the delegates in mind of a meeting with His Holiness the Pope, which in some ways it resembled since they had the distinct feeling that genuflection in his presence might not be entirely out of order.

'The Life President has a tight schedule' Makau went on, 'and has agreed to afford you an hour of his valuable time.'

'How should we address the President?' Jane Radcliffe asked. 'Does he have a favourite title that we should employ?'

Without the slightest trace of irony, Nixon replied: 'The President has many titles and you may use any one of them. He is: Life President of the Republic, Saviour of Zambelia, Founder President of the Massuyu Conference Party, Supreme Magistrate, Supreme Commander of the Armed Forces, and Marshall of Zambelia. I think for the purposes of this interview though, Life President is the one he would favour. One word of warning. As I tell all visitors, try not to provoke him with offensive or disrespectful questions, especially if he is wearing his dark glasses for that could mean he is in a bad temper and you won't find your audience with him very productive.'

The delegation knew full well what he meant by "offensive questions", that is any questions about Zambelia's human rights record or stories emanating from the Matata Research Bureau, which might make the Chief throw a "wobbly". Sir Michael though felt that, as a representative of Britain, he ought to assert his own authority and not feel that

356

he had to avoid unpalatable subjects in case they ruffled the feathers or irritated the President of this country which had such an abysmal human rights record.

'Perhaps I should point out Mr Makau that we have not come all the way from London in order to have a pleasant *tete-a-tete* with your President. We are here to discuss and examine the suppression of democracy and the freedom of the Zambelian people and…'

As they were talking, there came a sudden burst of laughter from behind the main door and Nixon visibly relaxed and smiled. 'You're lucky,' he said, looking relieved. 'You have caught him in one of his better moods.'

***

The door opened and the ageless Messiah of Zambelia, Life President Samson Matata accompanied by the rest of his executive committee Marie Antoinette, Colonel Kiboko and Dr Schneider, entered the room and went to their appointed places. The visiting delegates got to their feet and, though they did not actually genuflect or make the sign of the cross, they bowed from the waist. Matata was carrying his ubiquitous fly-whisk, potentially a bad omen, but today he was smiling, definitely a good sign. His leathery, copper-skinned face looked on the company benignly as he greeted them: 'Ah, so you have brought two lovely female *wakahaba (concubines)* for me. I am so happy to see them here. I shall take them both with me back to my private *nyumba (bordello)*. I love all women and they love me. Wherever I go in Zambelia, the bibis sing and dance for me. Is that not so, Marianne?'

'Yes, Mr Life President, it is so. The women love you and dance for you.'

Margaret Donaldson, a Scottish barrister famous for fighting cases of sexual discrimination, and who had spent

357

three days inspecting Gereza's women's prison didn't look as if she concurred with this statement about universal female adulation of Matata. For a moment, it looked as if she might retort with something offensive which might have landed her in Gereza, not as a researcher, but as an inmate.

Anxious not to be distracted by this red herring, Sir Michael got down to the business in hand. 'Mr Life President, we have been here in your beautiful country for five days talking to your people and I wonder now if we might ask you a few questions to clarify various queries which have arisen during our tour.'

'Fire away,' President Matata said, waving his fly whisk in Sir Michael's direction.

'How true is it, sir, that Zambelia is one of the poorest countries in the world with one of the highest infant mortality rates of over fifteen per cent and an average life expectancy of only forty-five years?'

The face of Nixon Makau, the presidential aide, paled and grimaced as if he were about to have a heart attack. The rest of the delegation waited for the explosion and the slamming of the fist on the desk but the expected responses never came. Perhaps Big Mama's hand on the president's shoulder was a factor in keeping him calm. Or maybe he had taken a strong tranquillizer pill in preparation for the meeting. Whatever the reason, Matata retained his composure.

'Lies!' the President declared. 'Damned lies and statistics!! Zambelia is the richest country on the African continent. The IMF and the World Bank sing our praises. Our people are prosperous; they grow maize, tobacco and groundnuts. They have plenty of food, houses with roofs that do not leak. My people are happy. Zambelia is like a huge village. Wherever I go, the people want to dance and sing in my honour. They come to glorify me. Is that not so, Marianne?'

'All true, Mr Life President,' Big Mama purred.

'Thank you, Mr President, for that full and honest answer,' Sir Michael continued with an almost imperceptible grimace. 'There has been concern in world opinion about the rule of law in your country. You say you have adopted the British rule of law but in Britain we don't beat our politicians to death or put them in prison for challenging the government as you do here in Zambelia. How would you answer that accusation?'

The look of consternation on Nixon's face said: 'This Englishman's been and gone and done it now with that question. We can expect a flash of anger followed by flying objects any moment.'

Matata's eyes became narrow slits. 'Let me remind you, Mr Englishman, that we are not Europeans. We are not Westerners. We are Bantu. Don't think that because Westerners colonised us, *we* have become Westerners. We remain Bantu and have our own moral code, which isn't yours and never will be yours.'

'So in your opinion democracy as we understand it doesn't apply here?' Sir Michael persisted. 'Is that what you are saying?'

'We can apply it but not to the letter. Our social structure is like a pyramid with the chief at the apex and the people at the base below. And the most important thing in the pyramid is respect for the chief and that's sacred. You can't play around with the chief. He decides and that's it. And in Zambelia, I am the supreme chief. Our people are like children and don't understand what it means to vote for someone. I, as the chief chosen by our God, Mungu, decided I would rule Zambelia for life. Our system of democracy is the best in the world. The people in the towns and villages choose several candidates for the Chamber of Deputies. The names are given to me and I go through the list and pick out those I know will make good Deputies and reject those who would be bad for the country. Zambelia is no longer in the hands of the politicians and the money men. As for politicians who try to turn the people against me, I always have them executed. We cannot have people stirring up disorder and unrest and I have to make an example of them.'

'You say, Mr President, that *you* decided to execute them,' Sir Michael went on. 'Do you no longer work through the judiciary and the courts of law?'

Matata adopted a gentle paternal tone as if explaining things to a small child. 'I have seen your British courts at work and the way they release murderers and thieves. And you call that justice! Our tribal system is far superior. Our traditional courts mete out true justice and punishment without mercy to the guilty. When we know for sure that a man has committed a crime, we don't waste time and money on lawyers defending him as you do in your country. We don't have miscarriages of justice like your Birmingham Six, the Guildford Four, the Maguire Seven, and the rest. Our judgements are just, swift and effective.'

The British Member of Parliament, Richard Sullivan, decided to take a chance on a question. 'Mr Life President, we see that there is only one legal political party, the Massuyu Conference Party, allowed in Zambelia. Why is this?'

'It is so,' Matata retorted, waving his fly whisk at Sullivan, 'because I said it is so. My object was to destroy all echoes of the colonial era which so enslaved my people for centuries. I set up a popular movement by creating this party which everyone now has to join.'

'Do you think having a single party is democratic, Mr Life President?'

'There is no such thing as a single party here in Zambelia,' the President rasped thrusting his fly whisk at Sullivan as if it were a sword. 'We are a *national* party, not a single party. A single party means that something has been coerced. I have never coerced anything. A single party means there's some kind of opposition. There *is* no opposition. We don't need

360

opposition. We are Bantu. We join together, think together and build together. That's it.'

Sir Michael thought it might be safer to turn the questions to an area dear to Matata's heart, his own security.

In our travels around Zambelia,' he said, 'I have heard it said that you have created an extremely efficient army, A Special Presidential Division, a Praetorian Guard, to protect you at the palace and that, in so doing, you have neglected building up a strong national army. What truth is there in that idea?'

'Yes, it's true,' Matata retorted, 'and it is with good reason that I have strengthened the Civil Guard to protect the palaces. If you had studied other African countries as I have, you would have noted that civil wars always begin by insurrection in the national armies. It's not going to happen here in Zambelia. My special Presidential Division and my Matata Youth Brigades can fight off any attempt to attack us.'

Professor Jane Radcliffe felt it was time she said something. 'I'd like to ask you Mr Life President about your attitude to religion and politics. It has been reported that you have put the Zambelian bishops under house arrest. Is that true?'

'Yes, that's certainly true, madam,' Matata barked, brandishing his fly whisk like a scythe. 'I don't want my clergy to get involved in politics. It's out of the question. It may take place in Britain but here it's unacceptable. The two things don't mix. Christ himself was unequivocal on the subject. "Unto God that which is God's and unto Caesar, that which is Caesar's,".'

Richard Sullivan decided to return to the fray once more and chance his arm by raising a provocative matter. 'It has been reported to us that you have exploited the wealth of your country in order to spend a vast fortune on an ostentatious life style, on extravagant projects, like three palaces in Zambelia, a Swiss chalet, and luxurious residences in Paris, Venice, and Rome, providing expensive homes and presents for favoured

Zambelians, and exorbitant gifts even to foreign politicians in order to win their support. How far is any of this true?'

This time the cat had been put among the pigeons for the president exploded with uncontrolled fury and crashed his fist on the desk producing the inevitable aeronautical flying objects.

'How dare you, an Englishman, talk about palaces and state expenditure! I could not even begin to imagine the wealth of your Queen Elizabeth nor to count the number of residences, palaces and castles owned by your royal family. That is before I even mention the Crown jewels and the innumerable members of the family that live off these riches. And when it comes to exploiting Africa, have you forgotten your own European people? Such names as Leopold II of Belgium, and your own Cecil Rhodes in what used to be Rhodesia spring to mind. As for extravagant living, my life style does not compare with that of the late Idi Amin in Uganda, Mobutu in Zaire, Gaddafi in Libya, nor with Mugabe in Zimbabwe. That is enough on this suggestion that we are spendthrifts here in Zambelia. I will take no more questions on this subject. It is tabu.'

Big Mama sitting by Matata's side looked concerned at this outburst and, at the same time, relieved that the subject was not pursued to include her own extravagant trips abroad and the swanky foreign cars given to her sisters on their birthdays.

Nixon Makau felt it was time that he brought the audience to a conclusion as there was danger that it might get out of hand. 'I think the President will take one more question and then we must bring things to an end,' he announced.

Dr Robert Lovell raised his hand to signify that he would like to ask this last question. 'Mr Life President,' he began, 'I have spent some considerable time studying your medical facilities here in Zambelia and, on the whole, found them adequate. I am extremely concerned about the Research

362

Bureau however and its practice of selling human organs for transplant. I would appreciate your comment on the matter.'

'What we do in our Research Bureau is our own business,' Matata snapped, 'but since it is the last item for discussion this morning, I shall ask our Dr Max Schneider to explain our views on the matter.'

Schneider stood up and, giving his listeners a confident smile, began to outline the Zambelian policy on organ donation and transplants.

'First, let me say at once that I can see no objection to the sale of body parts on the open market. There are already many precedents for this. For example, blood is regularly bought and sold in the free market economy. Why, I've even seen advertisements, admittedly in America where bizarre things often happen, in which people have offered their own organs, and occasionally those of other people, to the highest bidder. Surrogate mothers hire out their wombs for the best price whilst there is open commerce for the buying and selling of human semen and ova which, though not organs, are products of them. There is also a thriving market in the sale of kidneys from volunteer donors though this is not widely publicised. In China, organs are regularly procured from executed prisoners. In Iran, the sale of kidneys is legal and as a result, there is no waiting list there. This has got to be a good thing, surely.

'As medical advances in human transplants have become more possible and more sophisticated, so there has developed a world-wide shortage of organs available. Not only kidneys, corneas, and livers which are the ones most successfully transplanted but also hearts, lungs and even testes. People everywhere are unwilling or too lazy to donate their organs after death and so these vital organs are simply consigned to the worms or to the flames of the crematorium. A simple law of economics takes effect. If you have high demand and a limited supply, someone somewhere is going to make a business and a profit out of it. Why not us here in Zambelia?

'Many countries have orders banning trafficking in human organs and rely on government agencies to ensure no-one will ever have to pay for these body parts. How far has it got them? Nowhere is the answer. The shortage has become more and more acute and will remain so until governments recognize that the only way to ensure an adequate supply is to start recompensing people for agreeing to donate their organs. Until that time arrives, we in Zambelia can see nothing wrong with extracting organs and transplanting them into useful and creative people.

'There are hundreds of thousands of good people desperately waiting for human organs to become available. So much of our population leads useless and pointless existences for example in psychiatric hospitals or as layabouts on our streets. What's wrong with passing on their organs to people who can make better use of them in more constructive, creative lives. In this way empty lives become of some value and worth to society. That is the essential work upon which we are engaged at the Matata Research Bureau and I hope that we shall be able to continue our vital work for many years to come.'

'Thank you, Dr Schneider,' the Life President said, 'for that masterly explanation of our position. I now declare this meeting closed. No further questions.'

Sir Michael was on his feet. 'Thank you, Mr Life President, for permitting us to visit your country and carry out our inspection of your facilities. I hope as my final word that I shall be allowed to say that it is not within our remit to comment on our findings during our five day visit. The delegation will now return to London to consider all the evidence. Our report will be passed on to the British Commonwealth Office and, after they have added their observations, the final document should be with you for your deliberation, discussion, and possible action. Thank you once again for your generous hospitality.'

364

The other four members of the delegation were on their feet to acknowledge their agreement with what Sir Michael had said. The executive committee of Zambelia filed out of the room and the British delegation made its way back to their hotel, to prepare for their flight back to Heathrow.

****

Chapter Thirty-Four

Delegation's Findings

A week after the delegation had departed from Zambelia, a High Priority Document from them came by Diplomatic pouch addressed to the president. As Senior Aide, Nixon Makau was the first to read the report and recommendations. After a quick skip-reading through the circumlocutory legalese, he turned impatiently to the back of the document seeking out the gist and main recommendations. As his eye took in the import of the words on the page, he knew that what he held in his hand was the legal equivalent of a nuclear weapon. In order to verify that his eyesight had not deceived him, Nixon read the document a second time, only this time more slowly, absorbing every word. He read:

CONCLUSIONS AND RECOMMENDATIONS
OF THE DELEGATION

Given the importance of attracting international funding we urge the adoption of the reforms listed below. Our support for such funding will be contingent on immediate attention being given to these matters.

We of the delegation were extremely concerned at the many examples that we found of breaches of human rights and natural justice in prisons, hospitals, and broader society. We were particularly concerned to learn of allegations of death threats, and intimidation of judges and legal representatives who had expressed dissenting views or criticised the Government ruled by the Massuyu Conference Party. All threats and intimidation of the legal fraternity must cease forthwith. Urgent action as a matter of priority is required to rectify these gross injustices.

Allegations of corruption and lack of checks and balances must be investigated and rectified.

We delegates insist on the acceptance and instigation of fundamental democratic principles, as enshrined in four pillars of democracy:

a) Presumption of innocence before the law;

b) The Rule of Law and Due Process. i.e. No more arbitrary arrests and imprisonment without charge and there must be trial before impartial judges;

c) Open justice. Not only done but seen to be done; this means the abolition of traditional tribal courts which are held in secret and without recourse to witnesses.

d) New and fair multi-party elections (i.e. there must be more than one party from which the electorate can choose; the former People's Freedom Party which has been suppressed for so long could possibly be resurrected. Such elections to be monitored by United Nations observers.

In particular we would insist on:

i) The release of all political prisoners and prisoners of conscience; immediate improvement in prison conditions, especially with regard to overcrowding and levels of nutrition;

ii) A thorough investigation of the activities of the Medical Research Bureau and its Head, Dr Max Schneider, and his possible participation in the illegal sale of human organs.

iii) The abolition of the Medical Research Bureau and its incorporation into the general hospital system;

iv) A thorough investigation of the activities of the Public Safety Unit and in particular those of Colonel Kenneth Kiboko and his participation and connivance in the inhuman treatment of prisoners;

v) A United Nations investigation into the unexplained disappearances of public and private figures.

It was Nixon's duty to take the document straight to the President where no doubt Big Mama would interpret it for him. Before he did so, Nixon thought it might be more productive if he gave Kiboko and Schneider a few hints as to its contents for there were profound implications for their future careers and life prospects. With this in mind, he phoned both of them and arranged to meet up with them in Kiboko's private office in State House.

'Colonel Kiboko,' Nixon began, 'What I have to tell you is of the utmost importance both to you and Doctor Schneider. Can you guarantee that this office of yours is not bugged as I'd hate for any of our conversation to leak out of this room. What I am about to tell you is dynamite.'

'Let me give you every assurance, Makau,' Kiboko replied, puffing vigorously on the cheroot that he always lit when faced with something that promised to be explosive, 'that this room is one hundred percent safe. I'd stake my life on that.'

'If it's as hot as you would have us believe, Makau, and involves me also,' Schneider exclaimed, 'then get on with it, man. We're perfectly safe in this office.'

'Very well,' Nixon said *sotto voce*. 'I have passed on to the President the highly confidential paper from the British delegation. Their recommendations are not good and, if carried out, will mean the end of our Inner Circle. It spells ruination for you, Colonel Kiboko, and for you, Doctor Schneider, and me also. We must stop the recommendations being implemented, no matter what but I know from the initial reaction of the President and Big Mama that for us it's all over and we'd be down the pan. The delegation recommends that Zambelia adopt free, multi-party elections, that both your operations be shut down, and finally that both of you should be fired. The President is bound to follow your dismissal by having you arrested. The same probably goes for me, I fear. Now that we are together and can talk securely without fear of being overheard, I want to hear your initial reactions.'

368

'That's easy,' Kiboko said immediately. 'We must stop the President from adopting the recommendations. We must use our influence to convince him that it would not be in Zambelia's best interests to have free elections nor to close down our operations. Why, our arrest could possibly mean execution for the three of us.'

'Damned right,' exclaimed Schneider. 'If it ever became public knowledge that we had been extracting human organs without the owners' permission, we're kaput and no mistake.'

'I understand what you are both saying,' Nixon agreed, 'and I think we must do all in our power to persuade the President to reject the delegations. But what shall we do if he accepts the delegation's proposals?'

Kiboko and Schneider exchanged confidential looks and stared into each other's eyes for what seemed to Nixon like an eternity.

It was Kiboko who finally spoke up. 'I think we can trust him, Max,' he said finally. 'After all, he's up to his neck in it just as much as we are. Agreed?'

'Very well,' Max said. 'I'll tell him. It's like this Makau: the Colonel and I have already discussed the possibility of taking over the government.'

'You mean a *coup d'etat*?' Nixon gasped.

'We mean exactly that,' Kiboko replied. 'If the President accepts the delegation's advice, and only *if*, then Max and I are not prepared to sit idly by while Matata and Big Mama order our executions, which they most certainly will, if the delegation's paper is accepted and acted upon.'

'The colonel and I have already talked it over,' Schneider said. 'Consider the opposition! A doddering, senile old fool and a dancing queen. It shouldn't take much to topple them both off their perches.'

'I can't see how such a pair could offer much resistance,' Kiboko said, puffing furiously at his cigar and nodding in agreement. 'Don't forget I control the Public Safety Unit and have several thousand officers and men under me. I'm sure I can persuade Major Nyoka and Captain Gumbo in Hekima to come over to us. There are probably a few other officers who would like to see a change of leadership and would back us if push came to shove. I've thought this thing through and, if we can retain the element of surprise, it'll be a piece of cake simply to walk in on them one morning and clap Matata and Big Mama in irons.'

'Next, we throw the findings and recommendations of the delegation out of the window,' Schneider added.

'We plan to mount the attack in three days' time as soon as we've got the support behind us organized,' Kiboko said, lighting yet another cheroot. 'A few phone calls to the right places and we'll be ready to strike.'

'You've certainly designed your scheme down to the last detail, I'll give you that,' Nixon said warmly. 'I must congratulate you on that but what would you do with the President and Big Mama when you've seized power?'

'Well, since Matata is already over the hill, we'd put him out to pasture,' Schneider said, smiling his evil smile. 'Maybe, confine him to an old peoples' home.' He laughed. 'Or even find him a bed in my Medical Research Bureau though his organs are probably knackered by now and of no commercial value. Big Mama would be permitted to stay with him of course to look after him until he finally pegs out, which hopefully wouldn't be too long if he were fed the right drugs. As for Big Mama's sisters, they can go back to their home villages where they belong. They've milked the system thoroughly and have become too big for their boots.'

'Well, what do you think, Makau?' Kiboko asked. 'Are you in?'

Nixon knew that his life depended on his reply. 'I am not sure how I can be of any assistance,' he answered carefully, 'since you seem to have it planned so carefully and have omitted nothing. My best contribution will be to offer you my advice and expertise in financial and administrative matters whenever you require it. I shall be intrigued to see how your scheme works out. Thank God, this little meeting has taken place in your office, Colonel, because if any of this

370

got out, that would be the end of the three of us. As you implement the various stages of your coup, remember I am here, ready and available, whenever you need me. I think now we should part company and I shall await developments eagerly.'

'Remember Makau,' Schneider said putting his finger to his lips, 'Mum's the word.'

'And Bob's your uncle,' Kiboko chuckled, lighting yet another cheroot.

***

An hour after they had parted, Nixon was in Big Mama's office.

'Well, what we've been expecting for some time has finally happened, ma'am,' he said when he was seated before her desk. 'The evil pair have approached me with a view to enlisting my help to usurp the president. They are hoping to recruit Major Nyoka and Captain Gumbo plus the militia of the Public Safety Unit. Let me play back the recording of what they said.'

'How did you manage to record it, Nixon? Surely the Colonel's office has been completely cleared of bugs. By the way, I'd like you to start calling me Marianne if we are to be working so closely together.'

'Yes, Marianne. I put the colonel at his ease by giving the impression that *I* was the one worried about security when I asked him if his office was completely de-bugged. I forgot to mention that I was wired myself. My Massuyu Conference tie-pin is a miniature transmitter and the whole conversation was recorded back in my private office. If Kiboko had suspected any of that, I doubt I'd be here talking to you now. Anyway, I am sure you're anxious to hear what they said.'

Nixon switched on his tape recorder and played back the discussion with Kiboko and Schneider. Big Mama listened stony-faced to the playback until they reached the reference to her and the President as "a doddering, senile old man and a dancing queen" and how "it shouldn't take much to topple

371

them both from their perches" when she frowned angrily and muttered something incomprehensible under her breath.

At the end of the recording, Nixon said, 'I take it, Marianne, that we now operate Plan A as agreed?'

'Yes, Nixon, put Plan A into motion. Even though we have been anticipating a move like this for some time, it still comes as something of a shock when it actually happens. Mark my words: before I've finished, I shall make them eat those words: "doddering, senile old man and dancing queen" indeed! Now you must contact Nyoka and Gumbo and forewarn them that an approach will be made to them shortly. They must give the impression that they are ready to go along with the projected take-over. Of course, they must do nothing until we issue the next instruction. Meanwhile, whatever happens, our president must not hear a word of this until we are ready. I'm sure that the moment he learns of the planned treachery he will have them both executed immediately. That would be no good. It's too soon. We have to bide our time and wait for the opportune moment. If the President decides to ignore the suggestions of the delegation, there will be no attempted coup and things will simply fizzle out. But if our inner circle accepts and implements the delegation's recommendations, all hell will be let loose and the President must be told of their treacherous intentions.

**

Later that evening, Nixon put in a confidential phone call on the same line to the two people in Hekima.

'Good evening, Major Nyoka and Captain Gumbo. This is Nixon Makau, Private Secretary and Senior Aide to President Matata. I am speaking to you on a secure line from the President's Office here in Lundazi. In ten minutes' time I shall phone you back on this same line. What I shall be communicating to you is a state secret and will require confidence of the highest order. Make absolutely sure that you cannot be overheard in your office and that there's not the faintest possibility that anyone but the three of us will be able to listen to what I shall have to say. Is that fully understood?'

'Yes, sir,' the officers said in unison. 'Our offices will be one hundred per cent clear when you phone back. We shall attend to it this very moment.'

'Very well. You should go about clearing your office of people and listening devices immediately.'

***

Ten minutes later, Nixon rang them back.

'Good evening. Nixon Makau again. May I take it that we have complete security on this line? Your lives and your jobs will depend on it.'

'Yes, sir,' they chorused. 'We have cleared the line for you.'

'Very well. We believe that shortly there will be an attempt to overthrow President Matata by force. Most likely you'll be approached to co-operate in this *coup d'etat*. It is imperative that you give the impression that you are willing to go along with the attempt and a little later I shall give you instructions and details as to our next move.'

***

The following morning, Nixon distributed copies of the delegation's document to the inner circle of five, and awaited the inevitable nuclear reaction. He hadn't long to wait. An hour later, after the President had had time to absorb the import of the paper, he went into the expected rage and, mouthing every kind of imprecation and abuse down the phone at Nixon, commanded him to summon an immediate emergency meeting of the inner circle.

'Call it now, at once! Within the hour!' he screamed. 'How dare a bunch of foreign delegates visit us and try to dictate policy to us!'

'Uh-oh,' Nixon thought. 'Big Mama is going to have her work cut out persuading him to accept the recommendations. Nevertheless, if past experience was anything to go by, she

373

could do it. Zambelians think that Matata uses juju methods to accomplish things but they've got the whole thing wrong. The real black magic ju-ju is exerted by his consort, Marianne.'

Promptly at eleven Matata stormed into his private office still beside himself with fury. Matata belching fire and smoke had become the normal response to any communication from the British government. But this one had been the worst that Nixon had ever witnessed and there was danger that the president would blow a gasket. Nevertheless, Nixon noted, Matata had calmed down a little since the phone call.

'We must send a telegram at once to the British Commonwealth office rejecting their delegation's recommendations immediately,' he roared. 'What I object to most in their document is their implied threat that unless we agree to their proposals, financial aid will cease. He consulted the document and read out loud:

"Given the importance of attracting international funding we urge the reforms listed below. Our support for such funding will be contingent on immediate attention being given to these matters."

'I deprecate most strongly this notion that we receive financial assistance at the price of relinquishing our freedom, that we are given aid in return for political concessions. It's like giving a banana to a monkey and asking it to dance. We are *not* monkeys. We are proud and independent Zambelians.'

'I agree wholeheartedly with you, Mr President,' Colonel Kiboko grovelled. 'We should tell the Commonwealth Office to stick their money. We're not their lackeys. We can get by without their pieces of silver.'

'How right you are, Colonel,' Schneider echoed. 'The phrasing of "our support is contingent on" amounts to blackmail and we should reject it in no uncertain terms.'

374

'Before we go off at the deep end,' Big Mama said calmly, 'let us consider our financial position. Can we afford to cock a snoot at the British Government? Perhaps Mr Makau, our trusty financial adviser, can enlighten us.'

Nixon grimaced. 'That's easy to answer. Zambelia is broke. Bankrupt. The kitty is empty and, unless we receive a big injection of funds soon, we shall have to appeal to the International Monetary Funds for assistance and they will insist on much tougher conditions than the British Government, I can assure you.'

Kiboko and Schneider were now scowling and looking daggers at Nixon and, if looks had the power to kill, he would be already lying on the mortuary slab.

'A load of old cobblers,' Kiboko snorted. 'We have only to imply that we shall go to Russia or China if the British are not forthcoming, and watch them pour the money into our coffers so as to keep us out of the embrace of the nasty reds. As for the idea of releasing political prisoners! I've never heard of such a mad idea. It would be suicidal.'

'Hear, hear,' Schneider sang. 'We have only to whisper "Mao Tse Tung" to the British and the Americans and they would pour out their largesse. We should try that tack first before we think of reforming our constitution and handing our government over to a gang of cockroaches.'

'Not only that, Mr President,' Kiboko continued, taking up the baton., 'As you yourself have said, our people are like children and not yet ready to vote in elections. Most of them don't know what an election is. They are accustomed to being told what to think by their tribal chiefs who in their return rely on you for advice. As for multi-party elections, the idea is so ludicrous that it's not worthy of serious discussion. Are we to place our country's future into the hands of a bunch of ignorant peasants?'

'These are fine words,' Big Mama said, 'but they butter no parsnips. The stark truth is that the treasury chest is empty. If we reject the suggestions of the delegation,

375

Zambelia is in Queer Street and we may as well pack our bags and go to "I don't know where". This country of ours has few natural assets like the mineral wealth of the Congo, the gold of South Africa, the copper of Zambia, the oil of Nigeria. The loss of international aid would have serious repercussions.

'We can kiss goodbye to our wonderful ambitious projects, like: new roads, railways, new sewage and water supplies, the proposed hydro-electric schemes, the new palace on the Lake that will rival Buckingham Palace and Versailles. And how, may I ask, do we pay for our Public Safety Unit, and our little navy on Lake Zambelia? I could go on but I would conclude by asking the president what he will do when we have to disband his Special Presidential Division. Who will protect and defend him and us then?'

Tapping her nose confidentially and giving the President a knowing look, she said 'As for elections, there are ways and means of producing the results we want. Let me remind you all once again of what Stalin once said: "It's not who *votes* that matters but who *counts* the votes…" '

There was a pregnant pause after Big Mama had finished speaking. The result was a foregone conclusion for the President was smiling broadly and nodding his approval of Big Mama's words.

'I have heard enough,' he said. 'When I came to this meeting this morning, I was angry that the British were trying to blackmail us into accepting their recommendations but, as usual, Marianne's wise words have persuaded me otherwise. I see now that our country's survival and future prosperity depends on our agreeing to what has been proposed. Let us take a vote on it. Do we accept the recommendations of the British delegation? First, that we release political prisoners and agree in principle to hold multi-party elections. Those in favour?'

There were three votes.

'Those against?'

There were two votes.

'Motion carried,' The president announced, bringing down his gavel. 'Mr Makau, you will communicate our decision to the British Commonwealth tomorrow. I now declare this meeting closed.'

****

Chapter Thirty-Five

Sue is free.

In the same way as the outer crust of the earth may appear calm and peaceful while an inferno rages deep within its bowels, so it was with Nixon Makau. His face wore an impassive, deadpan expression, quietly mournful in repose, but deep within his soul there were powerful emotions which rarely made it to the surface. As Presidential Aide-Adviser, he could not afford to manifest his innermost thoughts and had spent a lifetime dissembling his true feelings. But when he heard the president pronounce those words, "Motion carried", his euphoria almost came bubbling to the top. Almost. Because he managed to control himself only just in time. It was still important not to show his hand to Schneider and Kiboko who had been eyeing him suspiciously throughout the meeting. Once the meeting broke up, it was a different matter.

As he came away from the presidential suite, he practically skipped across the compound back to his own domain. 'Stage One of my plans! Accomplished!' he chuckled to himself rubbing his hands together. 'Now I must get the joyful news over to Sue! As quickly as possible!'

Back in his living room, he rang the bell for his two servants, Rafiki and Mlima.

'Rafiki,' he said, 'Did you bake the special cake I asked you to prepare?'

'Yes, sir. Exactly as you ordered. A chocolate cake with the words "Uhuru! for Sue!" written in icing on the top.'

378

'Excellent. Now get out our best china and prepare the best tea you are capable of.' Turning to Mlima, he said, 'Go over at once to Doctor Delamere's cottage and tell her to come over here at once as I need to give her immediate and urgent news. Have you both got that?'

'Yes, sir,' his two servants said in unison.

Fifteen minutes later, Mlima was back with Sue.

'Come in, Sue,' Nixon said gravely. 'Please come in and join me for tea.'

Rafiki brought in the tea first and on a nod from his master solemnly poured two cups.

Sue anxiously searched his face. 'Come on, Nixon. What's going on? Why have you asked me over?'

Nixon said nothing but gave a signal to Rafiki to bring in the cake. Nixon cut two slices and handed one on a plate to Sue. She still didn't get it even though her slice said "Uhuru!" on the top.

'I have come from a meeting of the pentarchy, our inner circle,' Nixon began.

'Yes, yes….and…and…' said Sue nervously searching his face. 'What is it, Nixon? Is it bad news? Has something happened? For God's sake, tell me. Has something happened to Mike?'

No use. Nixon could contain himself no longer. The broad smile that lit up his face was like the sun coming out from behind a cloud. 'The inner circle has agreed to release political prisoners forthwith.'

'Yes, yes, Nixon and so…'

'Read the word on the slice of your cake, Sue. "Uhuru!" It means you are now free! You can go home or at least go back to Hekima!'

Sue could do nothing but stare at him incredulously. 'Nixon! Oh Nixon! Please tell me you're not joking. It would be too cruel if you were.'

379

'No joke, Sue. Only half an hour ago, the President agreed to release all political prisoners and prisoners of conscience. Your three months of enforced residence here at the state house villa are over. Furthermore, you are free to phone Dr Goodman on a secure line from your cottage and ask him to come and collect you and take you back to your house in Hekima. Now I shall have to excuse myself as I need to phone the news to Major Nyoka and Captain Gumbo in Hekima. They will have to make arrangements to release their political detainees tomorrow. I think there's going to be some rejoicing in Hekima when the news finally sinks in. For those inmates who've suffered serious illness or maiming during their captivity, the news will be tinged with a certain amount of sadness of course.'

As in a dream, Sue left Nixon to continue with his phoning.

***

First, Sue contacted the Hallidays and gave them the thrilling news. They left what they were doing immediately and, overwhelmed with delight, rushed over with a bottle of the palace's best Cristal champagne to celebrate.

'Here's to the rest of your tour in Zambelia!' Helen said, raising her glass.

'And let us hope that you find the happiness we promised you in our letters!' Peter said, lifting up his bubbly.

When Mike Goodman heard the news from Sue's own lips, he too could hardly believe his ears. When the message finally got through to his brain, he excused himself from the committee meeting he was attending and drove through the gathering dusk to collect his beloved Sue. They quickly collected her things together and within a couple of hours they were on their road back to Hekima and to what she hoped would be a normal life.

All the way back, Sue talked incessantly about the things she missed when cooped up in her little "rondavel" cottage.

'Oh, Mike!' she exclaimed. 'I can't begin to tell you how overjoyed I am to be going back! Nixon did his best to make me comfortable but I feel that I have been imprisoned for so long. How I missed the university atmosphere, the teaching, mixing with the staff at college and socially at the club. Why I'd even welcome another of Bugsy's braaivleis and that's saying something. Most of all, I've missed your company, my dear and lovely Mike. Seeing you at weekends only was as if you were part of the timetable and our meetings were strictly regulated by an academic curriculum.'

'I hope I passed my exams, Sue.'

'With distinction, my love. You became my hope and my inspiration. My knight in shining armour.'

'And you my beautiful Lady Guinevere and I love you deeply.'

'Thank you, my dearest Mike. We'll forget for a moment about Lady Guinevere though,' she added laughing, 'because according to legend, she ran off with Sir Lancelot. I promise you, Mike, I'll not run off with anyone but you.'

They arrived back at Sue's home and, like a little girl exploring her new home, she rushed inside and examined every room, every cupboard, every book shelf, every little thing in the home she'd had to leave so abruptly and cruelly three months before.

'Many of my books have gone,' she exclaimed, 'but my kitchen and my bedroom are still intact and exactly as I left them, thank the Lord.'

Finally she sat down in her easy chair and sighed. 'Gosh, it's good to be home again, Mike. Thank you for your love and support for the last twelve weeks. I couldn't have survived without them. I'd have simply given up hope and accepted Nixon's offer of a passage back to England.'

***

The week-end following the release of the political prisoners saw a number of big "Welcome Home" parties. Notable among them were two in particular. The one held at the home of Tarak Tulshidas in Lundazi was a lavish affair since it was organised and financed by him with invitations extended to the families and friends of former members of Cell Number 8, Tagooma Branch. It was like a reunion of old comrades-in-arms who had shared wartime experiences which, in many ways, their imprisonment at Tagooma had resembled. Among those present with wives, girlfriends and younger members were: Chifunza Government Deputy; Chimanga, the Union man; Bazuka, the farmer; Mitinda, the teacher; Masiku, the banker; Shairi, the poet. Talk flowed animatedly, touching on the sad stories of Gwelo, the singer, and Frank Johnson the university teacher both of whom had been shot on the orders of Kiboko in his grotesque game of musical chairs. Not every story recalled was sad however and an outsider would have been intrigued by the number of times that reminiscences began with "Do you remember the time that the spotty-faced guard...." or "Do you recall that time we got one over on Fatty the gaoler?"...

Missing from Tarak's reunion was Jack Zulu who had decided to attend another "Welcome Home" party, this time at Hekima University. Mike Goodman was so beside himself with joy at having Sue back in the safe, familiar surroundings of Hekima that he threw a huge garden party inviting colleagues from every faculty. Bugsy Moroney did offer to organise one of his braaivleis in honour of Sue's safe deliverance but, after thanking him profusely for his kindness and his generosity, Mike decided most reluctantly to pass on his offer.

During the festivities, Bugsy came up to Mike a-quiver with excitement.

'Say, Mike and Sue,' he gushed. 'I forgot to tell ya. Good news! You remember that attache case I lost in the London cab? They found your dossier! Still there filed among my bird papers! Do you still want me to send it over to the Commonwealth Secretary and the Justice and Peace Commission in London?'

'No need now, Bugsy,' Mike said.

'So, what do you want me to do with the dossier you gave me?'

For a moment, Mike was tempted to give him the answer that sprang to his lips but resisted and said simply: 'No, Bugsy, it's all yours. Keep it as a memento. Why not file it among your bird souvenirs?'

'Yeah, yeah, Mike, but where would I file it?'

'How about African cuckoos?'

The party was a truly happy affair and colleague after colleague came to Sue to rejoice at her safe return and to congratulate her on her perspicacity in avoiding the clutches of the Public Safety officers.

'How on earth did you do it?' they asked. 'The eyes of the Public Safety people were everywhere. They turned the country upside down looking for you. How did you pull it off?'

'Friends in high places,' Sue answered, with a knowing look and tapping the side of her nose.

Sue's greatest joy, however, came a few days later after she had put on her teaching mantle once again. She faced her English Literature class again after a gap of twelve weeks, bringing the house down with her opening gambit.

'Good morning students. Now, as I was saying in my lecture on *Macbeth* before I was so rudely interrupted…..'

***

Some time later, in another part of the university, the National Union of Students had called an emergency meeting to discuss the political developments in the country. It was a stormy affair which almost came to blows after many angry verbal exchanges.

One angry faction demanded an immediate strike and a march on the Lundazi government for the scorn and derision it had shown to the university, its staff and its students.

'Look at the disgraceful, contemptuous way we've been treated,' a firebrand speaker named Jonah Moshi harangued. 'One of our best teachers, Dr Frank Johnson, has been imprisoned, tortured, and shot dead; another, Doctor Sue Delamere was forced into hiding and has only recently come back to us; two of our young medical students have been murdered, while their older brother who is present here today was badly beaten up and thrown into Tagooma.'

'And what about Monsignor McGinn, our chaplain! Don't forget him!' a Catholic student called out. 'He was deported for unspecified reasons.'

'All the more reason we should take action,' Johan Moshi bellowed. 'How much more are we supposed to tolerate before we do something? I say, we rise up today, walk out and move on to Lundazi palace and set fire to the bloody place!'

'And hang President Matata from the nearest tree' called another.

'And his bit of fluff, Big Mama, Marianne!' yelled a third.

The meeting was being stirred up to fever pitch by a succession of speeches along the same vein and it looked as if the students, given the slightest excuse, were in the mood to revolt. Their anger was cooled however by the next speaker.

'Students! I appeal to you to wait before you do something you may regret for the rest of your days. I am Jack Zulu and I am the one who was banged up in prison by Kiboko's goons. I, more than any of you, have good reason to march on to Lundazi state house but I say we bide our time. President Matata has agreed to the demands of the recent delegation. He has released political prisoners and has agreed to hold fair and free elections. If he's as good as his word, we shall soon see a new government and a multi-party democracy. I say we wait and see before we act or we may find that some of us will be shot dead in a confrontation with Matata's Presidential troops.'

Jack Zulu's words won the day in the end although some students agreed only with reservations.

'Very well,' said the firebrand, Moshi. 'We'll adopt a "wait-and-see" policy but I don't trust Matata nor his inamorata, Big Mama. Let's see if we really do get a free election and a new government but I wouldn't hold your breath if I were you. The president's Youth Brigade thugs are sure to be at every polling booth putting the frighteners on the voters. We should have student representatives there to counteract them.'

****

Chapter Thirty-Six

Coup d'état foiled

The day after Sue had been informed that she was free to go, Big Mama felt the time had come to inform the president about Kiboko and Schneider before these two gentlemen took it into their heads to instigate their planned *coup d'état*. With this in mind, she and Nixon called on the president to apprise him of the plot. Her worry was that the shock of learning of the treachery might give him a heart attack.

'I have called this urgent meeting with you today, Mr President,' she said carefully, 'in order to give you full information about a certain dangerous matter that has been developing behind your back.'

'Information! Dangerous matter! Developing behind my back!' President Matata barked. 'What's been going on, Marianne?'

'I'd rather not be the one to inform you, Mr President, because what we have to reveal may shock you to the core. I should like to hand over to Nixon because he knows first hand what contemptible, underhand perfidy has been plotted by two members of our inner circle. Nixon, over to you.'

In response, Nixon placed a cassette recorder on the president's desk. 'Thank you Marianne,' he said. 'Well, Mr President, the situation is as follows. After our last meeting when we discussed the findings of the delegation, Colonel Kiboko and Dr Schneider approached me and expressed concern that you might decide to accept the British recommendations about releasing political detainees and holding multi-party elections. They also suggested that if you did, it might be necessary for them to carry out a *coup* and take over the presidency.'

For a moment, it looked as if Big Mama's anxieties about a heart attack might have been justified because the complexion of President Matata turned purple, his eyes bulged from their sockets, and he stared uncomprehendingly at Nixon.

'*Coup*! Take-over!' he roared. 'What evidence do you have for such grave accusations?'

'We have it on tape, Mr President,' Big Mama said, answering for him, omitting the fact that what he was about to hear was an edited version. 'Before I hand over again to Mr Makau, may I now have your permission to bring in our new inner circle members, the ones that you agreed to last night at our aromatherapy session?'

'New inner circle members? Did I really agree to them? I don't recall but if it will throw light on this crisis, Marianne, by all means bring them in. Who are these new members again? And I agreed to accept them, you say? What are their names again?'

'Major Nyoka now promoted to Colonel and Captain Gumbo now raised to the rank of Major and commander of the Presidential Guard. Also Dr Simon Timothy our new head of the Medical Centre.'

'Yes, yes, I remember them now,' snapped Matata, fearing that his memory lapses were getting worse. 'Very well, let's have them in if it's going to help.'

The three new members who had been waiting in an adjoining room now joined them.

'Welcome to our inner circle,' Big Mama said. 'We shall get down to the business in hand without delay. Top of today's agenda is the matter of the two conspirators.'

At a nod from her to the sergeant on the door, the two accused were escorted in handcuffs into the room where they were made to stand before the committee.

The President now addressed the pair.

'Colonel Kiboko and Dr Schneider, you have both been accused of plotting to overthrow the presidency. What have you to say in your defence?'

'A pack of lies from beginning to end,' Kiboko snorted. 'Dr Schneider and I are the victims not the conspirators here.'

'We have always been loyal citizens and worked for the good of the Zambelia,' Schneider protested. 'We have nothing but the highest respect for the presidency and we hold you, President Matata, in the highest esteem.'

'Then how do you explain the recorded conversation you had with our presidential aide?' Big Mama asked. 'Mr Makau please play back the recording.'

Nixon stood up, walked across the room to the tape recorder and pressed the play button.

'Very well,' (Schneider's voice). *'I'll tell him. It's like this Makau, the Colonel and I have already discussed the possibility of taking over the government.'*

'You mean a coup d'etat?' (Nixon's voice)

'We mean exactly that,' (Kiboko's voice). *'If the President accepts the delegation's advice, and only if, then Max and I are not prepared to sit idly by while Matata and his consort order our executions, which they will certainly do, if the delegation's paper is accepted and enacted upon.'*

'The colonel and I have already talked it over,' (Schneider's voice). *'Consider the opposition! A doddering, senile old fool and a dancing queen. It shouldn't take much to topple them both off their perches.'*

'I can't see how such a pair could offer much resistance,' (Kiboko's voice) *'After all, I control the*

388

Public Safety Unit and several thousand officers and men. I am sure I can persuade Major Nyoka and Captain Gumbo in Hekima to come in with us. There are probably a few other officers who would like to see some change of leadership and would back us if push came to shove. I've thought this through and if we can retain the element of surprise, it'll be a piece of cake simply to walk in on them one morning and clap them both into irons.'

'Next we throw the findings and recommendations of the delegation out of the window,' (Schneider's voice)

'We plan to mount the attack in three days' time as soon as we've got the support behind us organized,' (Kiboko's voice) *'A few phone calls to the right places and we'll be ready to strike.'*

But what would you do with the President and Marie Antoinette when you've seized power?' (Nixon Makau's voice)

'Well, since Matata is over the hill, we'd put him out to pasture,' (Schneider's voice) *'Maybe, confine him to an old folk's home or even to my Medical Research Bureau though his organs are probably knackered and of no commercial value. Big Mama would be permitted to stay with him of course to look after him until he finally pegs out, which hopefully wouldn't be too long if he were fed the right drugs. As for Big Mama's sisters, they can go back to their home villages where they belong. They've become too big for their boots.'*

Nixon pressed the "Stop" button.

By this time, President Matata was apoplectic and spluttering with rage and finding it difficult to speak.

'You are both guilty of treason,' he bellowed at last. 'Guilty of heinous insults against the legal authority of

389

Zambelia. So I am a doddering, senile old fool who is to be put out to pasture, am I? I'll show you how doddering I am!'

'Mr President, we are being quoted out of context.' Kiboko pleaded. 'Your Aide, Nixon Makau, provoked us into these utterances. This was an entrapment. We were duped and we said these words on his instigation and encouragement.'

'I absolutely agree,' Schneider quaked. 'Makau is an agent provocateur who inveigled us into saying these things. He is the one who should be punished, not us. When our case is judged in a court of law, our innocence will soon become apparent.'

'Unadulterated rubbish!' President Matata raged. 'Was it Makau who induced you to describe me as a doddering, senile old fool? As for a court of law! This meeting today of the inner council *is* the only court of law you're going to get.'

'In addition to the tape recorded evidence,' Big Mama continued, 'there is yet more proof of their traitorous intentions. I turn now to Colonel Nyoka for his contribution.'

'Thank you, ma'am,' Nyoka fawned. 'Two days ago, I received a phone call from Colonel Kiboko on my secure line. He asked me if I would be willing to join him in an attempt to depose the President. Naturally I turned him down immediately as I have the greatest admiration and the deepest loyalty for our beloved Life President. I reported the matter of course to the presidential aide, Mr Makau.'

It was Gumbo's turn to add to the evidence. 'When I was in charge of the prison at Tagooma, I too was approached in exactly the same way. It goes without saying that I rejected such a wicked proposal right away and reported the matter to the presidential office.'

'I note that these two officers,' Kiboko sneered, 'have recently been promoted. Is their promotion a reward for the vicious, wicked lies they have concocted. Of course they will say anything and implicate anybody in gratitude for their sudden and undeserved career enhancements.'

'Take care how you go,' President Matata said through clenched teeth. 'Remember there are things worse than death in our repertoire of punishments.'

'In assessing the extent of their guilt,' Big Mama now added, determined to add yet more crimes to their portfolio, 'we should also take account of the numbers of unexplained deaths which have taken place in their institutions. Major Gumbo and Dr Simon Timothy can perhaps enlighten on these matters.'

'I can confirm that over one hundred and fifty bodies have been recovered from the grounds of Tagooma Prison,' Major Gumbo said. 'Most of these were murders ordered by Colonel Kiboko on a whim in his crazy, madcap games. Officers under him were forced to carry out these assassinations under threat of losing their own lives if they disobeyed.'

'I can add similar corrupt activities at the Medical Research Bureau in Lundazi,' Dr Timothy said, speaking up for the first time. 'The medical staff have been disgusted at the way Doctor Schneider engineered the deaths of many patients who came to us with relatively minor ailments and died when major organs were removed to be sold abroad for transplants. Most medical staff have been horrified by what they have been forced to do under pain of becoming victims themselves. Most of the dead were cremated but not all and some were buried in the grounds of the Research Bureau. On orders of Mr Nixon Makau we have exhumed some of them and the evidence of missing organs is there for all to see.'

'That is grossly unfair,' Max Schneider called out. 'Madame Marie Antoinette was fully aware of the policy of extracting human organs for sale. She gave her full approval.'

President Matata leapt to his feet and, having once again removed his shoe, thumped it on the table like a gavel. 'Are you determined to make your fate even worse by implicating a beautiful lady like Marianne in your evil, sadistic schemes?

'I have heard enough today to make me profoundly sick at heart and to despair of the human condition when I learn of the depths of wickedness to which some men can descend. But to go and try to bring innocent others down with them, oh it is enough to make one give up hope of redemption for mankind. No more evidence is required. I find the two litigants guilty as charged of plotting with treasonous intent to depose the President of Zambelia. They are hereby condemned to death by public hanging in Lundazi football stadium one week from today on the anniversary of Zambelia's independence. Meanwhile, they will be imprisoned in Tagooma to await their execution. And may God have mercy on their souls. Take them away.'

***

The public hanging in the Lundazi football stadium did not however take place.

Kiboko and Schneider arrived in handcuffs at Tagooma Prison in accordance with the president's order all right. As was the custom with condemned prisoners, they were locked up in different cells to await their execution. Then one day, Major Gumbo read (some later said "deliberately mis-read and misinterpreted") something somewhere about the enlightened practice employed in Ulster in the U.K whereby prisoners were granted a so-called shackle-free "unlock" period that gave inmates access to decent sanitation outside their cells during the night. Anxious to show that he was willing to adopt a more liberal policy as recommended in the delegation report, he rang Nixon Makau for his views.

'By all means, try this civilised practice with your prisoners, both for the condemned and the others,' Nixon advised, 'and let's see how it works out. The Ulster authorities found there were serious risks involved in seeking to enforce strict lock-ups at night because prisoners got up to all kinds of mischief. It's only right and humane that they can reach clean and decent lavatories during the small hours.

Keep the actual prison blocks tightly restrained of course but let individual cells be unlocked during the night enabling freedom of movement within the block.'

Unfortunately the new liberal policy meant failure to pin down the wilder, more dangerous inmates in Cell Block 13 (known to all and sundry in the prison population as "the powder keg") and made it easier for them to cut the wires in a yard fence and to climb down into the exercise yard where Kiboko and Schneider were incarcerated. Many of these fierce prisoners had held long term grudges against the pair for past atrocities suffered at their hands. That night, these more violent elements found out where the condemned pair were being held and ran amok. They dragged the two of them into the courtyard and subjected them to indescribable tortures. Their eyes were pulled from their sockets, their testicles ripped out, and their arms and legs lopped off one by one. To round off their frenzied massacre, the insane prisoners took the two bloodied torsos and strung them up from the prison flagpole leaving them dangling next to the Zambelian flag where they were found the next morning.

The "unlock" experiment was abandoned immediately as not only unworkable but a dangerous mistake. Major Gumbo denied that there had been any duplicity between the prison authority and the government. An official report later highlighted a number of security failures and expressed its regret at these errors of judgement which had led to the massacre but found no proof of state involvement. The report concluded: "While we could perhaps be critical of certain individuals, institutions or state agencies, we were not persuaded in any instance that there was evidence of collusive acts or collusive conduct."

****

Chapter Thirty-Seven

How to rig an election

'One man, one vote' said the democrats. 'One man, one vote, once,' said the despots. 'One Party, One Leader, One Government, and no more nonsense' said Matata after achieving power in Zambelia and declaring himself President for Life.

On the morning of polling day, Big Mama was giving the President his usual aromatherapy session.

'Are you not worried, Samson,' she asked as she massaged his lower back, 'that you may lose this election and be voted out of office?'

'Not in the least, my dear Marianne. I have not remained in office these many years without learning a trick or two on how to rig an election. Maybe I'll write a book on the subject one day.'

'Fascinating, Samson,' she said as she applied rosemary oil to his shoulders. 'Well, how *do* you rig an election? I may need to know this for myself one day.'

'As easy as falling off a log, Marianne. Listen carefully and I shall reveal to you some of the secret techniques of how to manipulate a poll. It has taken me many years to accumulate this wisdom and I give it to you, free of charge.

'First, remember what I have said to you many times. It's not who *votes* that matters but who *counts* the votes. We collect the ballot boxes and take them to a secret place where we can alter the votes to suit ourselves. For example, we can spoil any papers in favour of Chifunza by simply adding an extra X and all such papers then become invalid.'

'Clever, my dear Samson but what about the UN observers? Won't they be watching you?'

'True, Marianne, but it is *our* electoral officers who take charge of the ballot boxes after the booths have closed and take them away to a safe place. That is, safe for us to alter the votes.'

'Ingenious, Samson.'

'The next technique is to intimidate the punters by installing our Matata Youth Brigade lads at the entrance of each polling booth supposedly as canvassers or vote counters. Out of earshot of the observers, they will petrify the peasants by telling them there is no such thing as a secret ballot and we'll know exactly who they've voted for. Chifunza supporters will be promised a good thrashing. This will definitely work.'

'Fine, Samson, as long as the observers don't see you.'

'The UN monitors shouldn't be a problem, Marianne, as they stay inside the booth out of the hot sun and their officials are looking for a quiet, comfortable life. We use stick and carrot methods. The intimidation I'm talking about takes place outside in the queue. We can even send in a gang and take over the whole booth if we have to and cast the votes of legitimate voters by threatening them with a good beating. In the last resort, if we don't manage to terrify the voters that way, we can use the carrot approach by bribing them with promises of a job, food, beer, money or even a goat or two.'

'That should certainly do the trick, Samson. Is that the lot? Now turn over and I'll do your front.'

'We can also get our people to go round several booths casting their votes at each one. The checks made on individuals casting their votes several times over are minimal. One man can vote a dozen times.' He chuckled and then it is a case of "One Man, One Vote, Twelve Times".'

'But I thought voters had their fingers marked with indelible ink to prevent that.'

'Nah, that's no problem. A little pumice stone soon removes the ink. And if that fails, Marianne, we can take away the ballot boxes and stuff them with multiple ballot papers. Don't forget that in Zambelia there's always a gap of a week to ten days before the results are announced because of the numerous remote rural polling stations and it takes time to gather in the boxes.'

'It looks as if you've got it sewn up, Samson.'

'Too right, Marianne. It's in the bag, I tell you. So much for that British delegation and their dreams of Utopia.'

***

The people of Zambelia had not had the chance to vote in an election since Matata had entrenched himself thirty-odd years previously and they hardly knew what "having the vote" meant. In the past they'd taken part in sham elections for the Chamber of Deputies with only one party to choose from and even that had been simply a list of candidates drawn up and approved by the President. Now they were to be faced with two parties – the Massuyu Conference Party and the revived People's Democratic Party. When it came to the presidency, in the past there had been only one man standing for the job and they had no option but to re-elect Samson Matata. Now there were to be two men up for the office. They could put Matata back in office or they could go for the new man, the ex-prisoner and Deputy Minister, Lazarus Chifunza.

When people were told that they would soon be able to cast their vote, there was a certain amount of confusion. "Cast"? Did it mean they had to throw something like a fishing net or a spear? They'd heard it in the Bible with references like "cast thy bread upon the waters." They'd heard about people being cast into prison. Surely that couldn't be it! Or there was a cast of actors in a play. They were also told that there would be two ballot papers: one for the Chamber of Deputies and one for the office of president. That word "ballot" worried them a little though as it sounded a bit too much like "bullet". No matter. When it was announced that there would free elections, the people went mad with joy though they weren't altogether sure what it was they were celebrating. There was dancing and singing in the streets and some over-enthusiastic voters announced that they would vote five hundred per cent while others went one better and raised it to one thousand per cent.

A day's holiday was granted on the day of the election so that the populace could go out and exercise their right, most for the first time. The queues, six deep, outside the polling booths began to build up from six o'clock in the morning even though the doors were not due to open until eight. The lines of would-be voters stretched off into the distance and were at least three miles long even at that early hour of the morning.

'It's amazing,' Sue remarked to Mike when she heard about it. 'Back home in England, it's all they can do to persuade people to come out of the house to vote. Often we have to send a car to get them out and even then a turnout of fifty per cent is considered good.'

'The difference,' Mike said, 'is that here in Zambelia, the right to vote is considered a great privilege as they have been deprived of it for so long. In the UK, people have become blasé about universal suffrage. It's a depressing thought when you consider how bitter were the struggles of the past to win the right. Emmeline Pankhurst and her Suffragettes would turn over in their graves if they knew how much value British women put on the right to vote today.'

'I don't know if you agree with me, Mike,' Sue said passionately, which meant there'd be big trouble if he didn't, 'but I often think that we British believe in our conceit that our customs and practices are perfect so it's only right and proper that we foist them on to developing nations. In a way, it's a form of cultural assault, insisting as we do that they adopt our ways. We do it in so many other fields that we teach: in literature, music, history and the rest. Now we're doing the same in politics. We'll only grant independence if the third world country accepts a parliamentary democracy of the Westminster type with universal suffrage, secret ballots, and the rest of the shooting match. Practices which have taken thousands of years of struggle and strife to evolve.'

'And look how long this exported democracy lasts,' Mike laughed. 'As soon as the imperialists have gone home, it's straight back to the *status quo* with all-powerful tyrants boasting megalomaniac titles like "Saviour of the Nation", "The Messiah" "King of All Africa" or something similar.'

***

Throughout Zambelia, election day was treated as a major event and for many, the most thrilling and the most important event in their lives, especially as Matata had snatched the right away from them shortly after independence all those years ago. Tens of thousands of rural peasants came pouring down from the hills and villages outside the towns, many of them with feet bleeding, having walked barefoot over rough, rocky terrain. As they waited patiently for the booths to open, many in the crowds raised umbrellas against the blistering sun and there was much cheering, singing, and shrill ululating as they waited to exercise the franchise.

It was not all laughter and gaiety however. Outside every station, there were stationed louts of the Matata Youth Brigade and, as electors jostled their way through the entrances into the crowded booths, one or two of the thugs were seen to raise a clenched fist and hiss, 'Remember, we'll know who you voted for. Vote for Chifunza and we'll be coming to pay you a visit. We know where you live.'

Fortunately as a counter measure, university students were also standing outside the booths keeping a watchful eye on the Youth Brigade bullies. Scuffles and fistfights broke out at many polling stations between the two factions and it became commonplace to see bodies rolling around in the dust. One of Matata's yobs tried trickery by telling obvious Chifunza fans to place an X on the one they *didn't* want just as a teacher at school did when a sum was wrong. As for the United Nations observers, they stayed, as Matata had predicted, mainly inside the booths to keep an eye on things and see that election procedure was adhered to. Inside there was also likely to be less trouble.

***

A week passed after the elections and still no results were announced.

'Jiggery-pokery, as expected,' the people muttered among themselves. 'Matata and his gang have got at the ballot papers and rigged the election. It's no use: we can't win.'

This time they were wrong. Despite the efforts to juggle the results, the Massuyu Conference Party lost to the People's Democratic Party who won with an absolute majority over them in the ratio of 60/40. The competition for the presidency was equally intense and, though not so clear-cut as for the parties, the result was decidedly in favour of Chifunza who defeated Matata 55 to 45. A momentous day! And time for "The Old Man" to step down after reigning over Zambelia with an iron fist for more than three decades.

A jubilant Chifunza along with his triumphant Deputies and numerous supporters and party workers made their way to the Intercon as the Lundazi Intercontinental Hotel was known locally. There they took over the whole of the ground floor celebrating victory in grand style: drinking, laughing, joking as they waited for the Matata's government to vacate their offices so they could move in and begin putting their plans and policies into practice. A thousand and one questions needed to be resolved and the discussions stretched well into the early hours of the morning. Who would move into which bureau, who would occupy which house, which party officials would be rewarded with which positions?

399

Even the thorny question as to what to do with the outgoing Matata was discussed.

'We could charge him with murder and corruption for a start,' suggested one of the new and radical Deputies.

'No,' said Chifunza. 'We must treat him with mercy and compassion because, let's not forget that it was he who discarded the colonial mantle and won the country's independence. Matata's now an old man and deserves to be treated with respect and dignity. I would suggest we honour him with a title which will take account of his achievements. Why not a position such as Emeritus President of Zambelia or some such. We are offering him an olive branch and the chance to renounce his life presidency with dignity. At a pinch we could include him in a coalition as adviser. If he resists our overtures though, he will be disgraced instead of being accommodated and held in reverence. Remember that our chief aim is not to exact revenge but to build a new Zambelia founded on freedom, democracy and social justice.'

When the results of the elections were announced on Radio Zambelia, there was rejoicing throughout the kingdom except for those Massuyu Conference party zealots who had contrived to wangle and manipulate a Matata victory. Thousands of celebrants took to the streets dancing and singing; a relay of bonfires blazed across the country, and triumphant street parties were held in every town and the village; the taverns throughout the land were full to overflowing with noisy, jubilant revellers unable to take in the momentous fact that Matata's repressive regime had finally come to an end after so many long years of repression and suffering. In the Lundazi and Hekima townships, the festivities continued well into the night with drinkers wearing silly hats, waving the Zambelian flag, leading conga-line dancing, beating drums, blowing whistles, and letting off fireworks.

'This election,' they laughed through their tears of joy, 'was unriggable! The will of the people has won the day. It's a new birth!'

"The Dawn of a New Age!" proclaimed *The Zambelia Herald*.

Then it all turned sour when Matata, urged on by Big Mama, refused to step down.

****

Chapter Thirty-Eight

Two Presidents and two cabinets

As the results were gradually released, and it slowly sank in that he had lost, Matata was filled with dismay and self-pity. His senility had begun to get the better of him and he depended entirely on Big Mama to tell him what to do next.

'My people no longer love me,' he sobbed on her shoulder, 'this is my reward after all I've done for them. I have devoted my life pursuing a policy for the good of the country and to improving the welfare of my people and they reward me finally by rejecting me, throwing me on to the scrap heap and choosing that idiot, Chifunza. What am I going to do now, Marianne?'

'Nonsense, Samson,' Big Mama said. 'They can't reject you. If Chifunza is claiming to have won, it can only be wishful thinking on his part. Have you forgotten you are the *Life* President? Not for a year or two, Samson, but for life!'

'You're right, as usual, Marianne. Life means life and all things considered, I was chosen by the people, was I not? And then to be offended by that upstart, that gaolbird, Chifunza,' he barked, conveniently forgetting that he too had once been a gaolbird and had forcibly appointed himself as Life President. 'As for that offer of Emeritus President and to be part of a coalition government, I consider that to be an insult to someone like me. It's like offering me a ceremonial wheelchair and a ticket for a place in a retirement home.'

'You must go on the radio and speak to the people, Samson,' she urged. 'You mustn't take this lying down.

Remember who you are! The great Samson Matata, the Messiah, the leader of the people and Captain of the Ship of State. Announce to them that you are not willing to hand over to a bunch of good-for-nothings like Chifunza and his gang. Oh, how I regret not telling Kiboko to push him out of the helicopter into Lake Zambelia along with his fellow conspirator, Deputy Chilolo! Tell the people how they were cheated at the election and how Chifunza rigged it and terrified the voters by positioning so many thuggish-looking students outside the polling booths, menacing the electors as they went in to record their votes. Reveal how they have resorted to ballot stuffing by having students vote at many different polling stations. Tell them how crooked the count was with so many of Chifunza's boot-lickers employed on the actual job of totting up the voting papers. Throw out a few hints that you'll appeal to the East for support; the Russians have long wanted to use Zambelia as a stepping stone into Africa. If the Soviets thought that you were a potential ally, they would come to your aid immediately. The notion that you might turn to communist countries for help will unnerve the West and should bring about a swift resolution of the problem. You could also suggest that Chifunza was a crook ripping off his fellow Zambelians by stealing money from charitable organisations in order to fund his election expenses. Finally, my dear Samson, don't lose sight of the fact that you still control the purse strings and the militia. Whoever has charge of these two things calls the tune. Be like the Samson we know and love! Show 'em who's boss!'

Matata did as Big Mama ordered and gave his speech on Radio Zambelia reading from the autocue Big Mama had composed for him.

'My dear people of Zambelia, this is your true and only president speaking, Life President Matata who won your liberty and independence from the imperialist oppressors; the president who has served you faithfully for over thirty years. Do not believe those people who try to trick you into believing that the People's Democratic Party won at the recent election. It's a wicked lie as the PDP resorted to deception by rigging the votes and intimidating the electors. I will not allow it. Any citizen claiming to have won a seat in the new Chamber of Deputies votes will be arrested and thrown into gaol. I have taken steps to see that these liars and cheats do not prevail in our beloved Zambelia. Of course you returned me to serve as your president once more and, for this, I thank you from the bottom of my heart for your love and your trust. Now you have given me the chance to finish my task of building a new strong Zambelia. It will be a glorious monument that I can bequeath to posterity. Uhuru!'

After the broadcast, Big Mama advised Matata strongly that he had better instruct Colonel Nyoka to put the five thousand armed Public Safety Militia under him on high alert in the capital to deal with any insurgents. To the Intercon Hotel, she dispatched a highly trained contingent of the Presidential Guard to surround and forbid anyone to enter or leave, effectively putting Chifunza and his Deputies under close house arrest. Next, he cordoned off the area round the villa complex at his palace with the crack troops of his Special Presidential Guard under Major Gumbo. Finally, sentries were positioned at key points around the outskirts of Lundazi and access to the capital was strictly controlled through military checkpoints. There was no hint of compromise in his radio speech and the country appeared to be drifting towards a violent showdown.

Zambelia was also now in the surreal position of possessing two presidents and two cabinets. In the besieged hotel, the new cabinet and president-in-waiting were surrounded and confined.

***

Meanwhile, the Students' Union had reacted to the electoral news by sending out an e-mail to all student organisations not only at the Hekima University campus but also the Polytechnic in Lundazi and the Odongo College of Agriculture in the Northern region calling an emergency meeting.

'It's exactly as I predicted,' the hot-tempered Jonah Moshi thundered to a hall packed with angry students. 'The time for talk and negotiation is over. Matata is a liar and a cheat and has been for the last thirty years, from the moment he came to power. He has never been true to his word. He has wreaked blood-stained destruction on our country by torturing and murdering his way to the top and our people have suffered under his brutal oppression. Now he refuses to hand over power to the legitimate winner of the election. He's playing for time in order to bring in more arms, munitions, and mercenary troops from the East so's he can stay in office. But it won't work. If he won't step down voluntarily, I say we march on his palace at Lundazi and remove him by force of arms. String him up from a tree if we have to.'

This speech was greeted with a great roar of approval. Encouraged, Moshi continued, 'If we can bring out our fellow students at the Poly the Odongo College, we should be able to overwhelm them. We might even persuade the soldiers to come over to our side.'

An e-mail message went out that evening:

TO ZAMBELIAN STUDENTS EVERYWHERE!

THE TIME FOR TALKING IS OVER. NOW IS THE HOUR FOR DIRECT ACTION TO REMOVE THE TYRANT, MATATA. STUDENTS WILL ASSEMBLE AT 9 A.M. ON MONDAY, APRIL 24TH OUTSIDE THE MAIN POST OFFICE IN LUNDAZI TO MARCH ON THE PALACE. BE THERE!

That week-end, thousands of students from the three educational institutions grabbed their belongings and what

405

food they could lay their hands on and started the march on Lundazi.

At eight-thirty, the protestors, their numbers swollen by workers from every sector of society, began gathering at the agreed assembly point. Ninety minutes later, the biggest rally ever seen in Zambelia's history began marching down the Samson Matata Highway in Lundazi. Around ten thousand demonstrators who had walked, hitch-hiked, cycled or bussed in from all points of the compass, could be seen and heard raucously chanting: "No Ifs, No Doubt! We Want Matata Out!" Howling and gesticulating, with faces covered in scarves and black balaclavas, they headed into the city centre. It wasn't long before the rally was hi-jacked by a rabble of rent-a-mob anarchists, masked and hooded and with their own revolutionary agenda. What started as a peaceful protest quickly deteriorated into chaos as the demonstration turned into a snarling, malevolent assault on every symbol of government, edifice and monument alike. Nothing was exempt; no official building left unvandalised; the Chamber of Deputies, the Supreme Court, and the Ministry of Finance were surrounded by a wild, angry, gesticulating mob.

Colonel Nyoka who had been put in charge of defending the capital from the marauders said: 'The marches have become a magnet for unruly elements who are intent on violence and mayhem. The demonstrations are being used to cloak dissident factions determined to attack the legitimate authority and destroy property. Let them understand! They will be met by a firm and unwavering response.'

Radio Zambelia reported developments on the evening news bulletin that evening:

As the mob reached the monument dedicated to our beloved Marie Antoinette in Samson Square, a small group of hard-core demonstrators in black balaclavas detached itself from the main body of the rally and climbed up the base and gave a clenched fist salute to a baying crowd. A rope was attached to the head of the stone statue and the image of our respected presidential consort was pulled on to her face and broken up with sledgehammers.

Nearby, half a dozen masked thugs began smashing the windows of the Ministry of Education on First Street. Soon, over two hundred rioters had forced their way inside after battering their way past the half dozen local guards on duty outside. It didn't take long before a screaming, baying horde of around three thousand protestors had invaded the courtyard and ceremoniously set fire to an effigy of our beloved president.

The more violent elements next broke into the building and began wrecking all three floors. The small number of uniformed officers of the Public Safety Unit could only watch as louts, faces hidden, linked arms and methodically kicked in every window in the central hall. They followed this up by putting in every other window they'd overlooked by throwing heavy metal chairs and electrical apparatus from inside. Not content with this, they completed their destruction by pulling down ceilings, cutting up sofas, jumping on glass topped tables, paint-spraying walls with slogans like: "Death to Matata" and "Off with His Head".

Outside, the insurgents erected barricades of burning tyres and logs on the main road between the American embassy and the Central Bank of Zambelia. We conclude this special report with a statement from Colonel Nyoka, Head of the Zambelia militia.

'Let the rabble that is at present rampaging through the streets of our capital get it into their thick skulls that no mercy will be shown if they try to attack the presidential villa. Major Gumbo and I will have no hesitation in ordering our troops to fire on any rioters who approach the palace. I hereby command the protestors to return immediately to their homes or face the consequences.'

***

Nyoka's words were no idle threat. Before long, a large contingent of militia dressed in full riot gear arrived on the scene to which the rebels responded by throwing urine-filled bottles, rocks, paving stones, flares, petrol bombs and even spears. Palls of black smoke rose above the skyline as gangs of wreckers continued random attacks on shops and businesses. The barriers, erected to hold them back, were now employed as weapons, the metal structures being used as battering rams against both foot soldiers and the cavalry.

The Colonel was fully up-to-date in riot-control methods having received his training in crowd control at the Public Order Training Centre, at Gravesend in England and was not slow to react to this mindless violence. One of the first tactics he employed was a slowly advancing wall of men with batons, and mounted officers forcing the protestors back. But when the wilder elements among the dissidents began jabbing officers and horses with long scaffolding poles, he moved his weaponry up a gear by ordering the use of truncheons, tear gas, rubber bullets, and finally water cannons. To quell the most aggressive and destructive of the wreckers, he had no hesitation in ordering the use of more sophisticated weapons such as pepper sprays and the electroshock Air-Taser gun.

A large contingent of marauders, numbering two thousand protestors broke away from the main body and marched out to the outskirts of the city. Their destination was the presidential villa and Matata's palace. There, the presidential Praetorian Guard led by Major Gumbo - but under direct orders of Big Mama - was waiting for them, and they were a different kettle of fish from Nyoka's Public Safety men for they had no compunction about using lethal weapons.

The rebels arrived at the main gate of the palace and began taunting the officers at the checkpoint.

'Traitors!' they yelled. 'Matata's a thief and a liar! 'Come and join us in the protest!'

They proceeded to stage a sit-down demonstration blocking the highway so that no vehicle could get in or out of the villa. At that moment, a presidential Land Rover carrying four of Matata's elite Guards arrived and attempted to enter

408

the palace gates. A crowd of rioters surrounded the vehicle and dragged the soldiers plus their two drivers out on to the road and began kicking them and beating them up with baseball bats. That was enough for Major Gumbo because he now suddenly appeared with his crack troops from behind the large iron gates and attacked the rebels firing tear gas. Through the clouds of smoke there emerged a dozen guards armed with rifles and fixed bayonets. Without pause they charged after the rebels shooting and bayoneting indiscriminately and without mercy. Pandemonium broke out and the mob dispersed running pell-mell back into the centre of Lundazi.

Doctors and university professors later confirmed that twelve students had been killed and more than thirty-six seriously maimed. Among the deceased was the firebrand student Jonah Moshi. Families gathered at Lundazi General Hospital later that week to mourn their dead and arrange for their funerals.

Though the Presidential guard had effectively cut off the Intercon Hotel's communication with the outside world, the BBC managed to get a foreign correspondent through the blockade and in the lobby of the hotel, the interviewer met the legally elected President Chifunza.

'The tragic deaths of these young people are a dark episode in Zambelia's history,' he said, 'and the more so when we realise that they were unnecessary and due entirely to Matata's unwillingness to hand over the reins of office. These deaths must be added to the crimes of this dissident president who ordered his guards to fire on protestors. We learned from his recent broadcast that he has no intention of stepping down and relinquishing power over to the true government chosen by the people of Zambelia. He knows full well that he has lost the election but he is clinging to office in the hope that foreign troops from Russia or China will come to his aid. At the present time he has his militia and his thuggish Youth Brigade protecting him. Our only hope is that the international community will put pressure and use force if necessary to depose him. If Britain could only send in the SAS to grab Matata and remove him from the scene, the presidential guard would capitulate and Zambelia's troubles would evaporate overnight.'

Both the President of the USA and the Prime Minister of Britain took up this suggestion and began putting subtle consular pressures on Matata to resign. They even tried to phone him but he was adamantly defiant and refused to take their calls. Appeals from the United Nations also proved to be in vain. There was nothing doing and Matata was sticking to his guns in every sense of that expression.

***

At a meeting of the British cabinet to discuss the Zambelian crisis, it was decided that a policy of military intervention was a dangerous course of action and could have serious international consequences if other national governments like Russia or China took a contrary view. After long and heated discussion, it was agreed at the end that a series of diplomatic overtures might be more effective as well as being less provocative.

'I have visited Zambelia,' said Sir Hugh Baxter, the Commonwealth Secretary, 'and so I know the country and the people well. I suggest firstly that we send a diplomatic note to ex-President Matata telling him that we no longer support him nor accept his envoys. Secondly, we should impose severe financial controls on him by blocking his access to state funds. The USA and other western NATO countries along with the African Monetary Union have agreed to follow suit and exert pressure; the World Bank and the IMF will boycott the place and Zambelia will become a pariah state.'

'What would be the point of that and what would that achieve?' the Foreign Minister asked.

410

'If Matata cannot pay his soldiers, they'll soon stop backing him and he'll have no alternative but to hand over to the legitimate president, Lazarus Chifunza.'

Big Mama anticipated this move by the British government and was quick to instruct the president as to his next move.

'The British must think we're stupid, Samson,' she said at one of her massage sessions. 'We'll show 'em we're not done yet. First thing we do is kick out their ambassador along with any other envoys who support Chifunza. Next, we'll print our own new money. Let's call it the Matata dollar and we can use it to pay our soldiers. Let the British put that in their pipe and smoke it! Our new dollars will have a picture of you emerging from the clouds on one side and our national flag on the other.'

Big Mama's plan went down well and everyone, soldiers and citizens alike, was happy with the new currency of beautiful, crisp-new dollar bills. For a couple of months, it looked as if the sham President had sidestepped the international attempt to cut off his funds. Until, that is, traders, and shopkeepers in particular, discovered that the lovely brand new notes were worth about as much as Monopoly money and began refusing to accept them.

It wasn't long before anger and frustration flared up and the hungry populace began a frenzied pilfering of the shops for groceries and provisions. Looters armed with knives and clubs proceeded to pillage at will. Next, regular soldiers of the Public Safety force who had not been paid for weeks joined the rioters, seizing food and drink from stores and supermarkets. Offices, warehouses and stores were ransacked and anything of the remotest value was pilfered. Some of Nyoka's men could be seen pushing wheelbarrows and handcarts containing printers, computers, and one enterprising soldier had taken possession of a large fridge. Only the Special Presidential Division guarding Matata and the palace grounds appeared to be exempt from the privations

411

since the president had managed to pay them from his own resources.

Such was the level of vandalism that it was only a short time before shops and stores had been gutted and the streets of the towns, big and small alike, were littered with the debris of broken glass, smashed wooden counters and shelving, shredded packages and boxes, and doors torn off their hinges.

'They've completely cleaned me out,' wept Tarak Tulshidas recently back from his term in Tagooma. 'To think I spent all that time in prison only to find on my return that these thieves have not only emptied my shops but keep coming back in case they missed something. What's more, I have no idea when and where I am going to replenish my stock.'

It was the beginning of a three-month long period of plunder as people struggled to survive in a country that was rapidly descending into anarchy. The mayhem spread to the prisons where there were disturbances throughout the system with three hundred inmates escaping from Tagooma. Prison officials reported that ten people had been killed and they'd been forced to open the gates to prevent further bloodshed.

Even in the university town of Hekima, the ransacking spree continued unabated and urchins could be seen trundling their soapbox carts loaded not only with food and bottles of drink but also items of office equipment such as table lamps, computers, monitors, typewriters and even electrical fittings. One enterprising individual was seen hurrying away with a central heating radiator hoisted on his shoulder.

***

'This is my worst nightmare come true,' Sue Delamere sighed to Mike Goodman as they stood one afternoon helplessly watching the wholesale pillage from a window in the university. 'Where are the police?'

'Many of those carrying away the loot *are* the police,' Mike said. 'We can only stand and watch as law and order unravel.'

412

'Why doesn't the British Government intervene?' Sue asked bitterly. 'The most we have heard so far is a speech from our Foreign Secretary urging restraint from all sides and appealing to the vandals' commonsense to return to law and order. A fat lot of good that will do. Surely there's *something* they can do to stop this destruction.'

'The question is "what", Sue. Now that Zambelia is independent, Britain must wait for a request to intervene. They're afraid that if they simply walk in and try to knock a few heads together, they could start World War Three if other hostile countries object to our interference and come in on Matata's side.'

'You know, Mike, when the country held multi-party elections and Chifunza was made president, I thought our problems were over but it seems they'd only just begun. There'll never be real elections in Zambelia as long as the people believe that Matata can simply arrest or kill the winners. We seem to be going from bad to worse with some of our students killed and wounded in that affray at Lundazi palace.'

'And the true President-in-waiting trapped at the Intercon,' Mike added. 'The country has gone to pieces and there's chaos everywhere. I've got to admit, Sue, I don't know what the answer is to this impasse. Maybe the United Nations might have the solution but I don't know what it would be as *their* hands are tied as well.'

'I certainly don't know what anyone can do, Mike, but I liked what Chifunza told the BBC the other day in his interview at the Intercon Hotel. Do you remember what he said? "If Britain could only send in the SAS to grab Matata and remove him from the scene, the presidential guard would capitulate and Zambelia's troubles would evaporate overnight".'

'Brave words, Sue. There's absolutely no chance of Britain sending in a force to do such a thing.'

413

Sue sighed. 'I suppose you're right, Mike. But if only some power could somehow spirit Matata out of his palace and hide him away, our problems could be over.'

'Right, Sue, and if only I were God and could make myself invisible, I could descend unseen on the palace and lift Matata out and take him to my secret lair. Pipe dreaming, Sue.'

'Wait a minute, Mike. You've suddenly put a mad, crazy idea into my head. Listen. I am about to be brilliant. *We* could do it, you and I.'

'Uh-oh,' Mike exclaimed. 'I don't like that wild look in your eyes, Sue. You're not thinking what I think you're thinking! Surely not! It'd be utter madness.'

'Not as mad as simply standing here and watching the world disintegrate around our ears, I only know that Zambelia is on the edge of an abyss and desperate times call for desperate measures. Look, let *me* tell you what I have in mind and then, and only then, *you* can tell me I'm mad. But before you do, let me put on a pot of coffee, and I shall reveal my cunning plan.'

****

414

Chapter Thirty-Nine

Sue's plan

'What I have in mind,' Sue told Mike as she handed him a mug of coffee, 'involves me going back to live in the rondavel at the Lundazi villa complex. Do you think we could organise a return visit for me and keep it secret as we did last time?'

'You mean sneak you back into the rondavel! That'll be extremely difficult, Sue, as the Presidential Guard is now on high alert. But why? Tell me what it's all about!'

'I remembered the words of Chifunza when he said that if we could pick up Matata and take him out of the scene, the Presidential Guard would capitulate and our problems would be over.'

'Yes, I remember, Sue. You're not proposing that we go in and assassinate Matata, I hope.'

No, Mike. Nothing as drastic as that. I propose we return to Lundazi and kidnap him.'

'Kidnap Matata! Sue, then you are crazy! That's almost as drastic as assassinating him! And just as risky. Hell's bells, how do you propose we do such a thing?'

'You may have forgotten, Mike, but you said something about descending unseen on to the palace, lifting Matata out and taking him to your secret lair. That is more or less what I propose we do.'

'What madness is this, Sue? You do realise of course that if we tried and failed but were caught in the act, we'd be

415

summarily executed on the spot. And don't say: nothing ventured, nothing gained. What you are proposing is potentially lethal. Why, even to be overheard talking like this, would be enough to land us both on death row.'

'Right, Mike. I know full well how dangerous the whole thing is but I'm damned if I can see any other answer to the problem. Here in Zambelia we've got complete stalemate and we're stymied good and proper. Let me get you another coffee and I'll explain my idea and how it can be done.'

Talking well into the rest of that evening, Sue outlined her scheme for "taking Matata out of the scene."

***

Next day, Sue was on the phone to the Hallidays on a secure line explaining her idea to Peter.

'Wow!' he exclaimed after she finished outlining the plan. 'That's a mighty daring thing to do and I'll take it on trust that you've thought it right through. As for coming to stay here, yes, Sue, maybe we can repeat the process but we'll have to be doubly careful this time as security around the palace complex has become unbelievably tight. We could adopt the same routine as last time. So if you can get Mike to drive you up to the Lundazi Inn, Helen and I will meet you there. Fortunately, it is still Jason on the rear sentry box and we shouldn't have any trouble sneaking you in. Meanwhile, I'll clear things with Nixon and get his reaction. I'm sure he'll be glad to see you again. Until Friday then. All our love. You're certainly one helluva daring young lady and we admire you for it though we must also admit you've got us a bit nervous!'

***

The Friday drive from Hekima to Lundazi was the same as the trips before except Mike was able to use his own car instead of the ambulance as Sue was no longer a fugitive on the run. Mike parked in the long term stay section of the Inn and there they met up with the Hallidays. The four of them piled into Peter's BMW and drove over towards the rear

416

section of the palace estate. They stopped a good mile before reaching the sentry post and Peter explained the routine to be adopted for entry to the villa.

'As usual, we'll be taking Mike in as Doctor Finlay, the chiropractor, as Jason the sentry on duty, is well acquainted with his Friday visits to treat Helen's back trouble.'

'Good,' said Sue, 'but what do *I* do? I don't want to be seen going into the villa as I intend spending a week at my old rondavel and it's imperative that I remain invisible while I conduct a reconnaissance of the area and prepare the steps for the taking of the president.'

'Sorry, Sue,' Helen replied. 'Peter and I have talked it over and there's no alternative but for you to hide once again in the boot under some blankets. I doubt Jason will want to look in the back but better to be safe than sorry. Hopefully, it shouldn't be for more than half an hour or so.'

'Don't worry, Helen. I'm getting used to hiding under blankets at the back. Anyway, it's my plan and so I can only blame myself if it's uncomfortable. Perhaps I can get a job with M.I.5 if ever I get the sack from teaching.'

Sue got out of the car and climbed into the boot and Helen covered her over with a large blanket. They drove up to the rear gate and approached Jason who was standing in his sentry box. He wasn't alone on this occasion for next to him stood a smartly dressed lieutenant in the Presidential Guard Division.

'Good afternoon, Jason,' Peter called. 'You remember Dr Finlay? He's come to give Helen the usual treatment for her back.'

'Yes, Mr Halliday. Of course I remember Dr Finlay. Good evening, doctor. By all means, go in. I'll open the gate.'

'Wait a minute,' the presidential lieutenant snapped, placing his hand on the handle of the revolver in the holster.

'Who *is* this stranger? You know we have strict orders to vet everyone coming into the villa.'

'It's all right,' Jason said. 'Dr Finlay is no stranger. He's been coming for some considerable time to give Mrs Halliday treatment for her back; he's an expert. There's no problem.'

'All the same,' the lieutenant barked. 'I have my orders to search all vehicles.' The young man went over to the car, peered in and stared at Mike suspiciously. 'You say you're a doctor that treats backs? Is that right?'

'Yes, that's correct,' Mike said carefully. 'Why? Anything wrong, officer?'

'Yes, there is,' the young man said. 'Something very wrong.'

'Uh-oh,' Mike thought. 'What do I do now if he asks to look into the boot? Make a run for it? Fight him? Wrestle him to the ground?'

The dilemma resolved itself however for the officer said suddenly, 'I have this terrible pain in the small of my back. What would you recommend, doctor?'

The relief on Mike's face was apparent to everyone. 'Pain in your back, eh? I may have the very thing for it right here.' He reached into his medicine bag and brought out a bottle of Sloane's liniment. 'Here take this with my compliments. Try it before you go to bed tonight. Massage it in well into the affected muscle but be careful not to rub into any sensitive part of your body such as...' He left the body part unsaid. 'You'll find it burns like hell but it should do the trick.'

'Thank you, doctor,' the young officer said. 'I shall try it tonight. I was lucky to meet you.'

'Yes, it was a piece of luck,' agreed Mike.

With a big smile, Jason waved them on.

'I've only one thing to say,' Mike remarked wiping the sweat from his brow and with a big smile on his face as they entered the palace complex, 'and that is: Phew!'

418

They drove on and when they were a mile into the grounds, Peter stopped the car to let Sue out. 'That was a close call,' she said. 'I thought the game was up. If I'd had a gun, I'd have shot that young guard if he'd opened the boot.'

'You wouldn't have had a chance,' Mike chuckled, 'for I'd have strangled him before he got the key into the lock.'

***

Late Friday afternoon, the four of them met with Nixon Makau in his cottage for tea and to hear details of Sue's plan for kidnapping Zambelia's president.

When everyone was settled, Nixon said, 'I've already spoken privately to Sue by telephone and the rest of you and we are agreed that, after the recent upheavals and the disputed election results, Zambelia is in dire straits and possibly teetering on the edge of a complete breakdown of law and order, even civil war. Something profound and drastic is needed if we are to avoid catastrophe. Right, Sue. Let's hear it. I can't wait to learn the intricacies of how to snatch a president from under the noses of the Praetorian Guard. Before you begin, let me say that I support this attempt to get Zambelia out of the quagmire into which we've sunk. I've racked my brains and I cannot see any way out of this cul-de-sac. Something severe is required and this scheme of Sue's may well be the only answer we have. Let me begin by supplying you with a few relevant and important details. First, the President's nurse, Florence, is an Umbuka, that is, one of my own tribe and also a distant relative. She has agreed to cooperate fully with the attempt.'

'It's an extraordinarily brave thing for her to do,' Mike said. 'While on the subject of the president's nurse, the one thing that's been puzzling me all day is why the president is not more closely guarded. One middle-aged nurse hardly represents tight security.'

'I can answer that,' Nixon said. 'The reason is because the presidential guard is so proud of its outer defences, they have become complacent and regard the palace complex as an

419

impregnable fortress surrounded by two huge impenetrable fences of Mauritius thorn; furthermore there are crack troops everywhere. For them, the idea of anyone getting on to the premises is unthinkable but, as we know, every defence system has its Achilles heel and we've found it. On this point, I shall get my gardener, Mlima, to cut a passage through the thicket of thorns in the north of the palace grounds. It will be well hidden and known only to Mlima, Florence and myself. The passage will open on to the main road running around the villa. Now, Sue, having got those little details out of the way, please continue.'

'Thank you, Nixon,' Sue replied. 'Those little details, as you put it, make my explanations a little easier and a little clearer. Right. Here goes. I've put a lot of thought into this and I've had a few sleepless nights formulating this plan. This is what I propose.

'From a vantage point in Nixon's 'rondavel' garden which overlooks the palace grounds, I shall spend the rest of the week observing the president through binoculars taking his daily constitutional walk-cum-ride accompanied by his nurse, Florence. I shall study them every day until I have their routine off pat. What time they set off, how fast they walk, where they go and where they stop and for how long. By this time next week, I should know exactly their routine and where the best place is to do the snatch without being seen. From preliminary inquiries of Florence herself, it should be between eight and nine in the morning. Florence could fix it so that she stops the wheelchair at around eight thirty in a given spot where we could pick him up.'

Peter raised his hand here. 'He might resist. Did you think of that?'

'Yes, he might,' Sue said, 'but we've anticipated that. We may have to put him out for a short spell. Over to you, Mike.'

Helen paled a little at this point. 'You mean give him ether?'

420

'Not necessarily ether,' Mike said. 'I would give him a shot of sodium pentothal which should put him under in about forty-five seconds.'

'Isn't that dangerous?' Helen asked anxiously. 'I mean: we don't want to kill the poor old man, do we?'

'No danger, Helen. He's old, so I shall give him only about three or four milligrams which is practically nothing. I assume he's not suffering from anything serious, like liver or heart disease.'

'No, nothing like that,' Helen answered. 'The only thing I do remember is that he once injured his left arm when he fell off a rostrum during a speech. He became so excited that he forgot he was three feet off the ground.'

'Any lasting damage?' Mike asked.

'Nothing serious,' Helen replied, 'except that his arm gives the occasional spasmodic twitch but there's nothing more.'

'Well, the small shot of pentothal that I shall give him won't do him any harm. He should come round again after about five to ten minutes. Enough time for us to whisk him off the premises.'

'And what if he persists in being resistant after that?' Peter protested.

'I shall put him under for a longer spell though from what I've heard he is senile and amenable. A tiny dose of Nembutal should keep him in a sleepy but happy state after that. If all goes to plan, we shan't be detaining him for more than three or four days. That will depend on how co-operative Big Mama is in releasing Chifunza and his cabinet from the Intercon Hotel so that they can take up their rightful place in government. OK back to you, Sue.'

'Thanks for that. Next Friday, Mike will return to the palace bringing the ambulance with the leper signs prominently displayed. He will also be carrying a couple of friends of ours from Hekima market, Liza and Jonathan, who

421

were once severe cases of leprosy but have now fully recovered, though the disease has left them severely ravaged. They are more than happy to be going on the expedition as the hospital at Mombo Island has special facilities for the treatment of their condition and it will give them a welcome holiday from sitting around at Hekima market begging alms. They will be accompanying the president to Mombo Island where they will stay until Zambelian authorities come to their senses. I should also like to include in our party young Jack Zulu, a fifth year medical student, who can sit in the ambulance with Matata to see that he comes to no harm while I will sit with Mike in the cab at the front. Jack and I will be kitted out of course in full medical uniforms in case we are stopped *en route* by curious militia. Jack will be useful on Mombo Island as he knows the lay of the land and the patients there very well.'

'What happens to poor old Florence, the nurse?' Helen asked. 'Is she to be left with an empty wheelchair? If so, that's the end of her because she'll be arrested right away and slapped into Gereza.'

Nixon now joined in the discussion. 'No, I have discussed it with Florence and she has agreed to go with the president, wheelchair and all to Mombo Island where she will continue to look after him until he can return.'

Peter asked: 'What if the weather is against you and Florence cannot take him on his daily constitutional on the day you've planned?'

'We shall simply postpone things for a week until the weather is fine but I doubt we shall get rain as it's not the season for it. Only high winds could stop us.'

Mike now spoke up. 'I have a question for Nixon. How will I know where the gap in the hedge is if it's so well hidden? And will the gap be wide enough to take a wheelchair containing a sleeping president?'

'You can leave that side of things to me,' Nixon replied. 'First, I shall indicate the exact spot on the map of the palace

422

grounds that I have here. The gap will be wide enough to take the wheelchair and, in order to be sure that you know where it's located, I shall ask my gardener, Mlima, to wait on the road until you arrive. After you have driven off, he will make sure that all traces that there was ever a gap there are removed.'

'That's excellent,' Mike said. 'I shall expect to see him next Friday when I drive up in the ambulance. Meanwhile, I'll go over to Mombo Island with Jack Zulu this week-end to make preparations for our guest. I shall warn Dr Benvenuta at the refugee camp and Joseph, the orderly, on Mombo Island to expect us at some time on Friday evening. I'll get in a good supply of food – lots of canned goods – for a possibly extended stay and tell Joseph to prepare the master bedroom for a distinguished visitor. We'll need odds and ends like extra bed linen, towels, soap, kitchen utensils, and so on all of which I shall buy this week-end. Finally, I'll get in a few extra cans of fuel to avoid stops at petrol stations, which could draw attention to us.'

Peter said: 'You certainly seem to have thought of all the angles. It looks to me as if it's going to work but I hope you know how dangerous all this is. If anything goes wrong, that'll be the end of the lot of us. I should think Big Mama will order us to be hanged, drawn and quartered in Marie Antoinette Square.'

'Mike and I,' Sue said, glancing at Mike who nodded in agreement. 'have talked it over and we're aware of the immense risk involved. But without something as fundamental as this happening, nothing will change in Zambelia and there's a strong possibility that we could have total anarchy involving much bloodshed and probably many deaths. The mayhem we have seen in the past few weeks could be the preliminary to a full scale civil war and then it's God help us.'

'What will happen after it is discovered that Matata has gone?' Peter asked. 'Won't there be a general alert and recriminations?'

Nixon thought that he'd better say something here to reassure everyone. 'I think you will find that the kidnapping of the President will be hushed up. There won't be a hue and cry. I shall persuade Marie Antoinette that it won't be in our interests to broadcast the news that the old president has gone as it might trigger off unrest, a fresh wave of strikes and a demand that Chifunza be installed immediately in his rightful place. She may alert the Presidential Guard about Matata's disappearance but I believe firmly that, when the president has gone, Major Gumbo as commander of the Presidential Guard, won't be too keen on defending an empty throne. I have noted already a certain antipathy on his part towards Matata and his consort. Besides, the Major is fully aware that the legitimate president, Deputy Chifunza, and his cabinet are held against their will in the Intercon. With Matata gone, Gumbo will press for the release of the elected Deputies from the hotel so that they can take up their rightful places as the true and legitimate authority in Zambelia.'

'What happens to Matata and Big Mama afterwards?' Helen asked, solicitously

'That remains to be seen,' Nixon replied, looking deliberately vague.

****

424

Chapter Forty

The plan in action

During that fateful week, Mike and Jack made their preparations in Hekima for the kidnapping of President Matata. Sue continued to monitor Florence and the morning 'constitutional' and everything seemed to be going like clockwork. It was Thursday night that Sue had the panic attack during sleep. Distraught, she phoned Mike in Hekima.

'Mike, we've got to call it off. I'm scared. I had a nightmare last night in which the lot of us were on trial and later subjected to unbelievable torture in the dungeons of Tagooma and Gereza. I believe hanging, drawing, and quartering featured somewhere in the dreadful visions that ran through my mind. Maybe this kidnapping idea of mine is crazy and I am simply leading the people I love into a dreadful fate. We're normal, respectable people and we live quiet, decent lives. We're not the types who go out and kidnap presidents and try to change governments by force. What I am trying to say is that originally I got caught up in the excitement of planning to change things in Zambelia but somehow deep down, I now sense that it's not going to happen. Perhaps it would be best for everyone all round if we simply soldiered on under the present regime. At least we're not in gaol and we're still alive!'

'Sue, you've simply had a bad dream and I don't believe you're thinking straight at the moment. The plans we made in our small group last Friday were perfect and there is absolutely no hitch that we've not anticipated. We've been over every step a thousand times to see if we've forgotten anything. Every possible contingency has been covered. There's no hitch that has not been anticipated. Nothing can go wrong. Remember this is not a true kidnap in the real sense of the word. Matata is an illegal president and it is he who is breaking the law by not standing down. He has to be removed by force and, as we have discussed so fully, taking him out of the picture is the only way. It's up to us to give the people the justice that's been denied them so long. Do you want to continue to live under his repressive regime? Have courage, Sue. It will come out right in the end, never fear. Remember the Edmund Burke maxim that you're always quoting at me. "Evil flourishes when good men do nothing".'

'You're right of course, Mike. All right, we'll do it. I'm so sorry to have worried you at this late stage. I suppose I let my imagination run away with me and I panicked. Simply to hear your voice is reassuring. The idea of spending the next ten years under Matata and his corrupt government makes me shudder. OK. So it's on again and I shall see you on Friday morning bright and early when I shall be dressed in my smart nurse's uniform. Oh, and I almost forgot, do you think you could bring a box of talc or French chalk in your medical supplies? I'll explain why on Friday.'

'Sounds mysterious, Sue, but I think I can find some among my supplies. See you Friday and rest assured, it'll run without a hitch, you'll see.'

***

It was Friday morning of 'D' Day. Sue was up with the crack of dawn and after a shower, she donned the nurse's uniform, had a light breakfast, and was ready for action. Through binoculars, she watched the route normally taken with the president. At ten past eight, Florence appeared pushing the Matata in his wheelchair as usual. 'Right on time,' she thought. At eight-fifteen, with heart fluttering, she set off carrying her things in a small valise.

426

In the mean time, Mike and Jack Zulu had driven up from Hekima with the two lepers, Liza and Jonathan, in the back of the ambulance. At the appointed spot in the hedge, they met Mlima, the gardener, parked the vehicle and waited with the engine running until eight twenty. Shortly after that Sue appeared looking extremely tense and worried. 'Come quick,' she gasped, 'your help is required, now! A wheel has come off the invalid chair and the president has fallen on to the gravel path. This *would* have to happen on this day of all days!'

'Oh, hell!' Mike exclaimed. 'Right, Jack, you and I had better go to their aid.'

Gripping his medical bag and running as fast as he could, Mike pushed his way through the hole in the hedge and saw the overturned wheelchair about a hundred yards back. 'Come on, Jack, let's move! Quick as you can! It'll need both of us to fix the wheel and get the president back into his chair.'

The two men broke the record for the hundred yard dash. Jack picked up the wheel and rammed it back on its axle securing it with the pin which had fallen on the path and soon righted the chair. Mike hoisted the President back into his seat.

Florence the nurse stood helplessly by wringing her hands.

Mike ignored her but went straight to Matata. 'Good morning, Mr President,' he said cheerily. 'I am Doctor Finlay. A slight mishap and I have come to your aid.'

'Good morning, Doctor,' Matata replied amiably. 'A nasty accident. I must congratulate you on your speed. I have only this moment fallen out and in a flash there's a doctor on the scene. That's what I call efficiency.'

'All part of our service, Mr President. I know you once fell off a rostrum and injured your arm and so, to make sure there's no recurrence of the spasms you suffered, I'm going to give you a small injection. Please roll up your sleeve.'

427

'Incredible service,' murmured Matata appreciatively, rolling up his sleeve. 'By all means, do go ahead. If only the rest of the country were as nimble as you, we'd have no problems.'

Mike administered the injection and in thirty seconds, the President's head lolled forward and he was asleep.

'Oh, I'm so sorry about this,' Florence wept. 'This has never happened before. I should have checked the wheelchair before we set out, especially this morning.'

'Never mind that now! Let's move! Now! Come on, Jack!' Mike snapped, gathering up his things and scanning the area to check there had been no witnesses. As far as he could see, there were none. Summoning up all his strength, Jack pushed the chair containing the sleeping president through the gap in the hedge. Mlima had done his work well for the space he had created was exactly right to take the width of the chair. Sue already had the doors of the ambulance open and with a mighty heave, ex-President Matata was safely stowed aboard to join Liza and Jonathan who were waiting for their fellow traveller en route for Mombo Island. Sue and Jack lifted the recumbent Matata on to one of the two beds.

'I shall now join Mike in the cab,' Sue said, 'but before I go, there's one small thing I must do.'

She took the talc that Mike had brought with him in his supplies and applied a liberal amount to Matata's face making him look like a corpse.

'Now, Florence, I'd like you to do the same to your own face. Don't stint in applying the powder. Next, I want you to lie down in the second bed and cover yourself up to the chin with the blanket.'

'Is there a reason for this?' Jack asked, 'or shouldn't I ask?'

'Maybe you'll see in due course though I'm hoping you won't.' Sue said mysteriously. 'Now, I shall join Mike at the

428

front and we can be on our way.' She got out of the back and having secured both doors behind her, clambered into the front to be Mike's companion.

'Right, Mike,' she said. 'Let's go. Fingers crossed that we reach Mombo Island unscathed and undetected.'

***

Mike had worked out a short cut from Lundazi to the lake. Instead of taking the main highway and heading east, he chose a minor road which took him north for a short stretch as far as the small town of Ponelma. From there he had no alternative but to swing east on to the main road which ran parallel to the lake. He glanced down at his hands and saw how white they had become because of the vice-like grip he had on the steering wheel. Even though Nixon had assured him that no general alert would be put out, he was still extremely tense, expecting to hear any moment the wail of police sirens in pursuit. Every passing police car sent his blood pressure into the stratosphere. Every motor cycle he saw in his rear view mirror sent his heart racing. Surely by now, Nyoka's Public Safety men would be aware of the kidnapping and would be on the lookout for them!

'Take it easy, Mike,' Sue said, sensing his anxiety. 'It's all gone to plan; it ran swimmingly like a dream. It's downhill from here both literally and figuratively. So relax.'

Easier said than done, Mike thought as he drove on observing the speed limit carefully so as to remain invisible in a line of commercial vehicles. He avoided overtaking unless it was absolutely necessary and, though his instinct urged him to step on the gas, he resisted the temptation as this would be sure to attract traffic police. On the other hand, best not to drive too slowly either as this was likely to frustrate other drivers and cause them to sound their horns. The best policy was to match his speed to the flow of the traffic. A nice, steady 100 kms an hour seemed to be ideal. Then the thing he'd been dreading happened. In his mirror, he saw the headlights of a police car flashing him and telling him to pull

429

over. Ever so carefully Mike turned on to the verge by the side of the road and stopped.

Mike wound down the window of his side but it was Sue who spoke up.

'Can I help you officer?' she said ever so sweetly.

'Can you both please step out of the vehicle?'

'Certainly, officer,' Mike said. 'Anything wrong?'

'What is your name and what are you carrying?'

Standing on the grass verge, Mike pointed to the notice on the ambulance: ANGALIA: UKOMA. (BEWARE LEPROSY).

The older officer turned pale when the message sank in. 'O.K. You can be on your way,' he said quickly.

The younger officer, however, was more persistent. 'No, no. Wait a minute. I'd like to see for myself exactly what you have on board.'

'Certainly, officer,' Sue purred. 'I'll knock on the back doors to tell my assistant to open up. Perhaps, I should warn you that we have on board four severe cases of advanced leprosy. All are highly contagious but if you insist on inspecting, and don't mind taking a chance, I shall be glad to oblige. It's at your own risk. You'd be advised to hold a handkerchief to your nose and mouth.'

Sue banged three times on the rear doors (a pre-arranged signal to Jack Zulu to be on the alert). The rear doors swung open and the young officer looked in. The blood drained from his face and he turned a sickly colour when he saw the patients inside.

'Good morning, officer,' Jack said brightly. 'Please come on board if you'd like to take a closer look.'

The young policeman looked as if he was going to be sick and his complexion had become as sallow as the patients in the ambulance.

'That won't be necessary,' he muttered, hurrying away to join his colleague in the car. He was heard to say to the older officer, 'Oh, my God, Julian, those cases were bad! Straight out of the Old Testament. The two with the facial deformities were bad enough but you should have seen the two in the beds – as white as sheets and both at death's door. Let's get the hell out of here before I throw up.'

Sue closed the rear doors and bolted them down and they were on their way again. The rest of the journey was uninterrupted and they arrived at Mombo Island late afternoon, having crossed the river on the ferry. Matata was still out for the count and enjoying a deep slumber. A smiling Joseph was waiting for them as the ferry docked.

'Greetings to our new patients and hearty welcome to the Mombo Island Leproserie. Good to see our old friends once again. Everything that you requested, Doctor Goodman, is ready. The refrigerator's full and the master bedroom is waiting for your guest.'

***

For the rest of that Friday, ex-President Matata slept as sound as a baby. When he awoke on Saturday morning, he was still drowsy. The sunshine streamed through the window and when he opened his eyes, Mike was ready to receive him.

'Good morning, Mr President,' he said cheerfully. 'I trust you slept well.'

'Indeed I did,' Matata mumbled. 'The best sleep I've had in a long time. Where am I? Where's Marianne?'

'You are here in a private hospital, Mr President. You remember you fell out of your wheelchair and I attended to you. We shall let Marianne know what's happened to you in due course. Meanwhile, we want you to have a good, long rest to recover your strength and your spirits. I shall get one of our servants to bring you breakfast shortly. I take it that you still like a mixture of tropical fruits: paw-paw, avocado and so on.''

431

Matata smiled. 'How I look forward to a rest! As you know, I have been under great stress fighting an election and dealing with riots and strikes. This is a beautiful room. It reminds me so much of my childhood. And yes, I should love a light breakfast of fruits. I know I'm going to like it here.'

Mike left the room to organise the breakfast with Matata still babbling happily to himself about his early boyhood.

'Thank God, he's peaceful,' Mike said to Sue. 'There shouldn't be any need for any more drugs to keep him under. He is senile and what a tragedy it would have been to have left him in power. He's in his second childhood and it would have been God help Zambelia if he'd remained in charge making decisions for the rest of us.'

'That's a relief,' Sue said, 'but as you well know, Mike, it wouldn't have been Matata in charge but Big Mama and things would have simply continued as before. Talking of which, I now have the enviable task of going to see her to put her in the picture. I shall contact Nixon Makau and he will arrange a meeting or maybe we should call it High Noon or The Show Down.'

****

432

Chapter Forty-One

The Showdown

It was a week after the kidnapping and Big Mama sat in her office with elbows on the desk, chin on fists. She was distraught and at the same time angry and frustrated.

'Where in heaven's name had the President got to?' she asked herself over and over again. It was a complete mystery that weighed heavily on her mind. He had set off for his usual 'constitutional' outing only last Friday and had simply evaporated like a puff of smoke along with his nurse. No-one could offer a rational explanation and it didn't make sense. Neither Mr and Mrs Halliday nor the presidential aide, Nixon Makau, could account for it. One moment he was there; the next, he was gone. But how and where? It was like the mystery of the vanished *Marie Celeste* or some inexplicable disappearance in the Bermuda triangle. At first, she thought there might be some event or arrangement she'd not been aware of and that the President had made a private engagement of his own without consulting her. That was not only unlikely but unthinkable. When his absence had stretched to three days, she knew something dark and sinister was going on. Her main headache was keeping the matter a secret for had it leaked out, the consequences, especially for her and her family, would have been cataclysmic and there'd have been demand that power be handed over to that gaolbird Chifunza, at present holed up in the Intercon. She knew only too well that if Matata went, she and her family went too. Up to the fourth day, she'd entertained the hope, though faint, that everything might turn out right in the end. Perhaps Samson had been abducted and a demand for ransom could be expected any time. In some odd way, that would be welcome news for it would be something she'd know how to deal with. Again, perhaps he'd had a sudden bout of amnesia but that wouldn't make sense either since he'd still have to get past the sentry at the rear gate. Then there was the worst scenario of all and one she didn't even want to contemplate: perhaps he'd been murdered by political enemies and his body dumped in the lake. But if that had been the case, surely she'd have heard something by now. Now it was the fifth day, she'd still had no word, and her deepest anxieties had turned to fear, real fear that something was profoundly amiss and beyond her control.

She had checked with Major Gumbo, the new Head of the Presidential Guard, and he could throw no light on the enigma as there was no report of a break-in or of strangers getting on to palace property, which everyone believed anyway to be hermetically sealed. Gumbo had looked most unhappy at the notion that Matata was no longer around and she'd had to re-assure him that the president's absence was only temporary and that he'd turn up soon. In addition, some of the palace menial staff were beginning to mutter among themselves about the possibility of ju-ju and mumbo-jumbo visitations from underworld ghosts who had arisen from their graves and spirited the ex-President and his nurse plus wheelchair into the nether regions. As she sat there pondering possibilities, she recognized Nixon Makau's knock on her door.

'Yes, yes. What is it, Nixon. I have a lot on my mind at the moment.'

'There's a lady here to see you, ma'am,' he said. 'A European lady.'

'Lady? European lady? I don't know any European lady here in Lundazi. What does she want?'

'I don't know, ma'am, but it sounds urgent.'

Oh, very well, Nixon. Send her in but it had better be really important or I'll have her arrested for wasting my time.'

Sue was ushered into her office.

'Yes, yes,' Big Mama snapped. 'What is it? I am extremely busy and I don't have time for idle chit-chat. Who are you and what do you want? Be brief.'

Nixon Makau stood up at this point. 'Perhaps I should leave you two to speak in private,' he said.

'No, stay!' Big Mama ordered. 'I want you in on this. You're still the presidential aide and your advice is needed now more than ever.'

'Yes, ma'am,' he said obediently.

'I shall come straight to the point,' Sue continued. 'My name is Sue Delamere. I am a teacher at the University of Hekima and I come with news of President Matata.'

That was enough to make Big Mama sit up and pay attention.

'News? What news. Tell me quickly what you know!' she gasped.

'I know where the president is being held. If you want to know more, there are certain conditions.'

'Conditions! What conditions! If you know where the president is, you'd better tell me quickly or it will be the worse for you. What was your name again?'

'Sue Delamere and I am a teacher at the university.'

'Sue Delamere! I seem to have heard that name somewhere before. You were on our list of troublemakers, if my memory serves me correctly. The president was going to have you arrested but you vanished as soon as the police issued a warrant. You were a colleague of Frank Johnson's who met with an unfortunate accident in Tagooma. How do I know you are speaking the truth about our president and are not here simply to waste my time?'

'I believe this is his Rolex,' Sue replied, holding out Matata's wrist-watch. 'There's an inscription on the back which reads "To Samson from Marianne with love". That should be proof enough. The former president is safe and well and is being held in a secret location abroad which is inaccessible to you and your soldiers. I repeat: if you want him back, there are conditions.'

'Conditions! How dare you try to make conditions to me! Why should I listen to you? You're not from this country and so know nothing. You are not involved in political affairs.'

Sue's hackles rose when she heard this. She was seething and the innumerable frustrations she had bottled up since she had arrived in the country now came rushing to the surface.

''Not involved in political affairs!' she bristled. 'Now you listen to me Madame Marie Antoinette. Ever since I came to this damned country I have been *forced* to take part in your political affairs! I gave up my post in England, sold my home, left my family to come to this country to teach English Literature! And what has been my experience? I have found myself in an Orwellian nightmare characterised by graft, greed, corruption, nepotism, brutality, and terror. The people of Zambelia go about in mortal fear of being arrested and tortured without cause and without charge. I myself have been persecuted and spied upon ever since I got here. My lectures have been scrutinized for seditious content; the phones at my house and my office have been bugged; my home has been ransacked by your Public Safety snoopers; I've been given the third degree by your Censorship Board; finally I have been forced to flee and go into hiding for my life. And now you have the gall to say I am not involved in political affairs! If that's not being involved in political affairs, I don't know what is!'

'Do you realize who you are talking to?' Big Mama came back equally angry. 'I am the president's personal hostess and consort. How dare you, a mere teacher, a lackey, address me, a high presidential official, in such an offensive tone! I

436

have only to pick up this phone and I could have you shot for having the effrontery to address me like that!'

'What purpose would it serve if you arrest me and have me shot?' Sue said, having calmed down. 'You would be merely shooting the messenger. I am due to communicate your answer to my principals within the next two hours. If they've not heard from me within that time, you will never see your beloved president again. I promise you. Have I made myself clear?'

'Now I warn you Doctor Sue Delamere, you'd better tell us what you know about the president's disappearance. Otherwise I shall have you thrown into Gereza Prison? We'd soon see if you still have the insolence to talk to me as you have once we have you on the rack. Braver women than you have found it best to reveal all they know. You'd be well advised to speak and tell us what you have in mind now and be quick about it while you still have a tongue in your head.'

'I repeat,' Sue said equably. 'There are certain conditions.'

Big Mama gave a snort of impatience at having to kow-tow to this upstart, this nobody from the university. It hurt her deeply at having to answer at all but she managed to splutter the words out. 'Well, what are these damned conditions of yours?'

'First, and the most important, is that you call off the presidential guard from the Intercon Hotel and release Deputy Chifunza and his colleagues. Secondly, as they are the duly elected Deputies, that they be given their rightful places in government and, in this connection, it should be made public immediately on radio and in the press.'

'Never!' Big Mama exploded in apoplectic rage, realizing only too well that that would be the beginning of the end not only for Matata, but also for herself and her clan. 'Never!' she screamed once again.

'Then there's no point in pursuing this conversation further,' Sue said calmly. 'I shall communicate your decision to my principals and you will not see President Matata again. Thank you for talking to me this afternoon. Good day to you both.'

Sue stood up and made ready to leave.

'Wait!' a voice called suddenly. It was Nixon Makau. 'Could we talk privately for a few moments, ma'am?' he said addressing Big Mama. 'I think we should consider more fully what's involved here.'

'Very well,' Big Mama said reluctantly. 'Doctor Delamere, please be good enough to wait outside while I confer with the private secretary?' She rang a bell to summon her own secretarial assistant from the office outside.

'Very well,' Sue retorted. 'You'd be well advised not to take too long in reaching a decision. Remember that I have a deadline to meet and the clock is ticking.' Sue left the room and waited in the office outside. She had her fingers crossed.

***

As soon as Sue left the room, Big Mama turned angrily to Nixon. 'How dare this insolent nobody, this underling, this head-in-the-clouds, white trash of a woman try to dictate terms to me of all people, the president's confidante and companion! Well, Nixon, what shall we do about her? Have her banged up in Gereza or what? We could soon make her talk.'

'I think, ma'am, that we'd better do as she says if we want to see our president again. No doubt about it, we have no alternative and she has us over a barrel. Why not release Chifunza and his fellow Deputies and get our own president back? Once we have him returned to the fold, we can go from there. It shouldn't be too difficult to regain control. Let's proceed one step at a time. Remember we still have Major Gumbo's Special Presidential Division and Colonel Nyoka's Public Safety Unit under our command.'

Big Mama saw a glimmer of hope in Nixon's words.

438

'Of course!' she exclaimed. 'I had forgotten about them. Whoever commands the militia commands the country. Let's accept the conditions of this deluded female and go from there. Once we have our president back, it won't take us long to take back control of the situation. First thing we shall do is put Chifunza and his puppets now in the Intercon behind bars for daring to challenge our Life President. Second, it'll give me the greatest pleasure to frog-march this insolent woman into Gereza. I shall enjoy immensely watching her squirm and scream on the Gumbo long distance telephone machine. We'll see how brave she is then.'

She picked up her intercom and spoke to her secretary.

'Martha, bring back the visitor.'

Sue was ushered back into the main office and told of the decision.

'That's good,' Sue said. 'I'm glad you made the right choice. Now please call in Major Gumbo and tell him to remove his soldiers from the Intercon Hotel so that Deputy Chifunza and his followers can assume their rightful offices.'

Without more ado, Big Mama telephoned Major Gumbo and told him to attend her office. Within ten minutes, he was there awaiting orders.

'Gumbo,' Big Mama snapped. 'Take the Presidential Guard off the Intercon and tell Chifunza and his colleagues there that they are free to go.'

For the time being, she said to herself.

Gumbo could not hide the look of relief, even glee, as he saluted smartly and said: 'Yes, ma'am. Yes, ma'am. It shall be done within the hour.'

Colonel Nyoka was brought into the palace and told the news. He too looked mightily relieved for he knew that once the grievances in the nation had been allayed, it would mean that the political ferment in the country would gradually die down. Peace and normality would be restored and perhaps he could breathe easily again and maybe get a good night's sleep.

'This means,' Nyoka said to Gumbo in a private conversation, 'that we can open the university, the polytechnic and the agricultural college once again. The students can go back to their studies and we can begin the daunting task of restoring law and order in the towns.'

***

Deputy Chifunza and his cabinet were released within the hour from their enforced stay in the hotel. They'd had plenty of time to deliberate during their incarceration and were ready to take up the reins of government and move into their various ministries immediately. They already knew who was to assume which office and, before the day was out, they were installed in their rightful places, having got the Public Safety police to evict the old office-bearers. An announcement was made on world radio and it featured in the headlines of every major newspaper.

Once the situation was resolved and the new government was in place and in control of the militia, Mike Goodman brought ex-President Matata back to Lundazi and delivered him to Big Mama. If she'd thought for a moment that there was any chance of Matata and herself regaining their old positions, and taking command of the militia, she had another think coming. Not only that, Matata was in a state of advanced senility and was hardly aware of what was going on around him. The notion of his assuming presidential office again was too ludicrous for words and no-one, apart from Big Mama, gave it any serious consideration.

***

Once in power, Chifunza proved to be a man of justice and decisive action for he'd had ample time to consider the role he was to assume. He took possession of the palace and all state houses and began a thorough re-organisation of state finances. The houses and properties which Big Mama had

440

illegally granted her four sisters were forfeited to the government and the houses made vacant were awarded to the new ministers of state. The sisters returned to their native villages where they became the responsibilities of their own husbands and families. The new government was in favour of arresting Matata and Big Mama and charging them for their past crimes and their brutality but Chifunza overruled them. In his inaugural speech, Chifunza said:

'Let us take a leaf out of South Africa's book and work towards peace and friendship. In the spirit of National Reconciliation, all Zambelians should forgive and forget the offences resulting from the recent upheavals and face the future with tolerance and trust.'

The new President honoured his words by forgiving the pair for their past transgressions though he froze their foreign assets and bank accounts so that none of the vast riches they had salted away was accessible to them. Instead he awarded the ex-President a small pension and found a place for him in a private nursing home outside Lundazi with residential medical assistants, including Florence his erstwhile nurse, always readily at hand. Big Mama was granted a comfortably furnished apartment close by so that she could look after him and keep him company. Needless to say, she was extremely unhappy and discontented in the lowly position that events had accorded her. She had known the heights and was not content to tick over living such a humble and ignoble life-style. She took to drinking excessively in an attempt to drown her sorrows and forget her frustrations but there were no more expensive tipples like pink champagne or the Bordeaux wines she had once enjoyed and been accustomed to. Late one Saturday evening, she visited the local supermarket and, along with a few groceries, chose a bottle of Chateau du Pape to put in her shopping trolley intending to consume it that night in the forlorn hope of banishing her perennial depression. She reached the check-out and presented her credit card in payment for the modest sum involved.

441

'Sorry, madam,' the cashier announced in a loud voice so that onlookers could hear and sounding, to Big Mama's ears at least, joyfully triumphant. 'Your card is rejected.'

'Try again!' Big Mama raged.

The cashier did as ordered with the same result. Rejected!

'Please return the goods to the shelves at once!' the cashier demanded.

Fuming, Big Mama took the bottle and returned it to its place on the shelf and chose another wine, a cheap brand. She went back to the checkout and paid cash with her last few coins.

'Thank you, madam. Will that be all?' the assistant asked sarcastically and winking at other customers in the line.

'What do *you* think!' Big Mama hissed, snatching the bag from the cashier. 'Do you realise who you're talking to?'

'Yes,' the cashier replied, peering at the credit card. 'I'm talking to Mary Ann Makubwa who's just had her card rejected twice at this till.'

Big Mama stormed out of the supermarket. She felt completely humiliated that an ignorant, peasant of a cashier could address *her*, the former consort of a president, so contemptuously. She, Marie Antoinette, formerly the toast of royalty, was now being rejected by such an uneducated, thick-headed shop assistant.

Distractedly she made her way to the exit, cursing the fact that life, fate, luck – or whatever one wanted to call it - had brought her so low. To think that she, Marie Antoinette Makubwa who had once dined with the famous and danced with princes and kings, should have ended up in the gutter like this. She saw it all clearly now. That snake-in-the-grass, Nixon Makau, had led her up the garden path by inveigling her into handing over control of the Presidential Guard to Chifunza and that vixen, Delamere. How she hated and loathed the lot of them! How she would have loved to have got that fishwife Delamere into the Gereza dungeons. By

442

heavens she'd have made her scream for mercy! Lost in these thoughts and cursing as she went, Big Mama walked through the exit and into oblivion.

*****

Around the time that Big Mama was buying her wine, Benjamin Bobozo, formerly a high-class ladies' footwear retailer on Lundazi's First Street, was finishing his day's work. It was the end of the shift and, as a special favour, he'd let his young work-mate out near his home leaving him to complete the final part of the job. It had been a series of tough shifts that day and he'd been carrying nasty, evil-smelling loads of sludge to the corporation dump throughout the afternoon but at last he was on the last run taking in the abattoir and the local fish and vegetable market. This final job was the worst of the day for he had on board a stinking load of rotting waste and bilge, the stench of which could be smelt all round the district. How he dreamed and looked forward to getting home where his wife and three children would be waiting! There he would take a hot bath with a liberal use of his wife's perfumed bath oil though even that never seemed to completely remove the fetid smell of the corporation dust cart. Thinking these consoling thoughts, he pressed on the accelerator, hoping to reach the corporation tip with his malodorous load before it closed at six o'clock.

As he was about to pass the exit of the local supermarket, some crazy woman who seemed to be in a trance walked out in front of him. He tried with might and main to stop the truck but didn't have a hope in hell of braking in time. She went under his cart and he knew from the speed that he'd hit her that there was no chance that she could still be alive. There was nobody else about so he reversed the cart in order to extricate the body. He recognized her at once. How could he ever forget that face! She'd been the cause of all his misfortunes and here she was lying dead at his feet. He

443

checked for a pulse though he already knew the answer. He looked all round; it was closing time all round and there wasn't a soul in sight. There were no witnesses. Without more ado, Ben Bobozo lifted Big Mama's body up like a sack of potatoes and threw it into the back of the compactor truck where it was chewed up and mixed into the market debris. Still shaken but amazed that no-one had seen the accident, he drove on to the corporation waste facility and caught them just in time before they closed for the week-end. He reversed to his usual dumping spot and operated the hydraulic tipping mechanism. The debris along with the remnants of Big Mama's corpse slid into the putrid mess which would be converted later into pulp and used as compost on the prison farms. Benjamin Bobozo returned the cart to the depot and continued on his way to his home and to his perfumed hot bath.

***

Nobody noticed her absence that week-end. People assumed that she had gone to visit friends and relatives. After a week with no news, the Public Safety police began investigating but could find no evidence to explain her sudden disappearance. No-one knew anything; it was an unexplained mystery like the time President Matata had gone missing a few months back. Simple-minded peasants began whispering and speculating about evil ju-ju practices; about ghouls, ghosts and spectres that had scooped her up and carried her off into their subterranean world. On Monday evening, a small notice appeared in the *Zambelia Herald*:

MYSTERY IN LUNDAZI

Police are investigating the strange disappearance of Madame Marie Antoinette Makubwa, formerly President Matata's official hostess and consort. She was last seen at a local supermarket where she bought a bottle of wine for

444

which she paid cash. She was observed by staff leaving the store but has not been seen since. Anyone who can shed light on the mystery is asked to contact Colonel Nyoka, Head of the Public Safety Unit, Lundazi. Police are treating the case as a possible homicide.

****

Epilogue

Where are they all now?

So ends the story of Big Mama. Readers who have come this far may be wondering what happened to the various characters who have featured in this tale.

Daniel Chitanda, the student, is now in his third year at university and hopes to become a teacher when he graduates. Although he was bullied into marriage by Colonel Kiboko, he is now happily settled in his father's village with Charity Gichuru and they have a son whom they called Solomon in the hope he might have more commonsense than his wooden-headed father.

Paddy Reilly and his side-kick, Jamesy, are still in charge of property development at the three palaces - one in Lundazi, another at the Lake, and the one at Hekima. Under President Chifunza's strict financial control, they have fewer opportunities for graft and jobbery but they find the challenges at work sufficiently stimulating. Paddy still lives with his young concubine and is even contemplating marrying her, if she'll have him.

Colonel Nyoka and Major Gumbo are happier working under President Chifunza than they were under Matata. The new President is fairer and wiser and always consults them before committing them to a course of action. The result is that they are not under pressure to act against their consciences or to do things they believe are immoral. After a year serving in the new government, they were both promoted again: Gumbo from Major to Lieutenant Colonel;

Nyoka from Colonel to Brigadier. The four Makubwa sisters (Cleopatra, Zenobia, Guinevere, and Nefertiti) had to surrender their substantial luxurious abodes to newly appointed Ministers on the orders of the new president and they were awarded more modest homes in recompense. They were also obliged to hand in the keys of the Mercedes-Benz saloons that Big Mama had given each of them as birthday presents.

Florence Umbuka, the President's nurse, continued to care for him in the nursing home where he ended his days. When the President died some years later she returned to her tribal village on a small pension.

Bugsy Moroney and his wife Betty Jo continued to prosper in Zambelia. He was never aware nor understood the political whirl that had been going on around his head as he was too preoccupied studying the mating habits of African songbirds.

Jack Zulu went on to gain a first class medical degree and, on the strength of this, was granted a full scholarship for advanced study at the University of Birmingham. He later became a celebrated consultant cardiologist.

Helen and Peter Halliday remained as Managers of the palace households and with their wide expertise and skills became invaluable to the new president. He came to rely on them entirely for the smooth running of his domestic affairs which included entertaining many diplomats and celebrated international figures.

Nixon Makau who had been so hurt by the contemptuous references to him as the "Dudu" (The Insect) now became more invaluable than ever as presidential secretary and aide to Chifunza. The President awarded him not only a substantial increase in income but also a sizeable portion of Lundazi palace land on which he was able to build a splendid new home. His new position and prospects were such that he felt himself worthy to propose marriage to the youngest Makubwa sister, Nefertiti, which she was happy to accept.

This meant good prospects both for her and her three sisters for, though Nixon would never stoop to extreme nepotism as Big Mama and Matata had, he was able to look out for their interests.

We come last to Mike Goodman and Sue Delamere who had worked so hard and taken such death-defying chances for the good of Zambelia. Mike was promoted to full professor in the Faculty of Medicine and Sue was made a Reader in Education but more important than their career achievements, was their decision to marry. Six months after the inauguration of the new president, they married in a grand ceremony at Hekima Cathedral. The Nuptial Mass was celebrated by the Archbishop himself, the Most Reverend Pius Kazembe and con-celebrated by the bishops of the seven provinces, and one monsignor, named Gerry McGinn, who returned as university chaplain to his beloved Zambelia when the new President took office. After the ceremony, there was a jubilant reception in the University Hall at which academic staff and senior students attended. For the honeymoon, Mike and Sue flew to Capri where they spent a gloriously happy fortnight.

'Oh, it's wonderful to be travelling with you again especially like this, Mike,' she purred, cuddling into him at the back of the taxi.

''I agree with you, my love,' he said, 'but I don't get it. What do you mean by "like this"?'

'This time, I don't have to get into a bed and hide under a blanket.'

'That will come later, my love,' he laughed.

***

Oh, and I almost forgot! There's still one more character unaccounted for - Benjamin Bobozo, the driver of the garbage truck. For a while he considered returning to the

448

retail footwear trade but thought it might be best if he kept a low profile. He did not report the accident with the mysterious lady who came sleep-walking out of the supermarket. As far as we know, he lives happily with his wife and three children. He is still driving the Mack Compactor.

****

THE END